Terror in the South

The Ku Klux Klan and the Union League

By

Dr. MICHAEL J. DEEB

Hi Carolyn:

Regards!

Michael J Deeb

D1526814

I

Terror in the South

The Ku Klux Klan and the Union League

Copyright 2019 Michael J. Deeb

ISBN: 9781091884236

Printed in the United States of America

My thanks to all those who encouraged me to continue the Drieborg Chronicles.

My undergraduate degree was in history with an emphasis on American studies. My Master's degree was also in history with a similar emphasis. My doctorate however was in management studies. Following the Master's degree, I was in education for nineteen years most of which saw me teaching American history.

My personal life saw me as a pre-teen spending time regularly at the Grand Rapids, MI public library reading non-fiction works of history. This passion continues to this day. Teaching at the college, university and high school level only increased my passion for such reading and research.

In addition to my historical novels, I publish a Civil War blog twice a month. If you would like to receive it, please send me your e mail address and name to gmail@civilwarnovels.com

Since 2005, my wife and I have lived in Sun City Center, FL. I write daily.

Novels by Michael J. Deeb

The Drieborg Chronicles

Duty and Honor

Duty Accomplished

Honor Restored

The Lincoln Assassination

The Way West

1860

Civil War Prisons

The Kennedy Assassination

Volume 1: Was Oswald the Only Assassin?

Volume 2: Why Was Kennedy Killed?

Terror in the South: The KKK and the Union League Reconstruction Terror Groups

By the end of May 1865, fighting between the military forces of the Union and those representing the Confederate States of America had ended. But the conflict between the two very different cultures of the combatants had not.

The two immediate questions facing the victors were, how to treat those who led their states into rebellion and war, and how to protect the four million former slaves still living in those states.

Put another way, the people of the South needed to rebuild both their destroyed economy and their disrupted social structure. Union forces had destroyed their homes, communities and infrastructure. Everything needed to be rebuilt. And, the people of the South faced the larger and more difficult task of making a new place for the four million freed former slaves left in their midst.

Before the fighting had ended, Lincoln had made it very clear that his policy was to bring the states in rebellion back into the Union quickly and completely. He also believed the freed slaves must be dealt with by the leaders of those states; that it was a State matter.

The Radicals of his own Republican Party thought otherwise. Their view of reconstruction was so different from his that many of them sought to replace Lincoln as the Republican nominee on the ballot in the Presidential election of 1864. Despite them, Lincoln won re-election.

Shortly after the Confederate surrender at Appomattox in April of 1865, Lincoln was killed. His vice president, Andrew Johnson took Lincoln's place. During the presidential campaign of 1864, Johnson had spoken clearly and repeatedly in favor of punishing the leaders of the South. He appeared to be one in spirit with the Republican Radicals.

The day after Lincoln's death, Congressman Ben Butler spoke to crowd at the New York Custom House. He praised Lincoln as a great and good man. But Butler also announced that the slain president was

"... a naïve sentimentalist unaware of Confederate perfidy.

"Lincoln had become the first victim of his own policy of clemency. Now, with the president's task completed, God had passed the mantle to Andrew Johnson, able believe me, and determined to treat this rebellion as we want to have it treated. Retribution, retribution, swift, unerring, terrible and just!

"We have our man now." (Andrew Johnson) The Radical Reconstructionist Butler concluded.

But he was mistaken.

*   *   *

In December of 1865, members of the House of Representatives and Senate returned to Washington City from their recess. Upon their arrival they were greeted by an astonishing challenge. Waiting to be sworn in were Representatives and Senators from every former Confederate state but Texas.

It appeared that during their absence the citizens of each state had complied with Lincoln's Proclamation of Amnesty and Reconstruction issued in 1863. His successor, Andrew Johnson adopted this plan as his own.

According to this executive order, as Ten Per Cent of the adult males in each former state of the Confederacy took the oath of allegiance to the United States, their legislative body rescinded the act of secession, adopted the 13tth Amendment in their state's new state constitution and held state elections, their state could be fully readmitted to the Union.

Thus, it was that representatives to Congress and two Senators from each of the former Confederate states (except from Texas) were waiting when members of Congress and the Senate from Union states returned from their recess in December of 1865.

These newly elected Representatives and Senators from the former Confederate states expected to be sworn in and then take the seats they had recently (since the end of the war) been selected to fill.

But the returning Union members of both legislative bodies refused to seat them. Instead, the Republican majorities in both houses of the legislative branch demanded that fifty per cent of adult white males pledge their allegiance to the United States; not the ten per cent required in the Lincoln/Johnson plan.

So, the sounds of Civil War battles had hardly faded away when the struggle for control of Reconstruction policy had begun. The Northern Radicals would win that debate in Washington. But their legislative and constitutional measures would be met with a secret and violent opposition in the former states of the Confederacy.

This historical novel focuses on that violent reaction in two southern states. In South Carolina, the military arm of the Democratic Party was the Ku Klux Klan. In Georgia, the military arm of the Freedman's Bureau was the Union League. Both groups used terror tactics to further the political, economic and social objectives of their support group.

Grand Rapids, Michigan

The homes on Prospect Street were all two -story and of frame or brick construction. Federal Marshal Michael Drieborg and his family lived in one of the frame houses. Their neighbors were among the more important and prosperous people in Grand Rapids.

The Marshal's house was just coming to life on this chilly November morning. Helen, the cook, had entered the Drieborg kitchen at her usual 6 AM arrival time. So, coffee was brewing and the odor of baking bread and rolls filled the room.

Unlike homes in the South, where most cooking was done in a separate building out back, for Prospect Street residents, the cooking was done in a room inside the house. It was called a kitchen. This room was just off a formal dining-room. It was the warmest room in the house.

It wasn't yet 7 AM, when Mary Jacqueline Drieborg entered her home's kitchen. She was already dressed for the day. Her cook, Helen, had once been a slave assigned to her when she lived in Charleston during the war as the wife of the late Dr. Charles Pope. She and Helen had come North in 1868 after Marshal Michael Drieborg had met, wooed and won the hand of the widow, Mary Jacqueline.

"Good morning, Helen," Mary Jacqueline greeted cheerily.

"Morning, ma'am," Helen responded. "Cold outside today, mercy! I don know how dese Yankees stand da cold. My poor southern bones just aching wit da wind cutting through me so."

"I know what you mean, Helen," Mary Jacqueline responded as she gripped her coffee-cup to warm her hands. "I was raised in

Philadelphia, but my years in Charleston with the Pope family seemed to have changed me. I just can't seem to get used to the cold here, either."

"I don know how da Marshal, your husband, and his daughter Eleanor stan it."

"It amazes me, too," her employer, Mary Jacqueline agreed. "They don't seem to mind it a' tall. It's truly a mystery to me how they do it."

Just then, the kitchen door swung open and Marshal Michael Drieborg entered the kitchen, dressed in his night clothing, robe and slippers. At six-foot two with blond hair and blue eyes he was a handsome man with a ready smile.

"You two leave any hot coffee left in that pot for me?" He asked as he walked over to his wife seated at the kitchen table. He gave her a hug, "Morning dear," He said. Then, he sat down himself. "Morning Helen." He greeted.

"Morning ta you too, Marshal," Helen answered. She quickly handed him a cup of the freshly made brew.

He raised his coffee mug and smelled the steaming hot coffee.

"Mmm," he mumbled. "Smells good, Helen. Thank you. It's so nice to walk into a warm kitchen on a cold winter morning. Isn't it, ladies?"

"Be better if'n it was warm outside like where I grew up down South." Helen reminded him.

"Now, Helen," Mike reminded her, "You and your husband, Amos have a good business here in Michigan and a nice home. Your two children attend a good school, too. Just remember, neither of you would have been allowed those things back in Charleston. Would you give up all of that for warmer weather?"

In South Carolina, Amos had cooked for Mike's cavalry troop during the last days of the war. Three years later when Mike and his deputies were in that state investigating conditions for a congressional committee, they met again.

He found Amos cooking in a local bar and being abused. He rescued his old cook and sent him north to Grand Rapids. There, Amos got a job cooking his specialty soups for Mike's brother-in-law at the local Cosmopolitan Restaurant. He soon became well established in town. Then, he wooed and married Mary Jacqueline's cook, Helen.

"You would have to go an remind me a' all da good things about lining up here wit you Yankees. Don get me wrong, Marshal, I know what you is sayin. But my poor bones ain't listenin. It's plum cold. Dat wind today is fierce. Don't tell me any different."

This kind of morning exchange was sort of a ritual between the two. Mary Jacqueline usually brought it to a close with something like,

"How about some breakfast for the Marshal, Helen?" Mary Jacquelin asked, changing the subject.

"I got some ham left over from da other night, Marshal," She told him. "How's about I fry up some 'a dat with eggs and friend potatoes?"

"That sounds great, Helen," Mike responded. "Can I have some grits with that, too?

"So nuff, marshal," Helen assured him. "Dat's one good ting you picked up in da South."

"Hey," Mary Jacqueline interrupted, "Don't forget me. He found me there, too." She said with a smile on her face.

"Oh, ya," I clean forgot dat. No offense meant. But I was only thinkin a' food, ma'am."

"Do I have time to clean up?" Mike asked.

"Not hardly, Marshal." Helen responded. "You just sip dat coffee a' yours an I'll have your breakfast in front a' you in a jiffy, including da grits."

"Not to worry," Mary Jacqueline said. "The Marshal isn't going anywhere, are you dear?"

"And miss a banquet like Helen is fixing? Not on your life. I'm staying put in this nice warm kitchen."

"Good choice, dear. While you're enjoying Helen's cooking and fresh bread, I'll get the kids going. Eleanor will probably be up already, washed and dressed, too. But Charles will most likely still be buried under his covers."

Helen piped in a comment. "Dat boy be a Southern, through an through. He know'd it be cold. Take his momma to get him out from under dose covers."

"Probably right, Helen." Mary Jacqueline said as she left the kitchen and went upstairs to her children's rooms.

She met her daughter Eleanor on the landing, coming down the stairs from her room. Eleanor was a lanky girl of seventeen. She had long blond hair and her father's blue eyes. Unlike her brother she looked forward to Central High School each day.

"Good morning, Mother," Eleanor greeted as they hugged on the landing. "Chilly this morning isn't it."

"Right," Mary Jacqueline agreed. "And, it's only November. It's a long time until Spring. Helen is fixing your father some breakfast. I'm sure she'll have enough for you."

"Lots 'a luck getting Charles out of bed," Eleanor warned her mother. "I pulled the covers off of him once. I won't tell you what he shouted at me. But I'm not going to be late for school again because of him."

"Just remember, Eleanor, he's not used to this kind of weather."

"I'm tired of his excuses, Mother," Eleanor declared. "If it wasn't the weather, it would be something else. He hates school and uses any excuse handy to avoid it. I'm leaving as soon as I finish my breakfast whether or not he is ready."

"I'll tell him."

Entering her son's room, Mary Jacqueline could only see a large lump under the blankets.

She gave them a yank.

"Leave me the hell alone, Eleanor." Charles shouted grabbing for the blankets.

His mother yanked back. "Don't you use that language or that tone with me, young man. You get yourself out of bed this minute. I'm tired of this every morning ritual with you."

"it's too cold!" he yelled pulling the blankets up around him again.

"It is for everyone, Charles! But children go to school and adults go to work; cold or not. If I don't see you downstairs in ten minutes, I'll send your father up here."

"So, it's the easy way or the hard way, eh?" Charles retorted.

"That's right kiddo," His mother reminded him. "You choose. Act responsibly or you will pay the price. Believe me."

Charles jumped out of bed and ran into the children's bathroom to use the chamber-pot. "Damn, it's cold" he shuddered.

"I heard that young man," his mother shouted from the stairway. "Watch your language."

"But it is!" he shouted back.

"I expect you in the kitchen immediately, if not sooner!" she demanded as she left the room.

Much to his mother's approval, he walked into the kitchen a few minutes later as she had demanded. He slumped down in a chair, elbows on the table.

"Don, I get even a good morning, Charles?" Helen snapped.

"Good morning, Helen."

"Dat's a little better," She smiled at him. "What can I get you?"

"Got any grits?"

"Jus so happens I fixed some fer yer father. So, I gots plenty," She told him. "Want some 'a my fresh warm bread with butter an sugar sprinkled on it, too?"

"Oh, yes," he brightened. "That sounds really good."

Helen put a glass of warm milk in front of him. Grits were next.

"Toast will be ready in a minute," Then Helen looked at him quizzically. "Did you brush your teeth dis morning, chil?"

"No," he admitted. "Momma made me hurry so, I forgot."

"After you eats, you will go back upstairs and do dat, you hear."

"Do I have to?"

"You want da teeth to rot in yer mouth?" She asked hands on her hips. "Not as long as I'm in dis house. So, afore you leave dis morning, you will brush does teeth like ya 'all is sposed to."

It wasn't long before Charles had eaten and brushed his teeth. He was getting his overcoat and scarf from the back closet. Eleanor, all ready for school, walked by him on her way out the door.

"Hey," Charles shouted. "Wait up for me."

"I'm not going to be late, Charles." Eleanor told him. "You just best catch up."

"Come-on, Eleanor, "he whined. "Wait up."

Eleanor took off running. "Whiner, whiner, can't keep up." She teased.

She didn't get very far when Charles caught up with her. They both laughed as they slowed to a walk. They weren't late for school after all. And, despite the cold, Charles played catch outside with his friends during their noon lunch break: without his coat or even his hat on, of course.

Eleanor observed her brother running around on the playground. She never heard him whining about the cold then. Not even once. He was having too much fun, she guessed.

"Boys!" she thought. *"What a pain."*

The Marshal's Office

The Federal Marshal had his office in the Federal building located in downtown Grand Rapids. Usually, Marshal Drieborg just walked from his Prospect Street home just up the hill. Today was no different than most others. The office and attached jail were both open twenty-four house a day. Usually, there were several prisoners housed there awaiting trial or convicts serving short sentences.

Bill Anderson was the Deputy Marshal in charge of the facility. Originally from Wyoming, Michigan, he and Mike Drieborg had met in September of 1862 during training camp when they had both volunteered for the Sixth Michigan Cavalry Regiment. The served throughout the war together.

Bill eventually became a platoon sergeant serving in Troop I of the Sixth Regiment. Mike was his Troop commander during that period.

Another training camp volunteer from back in 1862, was Stan Killeen. Hailing from up north n Cadillac, Michigan, he too became a Platoon Sergeant. Mike Drieborg had been his Troop Commander, too. Now, he served as a Deputy Marshal and was a field operator usually involved in arresting those suspected of crimes.

The Chief Deputy was Patrick Riley. Back in 1862, Riley had been the Platoon Sergeant in charge of training Drieborg, Anderson and Killeen. Later in the war, he served as the First Sergeant of I Troop when Mike was its commander. He finished out his military career out West in the Dakota Territory and later in Kansas with the first Negro cavalry regiment. Upon his retirement, Mike brought him to Grand Rapids as his Chief Deputy.

All three men were in the Federal Marshal's office when Mike arrived this morning.

"Any 'a that hot coffee left, Stan?" Mike asked rubbing his cold hands together.

"If ya can call it that," Stan grumbled. "Anderson's been heating it up fer so long, it's almost mud. It's so strong, make your hair stand up, actually."

"Always complaining." Anderson chuckled. "You're just a half empty glass kind 'a guy Killeen."

"I'm not that a'tal," Stan retorted. "Take a bit a' this coffee Mike," he urged. "Isn't it like sludge? Isn't it as strong as a plank?"

Riley was sitting back in his chair, feet up on his desk, coffee cup in hand, just waiting for Mike to respond.

"Fer once I think Killeen has a point," Mike judged. "I think it time fer a fresh pot, Anderson."

"See," Killeen snorted. "What I tell ya?"

"Damn it Mike," Anderson responded in disgust. "I hate it when you encourage Stan. He'll lord this over me for a week now."

Mike stopped laughing long enough to say, "You guys are a hoot. If you went on the stage, I'd buy a ticket to witness your performance."

"They ain't performing, Mike," Riley said. "That's just how the lads go on about most everything all day, every day. It's been like this since I know'd em back in your training camp days."

"I'd still buy a ticket just to listen. I love it." Mike bellowed slapping his thigh.

* * *

As the men were about to break up and go about their business for the day, a staff member came into the room.

"Telegram for you Marshal," he said.

Mike read the message.

He jerked erect in his chair. "Damn!!" he exclaimed.

"What is it, lad?" Riley asked.

"This telegram is from Bill Kellogg. It says that Craig Haynes has disappeared. Kellogg thinks he's been kidnapped."

"Damnation is right!" Killen snapped. "They're in Georgia fer God's sake. What does the Congressman want you to do about it?"

Congressman William Kellogg had been Mike's mentor since the 6th Michigan Cavalry had been assigned to Washington City back in December of 1862. On leave in the city one afternoon, Mike had saved Kellogg's daughter Patricia from being run over, and probably killed, by an out-of-control horse-drawn wagon.

Since that time, the two men had formed a bond much like father and son. This wouldn't be the first time one of them had asked the other for help. Neither had ever refused the request of the other.

Back in 1863, Kellogg saved the Drieborg farm from foreclosure by the local banker. In exchange, Mike became Kellogg's military aide. Following the Battle of Gettysburg, Kellogg took a seriously wounded Drieborg into his Washington home to recover from his wound. Following his return to duty as a Captain, Mike was captured during the Kilpatrick Richmond Raid and sent to Andersonville Prison. After he escaped. Kellogg had Mike promoted again and assigned to special duty in Washington City.

In Lowell, after the war, Mike's wife and son were killed by hoodlums hired by the revengeful Bacon family. Following their death, Kellogg brought Mike back to Washington as a US Marshal in charge of a fact-finding assignment in South Carolina for the House Judiciary Committee. His war-time fellow soldiers, Killeen and Anderson accompanied Mike on that assignment as Deputy Marshals.

Mike's Chief Deputy then was Craig Haynes. He had been the Chief of Police in Cleveland Ohio. He had been given that job because crime was out of control in Cleveland at the time. The leaders in Cleveland asked him to put a stop to it. During his tenure he had been very successful in dealing with that crime problem. He was too successful it seemed. While appreciating and prospering from his tough approach to enforcing the law, influential citizens of Cleveland had also chaffed under his strict but even-handed approach.

So, when the fact-finding mission to South Carolina was being put together in Washington, the Ohio congressman for the Cleveland area, Rep. Clark, saw an opportunity to get rid of Haynes. He suggested adding Haynes to Mike's team.

Mike was certainly pleased. He had heard of the no-nonsense tough Chief of the Cleveland police force and welcomed him to his team as his Chief Deputy Marshal. Thus, the two men began a close relationship. After the fact-finding mission was completed, Haynes accompanied Mike to Grand Rapids as his Chief Deputy Marshal there.

While in Charleston on that mission, Mike met the widow Mary Jacquelin Pope. The two fell in love and headed back to Michigan as man and wife. Kellogg had arranged for Mike to become the US Marshal for the Western District of Michigan.

Later, when Kellogg brought Mike to Washington to conduct the Lincoln assassination investigation, Haynes came along once again as his Chief Deputy. A year later, when William Kellogg was appointed to the Reconstruction government of the Georgia-Florida-Alabama Military District, he took Haynes with him as his Deputy.

Now, Haynes was in trouble and Kellogg was asking Mike for help.

"He wants me to contact him immediately."

"Then what, Mike? "Bill Anderson asked.

"He wants me to put together a team of people he can trust to do something about the problem."

"You mean, go to Georgia and rescue Haynes, ya think?" Killeen surmised.

"Would that be a problem for you, Stan?"

"Hell no!" Killeen virtually shouted. "Haynes was a friend 'a mine too, ya know."

"Mine too," Bill Anderson added.

"I'm afraid you can't go on this assignment, Bill." Mike answered without hesitation. "You need to hold down the fort here with Riley. Besides, I doubt if our bosses in the Justice Department would like it if too many of us left our jobs here and ran off to Georgia."

Riley asked, "Jus what kind of post does Kellogg have in Georgia, Mike?"

"Back in 1967, Congress passed the First Reconstruction Act. It is also called the Military Reconstruction Act because it divided the South into five military districts. The state lines of the former Confederacy were pretty will abolished.

"I thought Lincoln refused to endorse that plan." Bill interjected.

"Yes, he did, Bill," Mike agreed. "But after he was killed, Stanton and the Radicals in Congress made that part of their Reconstruction legislation. They even overrode President Johnson's veto of the bill."

"I remember that now," Riley said.

Mike went on. "Because of that act of Congress and their override of the president's veto, the powers of the state governments of the former Confederacy were taken over by a Union general. In effect, Congress virtually declared martial law in the former states of the Confederacy.

"With the election of Grant in 1868, the Act was implemented. Then, Grant asked Kellogg to assist the military governor in setting up a proper government in the military district that included, Georgia, Alabama and Florida.

"Kellogg accepted the challenge. He resigned his seat in Congress and went to live and work in Atlanta, Georgia."

"Is that when your deputy, Bill Hayes joined him?" Riley asked.

"That's right, Pat," Mike told him. "He got to know Haynes during the Lincoln assassination investigation. While my team was in Washington on that assignment, Kellogg's daughter Pat went missing. Haynes organized the search and eventually rescued her.

It was truly an amazing job Haynes pulled off that time. Kellogg never forgot."

"So, you let Hayes go," Riley surmised.

"Sure," Mike revealed. "His job as my Chief Deputy had become pretty routine. Kellogg's offer not only was a promotion but offered him a new challenge. I wouldn't have stood in Haynes way, anyway. So, off he went. That's when I offered you his old job."

"I'll be forever grateful, fer sure, lad," Riley commented. "My wife, the fair Colleen, and I love it here."

"And the Lord knows," Killeen added. "Drieborg surly needs the kind of looking after only Riley can give him."

"Thanks Stan," Mike said with a chuckle. "I appreciate all the help I can get; even from you, too."

"That's nice to know," Killeen responded.

Riley continued. "I assume Kellogg and his Deputy Hayes upset some folks down there or Haynes wouldn't have been kidnapped."

"That makes sense," Mike responded. "Let me get a map of the Military Districts for us to review before I respond to Kellogg. Best we get familiar with the area we're talking about. Give me a minute. I think I have what we need in my files someplace."

A few minutes later, Mike returned from his office with a file marked, Reconstruction Districts by the Reconstruction Act of March 1867.

"It appears that Kellogg' district includes Alabama and Florida in addition to Georgia. He just made his headquarters in Atlanta. "

"Look-in at tha map, though," Stan observed. "Montgomery Georgia would be more central to his area of responsibility."

"Still, Atlanta makes sense to me," Anderson responded. "Atlanta is still the railroad center for that entire area. Kellogg and his people could get most anywhere by rail pretty quickly."

"I'm reminded by my notes in this file that the voters in Georgia voted for Seymour, the Democratic Party candidate for president in '68, not Grant."

"I remember Kellogg tellin us that one of his jobs was to get the colored's registered and voting Republican before the next election," Stan wondered aloud. "That didn't appear to happen."

"I would guess the answer to that question would be, no; big time," Mike offered.

"I'm sure any effort in that regard would not be appreciated by the locals," Riley concluded. "The kidnapping of Haynes might be local push-back on that score."

"I suppose," Mike agreed. "Kellogg will fill us in when we get down there."

Mike left for the telegraph office to contact Kellogg in Atlanta, Georgia.

*   *   *

That evening at the dinner table, Mike told the family about the message from Bill Kellogg.

"How long will you and Mother be gone this time?" Eleanor asked. The sarcasm in her tone was not lost on Mike.

"Are you upset about our going to help Congressman Kellogg, Eleanor?" He asked his daughter.

"it just seems that you run off into danger at the drop of a hat," She responded. "Your job here as a Marshal is dangerous enough. But now you want to go down South with all the danger that puts you in. Why are you surprised that I'm worried and upset, too?"

The room was silent for a bit when Mary Jacqueline entered the conversation.

"Your father and I appreciate your concern, Eleanor. But the Congressman has looked after your father and this family several times in the past. We cannot ignore his cry for help."

Eleanor wasn't done telling her parents of her displeasure. "When I was a child, I didn't realize the danger you were in when you went running off to one place or another. Now I do. And, I don't like it one bit," she confessed tearing up. "Why can't you just stay home for once, and let someone else answer this request?"

Mike went to his daughter's side and knelt by her chair.

"Please understand, my friend needs my help"

"What about us?" Eleanor insisted. "We need you, too, you know? Don't we count?"

"Yes, you do, dear," Mary Jacqueline assured her. "And we need you and Charles here to look after Maxine."

"Of course, we would do that," Eleanor assured them. 'But you two are the parents. Isn't it your primary job to look after your children?"

Mike ended the conversation. "We'll talk about this more tomorrow."

"What's there to talk about, Father?" Eleanor snapped as she stood up. She walked out of the dining room. She paused at the doorway and said. "You made your decision without asking our opinion. Now, your children must live with whatever happens."

With that, she left the table and went upstairs to her room. Her brother Charles followed her upstairs having never said a word during the entire conversation.

"Whew!" Mike said. He left the dinning-room too and went into the adjacent living room.

Later, in the kitchen, Helen and Mary Jacqueline were putting away the food and cleaning the dishes Helen commented in her off-hand way,

"I wasn't trying ta hear you talkin jus now. But you folks was pretty loud. Dat girl a' yourn sure let you an da Marshal have a piece a' her mind. Mercy, is she a tough Yankee girl, or what?"

"She is that all right, Helen," Mary Jacqueline agreed.

"What ya gonna do about her and dis trip?"

"It has already been decided, Helen," she informed her cook. "The Marshal and I are going to Atlanta. We will be gone until he and his team finish the assignment. Eleanor and Charles will have to accept that, I'm afraid."

"Growing up is sometimes hard, ain't it." Helen concluded.

*   *   *

In their bedroom that night, Mike and his wife lay in each other's arms.

Mike asked. "What do you suggest?"

"About going to Atlanta or about Eleanor?"

"About our daughter."

"Since supper, I've been thinking about that," Mary Jacqueline told him. "Over the next few days, I'll have a chance to talk with her. I believe we have to give her some time to sort this all out. Hopefully, she'll allow me to help her. She's a teenager now, Michael. She's a young lady who is trying to figure out a lot of new things."

"Like what?" Mike said surprised by what his wife had said.

"Boys and girls her age must deal with all kinds of new emotions and worries. She is concerned about her looks, how she appears to others, what her role in life will be, how important she is in our eyes and in the eyes of her peers. All this is happening as she is maturing physically as well. It is confusing and I'm sure, oftentimes, frightening to her."

"Even so," Mike insisted. "What did I say that should have upset he so?"

"You are the foundation of her support system, Michael. By announcing our plan to leave, she believes you took away that support system. Now, faced with all the other uncertainties she is experiencing, it suddenly appeared to her that you just announced that she was on her own to face everything without either of us. She fears you are leaving her, possibly forever, when she needs you the most."

"Holy shit!" Mike exclaimed. "I never realized parenting could be so complicated."

"Of course, you didn't, dear." His wife assured him.

"What do I do about it?"

"Give her a few days to process your announcement and her emotional reaction. In the meantime, she and I will have a girl to girl talk. We'll see what happens."

"Damn!"

Mary Jacqueline hugged her husband. "If it hadn't been this, it probably would have been something else that triggered her outburst. It's part of the pains young people experience growing up."

"Surely took me by surprise," Mike admitted.

"Part of our growing up too, dear," Mary Jacqueline moved on top of her husband and kissed him. Then, it was his turn to hug and kiss her.

"I don't seem to have a problem with this lady," Mike said as he caressed his wife.

"You seem to know exactly what I want, my dear," She responded.

There was no more talk this night.

The Marshal's Office

"Do you have any responses to Mike's telegrams about the Atlanta assignment?"

Stan Killeen picked up a folder from his desk.

"Yep," He reported. "The one from Bose Faute is a classic."

"He's the one from Cade's Cove up in the mountains near Gatlinburg, Tennessee?" Riley asked.

"That's right."

"The one who was a Confederate cavalryman?"

"Yep. He was with Mike 'an me on that Lincoln assassination investigation. Anyway," Stan went on. "He and his wife also were with Mike and Mary Jacqueline out in Kansas investigating corruption among Indian Agents. You might remember that they brought Mike's brother back from some military hospital out there."

"Oh, ya," Bill recalled. "His brother got the Congressional Medal of Honor for helping to save a trainload of military wives who were being attacked by Indians. He was seriously wounded and eventually got a medical discharge."

"He also got to marry our Pat Riley's daughter out of the deal. The two kids first met during his training at Fort Leavenworth. Riley brought her with him when he came to Grand Rapids as Mike's Deputy Marshal. Mike's brother accepted a job as deputy marshal in Lowell and he and his new wife (Riley's daughter) bought Mikes sister Ann's farm near there."

"So, what does this Tennessee reb say to Mike's offer?"

"He's all for it. Just wants Mike to wire him the travel money. He and his wife are all in."

"What the hell is this business about wives going along?" Bill asked. "Seems to me that just complicates everything."

"Mike reminded me that he promised Mary Jacqueline before they married that he would always be with her for supper every day. He's pretty well kept that promise. And, she has insisted that he extend that courtesy to the men he has invited to assist him on these adventures of his. So, that's what he did for the Lincoln investigation and the trip west too.

"It appears that he's just continuing what seemed to work well in the past for this one, too?"

"Seems, so," Pat Riley said.

"Any others accept?" Bill asked.

"I just got a telegram of acceptance from two other southern boys, that South Carolina lawyer Bob Stephan and his wife, and the meat store guy Frank Stanitzek who lives in Macon, Georgia. His wife will be there, too."

"That's it?"

"You'll never guess who else is going?" Stan teased.

"Come 'on Stan," Bill urged. "I hate your guessing games. Who else is joining you on this trip?"

"Our old shave-tail lieutenant, Henry Austry."

"Well, I'll be horse whipped, "Bill exclaimed. "My old Platoon Leader. How the hell is he?"

"Since he worked with us on the Lincoln investigation a couple of years back, he's been working for his uncle, General Sherman in Washington City."

"I seem to remember that Sherman was made Secretary of War when Grant became president. So, Henry has a job with his office?"

"Appears so," Stan confirmed. "He never returned to his Illinois farm when our investigation was done. Stayed right in Washington City."

"As I recall," Bill continued, "Henry got shot by some renegade Washington policemen. What was that all about? I forget."

Killeen told the story. "Austry and our Confederate friend from Tennessee, Bose, were assigned to pick up a guy named Parker and take him to our secret farmhouse for questioning. The guy had been Lincoln's bodyguard the night of the assassination. He deserted his post at Ford's Theatre. You know what happened then."

"Did they just kidnap this guy?"

"Sure did," Killeen revealed. "They saw him coming home one afternoon from his job with the presidential security detail, busted into his house, tied him up and took him off in a carriage. They said his wife shouted up a storm. But they took him anyways."

"Did they use the old rope trick to make him talk?" Bill asked.

"In fact, they did. Bose told us that when Porter refused to talk about why he left his post at Ford's Theatre the night Lincoln was shot. So, they did use the rope."

Anderson was referring to an interrogation method used by Bummers in Sherman's army during his march to Savannah from Atlanta. While these bummers were out confiscating supplies in the countryside for his army, they also stole all sorts of things from the citizenry for themselves.

In the process, they encountered people who were reluctant to reveal where they had hidden valuables. These Bummers would then torture people into revealing where their valuables had been hidden. To get reluctant southerners to talk, they would throw a rope over a tree limb or a rafter with a noose at one end. Then they put around the noose around neck of the stubborn Confederate. The rope would then be pulled until the person's feet were clear of the ground. After counting to five or so, they would let the person back to the ground. After a few repetitions of this, the Union soldiers usually got the information they demanded.

"How many pulls on the rope did it take for Parker to break and answer their questions?"

"I recall Bose said they raised Parker off his feet three or four times. I think he said they got to a count of ten before he broke and answered their questions."

"So, how did Henry get himself shot?"

"After a few days at the place where they questioned Parker, the boys were running low on supplies. So, Henry took their carriage into town to report Porter's testimony and pick up some food. On the road to Washington, he was stopped by some hooded riders. They wanted Henry to tell them where Parker was. He refused and instead got his horse going and ran the carriage right through the guys who were blocking the road. They gave chase and, in the process, Henry got shot in the shoulder. He didn't stop though.

And, he ended up parked at the steps of the building where Congressman Kellogg had his office.

"Once Sherman was notified about his nephew's situation, he sprang into action. He sent troops to the hospital, got rooms in the National Hotel for his nephew and put guards all around. He threatened Henry's surgeon with reassignment to the Dakota territory if Henry didn't survive and sent more troops out to the farm house where Bose was stranded with Parker."

"I've heard Sherman is not one you want pissed-off at you."

"Watching him in action was a real treat. He just gets the job done, whatever it is, whatever he has to do. You get in his way and you are fried."

"Or sent to the Dakota territory?" Bill added chuckling.

"I guess. But Sherman took care of his nephew. And when Henry continued to run a fever, Mike sent for one of Enna Hecht's cures. It was a smelly poultice that she had used on Mike's wound during the war. When the doctor said he didn't want to use some backwoods cure, Sherman ordered the him to use it on his nephew's wound, or else."

"Let me guess," Bill interrupted. "He reminded the doctor about a possible reassignment to the Dakota Territory?"

"Right."

"Did the poultice work?"

"Surly did; like a charm. But that wasn't the worst 'a it.

"What?" Bill asked. "Something else went wrong?"

"Seems that an ol' flame of Henry's re-interred his life."

"I thought you said that he was just recovering from his wound an' all."

"it seems that this gal he had been carrying-on with in Washington looked him up at the hotel. Henry snuck her into his room, right past his uncle's guards.

"Sounds like Henry recovered really fast when she showed up."

"One afternoon, after the two of them had enjoyed themselves, she left. On the way out, she told the guards he was sleeping. Turned out somehow he got a dose a' poison. Damn near killt him, it did."

"Did she poison him?"

"They caught up with her at the railroad station leaving town. She claimed that Henry had taken something before she left. Nobody could prove anything. She joined her father in Europe somewhere. Before this happened, her father had been a Senator from Main and one of the radicals.

"So, they had to let her go. Couldn't prove anything, I guess," Stan concluded.

"I don't suppose he contacted her again."

"She's still over in Europe with her daddy," Killeen remembered. "But I haven't heard."

"And now, Sherman is allowing him to gallivant off to join Mike on this deal?"

"All I know is that Henry says he will meet us in Atlanta on the appointed date. However, he finagled it, he's coming."

"Wish I was joining you, too, "Bill bemoaned. "You be sure to give Henry my best, Stan." Bill asked.

"I will, fer sure, Bil," Looking at his list Stan commented. "It seems ta me like we got three men from the North and three from the South on this adventure."

"Makes sense, don't you think?" Bill judged.

"I spose it does," Stand agreed. "That mix worked the last time."

Doctor Murphy's House

Dr. Miles Murphy and his wife Judy lived on Cherry Street just around the corner from the Drieborg home. Mary Jacqueline, Mike's wife, was their daughter. The Murphy's had moved to Grand Rapids from Philadelphia, Pennsylvania after he retired from his teaching position at the University of Pennsylvania Medical School.

Once settled in Grand Rapids, Doctor Murphy had joined some local physicians to start up the first medical clinic to be established in that city. In addition to his clinic responsibilities, he worked out of an office in his home, too.

"So, you want me to take on Eleanor as sort of a medical assistant while you and Michael go chasing off to Georgia?" he said to his daughter rather testily.

"Yes, father, I do, "Mary Jacqueline responded calmly with a smile. "And, I want you and mother to take her and Charles into your home while we are gone."

"You want us to baby-sit, too?"

"Miles," cautioned his wife. "There is no need to get excited. You know we would love to have the children here. The only new thing is this business about Eleanor."

"Is that a problem, father?" Mary Jacqueline asked.

"I suppose you'd want me to pay her something, too."

His wife interrupted again. "My heavens, Miles. Of course, we would pay her for her work. Stop this nonsense right now and let's work this out before you talk with her."

"Father," Mary Jacqueline began. "As you know, Eleanor is a very bright young lady. She talks of you and your work all the time. I believe she wants to study for a role in the medical profession. This is an opportunity for you, a teacher, to bring her along to a clearer understanding of your profession."

"Now I'm to be a teacher again?"

"You are so exasperating, Miles," his wife snapped. "Here you are being given an opportunity to work closely with your granddaughter and possibly mentor her in the medical profession. And, what are you doing? Pretending it's an imposition. Rubbish! You are flattered. Admit it. And, stop all this blustering."

Miles smiled. "Forgive my play acting, my dears," He confessed. "I'd be delighted to have Eleanor enter my profession in some role. How about when she gets home from school in the afternoon, she could help my nurse, Kathy Lippincott for a couple of hours. And, on Saturday mornings she could assist me when I work at the clinic. There's a lot of walk-in activity there."

Mary Jacqueline rose from her seat and gave her father a hug. "Thank you, father," she said. "But remember, she is still a young girl who still needs to be a young girl. I wouldn't want you to overdue this."

"What the hell does that mean?" the doctor snapped.

"All she means, dear," Judy soothed. "Is that Eleanor should only work in the office three afternoons a week after school and half a day on Saturday; at least, at first."

"That's exactly what I meant, mother. Thank you."

"Would that work for you Miles?" Judy asked.

Mollified some, Miles said. "Exactly what I had in mind, anyway. When can nurse Kathy and I talk with her about her duties?"

"Would tomorrow be all right, father?" Mary Jacqueline suggested. "She gets home around 3:30 and has a snack. How about she and I walk over after that? We can be here by four."

"Just check my schedule," Miles responded. "If I'm open, I'm fine with meeting then."

'I already did, dear," his wife told him. "Eleanor, Mary Jacqueline and I will be here at 4 PM tomorrow to meet with you and nurse Kathy."

"Why are you going to be here, too, Judy?" he asked his wife.

"Eleanor is my granddaughter, too, remember. I just want her to feel comfortable."

Doctor Murphy had another question. "Hadn't we best talk with nurse Kathy first about Eleanor working with us here?"

His wife responded. "Oh, I already talked with her, dear. Nurse Kathy thinks it's a great idea. She is all for it."

Murphy grumbled, "Somehow I feel manipulated by you ladies. But I like the idea. So, I 'll overlook it for the sake of my granddaughter."

"Oh, thank you dear," His wife said as she gave her husband a kiss on the cheek.

The Cosmopolitan Restaurant and Bakery

Michael, Mary Jacqueline and Charles were sitting at a table in Susan and George Neal's restaurant. They were waiting for the owners to join them.

"I don't know why I have to work while you're gone, mother," Charles complained.

"Because it's time for you and your sister to get out on your own some," She responded quietly. "While your father and I are gone is a perfect opportunity for you to start."

Mike added. "You uncle George and aunt Susan are kindly willing to give you a job for a few hours each week. I had chores on the farm, you can regard this part-time job as your chores. Be good experience for you."

"Do I have to?" he whined.

His mother was the first to respond. "Yes. And, I expect you to do your very best without any complaints."

George and Susan Neal arrived and joined them at the table.

George spoke first. "I know you two ladies have talked this over. But please explain the arrangement for me."

His wife Susan, Mike's sister, explained. "Three afternoons each week, Charles will come here to work. He should be here by four and work for two hours. Our afternoon businessmen's coffee is normally over by then and we will be closed. Charles will be responsible for clearing the tables and sweeping the floors. He will then help the dishwasher dry the dishes and cups and take out any trash. One of our people will then walk him home.

"On Saturday, while Eleanor works at the medical clinic, he will work here doing the same jobs under the supervision of our manager. He will be here at 8 am to clean up after the morning coffee crowd and leave at noon. He will be paid $1.50 a week every Saturday.

"Do you have anything to add to that, dear?" she asked her husband George.

"I think you covered the job of a bus-boy pretty well." George responded.

"Do you have any questions, Charles?" she concluded.

'How will I know what to do, Aunt Susan?" he asked. "I've never done any of those things before."

"That's a good question, Charles," she replied. "On your first day I will be here to teach you exactly how I want you to do these jobs. I taught your Uncle Jacob and his friend Kenny Hecht years ago how to do these things just like I train all our new bus-boys and kitchen people. If you have any questions after that, ask the manager. I trained him too."

George Neal spoke. "I want you to know, Charles. Before the war, I started working at a bakery here in town doing clean-up jobs a lot like you are going to be doing. Now, your aunt and I own a very successful business in this town.

"Your cook Helen has a husband, Amos. He was a slave who came here with nothing after the war. Now, he owns a successful business in this town. He brought only one thing with him when he first came to work for me."

"What was that Uncle George?" Charles asked.

"He had a willingness to work hard and a desire to do well. Tell me, Charles. Are you willing to work hard?"

"I don't know what to tell you, Uncle George," Charles responded rather meekly. "I've never been asked to do anything except pick up my clothing and do my homework."

His mother covered her face to hide her smile. Mike sat impassively.

"Damn, if that isn't a great answer. This experiment might just be a very good thing for our son." He thought.

George continued. "That was a good answer, Charles. So. this will be a good challenge for you won't it."

"Yes, Uncle George, it will be," He answered.

"By the way, Charles," George added. "Don't call me Uncle George when you're in the restaurant."

"What do I call you?" he asked.

"While you're working, you address me as Sir or Mr. Neal and your Aunt as Ma'am or Mrs. Neal. And, I don't want you bragging to the other employees that we are your aunt and uncle. Got it?"

Charles looked at Mike who nodded to him.

"Yes, sir."

"That's good," he said. "As far as the others are concerned, you are just the new busboy. Oh, yes. Don't tell anyone how much you are being paid. No personal information like where you go to school and where you live should be revealed either. Keep your mouth shut about those things.

"Yes, sir."

"When do you want him here for training, Susan?" Mike asked.

"When are you two leaving for Atlanta?" Susan asked.

"Probably in about ten days." Mike answered.

"So, if we're going to do this, let's start the training tomorrow after school.

"Be here at four o'clock tomorrow, Charles?" she directed.

Not accustomed to making such decisions, Charles paused. He looked at his father. Mike nodded. Charles sort of straightened in his chair and took a breath.

"Yes, ma'am. Four o'clock tomorrow it is."

Susan concluded by looking straight at Mary Jacqueline.

"I have to ask you to stay away from the restaurant while Charles is working. Don't walk him here or wait for him outside at closing time. If he is going to succeed at this, he must do it on his own. Besides, it would be very hard on him if the other employees saw you hanging around, sort of looking after him. Do you understand, Mary Jacqueline?"

Charles' mother nodded.

"That goes for you too, brother Michael. No exceptions. Do you two promise?"

They both nodded.

Susan stood, "See you tomorrow, Charles. Don't wear your school clothing. Something you don't care about getting wet or dirty will do. If you don't have any work shoes go down the street to Kenny Shoes when you leave here. They'll fit you with something sturdy and water resistant. "

George stood, too. "You're a working man now, Charles. You have to act and dress like it. See you tomorrow, son."

The three Drieborg's left the restaurant and did as Susan suggested. They went to the Kenny shoe store and bought some work shoes for their son. Then, they went next door to Houseman's men store and bought a pair of work pants and a couple of shirts for Charles.

"Now that you're earning money, son," Mike told him. "I expect you to pay for your own work clothing, after this."

*   *   *

Back at the restaurant, George and Susan had a conversation with their store manager, Tom Russell.

"We've just hired new bus-boy, Tom," George told him.

"Yes, sir. When can I expect him to start work?"

"He should be here at four tomorrow and stay until six. I want you to walk him home afterwards. Can you do that, Tom?"

"Yes, sir. I understand."

"As usual, I'll train him when he gets here," Susan added. "Remember when I trained you, Tom?"

"Yes, I do, Mrs. Neal," He responded. "I remember back then. I was scared of making a mistake; scared silly."

"Just the same, you made a few and broke a few dishes too, didn't you?" She added.

"Yes, ma'am. I surely did."

"Remember that, Tom when this new kid makes his mistakes. And, he will, I'm sure. Correct him, but I want you to bring him along slowly, like I did with you. I want him to succeed. OK Tom?"

"Yes, ma'am. I get 'ya."

George concluded. "If any of the staff get rough with him or taunt him for any reason, you put a stop to it or let me know. I won't tolerate that."

"Yes, sir."

"Be sure, Tom," George emphasized. "I'd hate to have to find a new manager."

"Yes, Sir," assured him. "I understand completely."

On the way home, Susan said.

"You were a bit rough with Tom, weren't you?"

"Not at all, Sue," George explained. "I wanted Tom to understand how seriously I meant that I would not tolerate hazing by the other employees."

"I think Tom got the message, George."

"Good. I would hate to have to find a new manager."

Susan poked him. "You are terrible sometimes."

"But you love me just the same. Right?"

"Yes. But sometimes you make it hard."

*   *   *

At home that evening the two teen-agers were talking in their room.

"You're really going to work with sick people, Eleanor?"

"Someone has to, Charles, "she responded. "At least I don't have to clean people's dirty cups and dishes."

"Better than handling blood covered bandages and such," He snapped back. "You really like that kind of thing?"

"As a matter of fact, I do like working with people who are sick or hurt. I'm sure it will make me feel like I'm doing something good, something important."

"Uncle George told me that most every business person starts out sweeping floors and such."

"Do you want to be a business man?"

"I don't know, Eleanor," Charles admitted.

"So, this work is for you to sort of find out?"

"I suppose. I'll begin finding out, tomorrow."

"So, will I, at grandfather Murphy's office."

Charles shut off the kerosene lamp.

"Good night, Eleanor."

"Good night, Charles. "

*   *   *

Down the hallway, Michael and Mary Jacqueline were snuggled under their covers.

"Who would have thought helping Congressman Kellogg would cause such changes in our family." Mary Jacqueline said.

"Right," Mike replied hugging his wife.

"I think it will turn out to be a good thing for the children, though."

"I agree," Mike responded. "I must admit, I feel guilty not having required more of Charles before this. He was right when he told Susan that all that has been asked of him up to this point is for him pick up his room. That's hardly preparation for living and working in our world."

"It does seem that working at the restaurant is a good opportunity for him. But I worry, just the same."

"About what?" Mike asked.

"All kinds of dark thoughts are running through my head," she admitted snuggling closer to Mike. "How the other workers treat him. How he will react when he makes a mistake like breaking a dish or spilling something on the floor."

"I see your point," Mike agreed. "But he has to learn to get over such disappointments, follow instructions and perform. My father did that for me. Hopefully, this job will do that for Charles."

"Hopefully, it will. But I'm his mother. So, I worry."

"Just remember, dear," Mike cautioned. "when he comes home tomorrow night all tired out and whining about the hard work that was demanded of him, we can't be too sympathetic. We can't allow him to think we agree that he is justified in his complaints."

"It will be hard, Michael," Mary Jacqueline said.

Michael leaned over his wife and gave her kiss; a long one.

"Are you trying to take my mind off my worry about Charles?"

"Exactly," he said as he moved his hand under her nightgown and up her leg.

"Ummm," she growled. "I think it's working."

"Enjoying it, eh?"

"Don't stop, Michael," She moaned as she stretched next to her husband and enjoyed his touch.

He didn't stop.

The Marshal's Office

Chief Deputy Marshal Pat Riley was going over the arrest roster for the week with Bill Anderson.

"It appears the prison is not full, lad," He commented.

"No," Bill answered, "We have a few cells available. With the foul weather, the number of crimes always seem to go down. At least early in the winter, they do. By March everyone is sort 'a sick of it all. Cabin fever seems ta prey on folks, people get restless and the arrests go up. At least, that's my experience."

"It's a sad business we're in, lad," Riley observed. "But better this than bad people runnin' lose in the town, hurtin' others."

"That's a good way to look at it, Pat. Otherwise we might just get so hardened, we might become as bad as the folks in our cells."

Riley changed the subject. "How's the Marshal and Killeen getting along with their preparations for their Atlanta trip?"

"It seems that everything is going nicely. Killeen told me that our former Platoon Leader, Lieutenant Henry Austry is going to join their merry band."

"What do ya know," Riley responded with a smile. "Haven't seen the likes a' him since the Dakota Territory back in '65. When we get a minute ya 'll have to tell me what happened to him since."

"It quite a story," Bill revealed. "Over a pint after work some evening, I'll share the tale."

"Actually, why don't I speak to the fair Colleen and have ya' over ta' the house fer supper one evening soon. You can tell us the tale after we enjoy one a' her suppers."

"Sounds good ta' me," Bill responded. "Will yer wife allow us to enjoy our pipes in the house?"

"She'll make an exception fer you, lad. I'm sure."

"What a woman," Bill joked.

"That's fer sure, I'm tellin' ya." Riley concluded.

Atlanta, Georgia

Their carriage pulled up in front of the Kimball House, a six-story brick building on Peach Street in Atlanta, Georgia. The street was still unpaved and often muddy, but the hotel was new. Its front windows gleamed as they reflected the mid-morning sun.

A railroad man named Plant had purchased most of the ruined rail lines in the South after the war. As he rebuilt the rail system, he also built hotels to house his traveling passengers. The Kimball House was the pride and joy of the new Atlanta and his railroad line.

As soon as the carriage came to a stop, a uniformed door-man stepped forward to open the horse-drawn vehicle's door and two other men began to take the bags from the boot at the rear of the carriage.

"Good morning, ma'am," the door-man greeted Mary Jacqueline as he helped her out of the carriage. "Welcome to the Kimball House. My porters will take your bags."

"Thank you," she responded.

Then he led her and Michael into the hotel lobby.

"The check-in desk is to you right, sir."

It was only a few minutes later that they were on the hotel elevator.

"I don't remember being on an elevator before, Michael." Mary Jacqueline told her husband.

"You've forgotten the hotel in St. Louis last year, dear," He reminded her. "When we went West on that investigation of corruption among Indian Agents, there was an elevator in that hotel. Our friends Bose and Ellie joined us and we brought Jacob back to Michigan with us. Remember?"

"Oh, yes," She said. "I remember the trip but not the elevator. Strange that I should forget such an unusual gadget as this. Tell me again. How does it work"

"If I recall correctly, there are cables or ropes that pull this box we're standing in up to our desired floor. The rope that pulls this box up is pulled over a pully above us by a steam engine in the basement of this building. Quite ingenious, actually."

"Sort of scary, I'd say," Mary Jacqueline decided. "What if the rope breaks?"

"A man named Elisha Otis demonstrated a safety device over a decade ago in a New York City building. He invented a catch-device that clicks into place as the elevator moves up the building. Should the rope break, this box would drop maybe a foot, at most. But It's decent would be stopped by the device that fell into place below us as we passed over it.

"I read that Otis would demonstrate his devise's safety in each location where he installed an elevator. He would get on a platform, be pulled up and then someone would cut the rope. His device stopped the decent of the platform every time. It was always quite convincing"

"And this elevator has that safety device?"

"I hope so," Mike told his wife.

"So do I, Michael. But [please don't joke about this It makes me shiver just thinking about how high we are in this cramped little box. I'd feel safer if we walked up to our room."

Mike put his arm around his wife. "Hold on to me dear. We're almost to our floor."

*   *   *

Later, in the afternoon, Mike and his wife joined the other members of his team in a meeting room on the second floor.

The ladies hugged and the men shook hands.

Mary Jacqueline very quickly took charge.

"Michael," she said. "We ladies are going to go downtown and look around. You men have your business to discuss. We'd just be in the way."

"Hold it a minute," he responded. "Gerry and Linda Gostkowski are here for a reason. They will accompany you whenever you leave the hotel."

"Such a bother. Why do we need them, Michael?" Mary Alice Stephan asked.

"Mary Alice," Mike began patiently. "Have you forgotten what happened to you and these same ladies in Charleston the last time you went off by yourselves?"

A couple of years ago, this same team of men were in Charleston with their wives. They were part of the Lincoln assassination investigation team back then. Mary Alice wanted to take the

47

ladies on a tour of the city. She didn't want to bother with an armed escort, though. So, she dismissed the two men assigned by Mike to her group and went off with the other ladies to see the sights of the city. They ended up late that afternoon on Fort Sumter.

Just before dark, the last boat to the mainland left, without them. The ladies had been captured by some rogue Regulators who were under the leadership of David Pope, Mary Jacqueline's late husband's brother.

He had harbored a bitter hatred for her, calling her his brother's Yankee 'bitch'. Now, that he had her under his control on the island, he dragged her into the ruins of the fort and told her triumphantly that he was going to rape her.

As he began to tear at her clothing, Mary Jacqueline remembered the small pistol Mike had insisted she carry in her dress pocket. In the darkness, she managed to get it out, cock it and place it under the chin of her attacker before she pulled the trigger.

Back in town, Mike found the two dismissed escorts and also discovered that the ladies were stranded on the island as well. He and his team of husbands commandeered a boat and by the time they reached the island fort, they found that the ladies had killed their captors. They brought the alive, but very shaken ladies back to Charleston to their lodgings

"Are we in danger here in Atlanta, Michael?" Ellie asked.

"You could be Ellie," he answered. "We don't know yet. Some group has kidnapped Craig Haynes. The local authorities were no help and our friend, Congressman Kellogg found that he could not handle the situation either. He then asked me for help rescuing Craig. That's why we are all here. It is reasonable to assume that the same people who took Haynes, would not hesitate to kidnap you if it seemed to aide whatever agenda they are pursuing. So, please accept your escort or stay in the hotel at least until we sort this all out."

Mary Jacqueline entered the conversation. "I think we'll go to the lobby and discuss this, Michael."

Once they left the room, the husbands spoke up.

"I'm not sure they'll listen to you Mike," Bose said. "I know Ellie. She's tough as nails.
I'm not so sure she'll take your advice."

"Truth be told, Mary Alice is pretty head-strong, too," Her husband Robert Stephan revealed.

"You might remember, Mike," he went on. "That she was the one who said they didn't need the armed escorts back in Charleston. But she was pretty shaken over the incident back then. She might take your advice this time."

"I think Peggy will listen to you Mike," Frank Stanizeck offered. "She was very upset with that experience on Fort Sumpter. Today, she still carries that small pistol you gave her back then, too"

Mike ended the discussion. "Gentlemen," he stated firmly. "Let me be clear. I was not giving the ladies advice. I was telling them that if they want to wander about, it would be with the armed guards I hired to protect them. Gerry and Linda are trained former Pinkertons. There is no discussion about this. If any of the wives sneak off like they did back in Charleston, I'll send them home.

"Linda," he ordered. "Join the ladies now, please and stay with them. Gerry, you will follow them wherever they go. Make sure each of them has one of those small pocket pistols we brought with us. Do not take no for an answer and do not leave them whatever they say."

"Right, Mike," Gerry Gostkowski answered. He and Linda, left the room. "I will."

Mike turned to the three husbands. "I'm sorry to seem so harsh. But we are facing some pretty nasty people down here. If you have second thoughts about helping Kellogg and Haynes with this problem feel free to head on home. So, are you in or not?"

All three men assured him that they were staying to help. Stan Killeen and Henry Austry had no such concerns, but they said they were staying, too.

"That's great," Mike said. "Now, let's get down to business.

He began with Frank Stanitzek.

"Frank," Mike asked. "Have you been able to assess the situation in this area?"

"I contacted several men who are active in this area's Klan. They all know who Kellogg is and his efforts to set up a property tax system in this area. All of them also oppose the military occupation here. None of them know of the kidnapping. Frankly, they were surprised to hear of it. They don't' understand what purpose it could serve."

"Thanks Frank," Mike said. Then Mike turned to Henry Austry. "Henry. What information have you dug up on the Union League?"

"Sounds like a Yankee outfit, Henry," Bose commented. "What the devil is it anyways?"

"I'm not surprised you haven't heard of it, Bose," Henry commented. "Up in that mountain country of Cade's Cove, Tennessee, nothing seems to bother you."

"Dog gone right, Yank," Bose responded. "A little piece 'a heaven it is. Non 'a that big city stuff the rest 'a yas have. That's fer sure."

"Thanks for reminding us Bose. For the benefit of everyone, Henry," Mike asked. "Tell us about this organization."

"During the war this organization was founded up North. Its purpose was to promote loyalty to the Union and the war effort. Anyone talking disloyally would be reported to a federal marshal. Thousands of citizens throughout the North were arrested as a result of such reports. Even newspapers were closed down for allegedly publishing what was considered disloyal material.

"After the war, most of our troops were anxious to leave the army and return home. The government was anxious to reduce its costs, too. So, within months, the largest army & navy in the world was virtually disbanded. At the same time, the Johnson governments in the formers states of the Confederacy established state militias. Made up of former Confederate officers and enlisted men. These militias were used, it seems, to enforce the new Black Codes adopted by these post war southern governments.

"At that time, the War Department had only a few over 48,00 active troops left to handle the territories, the Indian conflicts and the military occupation of the entire area of the former Confederacy. So, when Congress abolished all the Johnson governments in the South, Congress also forbad these states to maintain militias.

"That's when the Union League moved into the South and began to recruit former negro Union soldiers and form para-military forces in the southern states. These units are now, in effect, the military arm of the Freedman's Bureau.

"You might find it interesting to note, the relationship of the Union League to the voting for president in the last election.

Where the League was found in large numbers, Grant won that state's electoral votes. Here in Georgia, where the League is not very strong, Seymour, the Democrat, won the state's electoral votes.

"Also, wherever the Union League operate, it is evident that they are hated by the locals."

"Why is that?" Killeen asked.

"Because they steal from the white population. You see, the War Department does not fund League activities; nor are any of the states in the South allowed to do so. Instead, the League must finance itself by confiscating and selling things they take from the citizenry. This is much like the Bummers of the war years who confiscated the possessions of Southerners in order to support military operations. Except now, the Leagues' effort is much more organized and thorough."

"You can understand why we Sothern's hate them so," Bob Stephan of South Carolina added.

"It doesn't help that their ranks are full of former slaves who fought for the Union in the late conflict," Frank added. "They are observed taking great pleasure pillaging people's homes and businesses, too."

Henry Austry concluded his update about the Union League.

"At the War Department, we see two para-military organizations operating in the South. The Union League is the military arm of the Freedman's Bureau. As such, they support the voter registration of freedmen, they get out the colored vote activities, they suppress conservative southern candidate efforts and conduct a good deal of pillaging and the destruction of southern property.

"On the other side of the road, we have seen the growth of the Klan. This para-military organization has grown rapidly as a counter to the Union League. Its members try to suppress the voter registration of freedmen and try to suppress the colored vote, too. Where the Klan is active, colored candidates for office are intimidated as well. Klan units appear to do their share of pillaging and burning of property, too. In many areas it is as widespread a practice as it is with the Union League.

"Basically, the League is devoted to changing the social order, and supporting the Republican Party. The Klan is determined to the restoration and maintenance of white dominance and supporting the Democratic Party."

Mike asked. "Would it be fair to say that it's six of one and half a dozen of the other?"

"That's too simplistic, Mike," Bob Stephan judged. "It all depends upon the region and the relative strength of the two organizations from place to place."

"Explain that, please." Stan asked.

"Sure, Stan. Where the League is the dominant force, freedmen vote in large numbers and colored's hold a wide range of political offices," Robert explained. "The opposite is true in those areas where the Klan is dominant."

"Thanks, Bob,"

"You're our Georgia guy, Frank," Mike decided. "How does this stack up in your area?"

"Allow me to explain it this way, Mike," Frank answered.

"I read that up North, you guys have a large organization called, the Grand Army of the Republic. They do all sorts of good in local communities and are a political force. Isn't that true?"

"Pretty much, Frank," Mike answered. "What's your point?"

"Down in the South, such an organization of Confederate veterans is outlawed. Where your guys wear their old uniforms and such in public, we cannot. We can't even have a funeral to honor one of our deceased Confederate leaders.

"Remember when Colonel Pope died back in Charleston?"

"Ya," I remember that," Stan said. "He had a rip-roaring Reb funeral; singing Dixie, rebel yell an all." Stan recalled.

"You're right, Stan. I remember that too," Frank agreed. "But that kind of funeral was illegal then and is still outlawed in today's South. Around here, no funeral processions, or uniforms are allowed, no singing of Dixie and certainly no Rebel Yell would be tolerated.

"So, we have meetings and even funerals in secret," Frank revealed. "In my town of Macon many of us veterans meet regularly. Our organization is called a Klan, pure and simple.

"Things are pretty quiet in our area. We have tried to keep it that way. I don't know what would happen if Union army troops came our way. Before the presidential election of 1868, we had an incident that merits telling.

"That fall, an armed force of over 300 colored's rode into the Camilla area, near Macon, to hold a Republican night rally. This Union League force was led by two whites, N.P. Pierce who was a candidate for Congress and a Major Murphy a candidate for Georgia Elector. Murphy was also the commander of the Union League in Albany, Georgia.

"The Sheriff of Camilla rode out to meet this force. He urged Pierce and Murphy to disband and return to Albany. His request was refused. So, the Sheriff returned to town and gathered a militia force. A battle ensued which resulted in eight of Murphy's men killed and another 25 wounded. Only two white militia men were killed. "

Bob Stephan interrupte4d. "I think I read about this. Was it call the Camilla Massacre?"

"In the Northern press it was," Frank responded. "The Albany Freedman's Bureau spread the story that a freedman's political meeting in Camilla was attacked. Of course, our Klan was blamed in the Northern press, as well."

Killeen asked. "What was the real story, Frank?"

"Bullock, our carpetbagger governor sent a committee to investigate. His people concluded that it was Pierce and Murphy who had started the trouble by attacking the town of Camilla with their armed force of Negroes."

"Funny," Stephan commented. "I didn't read about that part in the Northern press."

"How do you folks up your way handle such things, Bose?" Killeen asked.

"Life is pretty simple up on our mountain in Tennessee," Bose offered. "Not much of a Union presence there. We have had funerals and meetings of vets right out in the open. The Union guys meet openly, too. We all sort a' ignore such things. Live and let live. Works fer us."

Mike asked. "Frank, would a group like yours kidnap Federal officials, like our Craig Haynes?"

"We wouldn't. But I can't speak for the boys in Atlanta. There's still a lot of bitterness there about Sherman's burning of the city back in '64."

"Would you ask around about that?"

"Not a problem, Mike," Frank assured him. "But it may take a few days for me to find someone willing to talk with me."

"Wouldn't Kellogg know what's going on here?" Stan asked of no one in particular.

"I sent him a telegram asking him to meet us in this hotel tonight for supper. We'll meet him afterward for a run-through of the situation. Hopefully he'll be able to bring us up to date on the situation then." Mike told everyone.

"Are we supposed to go around here, armed," Stan asked.

"Absolutely," Mike responded quickly. "Each of us must carry a revolver in a shoulder holster; starting this evening. When we are on assignment outside of the hotel, you will each carry your Spencer rifle, too. We must be on the alert at all times."

"How are we to handle our expenses while we're here, Mike?" Stephan asked.

"That's one of the issues we will review with Kellogg tonight, Bob."

"Until then, though, let's join the ladies in the lobby," Mike suggested. "We have a couple of hours before Kellogg is scheduled to join us. I'll want you all in this room by six this evening. Plenty of time to catch a nap and clean up before then."

"That nap idea sounds good ta me," Bose offered. "Especially if my Ellie is in that nice soft hotel bed with me."

"You married guys get all the breaks," Killeen grumbled. "Right Henry?"

"We've both had our chances, Stan," Henry reminded. Him.

*   *   *

Mary Jacqueline, Peg and Ellie were sitting in the lobby chatting.

Bob Stephan asked about his wife.

"See that shop over there, Robert?" Ellie said and pointed to a sign that said Woman's Salon.

"What's that about?" he asked.

"She's getting all prettied up.," Ellie went on. "At least that's what she said."

Mike asked. "Why aren't you ladies in there, too?"

"Are you suggesting that I need prettying up, Michael?" Peg Stanitzek asked with a sly smile.

Stan laughed. "You're in trouble now, Drieborg."

"I thought you were here to protect me, Killeen."

"Sometimes I just can't protect you from yourself, though. Now is one of those times. You're on your own, my friend."

The ladies were chuckling at Mike's discomfort.

"I'll forgive you," Peg assured him. "But only if you treat me to a glass of wine at supper tonight."

"Thank you Peg," Mike said. "I will."

"But I'll not forgive you so easily, Yank," Ellie snapped. "Think I'll hold out for some good southern sipping whiskey. What about you Mary Jacqueline? You gonna forgive your husband easy or hard?"

"After we got back to our room, he'll find out what I have in store for him."

Ellie hooted. "Look at him, he's blushing," she laughed. "I think he knows what you have in mind, sweetie."

"He can only hope," Mary Jacqueline said with a coy smile.

The Kimball House Private Dining Room

Mike had reserved a small room for their evening meal and meeting with William Kellogg.

All of his team and their wives were present when Kellogg arrived.

As soon as he entered the room, Mike greeted him. "Congressman!" he almost shouted. "Welcome."

William Kellogg accepted Mike's offer of a handshake. "Good to see you Michael."

He turned immediately to Mary Jacqueline and asked. "How is little Maxine?"

Mike's daughter, Maxine had been born in Philadelphia shortly after the Lincoln assassination investigation was completed. Out of their regard for the congressman, Mary Jacqueline and Michael had named their infant daughter for Kellogg's late wife, Maxine. His fondness for Maxine was therefore understandable.

"She is fine, William," she told him. "I miss her terribly. But she is just too young to travel with us. And, the older children are in school."

"I understand," Kellogg responded after receiving a hug from Mike's wife. "It's a treat for me that you're here, my dear."

He turned to Michael, "If you wouldn't mind, introduce me to your men and their wives." He asked. "I confess. My memory is fading. I know them all by sight. But I'll be darned if I can remember all their names."

"Certainly, sir, "Mike assured him. "Mary Jacqueline will you accompany us. You can handle the introduction of the ladies."

Captain Austry was first,

"Of course, I remember you," The Congressman insisted. "You're a captain now, congratulations. I am so grateful that you could join us here in Atlanta."

"I'm sorry for the circumstances that prompted the invitation, sir," Austry responded. "I hope we can find and rescue Craig."

"I do too."

Kellogg turned to face Bose Faute

"I seem to recall that you're from some mountain in Tennessee. Is that correct." He said as he shook Bose's hand.

"Ya got that right, Yank," Bose responded with his usual disrespectful tone. "You're the second Yank I come to respect. Good ta see you again, sir."

"Who happens to be the first Yank you came to respect, my rebel friend," Kellogg asked with a broad grin on his face.

"Why you're very own Marshal Drieborg, a course."

"Of course," Kellogg agreed. "Thank you for coming to help.

"And, who is this charming lady at your side, Marshal Faute?"

"This be my wife, Ellie, sir"

"It is so nice to see you again, Mrs. Faute."

"My pleasure to be here," Ellie responded. "How is your daughter Pattie doing?"

"The last I heard she and her husband George are entertaining the dickins off the Washington City scene."

"She an' I hit it off real well," Ellie reminded Kellogg. "We seem ta be chips off a' the same kind a' block. I sure enjoyed her company."

"I'll let her know you asked after her, Mrs. Faute."

Mike continued the introductions, as he approached the Stanitzeks.

"This couple have a business in your area, Congressman. You might remember meeting Frank Stanitzek and his wife Peg when we worked on the Lincoln assassination investigation. They have a farm and meat store in Macon."

"It is good to see you again, Marshal Stanitzek and you too Peg. Thank you for helping us out on this problem with Marshal Haynes."

"We think a lot of Craig," Frank informed Kellogg. "We are happy to do whatever we can to get him returned safely."

Bob and Mary Alice Stephan were last in line. Mike introduced them.

"Bob and George Krupp were our legal team during the Lincoln assassination investigation. Bob and his wife Mary Alice hail from Columbia, South Carolina."

"Good evening," Kellogg greeted. "I seem to recall that Secretary of War Stanton did not enjoy your line of questioning."

"it was my pleasure putting the Secretary's feet to the fire back then, sir." Bob responded. "I was happy to read of his dismissal shortly after our report was published."

"He wasn't, I'm sure," Kellogg quipped. "Nice to see you Mrs. Stephan."

Mary Alice did a bit of a curtsey.

At the dinner table that evening, Kellogg played the perfect host.

"Mr. Faute," he said at one point. "Remember your old friend Congressman Bothwell??

Bose responded with a devilish grin. "Ain't he the one who Mike here put in chains an' locked up in a hallway closet fer a few hours?"

"I think he did just that Mr. Faute," Kellogg responded with his own grin.

"Mike. Didn't you put a hood over his head, too?"

"Yes, I did Bose."

"Ya, I remember him congressman," Bose admitted. "He called us Southerns traitors and got all heated up when I prodded him a bit. I recall saying something like, if we were such a burr under you're saddle why didn't you Yanks just let us go?

"He pretty well lost it, then."

"I remember that, Bose. Henry said. "That's when Mike drug him out a' the room in chains with a sack over his head. Only brought him back after lunch. The congressman had calmed down and cooperated some, after that."

Listening to all this banter, Ethie had something on her mind, too.

"I come with Bose to Washington City a few a' years ago. The size a' that town sure shocked me. Then, a year or so ago, Mike dragged me an Bose to St. Louis ta help him out on something. I thought Washington was big, But St. Louis seemed much bigger. How about this Atlanta a' yours, congressman? Should it be all right for us women-folk to walk around safe or not?"

"I'd be careful, Mrs. Faute," he responded. "Remember, my deputy, Craig Haynes was kidnapped in broad daylight a few weeks ago. Pretty bold, I'd say. And we haven't been able to find him or even get word about him since. Not a word from the kidnappers or help finding him from the locals.

"If the kidnappers aren't afraid of stirring up the Union army would they hesitate taking one or more of you ladies' hostage to further their purpose?

"So, Mrs. Faute, I'd be careful," Kellogg concluded.

"Marshal Drieborg," Peg Stanitzek asked. "I think I'm ready for that glass of wine you own me. I prefer a mild red, thank you."

"While you're at it, Yank," Ethie Faute added. "You can get me some sipping whiskey. I prefer a mild bourbon, if you please."

"What's this all about," Mary Alice Stephan asked.

"Seems that Mike stepped all over himself asking the ladies why they had not joined you in the beauty salon this afternoon." Mary Jacqueline told her. "They caught him at it. I think he is paying them off."

"Since my time in the women's salon this afternoon caused you some embarrassment Marshal Drieborg," Mary Alice decided. "I think I'll have a glass of sherry while you're at it."

Mike turned to his wife and asked. "Do you want something from the bar as well, dear?"

"Thank you, but no. I'll collect later."

Ethie howled. "That a' way dearie. You got him blushing again."

Mike left the table quickly to fetch the drinks.

While he was gone, the men explained the situation to Kellogg.

Mike soon brought the drinks for the ladies.

"Thank you, Yank," Ethie toasted. 'You can put yer foot in yer mouth anytime when there's good southern bourbon like this around. "

Kellogg joined the good-natured kidding.

"I'm surprised at your behavior Michael," Kellogg said. "I recall you being a pretty smooth-talker around the ladies."

Killeen finally broke his silence. "Yawl will have to forgive the Marshall, folks. He's been holed up in the far-away north country fer some time now. We don't need much smooth talkin' up there, don't ya know. Especially if'n you're the Federal Marshal."

"Isn't it time for you to go to bed or howl at the moon or something, Stan?" Mike snapped.

Everyone laughed, enjoying the good-natured kidding.

Mary Jacqueline stood.

"It is time for us ladies to take our drinks to the lobby and let these men have their cigars and conversation." Mary Jacqueline told everyone. "Good night gentlemen. Thank you for the fine dinner, congressman."

Kellogg rose to his feet along with all the men and said, "You are most welcome, ladies. Your presence at this table has been a real pleasure. I look forward to dinning with you again soon."

*   *   *

As soon as the ladies left, Kellogg passed out some cigars and the men settled down to work.

Mike began, "Please tell us as much as you can of the situation here, sir."

Grand Rapids

The family was sitting at the supper table in the Murphy home.

"Charles," asked Dr. Murphy. "Would you say grace please?"

Charles looked surprised, and hesitated.

"We can do it together, grandfather." Eleanor volunteered.

"All right, Eleanor," the doctor responded. "We'll do it together then."

"Bless us oh Lord

For these Thy gifts

That we are about to receive

From Thy bounty

Through Christ our Lord. Amen"

"Thank you, children," their grandmother, Judy Murphy said. "Now, Charles. Please begin passing the plates of food."

"I think I'll give each of you some of the stew, mother," Dr. Murphy said." It will be much easier than passing the hot bowl."

"Good idea, grandfather," Charles said.

"Thank you, Charles," His grandfather said with a surprised smile.

"Tell me, Charles," his grandmother asked. "How is the job going?"

"It's fine"

His grandfather snapped, "Charles. If you're not going to answer the question more thoroughly than that, you can leave the table and go to your room."

Charles pushed his chair back and stood to leave the room.

Eleanor almost shouted. "Charles! Don't you dare leave. Grandmother asked you a simple question. You need to give her a decent answer."

"Oh, all right, Eleanor."

He sat back down. "Every day, I just clear the tables, sweep the floors, help wash and dry the dishes and set the tables for the next morning crowd."

'Do you have to do this every day?" his grandmother continued.

"Yes, grandmother," he answered. "It gets pretty boring, actually. But that's all a bus-boy is supposed to do, I guess."

"What did you do with your first paycheck?" his grandfather asked

"I gave it to grandmother." he answered.

"And, what do you do with it, dear?" Dr. Murphy asked his wife.

"I give Charles twenty-five cents and put the rest into a bank account his uncle Joseph Deeb has set up for him at the Old Kent Bank & Trust.

"Grandmother does the same for me, grandfather," Eleanor said.

"What's this money being saved for?" he asked.

His wife answered for the children. "I think their parents want them to pay for their own work clothing and also for their own books when they go to college."

"I know college is a year away," Dr. Murphy continued. "But what do you intend to study in college, Charles?"

"I don't know, grandfather," he responded. "Uncle George thinks I should be a businessman. Uncle Joe says being a lawyer is best. Maybe I'll go back to South Carolina and run my grandfather Pope's plantation."

His grandmother joined the conversation. "Do you know anything about raising cotton or rice, Charles?"

"Not a thing, grandmother," he responded honestly. "But how hard can it be to supervise workers sticking seeds into the ground and watching it grow until it's ready to take to some market?"

"Got to be harder than that," Eleanor joined in.

"That's all I see grandfather Jake doing in his corn and wheat fields. He plants the seeds, the crop grows, he harvests it and then sells the grain."

"I hadn't realized it was that easy, Charles," His grandfather Murphy commented with a straight face.

Charles went on. "It seems to be, especially when someone else does all the work, like on grandfather Pope's land in South Carolina."

"Oh, yes," Dr. Murphy said, "I had forgotten about all those coloreds working the land."

"And, what about you, Eleanor?" her grandmother asked. "What do you see in your future?"

"I want to be a doctor, like grandfather Murphy," She answered without any hesitation.

At this point, Dr. Murphy put down his napkin, sat back and look at her intently.

"I have watched you working with my patients, Eleanor. Both nurse Kathy and I are very impressed with how you listen carefully to them. Our patients seem to trust you, as well. You have a real sensitive touch with them.

"But I must remind you that women have a difficult time becoming doctors. Those women who have achieved that goal are not widely accepted."

Eleanor sat back in her chair and looked directly at Dr. Murphy.

"Grandfather," she began. "Did you give up on your goal of teaching at the University of Pennsylvania just because you were Irish and Catholic? No, you overcame all that prejudice back then.

"Why should I not pursue my goal as well?"

"I can't think of a single reason you shouldn't my dear," He assured her.

* *

Later, Dr. Murphy sat in the family living room reading the town paper, The Eagle, and smoking a pipe.

His wife Judy sat knitting enjoying the warmth of the room's fireplace. The two children were in their study room on the second floor.

"What did you think of our discussion with the children at the dinner table tonight, Miles?"

"That Drieborg girl has spunk. No question about that." He said.

'You're right about her. She is one tough little girl. What do you think of Charles's comments?" his wife continued.

"I must admit, dear, that I worry about his attitude. I fear he looks for shortcuts. You know what I mean? He seems to see a challenge and immediately looks for a way to avoid it."

"Why is that so troubling?"

"it is troubling because you just can't successfully go through life avoiding challenges. You must be willing to confront them. You must be willing to work hard, to overcome obstacles; turn them to your advantage even. He seems unwilling to do that. That's why his attitude troubles me."

"I must admit, dear," his wife responded. "I have a similar fear. This job of his was a good idea. I hope it helps him mature."

"I hope so, too."

* *

At the Cosmopolitan Restaurant and Bakery, two workers were talking about Charles, too.

"What do you mean, that little spoiled brat?" his co-worker Billy asked. "You talkin' about the bus-boy, Charles?"

"Ya. The one who comes in the afternoon."

70

"What about him."

"I found out he's the nephew of the owner, George Neal."

"So, what?"

"I think we should have some fun with him."

"Like what?"

"You know. Make him trip and break some cups, or somethin."

"Why?"

"Be fun to see him suffer some. You know, spoiled kid an all."

"Howie. That's the dumbest idea I've heard all day. I like my job. Do you?"

"Well ya," Howie replied. "What's that got to do with havin some fun with this kid?"

"Cause that seems ta me to be a pretty fast way to get fired."

"Whose gonna know? Sides, its harmless fun."

"If'n you go any further with this, Howie, you're on your own." Billy concluded.

The next afternoon, Howie saw an opportunity to bump into Charles when he was carrying a tub full of dirty dishes from the front tables. Charles fell forward and dishes hit the floor and broken pieces flew all over the floor.

"Sorry, kid," Howie said. "Didn't see you coming around the corner. Best be careful next time."

The manager, Tom Russell saw the entire incident. He let Charles clean up the mess and get on with his work.

Later, Tom saw Howie.

"Hey, Howie," he greeted. "Come into my office for a minute."

Howie walked into the restaurant manager's office.

"Close the door, will you?"

"What's up, boss?" Howie

Tom looked across his desk at Howie.

"I saw you bump into the busboy," he began.

"Ya, he didn't look out carrying that tub an all. Ran right inta me."

"Yes, Howie, he did," Tom corrected him. "But I saw you waiting for him around the corner. You set him up for that collision. You bumped into him on purpose. I won't have that kind of thing in this restaurant. You're fired. Come back tomorrow and I'll have your last pay ready. "

"I want my pay now."

"Afraid not, Howie," Tom informed him. "I have to figure up the cost of all those cups and plates that got broken just now. I'm going to deduct the cost of replacing them from you pay. You come in after lunch tomorrow and we'll settle up. Now get out of here!"

Howie shouted. "Fired 'cause of some spoiled kid? You haven't heard the last of this, you bastard!"

He slammed the office door on his way out.

Tom thought about Howie's threat. *"That stupid ass just might try something. Wouldn't put it past him. If something happens to Charles, I might just lose my job. Best take special care of the boss's nephew."*

"Hey, Charles," Tom called out.

"Yes, sir?"

"Be sure to knock on my office door when you're finished with your work. Don't leave the restaurant alone."

"Yes, sir."

"I wouldn't put it past that dumb ass, Howie to try something with Charles on his way home. Not on my watch." Tom vowed.

Atlanta

"What do you have to report, Frank?" Mike asked.

"You asked me to check with Klan people in this area about Craig Haynes, right?"

"Right," Mike agreed. "What did you find out?"

"None of the Atlanta area Klan leaders admit to knowing anything about the kidnapping." Frank revealed. "They all know about it, but nobody claims any involvement."

"Right, but what is this about the Freedman's Bureau being involved?" Mike asked. "Where did you get that rumor?"

"The talk on the street up here in Atlanta is that the Freedman's Bureau leadership and their military arm, the Union League, pulled off the kidnapping of Haynes."

Henry Austry responded, "Why in holy hell would a Union supporting outfit kidnap a U.S. Marshal who is working for the Union's military governor here in Atlanta?"

Frank reentered the conversation. "Speculation around here is that the Freedman's Bureau leaders are trying to get something to blame on the Klan. It worked with the false stories they issued about the Camilla Massacre. They blamed all the killings caused on that occasion by their Union League troops on the Klan. It worked. The Northern press got all worked up condemning the Klan.

"My contacts think the Union League has no interest in a ransom. It is believed that group only wanted an incident to blame on the Klan. They also think Haynes was murdered a long time ago."

"Wouldn't be surprised," Bob Stephan said.

"Congressman Kellogg," Mike asked. "What are your thoughts about what Frank and Bob are saying?"

"My gut instinct is that they might be correct," he responded. "We've discovered some bad apples in the Freedman's Bureau and in their para-military arm, the Union League as well."

"What do you mean, 'bad apples?'" Henry asked.

"The Director of the Freedman's Bureau in Georgia is a prime example," Kellogg began. "His name is Richard Greenhoe. He was recently an Indian Agent in the Dakota Territory. Thoroughly corrupt, he bled the system for his own gain buying shoddy supplies with money meant for the Indians and corrupted them as well with whisky and prostitution. We, in Congress, believed large sums of money were funneled to his superiors in Washington City, too.

"When we got close to indicting him and others for that, they got a pass and Greenhoe got an appointment as Director of the Freedman's Bureau headquartered in Atlanta. Here he is supposed to pursue the mandate of protecting freedmen from economic and political oppression and the responsibility of seeing to it that they get educated and find a stable place in Southern society.

"With the support of his superiors in Washington and the backing of the Northern press, he appears to be completely free to use the para-military force called the Union League, to pillage the white community.

"Blaming their actions on the Klu Klux Klan is convenient and provides a cover for his completely amoral Federal government superiors in Washington and his corrupt Freedman's Bureau operation in Atlanta. It's a perfect setup for them both.

"I'm not ignoring the terror tactics used by the Klan, but the Union League should not be forgiven for their actions either."

"Don't Greenhoe's superiors in Washington care?" Bose asked.

"Some may not realize what he and others are doing here with the power they have given them. Some may approve of his actions because they have it in for the South in general and former slave owners in particular." Kellogg judged.

"I hate to say this but I have concluded that all any of them really care about is getting their share of the spoils, both political and monetary.

"So, that in the final analysis, they seem to be using the freedmen as a cover for pillaging the White community around here and gaining political control for the Republican Party in this reconstruction zone."

"But I read in the Northern press that the freedmen are being terrorized by the Klan." Henry stated.

"Excuse me for saying this Frank, a good deal of that is going on, Henry," Kellogg declared "Both the Klan and the Union League use brutal tactics in their attempts to intimidate the freedmen." Kellogg explained.

"The Klan tries to keep colored men from voting at all and to restore the old social system. The Union League uses terror and even murder to get colored people to hate all Whites and for colored men to vote for Republican candidates."

"It would appear, sir," Mike surmised. "That you and Craig are in the middle of a real tragic and violent mess down here."

"Correct, Mike," Kellogg responded. "It was like falling into quick sand for us. My boss, the military governor for this Reconstruction

District of three former Confederate states does not have ample resources to govern the territory under his charge. Henry here explained the reality of the military situation earlier tonight. So, here in Georgia, the Union League is the big gorilla.

"With all the former colored Union troops they want available to them, and ample arms available as well, the Union League controls this area, not the military governor or anyone in Washington City."

"What about that Henry," Bose asked. "Your War Department seems to pull the strings on that Union League puppet. Don't ya?"

"The way Congressman Kellogg tells it, ya, we should be able to," he had to admit. "But that's not the way it appears to us back in Washington City."

"So, you say you're sort 'a blind to all 'a this?" Bose continued. "Look at what you Yanks in Washington did. You kept the state authorities from having militia forces of their own.

Henry interrupted. "Sure, Congress did. They prohibited those because the state governments were using them to terrorize the colored communities."

But Bose Faute was not going to be denied. "Then, you tell the para-military Union League boys that it's all right to provide for themselves out a' confiscated goods. And, it appears that they somehow get their hands-on repeating rifles, ammunition and horses to equip and train their Negro troops.

"What in hell did ya think these former white Union officers who were hired to lead these Union League units were gonna do once they got troopers and equipment, Henry? They been terrorizing the white communities in the South; that's what."

Henry was red faced by now. "What the Congressman told us today about that was going on here was never approved by the War Department," he replied. "At least, I never heard a discussion about it or read a report about it.

"But I have seen a lot of reports of Klan activities," Henry responded. "While it changes from one location to another, Klan inspired violence is very widespread in the South. It appears that the purpose of the Klan is to terrorize the freedman community and by whatever means needed, to restore and maintain white control.

"The basic purpose of the Black Codes that were imposed after Appomattox, was to deny freedmen the right to move about and instead keep them working on the plantations where they had been slaves."

"I remember," Mike added. "We ran into a lot of that maneuvering when we were in South Carolina a few years back. Land owners needed workers. Workers didn't trust the land owners' their former masters. So, it was a bad standoff."

"Besides, former slaves were under the impression that freedom meant they didn't have to work anymore." remembered Stan.

"As I recall, Mike," Bob Stephan added. "The Freedman's Bureau folks around Charleston helped solve much of that mistrust by negotiating labor contracts between freedmen and land owners. Worked pretty well back in my area."

"But that hasn't been happening around here lately, Bob," Frank interjected. "Instead we've got guys like Greenhow using his military power to loot the white community for profit and terrorizing the colored people to keep them voting Republican."

"But that doesn't excuse the Klan from their terrorist activity either, ya think, Frank?" Killeen asked.

"I'm not saying it does, Stan," Frank protested.

Henry rejoined the discussion. "In South Carolina, Bob, there are more 'Gun Clubs' than in all the rest of the old Confederacy combined. They are well equipped and well- disciplined units used to keep the freedmen in line.

"Congress get a whole lot of reports every week of Klan people burning homes and schools and hangings or whippings of Freedmen; even women. Are they all lies?"

Mike commented. "When the war ended in 1865, the people in the North thought the fighting had ended. "

"Well, my friend, it hadn't," Bob Stephan insisted. "We may have failed on the field of battle, but we have only begun to fight for the restoration of the stable society you Yanks destroyed. And that fight won't stop until we do."

The startling comment made by Bob Stephan, usually the soft spoken one in the group. quieted the room.

Mike thought it was time to move on.

"Gentlemen," he interrupted. "We are not here to discuss the problems of the Reconstruction effort. We are here to find our friend Craig Haynes. I for one think we should sit down with this Greenhoe fellow as soon as possible and see where that takes us. Agreed?"

"Agreed," Bob Stephan said.

Killeen insisted on being heard.

"Just a minute, Mike," He said. "I got one more question. I get that you boys were fighting for independence. That didn't happen, So, now what a' you fighting for?"

"Control!" Stephan snapped. "The restoration a way of life you destroyed.

'You Yanks freed, in place, over four million slaves. This was a labor force that had been developed over the last two hundred plus years. Its existence was crucial to the entire economy and social order of the South. The slaves are ignorant and the majority of them only skilled to work the fields. In addition, you destroyed our towns and farms and all of our livestock. You left us no financial resources and you took away our slave labor force ta' boot. Then you just walked away.

"And to top it off, Stan," Bob concluded. "You Yanks expect us to stand around and do nothing while controlling our anger against you for the mess you've created."

Mike stood and held out his hands. "Look, guys," He said. "You can stay here all night and argue about this for all I care. I am going to join the ladies and maybe have drink in the hotel before I join my wife in her warm bed.

"Congressman," Mike asked. "Will you make arrangements for us to meet with Greenhoe?"

"I'll do my best, Mike," Kellogg promised. "He's a slippery one for sure. Might take me a few days to arrange it."

"Whatever you can do, sir," Mike said. "Now, gentlemen. We've done all we can this evening. I suggest we join the ladies downstairs."

"Good idea, Yank," Bose Faute said rising from his chair. "These old bones a' mine could stand a sip of good southern bourbon."

Grand Rapids

Charles Drieborg and Mr. Russell were walking up Fulton Street on their way to the Drieborg home. It was dusk, the moon had not risen and their path was in the shadows. Each man carried a three-foot length of wood; a club actually.

"Why is it you walk me home each night after work, Mr. Russell?" Charles asked.

"When you're some older you can walk alone," Tom responded. "For now, it's just safer for me to escort you. Besides, you uncle, who is my boss, asked me to."

Charles had to chuckle at that answer. "I can understand why now. But why are we carrying these clubs? Never did that before."

"Remember earlier today when you dropped that tray of dishes?"

"Oh, ya," Charles remembered. "I'm really sorry about that, sir. I suppose you'll take the cost of the broken dishes out of my pay."

"Not this time, Charles," Russell told him. "The reason I'm not going to do that is that I saw Howie waiting for you. He was standing around the corner in the kitchen. Your collision with him was no accident nor was it your fault. He bumped into you on purpose."

"Well, I'll be," Charles exclaimed. "Why would he do that?"

"Some men just like to pick on those they think are weaker than themselves. Makes them feel superior, I guess. Anyway, I confronted Howie and fired him. Then he threatened to get even."

"So, that's why we're carrying the clubs."

"You got it, son," Russell confirmed. "That's why we're carrying the clubs. Just in case."

"You think, Mr. Russell, that Howie knows that my father is a U.S. Marshal?"

"I doubt it, son."

'He would be in deep trouble if he attacked us on my way home."

"Maybe, Charles," Russell told him. "But Howie is not the brightest candle in the room. I doubt if that would make any difference to him. So, we'll see."

"I guess, sir."

*   *   *

It was nearly seven in the evening and he day shift at the Grand Rapids Federal Marshal's office was just leaving.

"Don't forget William," Deputy Marshal Riley reminded Bill Anderson. "The fair Colleen is expecting you for supper at seven, sharp."

"You can be sure I won't be late this evening. I hear your dear wife is a stickler for timeliness."

"You're right there laddie," Riley replied. "I'll see you then."

Chief Deputy Riley had hardly gone out the door than he returned dragging a man by the collar of his shirt.

"William!" He directed. "Find a cell for this brigand. Two men just attacked Mike's son and Mr. Russell the afternoon manager at George Neal's restaurant. We caught this thug. The tother attacker got away."

Riley dragged a stumbling disheveled man in front of Bill Anderson's desk.

Bill grabbed him by the collar. "Stand up straight or I'll give you a real reason to be on your knees."

"Damn kid hit my knee with a club," the man complained. "Then he hit me in the head while I was on the ground. I'll get that brat, believe me."

"Ya mean he banged yer head like this?" Bill grabbed the man by his hair and smashed his head on the top of his desk.

"Who was the other man with ya? Bill asked. "Who was the man who got away?"

"I don't know what yer talkin' about."

"Got a bad memory have ya?" Riley asked. He then stepped forward, his night stick in hand. "Did the lad hit this knee?" Riley wacked the man's left knee.

"Owww!" the man exclaimed.

"Or, did he hit the right one?"

Riley wacked the night stick on the man's right knee."

"Stop, stop!' The man shouted.

"Who was the other man with ya?"

The hoodlum was silent.

"Throw him in ta solitary, William," Riley directed. "We'll see about him in the morning. You might just as well come with me now. My wife's dinner is a' waiting for us. I'll not let this piece a' trash get her angry with me this night."

"Just give me a minute an' ill join you," Bill told Riley. "I'll just put this piece of trash in a cell, first."

"Hurry on with it, lad," He urged. "I'll not have the fair Colleen mad at me over this."

*   *   *

Meanwhile, at the Murphy home, Charles and his boss had just arrived and were standing in the front room.

"What you say?" Dr. Murphy asked. "You were attacked on the way here?"

"Yes, sir." Mr. Russell confirmed. "Just down on Fulton street a ways,"

"What's the commotion Miles?" Mrs. Murphy asked as she walked into the room.

"Charles and Mr. Russell were attacked by two ruffians on the way home, just now."

"Charles," she immediately asked. "Are you all right?"

Charles was still flushed with excitement. "Yes, grandmother, I'm fine. But those two guys who attacked us aren't. Mr. Russell and I gave them a good thrashing. Didn't we, Mr. Russell."

"Explain yourself, sir," Demanded Dr. Murphy of Tom Russell. "Tell us what happened."

"We were not far from making the turn at Prospect street on our way here, sir. When, two men jumped out from behind some bushes and ran at us. I, in turn, ran right at them with my club in hand."

"I saw them, too grandfather," Charles added. "So, I ran right behind Mr. Russell."

"Let him finish, son," Mrs. Murphy urged. "Then what happened Mr. Russell?"

"I don't think they expected us to attack them. I'm sure they didn't expect us to have clubs. Anyway, they sort a' stopped and turned like to run away. I gave a good whack with my club to the first fellow."

"And I hit the other one on the side of one of his knee," Charles added excitedly. "He really howled. And when he fell to the ground, I hit him on the head."

"I'm afraid the other guy got away from us, Dr. Murphy," Tom Russell said.

"Do you two always carry clubs when you walk Charles home in the evening?"

"No, sir," Tom Russell answered. "But today one of the dishwashers bumped into Charles when the boy was carrying a load of dirty dishes. I saw him do it. It was no accident. The man did it on purpose. I confronted the fellow and fired him on the spot."

"I still don't understand, Mr. Russell," Mrs. Murphy asked. "What does that have to do with you and Charles carrying clubs?"

"Because, ma'am, when I fired the man he threatened to get even with Charles; harm him in some way. So, I thought it wise for us to carry the clubs tonight, just in case."

"Well, I for one am happy you did, sir" Dr. Murphy said shaking Russell's hand.

"Mr. Russell," Mrs. Murphy said, "We are just about to have our supper. Won't you please join us. We are so grateful to you for protecting our grandson. Please allow us to share our meal with you."

"Thank you very much ma'am. That's very nice of you. I don't mind if I do. Can I wash up a bit before we sit down though? I'm afraid Charles and I are a bit dirty after our scuffle over on Fulton Street."

"Of course," she responded. "Charles. Show Mr. Russell to the wash-room. And you wash up too young man."

"Yes, grandmother."

Eleanor had entered the room and heard Charles and Mr. Russell explain what had happened to them.

She walked up to her brother and whispered. "Are you sure you're all right, Charles?" she asked.

"Oh, sure," he said. "I'm fine. You should have seen us, Eleanor," Charles continued excitedly. "We beat the crap out a' those two guys. It was great"

"Are you proud of hitting that man?" Eleanor asked. "You sound like you're boasting."

"Well, yah!" Charles said surprised she should ask such a question.? "Come 'on Eleanor. Two big guys attacked us. I whacked the one guy twice. He really hollered when he was on the ground and I hit him in the head. I would have hit him again, but Mr. Russell stopped me."

"What happened to him?"

"We dragged him to the Marshal's office," Charles said. "I 'spose he's in jail now."

"But you're all right? Truly?" Eleanor asked again.

"Yes, Eleanor. I told you already. I'm fine," Charles insisted. "I got to wash up now. Grandma has supper waiting an' I'm starving"

At the table, Mrs. Murphy sat their guest next to Charles.

"Charles," she said. "Would you please say grace?"

He sort a' rolled his eyes at this invitation. Under the table, Eleanor poked him in the leg.

He gave her a nasty look. Gave a sigh, and began without further complaint.

"Bess us oh Lord, for these Thy gifts, and for what we are about to receive in Thy name, we thank Thee Lord. Amen."

"Thank you dear," Mrs. Murphy said.

As the plates of food were being passed, Dr. Murphy asked.

"How do you like the restaurant business, Mr. Russell?"

"I find it very fascinating, doctor."

"How so?"

"The people I meet in the course of my shift make it so, sir.

"Of course, my employees are frequently a challenge for me, too," He added. "Today's situation is pretty unusual but day to day stuff keeps me on my toes, believe me."

"Do customers complain much?" Mrs. Murphy asked.

"That is sort of fascinating, too ma'am," He responded. "It doesn't matter if someone orders a cup of coffee or an entire meal; they want everything to be perfect. So, I have to be on top of every possibility of falling short of their expectations. George, my overall boss is a stickler for detail. But his wife Susan is the tough one. Nothing gets by her, believe me."

"How is Charles doing?" Doctor Murphy asked.

"Miles," Mrs. Murphy cautioned. "Not in front of our grandson."

"That's all right, grandmother," Charles said. "It's something I should hear anyways."

"All right, Charles. If you say so." She said.

"He's a good learner, sir," Russell revealed. "He listens to me when I give him instructions and corrections. I don't have to keep after him to finish his tasks. And he does a pretty good job at them, ta' boot. I know the drill pretty well, since his job is the same one, I started out with a few years ago, you see."

"Good for you, Charles," Dr. Murphy said. "Thank you for that evaluation, Mr. Russell."

*   *   *

Over their homework later, Eleanor asked.

"What Mr. Russell said about your work performance was pretty nice, don't you think, Charles?"

"I thought so, too, Eleanor," He responded. "But I still don't think I would want a business career. Working for someone else is not what I would want' for sure."

"Then, what do you want to do after we graduate from high school next June?"

Bothe of them were in their last year of secondary school at the new Central Hight School in Grand Rapids.

"I might go to South Carolina and see about running the Pope property on Edisto Island."

"But you don't know anything about farming rice and cotton." Eleanor reminded him. "How would you manage that land when you don't know anything about it?"

"What's to know?

"All right, smarty," Eleanor challenged. "In what month is cotton or rice planted and when are those crops ready for harvesting?"

"I don't know any of that stuff, Eleanor," Charles answered sharply. "But the man who runs the Pope land there, knows all that stuff. I'll just leave all those details to him; just like now."

"That approach sounds pretty shaky to me, Charles," Eleanor decided. "Why don't you go to the University of Michigan with me?"

"Is that where you're going?"

"Yep," Eleanor responded. "A couple of years ago they admitted women to study medicine there. I intend to be a doctor, so that's where I'm going."

"Ugg," Charles told her. "I've had enough of school. I've got southern blood in my veins. So, I think I'll go South and check it out for a while."

*   *   *

At the Riley home, the Riley's were entertaining Bill Anderson for supper.

"As ya were walkin' out the door Michael's son an his employer walked in with a thug who attacked 'em, ya say?

"Didn't I tell ya William," Pat Riley said to Anderson. "My fair Colleen would not be toleratin' us late fer her supper."

"That's what you told me Sarg," Bill remembered.

"Get yas to my table fore my food gets cold, you two."

"Yes, ma'am," Bill Anderson answered.

The prayer was said and the plates were passed. While eating, Colleen Riley asked.

"Tell me tha whole story, now."

Between swallows, Riley told his wife the entire story of why they were late to supper.

When he had finished, she said. "So, you two wouldn't mind cleanin up the dishes an such afterwards? Now, would you?"

"No ma'am," Bill agreed.

"I'm glad, it tis that the Drieborg boy came out a' this without damage. I sort a' feel sorry fer the two fellows who attacked him, when Michael returns, though." Colleen commented.

Riley laughed, "That's fer sure."

"The roast beef was delicious Mr. Riley," Bill said. "I don't often have a home cooked meal. This was a real treat. Thank you."

"You're welcome, William. An there's some a' me fresh baked apple pie after you two do the clean 'in up."

Later, over Colleen's apple pie and coffee, she was anxious to know why Bill Anderson wasn't married.

"You'd make a fine catch fer some nice lass, William," She judged. "Why haven't ya latched on ta someone. It's been years since the war ended, ya know."

"I know, misses," Bill responded a bit uncomfortably. "I just don't get out an' about much. I haven't met anyone who is attractive ta me, I guess. "

"Ya mind if I offer a suggestion, William?" she continued.

"No, ma'am. Not a 'tall," Truth be told, Bill didn't know how to politely decline her help on this matter.

"Pattie an I attend St. Mary's church just down the street, ya know," She began. "After Sunday mass we go to the parish hall an enjoy a nice potluck. I know of several ladies who would love to meet you. Would you go with us next Sunday, William?"

"That is very nice of you Mrs. Riley," Bill responded uncomfortably, "But I would want to intrude on your Sunday." Bill looked at Pat Riley for help.

Pat Riley was silent throughout this conversation. He showed no sign of intervening on Bill's behalf.

And his wife would not be put off. It seemed she was on a mission.

"Not a problem, William," She responded. "Is it husband?"

"No, not a 'tall, dear," he assured her.

'You just meet us here, at our home, at 9:30 next Sunday morn," She directed. "We'll all walk over to the church for Mass an' stay for the potluck afterwards."

Bill let out a sigh of resignation. "Thank you, Mrs. Riley. I'll look forward to it."

Atlanta

Congressman Kellogg and General Terry along with Mike and Bob Stephan entered a sparsely furnished room at the Freedman's office building. They were seated at the foot of a long table.

The door at the far end of the room opened. A rather short man entered. He wore his hair down to his shoulders, sported a thin mustache and clamped a cigar between his teeth. He dressed in a black suit and tie with a red vest.

As he sat at the far end of the table and looked at the four men seated at the other end.

"My, my," Greenhoe said. "The commander of the 3rd Military District and his staff. Such a serious looking bunch. Should I be impressed General Terry?"

General Alfred Terry, who was the commander of the 3rd Military District which included Georgia, Alabama and Florida, responded.

"Allow me to introduce Marshal Michael Drieborg and deputy Marshal Robert Stephan. You already know my Deputy, former Congressman Kellogg."

"Gentlemen," Greenhoe responded nodding toward them. "Nice to meet you."

"To get right to the matter, Greenhoe. I don't give a damn if you're impressed with me or my colleagues here. You're here because I ordered you to be, not because you are doing me any favors."

"Now that we have that settled, General," Greenhoe said. "I'm sure you didn't invite me here today just to meet these two marshals. Why am I here today?"

"You are here because word around Atlanta is that your bandits have kidnapped one of my people. I want him returned and returned without delay."

"That's pretty bold, general," Greenhow said. He leaned forward took the cigar from his mouth and smiled. "I don't much care what the word is around this town. Just 'cause some local rebs say I had something to do with you losing one of your people, don't mean I did.

"These rebs will say anything that suits them. Nor do I have any bandits under my direction. And, I don't know about any kidnapping. After all, it's not my fault if you can't keep track of your people"

General Terry was obviously upset with Greenhoe's disrespectful response.

"Sir," Terry responded with fury in his voice. "You are a scoundrel of the first order. I warn you. If I find that you or the brigands in your Union League had anything to do with the kidnapping of Marshal Haynes, I will clap the lot of you in jail; starting with you!"

Greenhow stood and returned Terry's fury with an infuriating smile. "When you do, general. you know where to find me."

He put the cigar back in his mouth, bowed slightly and left the room.

"If I had the troops I need to enforce my command here, I'd put that crook in jail right now, kidnapping or not." General Terry snapped. "But I don't and that bastard, Greenhoe knows it."

On the way out, Kellogg told Drieborg and Stephan. "See what we have to put up with. Greenhoe has the Union League's paramilitary organization behind him. We do not. That gives him the power to do pretty much as he damn well pleases."

"So, sir," Drieborg concluded. "It appears that it's up to me and my band to find Haynes on our own."

"I never thought otherwise, Mike," Kellogg responded. "And, as you can see. We don't have much to back you up in your effort."

*   *   *

Back at his office in the Freedman's Bureau building, Greenhoe met with the commander of the local Union League force, a Civil War veteran calling himself Captain Murphy.

"How did you meeting go with the Military Governor, Dick?" Murphy asked.

"Kellogg brought in some fresh faces," Greenhoe responded.

"A problem?"

"I don't know yet," Greenhoe said. "We need to test them."

"How do you want to do that?"

"It appears that these marshals have brought their wives with them; on sort of a holiday."

"Where are they staying?" Murphy asked. "In Atlanta?"

"My sources tell me they have rooms at the new Kimball House.

"That place has one of those new Otis elevators in it, doesn't it?" Greenhoe asked.

"As a matter of fact, it does," Murphy confirmed. "The owners of the hotel make a big deal about it, too."

"Don't you have one of your people on the maintenance staff there?"

"Sure," Murphy told Greenhoe. "We do. We also have some leverage with the Negroes who work on the household cleaning staff."

"The kitchen staff as well?"

"I wouldn't be surprised that a cook or two as well as a few waiters would be available to us." Murphy informed his boss. "What are you cooking up in that devious mind of yours, Greenhoe?"

"Nothing life threatening, ya' know. At least not at first." Greenhoe revealed. "Why don't you tell your man to have the elevator at the Kimball go out of order for a few days. Walking up several flights of stairs might get the ladies to whining."

Murphy laughed. "How about I have the waiters spill a few glasses of water onto the laps of the ladies."

It was Greenhoe's turn to laugh, now. "Sounds innocent enough. But just in case those messages don't get through, have the housekeeping people at the Kimball skip cleaning the rooms Kellogg's people are using skip their rooms for two or three days.

"I'll think of some way to inform Kellogg what is happening to his people." Greenhow concluded.

"Make sure he knows that things could get much worse, and dangerous for them."

"Right."

"What about Haynes?" Murphy asked.

"Keep him under wraps," Greenhoe directed. "Keep him alive. He's no use to us dead."

'Can he be slightly damaged?"

"Not a lick, Murphy." Greenhoe snapped. "If it turns out we have to trade him for something, I don't want his worth diminished. Not one lick. You hear me?"

"I hear ya," Murphy assured him. "Don't get your shorts in such a knot."

Kimball House

The following morning, Mike and Mary Jacquelin left their room on the fifth floor and went to the elevator.

"What's this?" Mike asked aloud.

On the closed door of the elevator was a sign that said:

"Sorry. This elevator is out of order."

On their way down the stairs Mary Jacquelin said:

"I don't mind the walk down. It's the walk back up that I don't want to face."

Mike told her, "Let me check the front desk."

Mike rang the bell on the desk bringing a gentleman from a back office.

"How can I help you sir?"

"We had to walk down from the fifth floor because your elevator seems to be out of order. What's that all about?"

"I noticed that," The man responded. "If you check back with me after you have breakfast, I should know by then the nature of the problem."

"Thank you," Mike said. "I'd appreciate it."

"Of course, sir."

In the dining room, the Drieborgs met the other members of the team, and the wives.

Ellie was the first to inquire.

"Hey, Mike," She began in her direct Tennessee way. "What's this about you're new-fangled Yankee elevator not working?"

"Don't know, Ellie., Mike responded.

"Hell of a way to start the day, ya ask me," her husband Bose added.

"We don't have a building this high in Charleston to worry about no elevator." Mary Alice Stephan informed everyone.

"This morning, that seems like an advantage doesn't it." Henry said. "This happened at the Willard Hotel in Washington City, the tenants would probably burn the building to the ground."

Not to be left out of the discussion, Keelean said, "I'd be one of the first to help light that fire, too."

"Don't any of you get any wild ideas, yet." Mike told them. "I asked at the front desk. Let's wait for an explanation before we complain too loudly."

"While we're waiting, I'm a hungry dude here." Keelean informed everyone. "Hey you, waiter. Can you take my order?"

A burly Negro man dressed in black pants, a white coat and white gloves stepped over to the table.

"Yes, sir," I can take your order."

Keelean give him his order and the waiter looked around the table. "Anyone else ready to order?"

Mary Jacquelin was first to speak.

"I think everyone would like coffee, first." She began. "Then I would like some scrambled eggs and toast, please. And, oh, yes, a glass of water."

"Right away ma'am," The waiter promised.

After all the orders were taken, a young boy stepped over to the table and began pouring water into the glass that was set in front of each diner. He hit the second glass he was filling with the pitcher and it went over pouring its contents onto the lap of Ellie.

"Whoops!" He said. "Sorry ma'am."

Ellie pushed back on her chair and stood avoiding most of the spilled water. She glared at the water boy, but said nothing.

The young man resumed pouring water. He spilled another glass on to Mary Alice Stephan's lap this time.

"Opps!" he Said. "Sorry ma'am."

It was some time before the food arrived. None of it was even warm.

Mike spoke to the head waiter. "We sat here for near an hour waiting for this food. And it is cold as ice. Did we sit here after our food was ready to be served?"

"I don't know, sir," The waiter answered. "I'll check with the kitchen if you wish."

The waiter returned shortly. "No one in the kitchen knows why the food was delayed, sir. Are you sure it was all cold?"

Mike stood and approached the man. "Listen carefully my man." He said. "Neither you nor your staff of waiters or kitchen people will receive a tip from any of us. In addition, we will not pay for this food nor will we eat here again."

Stan Killeen and Boise headed for the kitchen.

The head waiter shouted. "You can't go in there, sir."

Bose stepped in front of the waiter, pushed him toward the kitchen door.

"Did you serve the Confederacy in the last war?" Bose asked as he pushed the man through the doorway. "If'n you did, I'll bet it was behind the lines."

"I was the personal cook for General Joe Johnston."

"Yep, I was right. You were safe way behind us who were up front fighting." Bose said.

"Line up your kitchen people against that wall, and your waiters against the other." He ordered.

"Well, I never," The head waiter sputtered.

Killeen pulled his revolver and put it under the man's chin. "Do it. Now!

"My Tennessee friend here might be squeamish some," Keelean assured the man. "But I don't mind spilling some more rebel blood. If'n you don't move quick, it'll be yours." Killeen cocked his revolver.

A few minutes later, everyone was lined up as ordered.

"You there," Bose shouted. "You, the water boy. Come over here!"

Then Bose led the young boy into an adjoining room, shut the door and pulled his Bowie knife.

He twisted the boy's arm behind him and put the big knife against the palm of his hand.

"I'm guessing you won't be able to pour water very well if you're missing some a' these fingers.

"What da' you think, boyo?"

"Don't hurt me, sir."

"Tell ya what," Bose said. "You tell me who ordered you ta spill water on my wife, an I'll not cut off one a' you're fingers." With that he pushed the point of the knife into the boy's palm.

"Stop, please," The boil wailed. "I'll tell ya."

"It was the head waiter told me."

"An' the cold food. Whose idea was that?"

"The head waiter ordered your waiter to leave you sittin and allowin your food to get cold."

"Now, wasn't that easy?" Bose said. He put his knife away.

"But If I were you, I'd not work here anymore. Your boss, the head waiter will be awful mad at you fer tellin' me about him. So, you go out this other door here. All right?"

"Thank you, sir," the boy gushed. "I'll do just that."

"Be sure now," Bose urged. "I don't want ta' see you around here again. Never can tell what might happen if we have ta have another conversation, don't ya know."

"Don't worry a mite about that, sir," the boy responded. "You'll not see me again."

After the boy left, Bose returned to the kitchen and walked to the man who had brought their cold food to the table.

"You come with me, fella,"

Bose pulled him into the same room. He pushed the man against the wall and put the point of his knife under his chin.

"Will you still be a waiter if you can't use your right arm?"

"My arm is fine." The man answered.

"Right this minute, maybe," Bose agreed. "But what if one a' your arm muscles got cut, bad?" What about then? Would you still be able to carry that big tray full a' plates up on yer shoulder, like I seen ya' do today?"

"Suppose not."

"Tell ya what, my man," Bost said. "I'm going ta ask ya a simple question. If ya answer it, I'll let ya go. If 'n ya' don't one a' those big muscles in yer right arm's going ta get cut really bad.

"You listening ta me, now?"

"Yes, sir,"

"Yer hearing me, right?"

"Yes, I'm hearing you."

"You believe me, too?"

"Yes, I believe you."

"Here's tha question," Bose said. "Did you decide ta leave our food ta get cold all by yerself?"

"No, sir," The man said. "I didn't decide to do that."

"Someone told you to leave our food get cold?"

"I thought you were going to ask me one question."

"Oh, ya," Bose admitted. "I forgot. Answer my damn question anyways."

"I was ordered not to serve you until the food was cold."

"Who ordered you?"

"The head waiter.

"Good answer, my man," Bose assured him. "But if' n' you go back out there showing no bruises or such, your boss will be mad as heck. Right?"

"Yes, sir," the waiter agreed. "Probably will be mad."

Bose placed the blade of his knife up against the waiter's cheek. He cut the man's face with the razor-sharp edge.

"That ought ta do it, don't ya think?"

"You cut me, you bastard," the man moaned. "Just because of some cold food?"

"Teach ya not ta fool around with a reb cavalryman from Tennessee," Bose chuckled. "Now, you're goin out in that kitchen and get our whole order taken care of and delivered quickly nice an' hot to our table. Ya understand?"

"Yes."

"Go on now," Bose pushed the waiter out the door and walked directly to the head waiter.

Stan Killeen was still holding his revolver under the man's chin.

"What's going on, Bose?" Killeen asked.

"I'm just about done with this bunch. I just need ta talk ta this bozo. You can join me if 'n ya want to, Stan."

Bose turned to the waiter with the cut cheek. "What are you waiting fer. Get our breakfast going or I'll give yas other cheek a cut. An you better make sure no one messes with it.

"Unnerstand? Ya hear me?"

"Yes, I understand, I hear ya."

Bose then turned to the head waiter. "Come 'on, Mr. Head Waiter," he said while pushing the man toward the door of the vacant room.

Inside the room Bose told the man to have a seat.

"What's the story, Bose?" Stan asked.

"This bozo was behind the whole mess this morning. Weren't' you, Mr. Head Waiter?"

"I don't know what you're talking abouy," the man responded. "And, I highly resent the accusation. I Intend to inform the authorities about your highly irregular behavior this morning."

"We'll see about that," Bose responded. "Too bad we can't use the old rope trip, Stan."

"What do you suggest?" Stan asked.

"I think I'll use my Bowie knife ta get some truth out a' this bozo."

Bose put his knife under the left ear of the man in the chair.

"I'm told that a man can hear just as well with one ear as with two."

Killeen responded, "I don't know, Bose. That might just be an old wives' tale."

"If 'n it's not proven maybe we ought to see ya know, ta settle it, once an' fer all."

"Ya, Bose," Killeen responded. "I'd like ta know, too."

Bose was still holding the razor-sharp blade of his knife under the left ear of the head waiter. Now, he looked into the eyes of his prisoner.

"Here's the deal, Mr. Head Waiter. I'm gonna ask you a couple a' questions. If 'n ya answer 'em, ya keeps yas ear. If 'n ya don't give us good answers, we get to see if ya can hear as good with one ear as two. Yas unnerstan?"

"You're crazy," the man shouted. "You can't cut off my ear."

"Sure, he can," Killeen said. "I've seen him do it. Do you understand what's goin' ta' happen if 'n yas don't answer his questions?"

"Maybe if 'n I gave this knife a little nudge he'd understand that I'm serious about this. What do ya think, Stan?"

"That would probably work, Bose," Killeen said. "But don't cut it clean off: just a little cut the first time. We wouldn't want ta mess up his fancy suite too much."

"You too are crazy," the man shouted. "You would cut off my ear because your breakfast food was cold?"

"That's the plan, mister," Killeen confirmed.

"Who ordered you to mess with our breakfast this morning?" Bose asked. He gave the knife a little push.

"Aww!" the head waiter screamed.

"Well? Who told you to do it to us?'

"The commander of my regiment."

"Who is that?"

"Major Murphy."

"Is that the same man who commands the local Union League?"

"Yes."

"We appreciate that information," Bose told him. "Just one more thing."

"What?"

"If we encounter any more trouble in this hotel, anything a 'tall."

"Like the elevator not working," Killeen interjected.

"We'll hold you personally responsible and have another visit with you," Bose promised.

"I would still like to test that notion about hearing just as well with one ear as with two," Killeen added.

"That 'l be up to you, won't it Mr. Head Waiter," Bose threatened.

Back in the dining room, the rest of Mike's group waited.

When Bose and Stan joined them, Mike asked.

"What the hell were up to in there?"

"We just had a conversation with the head waiter and a couple of his staff."

"And?" Bob Stephan prompted.

"The problems we had with the spilled water, the long wait and the cold food will not be repeated," Bose promised.

"And," Killeen added. "Our head waiter promised that our stay here will be uneventful in the future."

Frank wasn't satisfied with that. "And just how did you guarantee that?"

"Because, my butcher friend," Killeen chuckled. "Our head waiter will be the subject of a painful experiment if our stay here becomes difficult."

"I don't think I want to know just what you promised him you would do in that case."

"No, Mary Jacqueline," Bose told Mike's wife. "You don't."

Killeen added. "Now it's your turn."

"Our turn fer what, Yank?" Elsie asked.

"Correcting the elevator situation and possibly housekeeping problems in our rooms."

"We discovered that the leaders of the Union League ordered the staff to hassle us.," Bose informed everyone. "Killeen an I took care of the kitchen problems. It's your turn to take car a' the other ones."

Mary Alice Stephan asked. "You mean the hotel people caused our elevator problem on purpose?"

"Shocking isn't it," Killeen said.

"Well, I never," She exclaimed. "But this hotel is run by Southerners."

"Hard ta believe, ain't it, dearie?" Bose concluded.

"Wait till ya'll get back to tha room," Killeen warned. "Bose an me were told there's a surprise fer us there, too."

"When we're done here," Mike promised. "I'll speak to the hotel manager."

"I know the man," Frank revealed. "It doesn't seem like him to allow his hotel guests to be treated this way. I want to hear this."

"A southern gentleman doing these things to guests," Mary Alice said. "I never imagined."

A waiter appeared at their table with a tray full of breakfast food. This time, all the coffee and food were served hot and in a timely manner. Everyone enjoyed their meal.

"Didn't I tell ya," Bose boasted. "Me and Stan here fixed this problem."

Grand Rapids

The owners of the Metropolitan Restaurant and Bakery talked with all the afternoon shift workers.

"Listen very carefully to what I have to say," George Neal began.

"Last evening your manager and our new bus-boy were attacked on Fulton street by two members of your crew. One of them is in jail. The other is being sought by the police.

"It seems that these two decided to hassle the new bus-boy. So, one of them purposely bumped into him as he carried a tray of dirty dishes into the kitchen. Your manager witnessed the incident and fired the man after he admitted doing it. He was the attacker who escaped.

"We are a team here. We work together to serve our customers. If you are not happy working here, leave now. I will not stand in the way of you working elsewhere.

Susan Neal spoke next. "For those of you who decide to stay and work at our restaurant, let us be clear, we will not tolerate any hassling of your co-workers. Any of you who try that sort of thing will be fired." She continued. "And we will see to it that no business in this town will hire you."

"Is that clear to everyone?" She asked.

None of the workers said a word. They just shuffled their feet, looked at the floor and nodded.

"Very well then," George concluded. "Thank you for your attention. You may return to your work."

*   *   *

At the marshal's office, Assistant Marshall Pat Riley and Deputy Marshall Bill Anderson were having their second cup of coffee.

"Ya, know lad," Riley began. "This here coffee ain't nearly as strong as you boys used ta make during the late war."

"Well ya," Bill responded. "We practically wore out our stomachs back then with that strong stuff. We make a fresh pot every couple a' hours now. Tastes better, too."

"Sort a' miss the old stuff though," Riley mused. "Kept me alert, it did"

"Ya got that right for sure."

"How's our new prisoner?"

"The fellow nabbed fer attacking Charles?"

"That's the one."

"I had a talk with the Grand Rapids Chief of Police on my way in this morning," Bill began. "We'll have ta turn the fellow over to him later today cause what he did was not a federal matter, but a local matter. But he understood that we need a bit a' time to question the man being as how he attacked the Marshal's son, an all."

"Let's get at it then," Riley proposed.

Anderson was in charge of the federal prison in Grand Rapids, So, he asked the Deputy on duty,

111

"How's the new man?"

"He's moanin' and groaning ta beat the band, Bill," the deputy related. "Claims that we're starving an innocent man."

"Have ya let him out since we put him in his cell last evening?" Riley asked.

"Not fer a minute," the deputy related. "He complained that he couldn't find his piss pot in the dark an he shits all over himself. We've been laughing till our sides hurt listening ta him moan and groan. I'd hate ta be the first one to go in his cell. Must stink ta high heaven."

"Get a couple a' buckets of water down here." Bill ordered. Include a scrub brush, soap, an' some prison clothing. Might as well get at it."

The Deputy opened the metal door to the man's cell.

"Whew!" he exclaimed. "Throw out all your cloths."

"Like hell," came the reply. "Then, I'll be bare-assed naked."

"Don't bother me if you stay in that smelly cell. But if you want to clean up and get something to eat, throw out your cloths. I'm here ta tell ya. You ain't coming out here like you is."

After a few minutes, pants, shoes, shirt and a jacket came flying out of the cell.

Two buckets of cold water were set inside with some rags, a mop and a towel.

"After you clean yourself and the cell floor, I'll pass in some clean clothing."

"This water is ice cold," The convict complained.

"You attacked a kid yesterday," The deputy reminded the prisoner. "You expect room service and hot water? Clean up or I shut the door until tomorrow morning. You can stay in there buck naked with no food for all I care."

Within a half an hour, after much complaining, the empty buckets flew out of the cell. "All right, where are those dry cloths you promised?"

The deputy threw orange colored coveralls into the cell.

"This all I get?" the prisoner shouted. "I'm freezing here and all you give me is some coveralls."

"Get 'em on and step out of the cell," He was ordered.

Bill Anderson put a three-legged stool on the floor in front of the cell. As the man stepped into the hallway, Bill ordered.

"Sit on the stool!"

The prisoner whined. "I'm starving, here. Ain't et since yesterday."

"First, we need a few answers. Then we can talk about food."

"What's your name?"

'Zeke Smith."

"Address?"

"Over on Pearl, above the laundry."

Riley told the deputy to go and check that out. "If 'n we find you're lying, it's back in the cell few another night, an no food.

"What's your partner's name?"

"Don't know what his name is?"

Bill hit the man on his knee with a night stick.

"Hey!" the man shouted.

"Answer the question."

"I ain't no squealer. Sides, he'll beat me up if 'n I tell ya."

Bill hit the man on his other leg.

"Hey! That's the leg that damn kid hit last night."

"What's the name of the guy who was with you?" Bill repeated.

"You gotta protect me from him. He's a crazy one."

"Unless you tell us, you'll spend so much time in that stinking cell, he will never get to you. What's his name?" Riley asked.

"Jake is all I know."

One of the deputies brought a platter of hot stew and set it down in front of the prisoner. It took only a few more questions to find out what they needed to know about Jake. Then, they let their prisoner eat.

"All right, back into your cell," Anderson ordered.

"I toll ya what ya wanted," The prisoner complained. "Sides, I ain't done nothin."

"We're gonna check out yas story," Riley told him. "Then we'll see."

That evening, with two local policemen along Riley took the prisoner to the bar where Zeke promised Jake could be found.

Sure enough, he was sitting at a table playing cards with some others.

One policeman kicked the chair from under the suspect. The other policeman grabbed the man called Jake and knelt on his back while tying his hands behind him.

"Hey! What are you doin' ta me?"

"Arresting you for assaulting a man and a boy last night."

"I didn't do nothing."

"We got witnesses who say otherwise, boyo," Riley said. "Your dish washing days at the restaurant are over. You're going ta jail. When ya gets out, I'm guessing Marshall Drieborg will be having a private conversation with ya., too"

"Who tha hell is that?" the man asked.

"The father of tha boy you attacked last night," Riley told him. "I'm thinkin, you'll be safer in jail when he finds out who it was attacked his son."

*   *   *

Dr. Murphy and his wife were sitting at the dining room table with their two grandchildren.

"Did everything go well at the restaurant this afternoon, Charles?" his grandmother Judy Murphy asked.

"Nothing unusual happened, grandmother," He said.

"No more bumping incidents with other workers?"

115

"No, grandfather," Charles reported. "The other workers were pretty quiet, though. No one said much of anything to me today. I thought that was sort of strange."

"Word of you being attacked last night got around, I suspect. I wouldn't worry about it. But I would not talk about it to any of them either. You hear me son?"

"Yes, sir," Charles responded. "I hear you."

Mrs. Murphy entered the conversation. "I wouldn't say anything at school about it either, Charles. It is not wise to brag about such a thing. You didn't, did you?"

Eleanor couldn't keep quiet any longer, it seemed. "Charles bragged about hitting those men with a club all over the place today. I won't be surprised if one of the older boys doesn't try to challenge him and stop all the bragging"

"Tattle-tale!" Charles snapped. "I only told a few of my friends."

"Eleanor is right, Charles," Dr. Murphy decided. "You'd be wise to keep this matter to yourself."

"Tonight, I want you to write a letter to your parents, children," their grandmother directed. "You can each tell them how your jobs are going. Charles, don't tell your parents about the attack. The sheriff has the men in custody, so it is over with. Your parents would only worry. Just tell them how you are doing in school and at work. OK?"

"Yes, grandmother," Both children said together.

*   *   *

Later that evening the children were sitting at the same table to write their parents.

"You go first, Eleanor," Charles urged. "I have to think about what I'm going to say."

"All right," she agreed.

Dear Mother and Father,

This is Eleanor. We decided that I would write something first.

How are you? We are fine. School is going well for both of us.

I am so excited about my work in Grandfather Murphy's office. Each time a patient comes in who is new to him, I conduct an interview. Then I put their name on nurse Kathy's list. Someone with an injury or really sick goes on another list because that person needs to be seen sooner.

Of course, I have to do a lot of cleaning up around the office. That's not so exciting. Last weekend I visited Grandmother and grandfather Hecht. While I was there grandmother told me a lot about ways to cure people of things. That was really exciting. It was also great to play with my two aunts. Isn't that so funny? I'll tell you more, later. Love you Eleanor.

Now it's my turn.

School is pretty much the same. Boring. Work is not exciting either, just work. I clean tables and sweep floors every time I go to the restaurant. After work on Saturday, I get paid. So far, I have earned enough to pay you back for my work cloths. Grandmother Murphy has the money.

When Eleanor went to the Hecht farm, I went to visit the Drieborgs. Grandfather Jake had me help him milk cows and clean the barn. I don't think I want to be a farmer. Work at the restaurant might not be exciting but it is a lot easier and doesn't smell so bad as a barn. I do know that I want to be a boss.

When you get back can I have a dog? All my friends have one. Eleanor says she wants a cat instead. Ugg! I miss you. Charles

We both love you and miss you. When are you coming home?

Eleanor and Charles

Atlanta

Marshal Drieborg was in the hotel manager's office. Frank Stanezek was with him.

"Bill," Frank began. "I can't believe the treatment we have received from your staff today. Nor do I want to believe you knew about it."

Clearly agitated, Bill responded. "And, Frank, I find it hard to believe you're working with these Yankees. After all we've endured here in Atlanta, you're helping them? No, I didn't know what was planned, but if it was our people who ordered it, I wouldn't have stopped it."

Mike interrupted. "Are you aware of the work Frank did in Washington City a year ago investigating the killing of Abraham Lincoln?"

"I heard something or other. What of it?"

"He helped clear President Davis of the charge that he, the President of the Confederate States of America, ordered the killing of Lincoln."

"We were at war with you blue-bellies," the hotel manager spat. "I would have expected Davis to give such an order; Lincoln was our enemy."

"It appears you hate has blinded you to what that would have meant for the South," Frank heatedly responded. "The Radicals in Washington wanted Davis to be involved in the assassination so that they could punish us even more harshly. We proved that he was not.

"Actually, President Davis told us when we interviewed him in prison, that Lincoln was our best hope for the future. As much as we all hated the man, Lincoln insisted we be returned to full partnership in the Union. He would have resisted the imposition of military rule in the South and other harsh measures insisted upon by those Radicals. His approach was inclusive not to punish.

'Now, we have a supporter of President Lincoln's policies in William Kellogg working here in Atlanta. And, what happens but his aide has been kidnapped. If that isn't provocation for the Radicals to be harsher I don't know what is. Their assumption is that the Klan did it.

"I am working with Marshal Drieborg in the hope that we can prove the kidnapping was not the work of the Klan. My investigation has thus far convinced me it was not. But we need to prove it."

The three men sat quietly for a few moments. Mike broke the silence.

"So, Mr. Thomas," he said. "Are we going to report that you were one of those standing in our way of solving the kidnapping of Kellogg's aide, or are we to report you were one of those Southerners helping us get to the bottom of this?"

"Put that way, Marshal Drieborg, I would be foolish and short-sighted not to assist you, or at least not to impede your investigation."

"Good to hear that, Bill," Frank stated.

"What do you need from me?" Bill Thomas asked.

"First we want you to order your people not to make our stay here unpleasant. Just treat us as you do all your other guest. So, this nonsense about the elevator not working must stop. We cannot walk either up or down all those stairs to the fifth floor.

"And, we discovered today that some workers here in your hotel were pressured by the Union League to disable the elevator and others to damage our food. We need such unpleasantness to stop."

"Going forward that will not be a problem, gentlemen," Bill Thomas assured the two men. "I may not like you Yanks, but I run a class hotel. I will not have its reputation tarnished by such nonsense."

"Anything else?"

"One more thing, Mr. Thomas," Mike revealed. "We do not want strangers given our room numbers. I have experienced some serious unpleasantness in the past when traveling up North. In the process the hotel was badly damaged. Help us avoid such attacks. In doing so you will protect your other guests and your nice hotel."

"I will warn my staff nots to reveal such information," Mr. Thomas promised. "Anything else?"

"I think we understand one another," Mike told the hotel manager." We'll let you know if anything else comes to our attention."

*   *   *

At supper that evening, the entire team and their spouses were sharing information.

"So, you had a chat with the hotel manager?" Bose asked.

"We did," Frank assured his Tennessee friend. "He was not behind the difficulty we had earlier today and assured us he would not allow any future problems."

"You have to twist his arm, Frank?" Stan asked.

"Not at all," Mike revealed. "Actually, when he realized that we were not in Atlanta to cast blame on all things southern, he was quite cooperative. In fact, he began to see that it would be helpful to assist us prove that the kidnapping of Craig Haynes was not the work of the Klan or any other southern group."

"Sounds to me like the voice of reason was just as effective as strong-arm tactics," Mary Jacqueline volunteered.

"My dear," Bose responded. Whatever works. You received a warm properly fixed breakfast shortly after our visit with the Head Waiter. Didn't you?

"And," Stan added. "Ours meal tonight was excellent. Wasn't it?"

"I can't deny it," Mary Jacqueline admitted. "Both meals were very good."

Bose couldn't help himself, "I rest my case." He concluded.

Mary Stephan said, "May I change the subject?"

"Of course, you can," Mike told her.

"I want to point out the simple fact that we had a marvelously safe jaunt this morning in downtown Atlanta."

"Hear! Hear!" Ethie Faute shouted and pounded on the table. "In fact, we shopped 'till we dropped."

"We did, actually," Peg Stanitezk agreed. "I suspect that we walked every inch of the six floors at Rich's Dry Goods. Their lunch-room on the third floor had an excellent menu, too.

"I was excited to see that they had three of those elevators for us to use as we went from floor to floor. They said they were the only store south of New York to have them."

"Jerry and Linda," Mike asked Gerry Gostkowski and his wife Linda. "Did you have any difficulty establishing security for the group?"

"Actually, not, Mike." Jerry answered.

Linda added. "I must inform you Marshal Drieborg that the ladies made our task easy. No one wandered off. In fact, they all stayed together as we shopped through the six floors of the store."

"That's good to hear, Linda. Thank you for your cooperation, ladies," Mike said. "What happened to us this morning with the elevator and the breakfast fiasco was only a mild sample what Greenhoe's Union League people have in store for us. Your shopping tour on Peach Street at Rich's was actually an open invitation to Greenhoe. Had it not been a last-minute thing, his folks could have made your tour downtown a nightmare.

"Worse, one of more of you could have been easily injured or kidnapped at virtually any time his people chose."

A quiet came over the table.

Finally, Peg broke the silence.

"Michael," she announced. "I expect this conversation will be repeated each time we attempt to venture out of the hotel. I for one will not be cooped up in this hotel like a prisoner.

"So, I intend to return to my home in Macon. You ladies are welcome to join me. We do not have all the highlights of Atlanta, but we should feel safe to enjoy what we do have in my smaller community. Any one wish to join me?"

Ethie Faute spoke first. "I agree with you Peg my girl. Thanks for the invite. I'll join ya."

Addressing Mike's and Bob Stephan's wives, Ethie asked. "How about you two? Will Join Peg an me in the grand city of Macon while our proud warriors fight the fight in Atlanta?"

"Oh, my goodness!" Mary Alice exclaimed. "Dear, would you mind if I left you in Michael's tender care?" That brought a laugh from everyone.

"No, dear," Bob Stephan responded. "if you would be more comfortable with Peg and the girls in Macon feel free to join them. But I expect Linda to accompany you."

"Of course, Linda is invited, too," Peg horridly added. "I never intended otherwise."

Ethie wasn't finished. "Now we must hear from Miss Mary Jacqueline. You staying close to the Marshal, Missy. Or are you the adventuresome type and joining us in Macon."

Mary Jacqueline Drieborg responded quickly.

"I was never much one for inviting danger, Ethie. But I don't fancy being a prisoner in this hotel however nicely appointed the jail. Besides, I've always wanted to taste some of that Stanitzek beef and sausage I've heard Frank bragging about for years. So, count me in, too."

"That 'a way girl!" Ethie shouted. "What ya think 'a them apples Mr. Marshal Drieborg?" she added.

"Fine with me Ladies, as long as Linda is with you," Mike responded causally. "And, I'm fine with it as long as you each carry that little pistol, I gave you. Remember how handy that was at Fort Sumter, ladies?"

"Ya got me there Mr. Marshal," Ethie admitted. "I'll give ya that promise. How about you ladies? Agreed?"

All the ladies nodded in agreement.

"An," she added. "As far as I'm concerned, Linda is always welcome ta be with us gals."

"Hey!" Bose Faute protested. "Don't we husbands got anything ta say about this?"

"Nope," Ethie spat. "Not your decision. We girls made it, an' tis' done with."

*   *   *

Back in their room that evening Mike and his wife were getting ready for bed. He asked Mary Jacqueline.

"When are you ladies leaving for Macon?"

"Peg said we would leave tomorrow after we attend church and have lunch."

"I understand why you ladies chafe at my insistence on security," Mike admitted. "Just the same, the danger is real and I don't know how else to approach the problem."

"I know, dear. I truly do." His wife assured him. "I think the ladies learned a lot back on Fort Sumter when that bunch of Regulators took us captive. I believe we'll be careful in Macon."

"Just the same," Mike responded. "While you girls were talking after dinner, we men were talking, too."

"Oh? And what were you talking about, prey tell." Mary Jacqueline said, smiling.

"Frank decided that his two sons will escort you ladies around town. He wanted to go to Macon with you himself, but his presence here is too essential. So, he intends to notify the local sheriff of your presence and request that his home be guarded by deputies and that they look out for you when you are in town."

"That will not go over well with the ladies, Michael." His wife snapped.

"My dear," Mike explained. "We are dealing with unscrupulous men here. The Union League men are bad enough. But I don't even trust the Klan people either. In spite of what Frank tells us, I believe that leaders of that terror group would think nothing of attacking you in open daylight or taking you captive for their purposes.

"I must admit that it was a mistake for me to allow you and the other ladies to join us."

"But you did," Mary Jacqueline reminded him. "And now you must live with that decision."

"I could just send you all home," He stated matter of fatly.

"I's too late for that, dear. We would never leave," His wife defiantly told him.

"You gals don't make it easy on a guy, do you,"

"You give birth to a couple of children and you'd understand why we wives are all so stubborn."

Mary Jacqueline moved closer to her husband on the bed and ran her hand up his leg under his nightshirt.

"Right now, I have something else I'm going to insist upon Mr. Marshal."

Mike lay back on the bed. "Are you giving me an order, Mrs. Marshal?"

Mary Jacqueline got a' top her husband and slipped her legs on either side of his hips.

"From what I feel right now, Mr. Big-Shot, you don't need much of an order to give me what I want." She added

"You got that right, lady."

There was no more conversation that night in the Drieborg's room.

*   *   *

Meanwhile, Bob and Mary Alice Stephans were having a conversation of their own.

"You really intend to go stay in Macon with the Stanitzeks?" Bob asked his wife.

Mary Alice Stephan was in her nightgown, seated on the bed, brushing her hair.

"Yes, dear," Mary Alice responded. "I really intend to do just that."

"Despite the danger?"

"Yes, dear," she replied. "Despite the danger."

"You know I'll worry."

"No more than I will worry about you here in Atlanta."

"That's different."

"How is that different, dear," Mary Alice prodded still brushing her hair.

"Will you stop doing that while I'm talking to you?"

"Doing what, dear?"

"Brushing your hair as if nothing is going on."

"Well, dear," Mary Alice said calmly." Nothing is going on. Tomorrow I'm going to Macon to stay with the Stanitzeks. I intend to stay there until your work here in Atlanta is completed."

"Well, I never," Bob Stephan said in exasperation.

"We're going to be parted for however long it takes you men to finish your work, here." Mary Alice reminded her husband. "So, why don't you come over here and sit beside me before we go to sleep."

"Well, I never."

"Don't you think it's about time, dear?"

There was no more conversation in their room that night.

*　　　*　　　*

Bose and Effie Faute were having a very different conversation.

"You know missy," Bose reminded his wife. "We haven't spent a night apart since the war."

"I don't like it any better 'an you, husband." Ethie responded. "But you big shots are bound and determined ta send us back home or lock us up in this here hotel here in Atlanta."

"Danger is danger, damn – it. Tough as you are lady, I have ta agree with Mike on this one. You gals are in danger here."

"Seems like ya do," Ethie snapped back. "It's getting late. We already settled this. So, jus get over here so's we can hug a bit."

"I spose," Bose conceded.

"You spose?" Ethie questioned. "A 'course, if 'n it too much trouble, you could always sleep in the hallway."

Bose joined his wife in bed.

After that, their room was quiet, too.

*　　　*　　　*

Frank was in bed with his wife. She was in his arms.

"I'm sure sorry you will be going home, dear," He said.

"Me too, Frank. But it's for the best. Mike is right about one thing. We would be a constant distraction for you and the others. You have accepted a mission here. We just get in the way."

"I know you're right, Peg," Frank agreed. "I think it would have been better if Mike had never invited the wives to join us here."

"Too late for that now, Frank," She reminded him. "We have to deal with the situation as it is, not as we wish it were."

"How'd you get so smart?" he asked with a chuckle in his voice.

"You're not so dumb either, Frank," she kidded. "You married me, didn't you?"

"I walked right into that one, didn't I."

"Say, Mr. Deputy Marshal," Peg asked. "This is our last night together for a while."

"Ya?"

"So why are we wasting so much time talking?"

"That's not too smart is it."

Peg turned in her husband's arms. There was no more conversation in their room either.

St. Patrick's Church, Atlanta

The ladies were going to leave on the Sunday afternoon train to Macon. So, that morning, four of the couples planned to attended church.

They walked to a Catholic church that morning. Mike and his wife, Mary Jacqueline, Bob and Mary Alice Stephans, Peg and Frank Stanetzek as well as Linda and Jerry Gostkowski interred St. Patrick's church for the ten am service.

"Tell me again about those ties you and Frank are wearing."

Bob responded. "You might remember that after we lost the war your government refused to allow us Confederates to wear any symbol honoring our cause. So, many of us decided to wear this red and blue tie with the white stars sewn on it. The idea spread throughout the old South.

"You have forgotten, Mike that many men wore them at Colonel Pope's funeral mass in Charleston a couple of years back."

"I guess I have forgotten."

"Look around you, Mike," Frank suggested. "You'll seem most of the men in church are wearing them."

But that wasn't the reason many at the service were staring at Mike and his men.

Why the stir? It was just odd that, despite their otherwise respectable appearance each man carried a Spencer rifle.

"Everyone's looking at us, Michael," Mary Alice whispered to her husband.

"They've never seen a man with a rifle before?" Mike quipped.

His wife snapped back. "Not in church at Sunday Mass."

By now, Mike was laughing.

"Don't you dare laugh," she told him. "You're in church. You shouldn't be laughing either."

"Yes dear," Mike continued to laugh, but quietly.

Mary Alice was blushing. "I've never been so embarrassed."

"You'll get over it, dear," Her husband said chuckling at her discomfort. "But you'll be safe. Isn't that a good thing?"

"Well, I never."

Peg warned her husband. "You will not take that thing with you up to the Communion rail," she insisted.

"Security first, dear," Frank whispered.

"You men are causing a scandal," she concluded.

"Choices must be made, dear," he whispered in response. "I'll take scandal any day in order to protect you and the others."

The Gostomsks took seats in the front row of the balcony where they could look down on the entire congregation and their companions seated below.

"You watch while I go to communion, will you Linda?" Gerry suggested. "Then, you can go."

"Sounds like a plan," she agreed. "At least you won't be lugging that rifle to the communion railing."

Atlanta

Richard Greenhoe was talking with the commander of his Union Brigade.

"Seems like Kellogg's marshals have put the clamps on your plan to disrupt the hotel services."

Bill Murphy responded. "I suggest we snatch one of their wives."

"I agree, that wouldn't be difficult," Greenhoe responded. "But taking a woman would cause too much of a stink. The military governor might wake up and make life difficult on us, don't you thing?"

"But we could get a few witnesses to blame the Klan for it."

"That gets sort a' old, Murphy," Greenhow responded. "We used it in Macon last fall. It worked with the Northern press until the Georgia governor looked into it an' blew the whistle on us."

"What da' we do then?"

"Fer now, jus' keep the lid on things. We'll figure it out," Greenhoe cautioned. "Keep 'em under surveillance. We'll get our chance. Who knows, maybe the dumb asses who lead the Klan here in Atlanta will do something stupid 'an help us out."

"What might that be?" Murphy asked.

"Maybe a fire starts on the floor Kellogg's marshals and their wives are sleeping on at the Kimball Hotel," Greenhoe grinned. "Never can tell what the Klan might do."

"I get ya'," Murphy responded.

At the railway station that afternoon, Mike and his men were seeing their wives off to Macon.

"You take care of yourself mister big shot marshal," Mary Jacqueline cautioned.

Michael hugged his wife. "You bet I will. You be careful too. Hear me?"

"Yes dear," Mary Jacqueline promised. "I will."

The other couples were saying their good-byes, too.

As the train was pulling out of the Atlanta station, Mike gathered his men.

"All right," he began. "Now, let's get to work. Bose has some information for us."

As the amen walked toward Kellogg's offices on Peach Street in downtown Atlanta, Bose Faute told Mike's group what he had found out.

"Remember when Stan and I questioned the cook staff back at the hotel?

"Well," he continued," The busboy who spilled water at our table that morning was one of those we questioned. I let him go and turned my attention on the Head Waiter.

"Anyway, the kid got back to me yesterday. He said that his girlfriend is a teacher at one of the Freedman Bureau's schools for colored's. After he told her about what had gone on at the hotel

134

restaurant, she insisted he return the favor by giving me some inside information about the Union League."

"She held out on him, did she?" Stan chuckled.

"I guess so," Bose said. "Anyway, he told me that they were getting ready to attack and burn down one of the Freedman Bureau's schools."

"Why the hell would they destroy a Freedman Bureau's school?" Stan asked.

"To blame it on the Klan; that's why," Frank surmised.

"Oh, ya."

"Maybe we should show up there and stop them," Bob Stephan suggested.

"While we're at it, that might be a good opportunity for us to take a prisoner or two." Frank Stanizek said.

"Exactly what I was thinking Frank," Mike said. "If they are holding Craig, I'll bet most of their men know about it."

"Be a good chance for us to squeeze some information out of them?" Stan suggested.

"Sounds like a plan to me," Mike responded.

*   *   *

Mike and his men arrived at the offices of General Alfred Terry, who was the military governor of the former Confederate states of Georgia, Alabama and Florida. They were shown in to a conference room.

Bill Kellogg soon joined them.

"Gentlemen." He greeted.

A couple of the men responded in kind. The others waited for Mike to lead the discussion.

"Bill," Mike began. "We are about to do something you don't want to know about."

"I take it, my boss, General Terry would not approve?"

"After talking with Greenhoe we believe the governor is regarded as a push-over, Bill," Mike responded"

Frank added, "The Klan leaders in this area think so too, Mr. Kellogg."

Mike continued. "Despite your best efforts, Bill, we think this military district is run like a Sunday school. Your general allows Greenhoe and his Union League thugs to terrorize the region for their own profit; the Klan seems to run wild, too.

"The freedmen under your protection are terrorized by the Klan and the Union League. But the general just collects his pay and does nothing to stop either group.

"If we want to rescue Craig, we need to be aggressive in our investigation. Sitting around has gotten us nowhere. We now have an opportunity to push the matter to a conclusion. I don't believe your boss would approve the action we need to take."

"So, you don't trust me or you just feel I'd be better off being able to deny knowing about it?"

"Not knowing in advance will be best, Bill." Mike insisted. "We need to act on some information we have and act quickly. Our follow-up will probably result in finding Craig alive."

"You're sure?"

"As sure as I can be. I have concluded that Greenhoe's Union League people are holding Craig."

"You're sure?"

"As I just said, I'm as sure as I can be."

"You men agree with what Mike is telling me?"

Bob Stephan spoke first.

"We not only agree with Mike, but believe that if Craig is still alive, we have to move quickly or bury what is left of him."

The room was quiet. No one else spoke.

"What about the ladies?" Kellogg asked. "Do they know of this?"

"They have been sent out of town," Mike revealed. "It is not safe for them to remain in Atlanta."

"I'm sorry to hear that gentlemen," Kellogg lamented. "I didn't realize they were threatened.

"Will you keep me informed?"

"Of course," Mike promised.

"If that's it," Kellogg concluded rising from his chair. "I expect you must get about your business."

"Yes, it is sir."

"Keep me informed, will you?"

"Yes, sir," Mike promised. "We will."

*   *   *

Later, as they road their horses to the site of the Freedman's school, Stan asked Frank, "Say, Frank," He began. "What is all this stuff about you guys in the Klan wearing white sheets an' stuff?"

'It's all about frightening the colored people," Frank admitted. "The white robes, head coverings and the torches are just for effect."

Bose added, "We don't have a Kan unit up in the Cove 'cause we don't have any colored people there. But if a group of you guys appeared in front of my place like that, I'd sure be frightened."

"Seems to work down Macon way," Frank added. "Negroes down our way seem to know their place."

"Is that what it's all about, Frank? Knowing their place?" Henry asked.

"Pretty much, Henry," Frank explained. "Before the war ended, we all knew our place in society. Afterwards, not so much. You see, we always believed that the Negro was an inferior race, meant to be at the base of the social order.

"But after you boys declared the Negro free and equal, the social order in the South was in chaos. Honestly, we don't know how to deal with that. In response, the Klan was formed to reestablish some sort of order; so, people would know their place"

Henry pushed back. "But the information we have in Washington is full of violent action by the Klan, Frank. Klan groups everywhere burned people's homes, men have been hung, women whipped, schools burned, too."

"How do you explain that?"

"Henry," Frank calmly responded. "All I can say is that my Klan in Macon has not done any of those violent things. I've heard of some of that elsewhere, I admit. But we have not done any of the things you mentioned.

"Remember, one of your own Congressional committees recently investigated those charges. That investigation did find some violence against Negro people by the Klan. But some of it was done by the Union League's military units and some by local Regulators and all blamed on the Klan."

"The Negro seems to be in the middle of all of this," Mike added. "In the northern magazine, The Nation, the magazine writers hoped that northern labor methods would solve the Negro work problem allowing free Negroes an opportunity for a new life. They said this opportunity and education would help establish a new social order in the South."

"The optimism of the folks at that magazine was shared by most sensible people in the South,
believe me. But reality has taught us otherwise. A Northern fellow took over a plantation in my area and hired Negroes to work the place." Frank volunteered. "He even had Negro supervisors. After two years, he abandoned the place."

"Why?" Bose asked.

"He told the local banker that his crops were not properly tended or harvested, "Frank reported. "He said that his supervisors couldn't get the field hands to work. He said, that his field workers thought freedom meant they didn't have to work. So, the Northern guy gave up the project and went back North."

"That's what that Northern magazine I mentioned, The Nation, reported, too," Mike said. After two years of observation they concluded that free labor methods used successfully in the North didn't work in the South in an agricultural setting with former slaves."

"Never-the-less," Frank broke in. "The former slaves expected everything to be provided them as in the slave days."

Stan Killeen spoke up. "Back North, nobody gets paid for sittin' around doing nothing."

"So, what do we as a nation do about this problem?" Henry asked.

"The Nation magazine people concluded recently in the article I read, that the 'Negro Problem' is the South's to solve," Mike added.

"I'm not surprised at that, Mike. You Northerners tell four million slaves they are free. You also abolish all the restraints on them and thereby turn social order in the South upside down. Then, you expect everything to run smoothly. Not too realistic, seems to me." Frank concluded."

Henry responded. "Probably not Frank. But what else could have been done after the Civil War? We couldn't just go home and leave slavery intact, could we?"

"Not claiming to know, Henry," Frank reminded everyone. "When your army, the carpetbaggers, and the Freedman's Bureau leave, we Southerners will be left with the problem. How do you think we should deal with it?"

No one offered any suggestions.

Back at their hotel that evening, Mike and his men gathered in a private ding room. Over drinks, they laid out their plans to confront the Union League's raid on the Freedman's school.

Mike had a map of the area spread on a table.

"When we surveyed the area this afternoon, we saw how narrow the road to the school is. There is a slope on one side of the road and a drop-off on the other. The school building is in a clearing to the hill side of the road.

"So, three of us will remain on the slope and allow them to pass. The other two will be stationed beyond the school to block any escape down that road.

"When they begin to fire the school, we'll block the road they came in on with some trees we'll have pre-cut, and then open fire on them. We'll have them in a crossfire."

Stan interrupted. "Sounds like a good battle plan, Mike. But how in hell are we going to end up with any prisoners?"

"Good question, Stan," Mike admitted. "We don't know how many men they'll have. But since they don't expect opposition, it will probably be a small force. So, those of us behind them will hold our fire but you guys in front shoot to kill. I'm guessing the attackers in the rear will attempt to escape back the way they came. We'll be there to take them."

"Sounds like it might work, Mike," Bob said.

Lowell

Eleanor was visiting her grandparents, Emma and Ruben Hecht for the weekend. Charles was given the choice of either milking cows at Grandfather Drieborg's or staying to work at the restaurant Saturday morning. He chose to stay in Grand rapids and work.

On the ride back to his farm in Lowell, Ruben and his granddaughter had a chance to catch-up.

"So," he said. "Your brother Charles decided to stay und scrub floors und wash dishes at da restaurant, eh?"

"The last time he visited the Drieborg farm he had to help clean out the barn and milk cows very early in the morning."

Ruben laughed. "I do dat all da time, Eleanor," He reminded her. "It is just da life of da farmer."

"I know that, grandfather," She responded. "But given the choice, Charles will avoid anything hard, dirty or smelly."

"Cleaning da barn is all of dat," Ruben chuckled.

"Und, what of you?" he asked. "How are you doing at Doctor Murphy's office. Isn't dat dirty and smelly sometimes?"

"Most of the time, grandfather," Eleanor told him. "But I don't mind. In fact, I think I want to be a doctor like Grandfather Murphy."

"I didn't know dat girls were doctors."

"It is still a bit unusual, grandfather," Eleanor told him. "But there are a few schools where women are trained in medicine. Besides, Grandfather Murphy will train me right in his office."

"Sounds like you have all dis figured out."

"I know what I want, grandfather," Eleanor assured him. "And, I'm not afraid of the hard work that will be required to become a doctor."

"Your grandmother Hecht is a healer you know." Ruben reminded his granddaughter. "Maybe you get dis need to work mit sick people from her, eh?"

"Probably, grandfather," Eleanor agreed. "I know I really look forward to talking with grandmother about those things on my visits to your farm"

Several years ago, after the Civil War concluded, the Hecht's saw their daughter Julia marry Michael Drieborg. He set up a farm just down the road from them and was soon pregnant with another Hecht grandchild. The following spring, she was killed while in Lowell on a Saturday morning by some assassins hired by men who hated the Drieborgs.

Shortly after the death of their daughter, Ruben and Emma Hecht's son Kenny ran off to join the Union cavalry. Then, they found themselves suddenly alone.

Emma Hecht reminded her husband of how quiet their house was. "I don't like the quiet, poppa."

"Ya, momma," he had agreed. "I miss all da laughter and even da fights da children had."

"Well then," Emma proposed. "Let us do something about it. Let us bring little ones back into our house."

"Momma," Ruben reminded her. "Ve are too old for dat."

"We are not too old to return to Saxony and find a little one in need of two loving parents, eh."

"Goot idea, momma. But in da meantime," Ruben proposed. "Can't we try da old-fashioned way, too?"

Emma just smiled, took her husband's hand and led him to their bedroom.

"Ya, papa," she said. "We try that, too."

*   *   *

Several months later, the Hecht's returned from the land of their birth with not just one infant, but two little girls, both hardly a year old. They also brought back a teen-aged niece to live with them to help with the little children

This morning, Ruben was in Grand Rapids to pick up his granddaughter Eleanor.

"Grandpa," Eleanor said as she climbed into the buggy. "When did you get this neat buggy?"

"When we got back from Saxony mit da little ones, I bought it for your Grandma Emma. When she leaves da house to help people, da weather can be very bad, especially in da winter time. Dis buggy is perfect for her. And, it helps on Sunday when ve got to church with da little ones."

"How are the children?" Eleanor asked.

"Dey are growing like nobody's business." Ruben told Eleanor. "Dey are into everyting. Dey love to work mit me in da barn mit da

144

animals und mit momma in da garden. Dey will make good farm wives someday."

"I'm looking forward to seeing them," Eleanor said. "I still can't believe they are my aunts."

Ruben laughed at the reminder. "Dat is sort a' funny," Ruben admitted. "Dey know you are coming and are all excited. Dey love it when you visit."

"I'm excited to see them, too, grandfather."

As they drove along Fulton street toward Lowell, they talked of many other things, too. Eleanor told her Grandfather of the attack on Charles.

"To attack a little boy like dat is hard to understand," He told her. "I don't know what gets into some people doing dat kind of ting."

"My daughter Julia und my grandson, Robert were attacked like dat in Lowell a few years ago. Men hired by dat evil Bacon man killed dem out of hate for Eleanor's fader. Later, Jake Drieborg und I picked up one of da attackers who got away. We tied him up und took him to my barn for a private meeting.

Ve untied him and gave him a chance to fight me, man to man. I hit him so hard, I tink my hands broken. Instead, he got broken up; face, ribs. Ven he tried to hit me mit a board, I broke his leg mit it instead. Ve turned him into sheriff Kalaquin in Grand Rapids. I accused him of assault und he vent to jail. I hope da man who attacked Eleanor's broder, Charles goes to jail, too."

Ruben pulled into the yard of his farm. He stopped the buggy in front of the doorway to the house.

"You go in while I put da horse und grandmother's buggy away," he told Eleanor. "I'll bring your bag in for you."

145

Eleanor jumped down. "Thank you, grandfather," she shouted as she ran into the house.

*   *   *

"Look who is here, children," Emma Hecht announced.

Ruth and Emily screamed and ran toward Eleanor. The three fell to the floor as the children jumped all over her. They rolled around laughing and giggling with joy.

Ruben hung up his coat and entered the room

"I tink dey love deir Eleanor," He observed.

"I think so, grandpa," his wife agreed.

"Eleanor," she said, "Get the children's hand's washed. Supper is almost ready."

Emma and the children's nanny, Heidie brought the food to the table. Once everyone was seated and Grace was said, the food was served.

Supper at the Hecht farm was the lightest of the three meals served each day. A hearty breakfast always began the day. The noon meal, dinner, was the main meal of the day, however. Left-overs from the noon meal were commonly served in the evening.

After the supper dishes were cleared and cleaned and everything put away, Once the children were cleaned up, and in their pajamas, Emma would read from the bible. Bedtime was shortly after dark for everyone. The Hechts would be up at dawn. Ruben had to milk his cows, Emma had to begin her day in the kitchen, baking bread.

Atlanta

Their meal and drinks finished, Mike and his men retired to their rooms.

By midnight, the hotel was quiet. Outside of the lobby and first floor bar, the only lights that could be seen were in the hallways. They were whale's oil lamps and their flame cast an eyrie shadowy light in the main floor lobby and in the narrow hall ways.

Guest rooms were located on either side of the hallways. The two stairways were at the ends of the hall with the elevator in the center.

The quiet was suddenly broken by a series of loud explosions followed by billows of smoke that filled the fifth-floor hallway.

Mike had warned his team about the possibility of such a night attack in the hotel.

*   *   *

He recalled another time, during the war, when he had to deal with this threat.

"I remember when Julia and I were staying overnight in Cleveland, Ohio. I was returning to Washington City and a military re-assignment after my leave and was escorting my sister-in-law Julia to her home in Maryland. After supper, we were in our sitting-room visiting when a grenade blew up right outside our door. The door was blown off its hinges and the room filled with smoke. We

both survived the blast without injury. But Julia was pretty shaken-up.

"I grabbed my revolver and looked into the hallway. There, I shot one man who I saw crouching to my left. Then, I noticed another man at the other end of the hall standing at the head of the stairs. I chased him down the stairs in short order and sent him tumbling with a shot to his shoulder.

"When I reached the bottom of the stairs, I grabbed him by the back of his shirt and, disarmed him. I took my knife out of my boot and put it under his chin.

"Who sent you?" I asked.

"My boss would kill me if I told you."

"Funny thing," I grinned. "That's what I have in mind if you don't tell me."

"I pushed the tip of the knife into the man's jaw. Then, I pulled it out.

"Ready to tell me who sent you?"

"Some guy up in Michigan, a banker in a hick town, paid my boss to kill you and whoever was with you. I don't know they guy's name."

"By this time two policemen were running up the stairway toward me.

"That'll be enough of that young fella." One of the uniformed men told me.

"The other policeman took charge of the man I was questioning and tied his hands behind him.

"We know this street hoodlum." He told me. "Did he cause the ruckus up on the next floor?"

"Yes, sir, he did." I told the policemen. "There's another man on the next floor just like this one. I think he's dead, though."

"You do it?"

"Yes, sir, I did."

"You have my thanks, laddie," the policeman said. "That's one less dirt bag on the streets for us to worry about."

"It was my pleasure, officer. "I told him.

"The three of us dragged the wounded man up the stairs to survey the damage.

"So, you shoot this guy, young fella?"

"Yes, Sergeant, I did. I caught him just after he blew my room's door off its hinges with a grenade. The fellow you have in custody I caught as he ran down the stairs.

"We know these two." One of the officers told me. "They work for a fellow named Billie. He has his men do most anything for hire."

"That's what the guy told me, too," I told the officers. "He told me his boss was paid by a banker in a small Michigan town to kill me."

"That cut under his chin tells me how you got him to reveal that much information. "

"Right," the other officer joined in. "They usually are more afraid of their boss than they are of us."

"I guess I convinced him that he should be more afraid of me, the guy with a knife at his throat.

"Just then, Police Chief Craig Haynes walked down the hallway. "You men have this situation under control?"

"Yes, sir. We do."

"Good. I'll read your report in the morning. Are you here alone, Major?" he asked me.

"No sir,

"I am escorting a young lady, my sister-in-law, to her home in Maryland. She is in the room waiting for me. I expect she is pretty shaken up right about now."

"I'll station two men in this hallway for the night." Chief Haynes told me. "You plan to leave Cleveland in the morning?"

"Yes, sir." I told him. "The 8 AM tomorrow for Baltimore. "

"I suggest you have breakfast in your room, Major. My men will then escort you and the young lady to the train station."

"Thank you, sir." I said. "If you don't mind, I'll see to the young lady.

On our way to Baltimore we were attacked once again; this time on the train. The thugs who survived that encounter were picked up by the Baltimore police. They told the same story: they were hired by a small- town Michigan banker. Had to be old man Bacon. Once we arrived at the Hecht hone in Maryland, I was escorted to Washington by a platoon of Union cavalry.

"Back in Michigan, Carl Bacon who was serving a sentence in federal prison at Detroit for an earlier attempt on my life, confessed to his role in the latest assassination attempt. His father Harvey Bacon, the banker, was arrested, tried and sentenced to join his son in prison."

By this time, Mike saw the men of his team hurrying out of their rooms and into the hallway, armed.

The men gathered in the center of the hall, by the elevator.

"Good thing the ladies weren't here," Bob said.

"You got that right," Bose added.

Mike gave instructions. "Frank, you and Henry go down that staircase. Henry, you come with me down the other stairway."

"What do you want me ta do, Mike?" Stan asked.

"You stay here, Stan. Watch the elevator for any strangers coming to this floor."

"When we meet in the lobby, I intend to roust the manager and have a little late-night talk with him."

Mike and his men did not find anyone on either staircase.

Now, in front of the manager's apartment on the main floor, Mike banged on the door.

"What the hell is all this commotion about, Marshal Drieborg?" the manager, Mr. Caldwell asked.

Mike pushed the man back onto the room.

"I thought we had an understanding that you were not to reveal our room locations.

"Even you must admit it would be near impossible for me to keep that secret," the man sputtered. "All types of my hotel employees service your floor and your rooms. They all know where the Yankee marshals are staying. It's no secret. Because all my employees know, so does most everyone in Atlanta."

"I see," Mike said. "So, if we move to another hotel, everyone in Atlanta will know that, too?"

"Yes, I expect that would be common knowledge pretty quickly." Mr. Caldwell predicted.

"How many bedrooms do you have in this nice apartment? Mike asked.

"I have two bedrooms," he responded. "Why do you ask?"

"Because my men and I are going to move down here for the duration of our stay at your hotel. That's why."

"Good idea, Mike," Frank said. "I never trusted that damned elevator, anyway."

"I know where there be five rooms available on our floor, Mr. Manager." Bose told him.

"This is outrageous," Caldwell. Charged. "I'll inform the Military Governor at once."

"You do that," Mike urged him. "If General Terrry moves as quickly on your complaint as he does on all the violence in this area, it will be a cold day in hell before anything is done.

"How fast can you and your family be out of these rooms?"

"Well, I never," He responded.

"Gentlemen," Mike said to his men. "Help Mr. Caldwell pack his belongings. Move them out into the lobby. Now!"

The lobby was soon full of clothing and other personal items from Caldwell's apartment. He and his wife sat in lobby chairs watching the parade of their worldly possessions being put in the lobby for all to see. She was crying.

"Gentlemen, will you join me on the fifth floor to bring all our gear down to our new rooms?"

"Henry," Mike added. "Will you stand guard down here. We wouldn't want any of Mr. and Mrs. Caldwell's things stolen while we're upstairs."

The entire transfer was accomplished within an hour. When they were finished, the Caldwell's were still sitting in the lobby. Mrs. Caldwell was still crying.

" I don't know about you fellas," Mike said to his men. "But I'm wide awake and hungry. How about some breakfast?"

"it's the middle of the night, Mike?" Frank reminded him. "The kitchen will probably still be closed."

Mike responded, "You can wait until it's open, Frank. But I fended for myself lots of times in the army. Besides, I don't need to be waited on. So, if you don't mind, we'll fix our own stuff."

It just so happened they didn't have to. The kitchen staff was already at work, baking bread and pastries for the day. They were sitting around having coffee. Mike just ordered them to toast some of the freshly baked bread, throw some bacon and potatoes in a pan and fry some eggs. Then he and the others enjoyed the coffee that the cooks had made for themselves.

After they finished their impromptu meal, the men sat smoking their cigars.

"I gotta say," Stan said to Mike. "this was a great idea. Got the whole place to ourselves."

"You are something Mike," Frank admitted.

"Now, what do we do?" Bob asked.

"I believe we rest," Mike told him.

Lowell

Eleanor played with the little ones until dinner-time.

Sitting around the table at noon, Emma spoke with Eleanor about her afternoon trip to an expectant mother's farm house.

"When you were working at Dr. Murphy's office, did you ever help deliver a baby, Eleanor?"

"I didn't because no woman has given birth in his office. He and nurse Kathy usually go to the home when a baby is due. They haven't taken me with them, yet."

"Well, the first thing we do after we get into the house is wash our hands. They will have water boiling on the stove. We'll use that to rinse off some strong soap I have in my medical bag.

"Only then do we go to the bedroom to examine the pregnant woman. Her husband stopped in last night to tell me how far apart her birth pains are. I think the baby will come this afternoon or this evening."

"You can't be sure, grandmother?"

"Only God knows, Eleanor," Her grandmother reminded her. "But the baby seems positioned correctly and the timing of the pains she is having are both good signs that Mrs. Muller is ready. I have helped her with birthing two children, already. So, this one should not be a problem for her."

"What am I supposed to do, grandmother while you're helping this lady give birth?" Eleanor asked as she spooned some ground-up vegetables into one of the children's mouth.

"You stand by my side," Emma answered. "I want you to hold a wet towel and be ready to hand it to me when I asked for it. The pregnant woman may perspire quite a bit. You must be ready to wipe off her forehead. Mine too, if I start perspiring.

"Once the baby is born, I will want you to help me cut off the umbilical tube and clean off the infant. So, you must have some hot water in a pan and clean towels by the bed, too.

"Your first experience with birthing might cause you to get sick to your stomach and even feel faint seeing all the blood and the pain involved in the birthing."

"I've seen plenty of blood and pain in Dr. Murphy's office, grandmother," Eleanor explained. "I should be all right."

"Good, then I won't worry about you."

Ruben added. "Just listen to your grandmother and watch her. Maybe you be a doctor someday. Eh Eleanor?"

"I hope so, grandfather.

"Your gramma saved your father's life back in da war, remember?

"I remember the story, grandfather. My father told me how you and grandma took my father from Washington City back to your farm in Maryland after he was wounded in some big battle.

"Yes,' she continued, "I understand grandmother knows a lot about healing and such. I'll pay attention. That's for sure."

Then, Eleanor helped Heidie, the teen ager brought over from Saxony with the children, to put Ruth and Emily down for their afternoon nap.

"Read to us, Eleanor, please." They begged.

So, she read to them until they fell asleep. Shortly, Emma was ready to go.

"Eleanor," her grandmother said." Get your coat and hat. It is time for us to go."

"All right, grandmother," Eleanor said. "Should I take my sweater, too?"

"Yes," Eleanor wad told. "Youi don't know how late we'll be tonight and it gets rather cool after the sun goes down.

"Papa," she continued her instructions. "Leftovers are in the icebox for tonight. You know how to fix them?"

"Ya, momma," He responded. "I have done it before."

"Yes, poppa, I know. I'm just saying."

"Your horse and buggy and in the back, waiting for you."

"Thank you, poppa."

Once they were in the buggy, Emma directed the horse on to Fulton street and headed west. The Muller farm house was several miles away toward the village of Ada.

"Isn't this buggy neat, grandmother?" Eleanor observed.

"Yes, it is," Emma Hecht responded. "Your Grandpa Hecht got it for me as a surprise after we brought the children back from Saxony. It is especially neat, as you young people say, when it is raining."

"I'll bet it will be nice during the winter, too."

"I expect so, Eleanor.

"When we arrive at the Muller house, I will introduce you." Eleanor's grandmother instructed. I 'IL do all the talking, too. They don't know you, Eleanor and might be a bit nervous with you around. Understand?"

"Yes, Grandmother."

*　　*　　*

Not much later, they arrived at their destination.

Rupert Muller opened the door for them.

"Good afternoon, Rupert," Emma greeted. "How is Irma?"

"Fine, I think, Emma. She is in the bedroom," he responded. "Her pains have not changed much. But I think she is anxious to get this over with."

"She'll be fine, Rupert. Don't worry.

"In the past, she gave birth rather quickly once the pains got a little closer together," Emma Hecht reminded him. "Irma should be fine.

"By the way, this is my granddaughter Eleanor. She is studying to be a doctor and will help me today. Do you mind?"

"Not at all. Good afternoon, Eleanor Welcome to our home."

"Thank you, Mr. Muller."

"Rupert," Emma asked. "Do you have the water boiling on the stove?"

"Yes, I do. Everything is ready as you instructed. Towels are on the table, too. "He responded.

"Come Eleanor. We scrub our hands first. Just like I told you."

"Yes, grandmother. "

Rupert told Emma. "I'll put your horse and buggy into the barn while you're washing. Do you need anything else before I go?"

"No," she responded. "We'll be fine. Just be sure to wipe my horse down please and give it some grain."

"I'll be happy to."

When Rupert Muller returned to the house, Emma Hecht and Eleanor were in the bedroom with Irma Muller.

Emma came out to talk with Rupert.

"How is she, Emma?" he asked.

"She is fine, Rupert." Emma assured him.

"Her pains are coming closer together now. I believe you will have a healthy son or daughter by supper time."

"As long as Irma and the child are healthy, that's all I pray for."

"I hear you, Rupert," Emma told him. Me, too. "Then, she went back into the bedroom.

Irma Muller was resting. But she wanted to talk, too. As she held Emma' hand she asked.

"How are your two little ones, Ruth and Emily?"

"They are wonderful; healthy and talkative and into everything."

"Still happy that you and Ruben adopted them?"

"Oh, yes," Emma responded quickly. "These two girls have brought life back into our home. Ruben loves them so. I do, too. How are your two doing?"

"Little Rupert is like another pair of hands for his father. They are always together in the barn working or talking about some farm thing or another. He is the shepherd for our flock of sheep, too. He loves his sheep. My Mary is a big help around the kitchen and in the garden. She loves her chickens and rabbits. What a dear she is. I wouldn't know what to do without her."

Then she suddenly squeezed Emma's hand. Emma told Eleanor,

"White down the time of the contractions, Eleanor. They are getting closer, Irma," she told the expectant mother. "It shouldn't be long now.

"Keep pushing," Emma urged.

Sure enough, the spasms began to come closer and closer. By early in the evening the baby was coming.

"See, Eleanor," Emma urged her granddaughter to look. "You can see the baby's head. Look over my shoulder as I help the infant slide out. "

Emma slid her hands on either side of the infant's head and began to gently pull.

"Look at its shoulders, Eleanor," Emma told her.

Irma groaned as she continued to push the unborn child out of her womb.

Emma pulled and the remainder of the baby slid into the open. Only the cord connected the child to its mother.

"Quickly, Eleanor," Emma ordered. "Give me the knife." Eleanor took a knife out of a container of hot water with tongs and laid it on a towel. Emma took it, cut the cord and tied it off at the baby's stomach. The rest of the cord and the placenta quickly slid out of Irma's womb.

"Give me that wet towel, Eleanor, "she directed.

With the towel, Emma cleaned the child, wrapped it in a dry towel and laid it on its mother's chest.

"Go tell Mr. Muller that he has a fine new boy in his family. I'll take care of this cord and placenta."

"That was so beautiful, grandmother," Eleanor sighed.

"Yes, this time, Eleanor, it was. This time it was easy and beautiful," Emma Hecht agreed with her granddaughter.

"But not always I'm afraid. I watched your mother die giving birth to you. I couldn't stop the bleeding. So, it's not always so beautiful child.

"Go now," she reminded Eleanor. "Tell Mr. Muller he can come in and see his new son."

Eleanor and her grandmother stayed at the Muller home for supper, too. Irma had roasted some chicken and fried some potatoes that morning for this meal. All her husband had to do was heat it up and get out some applesauce from the icebox and boil some coffee for himself and their guests.

Both mother and baby seemed to be doing well. So, Emma Hecht and Eleanor left the Muller farm shortly after the meal.

"Are you sure Mrs. Muller will be all right, grandmother?"

"No, child. Things can still go wrong. Your mother didn't start bleeding until a few days after you were born. You just never know about such things."

"Why then, don't we just stay at the Muller farm until we're sure?"

"Because Irma has given birth to two healthy children and had no complications. Besides, Irma will have Rupert come get me if necessary."

"While I helped Mr. Muller fix dinner, he told me that they're going to name the boy Boniface?' Eleanor told her grandmother.

"That is a good German name, don't you know."

"No, grandmother, I didn't know that."

"Yes," Emma told her granddaughter, "Back in the middle ages, he was a Bishop in one of the German countries. He was a famous saint, too."

"He must have been a good man to have been made a saint."

"I assume so, child. Tell me about your plans to become a doctor. Will you?"

"Grandfather Murphy tells me that it is now possible to enter a real university school of medicine. In fact, he says, that the University of Michigan has recently allowed two women to study at their medical school. That's what I want to do."

"Didn't he teach at the University of Pennsylvania medical school?"

"Yes, he did, grandmother," Eleanor told her. "But he told me that his old school doesn't allow women to study medicine there. At least not yet."

"That is so sad," Emma commented. "When we need doctors so badly it is hard for me to understand why such schools still bar women from the study of medicine."

"It won't keep me from becoming a doctor, believe you me." Eleanor vowed.

'I think I detect the Dutch and German stubbornness coming out in you. Good for you."

Eleanor changed the subject. "Isn't this buggy cozy?" Eleanor said.

"Yes, it is," Emma agreed. "especially with the side curtains down, like now. Here, child, pull up the blanket over your knees."

They continued to chat about this and that until they reached the Hecht farm.

"You want me to put the horse and buggy in the barn, grandmother?"

"No, child," she responded. "That's Grandpa Hecht's job. He always wants to handle such things himself. But thank you for offering."

"I think Grandpa Drieborg would feel that way, too," Eleanor judged.

"It's sort of a man thing, you know," Emma told her granddaughter. "We farm women have to be careful not to intrude on our husband's things like the barn, the animals and the crops. They learn to keep out of our way in the house. It works well most of the time."

"That sounds smart to me," Eleanor agreed. "I'll remember that."

They entered the house.

"Welcome home," Ruben greeted them. He gave both of them a hug. "Did everyting go veil at the Muller's?"

Emma sat by the fire and told him everything.

"Did you learn a lot, Eleanor?" Ruben asked his granddaughter.

"Oh, yes grandfather," Eleanor said. "It was so wonderful to watch the birthing. Grandmother was marvelous. She calmed Mrs. Muller and helped her deliver a beautiful baby boy. They're going to call him Boniface."

"Data's a goot German name," Ruben judged. "Did da buggy und horse work out, Emma?"

"They are both fine, grandpa," Emma said. "I left them both out in the yard for you to take care of. How were the children.?"

"Da children were fine, momma," He told her. "Dey finished der dinner and Heidie got dem to sleep on time. Oh, I almost forgot about da horse. I'll go an un-hitch her and give her some grain. Thank you for reminding me, momma. I be right back."

Emma winked at Eleanor.

"It is late already, child," She reminder her granddaughter. "Time for you to go to bed. Thank you for helping me today. It was very good to have you with me."

"You're welcome, grandmother," Eleanor said. "But you did all the work. I'm just grateful you took me along. Aren't you tired, too?"

"I am, child. But I will wait for grandpa to finish putting my horse away in the barn. You go to bed now."

*　　　*　　　*

In their bedroom, later, Ruben asked Emma about their granddaughter.

"Do you think Eleanor has 'the touch', Emma?"

Ruben was asking about the medical gift so many women have with healing. Most farm injuries are taken care of in the home or locally by such women healers. Emma was considered one of those by families in the Lowell and Ada area. She was called a 'healer'.

"It's too early to tell, papa," Emma said. "She certainly is not bothered by the sight of blood. And she does have great sympathy for those suffering pain. I think she will be very good with people who are suffering an illness or an injury. Working in Dr. Murphy's office is also good training for her I think."

"You vant her to spend more time mit you, den?"

"Yes, papa," She told her husband. "I hope she spends more time with me on my calls. She is eager to learn and it would be good for her. But it is up to her Grandpa Murphy. We will see."

"Enough talk, momma," Ruben decided. "Ve get up early, ya?"

It didn't take much time for Emma to fall asleep after Ruben turned off the lantern.

Atlanta

The Atlanta director of the Freedman's Bureau, Dick Greenhoe, was meeting with Major Tom Murphy He was the commander of the Union League para-military force for that area.

"How is your group doing Tom?" he asked.

"They need some action," Murphy replied. "Sitting around is not good for them. They get restless, start fighting amongst themselves and hard to control. They need something to focus on aside from each other.

"We need to confiscate stuff to sell. We're short of supplies," he told Greenhow. " Besides, it's been a month since the men have had a pay-day."

"You still got that school burning lined up for next week?"

"I don't know about that," Murphy mused. "Word has gotten back to me that Drieborg and his bunch may have gotten word about it. I'm thinkin' of putting it off or changing targets."

"You got a traitor in your force?"

"I don't know, for sure," Murphy answered. "Maybe I'm just getting skittish. But one of my boys has sort of disappeared. Maybe it's nothing. But it's troubling."

"Let's change targets, just to be sure," Greenhoe suggested.

"What have you got in mind?"

"The manager of the Kimball House is a guy named, Caldwell," Greenhoe began. "He sent me a message that all the wives in Drieborg's party have left his hotel."

"Went back home did they?"

"No," Greenhow responded. "As a matter of fact, they went to Macon, right here in Georgia."

So?"

"After that disaster of last year, haven't you wanted to return there and get some pay-back?"

"It has occurred to me."

"The wives are without their husbands down there. They're exposed," Greenhow told Murphy.

"You could sweep them up, no problem, Seems ta me."

"I suppose. Then what do we do with 'em?"

"Aside from frightening the very devil out a' them?" Greenhoe continued.

"Ya," Murphy wondered. "Then what?"

"Use your imagination, man," Greenhow prompted. "Four helpless white women under your control. Come 'on man. Think."

Back at his headquarters, Murphy called four of his platoon leaders together to discuss the Macon assignment.

"Why are we canceling the school burning?" Howie Hillbrands asked.

"None, a' your business," Murphy snapped. "All you need ta know is that we've been given a different assignment."

"I hope this one is smore profitable than the last," Another platoon leader said. "We hardly got enough out a' that last one to buy supplies after."

"Jones," Murphy commanded. "Keep your trap shut and listen. We're going back to Macon."

"We got our asses kicked by the sheriff down there, last time." Billy reminded everyone.

"This time it'll be different."

"How so, Major," Tom Alexander asked.

"We've got another kidnapping planned."

"Who is the target this time?"

"Four white women."

"Well I'll be. That's different," Jones decided.

"Sounds like it might be fun," Billy judged.

"Any particular four women?"

"The wives of the Federal Marshals in Atlanta trying to find Haynes."

"The women in Macon without their husbands?" Alexander asked.

"It appears so,"

"Sounds like a piece of cake," Billy said.

"How big a force we taking, Major?"

"A large force could create too much attention, Murphy told them. "So, I want you Billy and you Jones to pick two good men; guys you can trust. The five of us should be able to handle this."

"So, Howie and me are stayin' behind?" Jones asked.

"Seems that's the case," Murphy told his platoon leaders. "Somebody got to look after this bunch. I sure as hell can't trust, Billy ta' stay behind. No tellin' what mischief he'd get into left alone back here. Hillbrands will stay, too, and be in charge.

"Alexander's a steady hand, he goes with me, too."

After the meeting, Jones and Hillbrands were talking.

"Why'd he put you in charge?"

"Get over it, Jones," Hillbrands told him. "Between you an' me though, we gotta do somethin' or our men are gonna go stir crazy jus sittin' around."

"What do ya have in mind?" Jones asked.

"Maybe we'll jus take out that Freedman's Bureau school while those guys are having their fun down in Macon. You in?"

"I'd like that,"

"Keep it quite though, until Murphy is gone,"

*   *   *

Meanwhile, it took another day for Murphy to organize his team's trip to Macon. The horses and supplies were loaded on a freight-car, and, the train headed south to Macon. He met with his men in a passenger car during the trip.

"When we arrive, we'll take our horses and gear south of town and set up camp. The following day we'll go to town to watch for the women. We have some members in town. They've been instructed to find the women for me.

"The hotel manager in Atlanta provided the women's names. One of them, Margaret Stanitzek, is a resident of Macon. So, she shouldn't be hard to find. We'll check the local hotels first. If they're not registered, they are probably staying at the Stanitzek home."

"Sounds like shooting fish in a barrel," Alexander commented. "Don't seem hardly fair."

"Fair or no, you shit-head," Murphy snapped. "We need to get in, do the job and get out."

Macon, Georgia

The ladies were riding a six-passenger buggy into Macon. One of the Stanitzek's Negro farm hands was driving the vehicle. Gerry Gostkowski was riding a horse on one side of the buggy and Frankie, one of the Stanitzek's boys, was riding on either side. Both men were heavily armed.

"Maybe if we just ignore them, they'll get tired and go have a beer or something," Ethie," Faute said.

"They don't bother me, Ethie," Mary Alice said. "All I see is farm land and cattle; not the men guarding us, a 'tall."

"I for one, am happy to have them around," Peggy Stanitzek said. "All I have to do is remember what happened to us out at Fort Sumpter a couple of years ago when we left our security people back in Charleston. I wouldn't want to go through anything like that again."

"Neither would I, Peg," Mary Jacqueline Drieborg said. "I still have nightmares about that."

In fact, the memory was still fresh in her mind.

"When I was in Charleston with these same ladies a couple of years back, we decided to go downtown shopping. While there, we gave our two security guards the slip and took the ferry out to Fort Sumpter. While on the island fort, we walked around the ruins on our own. We were free of restraint. It felt good. What great fun!

"It was late in the afternoon and few tourists remained. Just before the last ferry boat left for the mainland, and with dusk approaching, a group of armed men suddenly appeared and took us prisoner.

"All of us got ruffed-up, but I think I got the worst of it. My deceased first husband's brother David was the leader of this gang of drunken thugs. He dragged me off into the ruins and began to tear my clothing. I know he was going to rape me. In fact, he told me as much.

"I managed to get a small pistol out of my dress pocket and in the darkness put it under his chin and pulled the trigger. The revolver was powerful enough to blow off the top of his head. I still thank my husband for insisting that I carry that small handgun. I then took my attacker's revolver so that as one, and then another, of his gang came looking for him in the ruins, I killed them. Linda Gostkowski managed to kill her captor, too.

"By this time, my husband, Michel and the husbands of the other four ladies had forced the ferry to return to the fort. While we had pretty well overcome our captives, we were very, very upset and shaken by the experience. So, we were most happy to see our husband arrive.

"When we returned to Charleston that night, we were all so shaken that we stayed at Colonel Popes home for several days under a doctor's care, and healthy doses of laudanum.

"That's the experience Peggy Stanizek was referring to. I guess the other ladies have chosen to forget it.

"Peg and I haven't."

*   *   *

The Stanitzek farm was some five miles outside of Macon. A two-story frame house, it had a porch on all four sides. Each room on the main floor had windows that opened outward to allow in all the breeze possible to each room. From the ceiling of each room, there hung a wide fan-like device that would circulate air when pulled back and forth. In the dining-room it also served to keep flies off the food during meals.

It was a beautiful day with a clear sky and a pleasant breeze.

"Tell us a little about Macon, Peg," Mary Jacqueline asked.

"I'm told the city was founded in 1823," she began. The Ocmulgee River runs through the town and provides power for several factories here. During the war we were considered a very important industrial center in the Deep South. Our city became especially important as such after you Yanks captured Nashville, Tennessee in the upper South early in 1862.

"During that war, your army tried to capture the city three times; and failed," Peg went on. "In fact, an entire Regiment of Sherman's cavalry rode here to liberate the Union officer's prison, Camp Oglethorpe. Instead, they were captured by us.

"So, we were never occupied as was Atlanta or Savannah. We escaped the destruction the people of those cities endured.

"Anyway, we operate a meat market here in town. Our son, Frank and his brother Fritz run it for the family. Their families live in town, too."

"Bose would sure love to visit that meat market, Peg," Ethie Faute commented. "He loves his meat."

"We sure sell a lot of it, Ethie," Peg told her. "Aside from various cuts of beef and port, our boys make and sell a lot of sausage. They slaughter cattle for others and dress deer for people, too. Around the holidays, they sell a lot of hams and turkeys as well. While Frankie is with us today, his brother Fritz will be working at the store."

"It appears that the war didn't stop the Stanitzek family much," Mary Alice Stephan said. "Sounds like you have a healthy business going, Peg."

"We were lucky that our boys and my husband came home safely from the fighting. And, of course, our town escaped Sherman's destructive march through Georgia, too. I thank God every day for those blessings.

"We do have a prosperous business, thank you very much. The whole family is involved and supported by it. We raise our own animals and run the local slaughter house, too. Tonight, we'll have some of our pork roast for supper with apple sauce and peach pie both from fruit harvested in our own orchards."

"Sounds good ta me, dearie," Ethie said.

"But now, we're going downtown to shop at our main dry goods store," Peg announced. "It's only a two-story structure, hardly as grand as the six-story place we visited in Atlanta.

"They don't have a restaurant in the place, but there are several down-town that are very nice."

"I'm sure they are Peg," Mary Alice assured her. "Don't you worry about it, one little bit."

"I'll bet they don't serve oysters like that place in Washington City, though," Ethie guessed.

"No, they don't Ethie," Peg assured her. "But just the same, the menus are quite extensive and as you might expect, sort of heavy on red meat."

"After that hearty farmer's breakfast," Mary Jacqueline observed, "I can't believe I'll have much more than a salad."

"Aren't you eating fer two again, dearie?" Ethie chided referring to her friend's pregnant state the last time they were together in Washington City.

"Not that I'm aware of, Ethie," A little color showed in Mary Jacqueline's cheeks.

"I'm surprised at that, dearie," Ethie continued. "The way that man of yours looks at you, mercy! A body would think you'd be pregnant all the time."

Mary Jacqueline blushed while all the ladies laughed heartily.

"Well, I never!" Mary Alice said.

Ethie wasn't through, though. "Maybe you could pick up some baby clothing at this store today, just in case., don't ya know"

Even Mary Jacqueline laughed this time.

Just before they entered the city, they passed four men seated on horses at the side of the road.

*   *

"Bingo!" one of the men said. "Seems like we found our targets."

"Maybe so," another responded. "See those armed men with them. Seems ta me they aren't going ta be as easy ta take as you promised, Murphy."

"Maybe yes, maybe no," Murphy said. "We'll watch an' see."

The four men waited a bit and then followed the women and their escorts into Macon.

"Drive down the main street and then go down to our river park, George," Peg directed the driver. "I want to show my friends some of the city. And so, the driver did.

The Oculgee River Park was spacious. Picnic benches and shade trees abounded. There was even a baseball diamond. Boat docks on the river held dozens of small boats, some with overhead canvas, most with oars for Sunday outings.

"This place is crowded on weekends," Peg told them. "We used to bring out children down here after church on Sunday. Now they bring theirs."

"Why don't we get some sandwiches or something and have a picnic while we're here, Peg?" Mary Alice suggested.

"Great idea," Ethie agreed. "Today, though I want to sample one a' those restaurants we jus passed over on Main Street."

"Great idea, Mary Alice," Peg said. "We can do that Monday, weather permitting. We'll pack a lunch for the day.

"Drive up past Saint Ann's church, George," Peg directed the carriage driver.

They soon passed a stately clapboarded church with a high bell tower. Children ran around in a playground located by a nearby two-story building.

"This is our church and the school our kids attended,"

"What order of nuns teach here, Peg?" Mary Jacqueline asked.

"We have the Franciscan Sisters in our grade school and the Franciscan Brothers teaching our secondary students."

"They are a tough bunch, but we think the children benefited from their firm hand," Peg answered.

The carriage found its way back to the main street and stopped in front of the dry-goods store.

Peg led the way. "All right ladies," she said. "We've got a lot of time before we're due at my favorite restaurant. So, shop you're hearts out. We'll meet back at the carriage in one hour."

The ladies were helped out of the carriage by their drive, George. They were joined by the fifth lady in their group, Linda Gostkowski. She and her husband were actually there to protect the party.

"Are you gonna shop or just look out fer us, Linda?" Ethie asked as they all walked into the store.

"I'll do some of both, Ethie," She responded.

"Don't let Mike scare you, ya hear. Shop right along with us."

"Don't worry about me, Ethie," Linda responded. "I'll do some shopping along with the guarding."

"That a' girl,"

*   *   *

The four men on horseback watched from across the road as the ladies entered the dry goods store.

"How we gonna handle this, Murphy?"

"We're gonna watch ta see what their escorts do," Murphy announced. "I'll tell ya when we go in. Jus you relax."

Of the three, armed men with the Stanitzek party, two stayed at the front door. One accompanied the ladies into the store.

Finally, Murphy announced. "There's gotta' be a back door to this place," he decided. "Billy, you go around back. Get out your watch. In ten minutes, I want you to fire a couple of shots inside the rear of the store. That'll draw those two, armed men standing by the front door into the store and back toward you.

"When they get drawn into the store, the three of us will hit the front door. You take the two ladies closest to the front. I'll watch for the two-armed guys and cover you're escape. We'll take them to our camp south of town. Billy, when those two guys enter the store, you leave, and ride around the front to help us get the captives out of town. Any questions?"

There were none. "Get on with ya, Billy,"

*   *   *

Linda and Ethie were taking their time near the front of the store. Mary Jacqueline, Peg and Mary Alice went to the second floor first. The armed driver, George when with them.

"They have some really nice table lamps up here I'd like you to see." Peg said. And up the stairs they went.

Suddenly, shots were fired in the rear of the store on the first floor.

Frank Stanitzek and Gerry Gostkowski left the front door and rushed into the store. Linda drew her revolver and stayed with Ethie. George stood at the top of the stairs prepared to protect the three ladies on the second floor.

It was then that Linda saw three men, armed with rifles, standing in the entryway of the store. Two of them moved toward her and Ethie. She assumed a crouch and shot one of them in the chest. The other man grabbed Ethie and began to drag her toward the front door.

Ethie was almost six foot tall and somewhat muscular. The man trying to drag her out of the store wasn't much over five feet five and around 120 pounds. That's the right size for a cavalryman, but not for an abductor of a strong Tennessee hill-country farm woman like Ethie Faute.

Initially caught off balance, Ethie got her feet under her, twisted away from her abductor's grip and hit him in the throat with her fist. He gaged, let her go, and grabbed his throat with both his hands. By this time, she had gotten her derringer pistol out of her dress pocket and shoved it under her attacker's chin.

"What 'ill it be, Yank?" she hissed. "You kneel down right here, right now, or I blow the top a' yer head off?"

He knelt.

Murphy had not fired at Ethie for fear of hitting his man. By the time he had a clear shot, Linda had gotten off one of her own, at him. Her shot was off somewhat, but she did hit the stock of his rifle. It flew out of his hands. Before she could get off another one, he fled out the front door.

He and Billie rode out of town as fast as their horses could carry them.

"So much fer shooting fish in a barrel. What tha hell happened back there Murphy?" Billie asked. "Where's Tom and Alex?"

"Just ride," Murphy shouted. "We'll talk back at camp."

*   *   *

It seemed to Linda that the Sheriff and some of his deputies were at her side almost immediately.

"What the hell is happening here?" he demanded.

Linda was standing alongside Ethie with her revolver pointed at the head of their captive.

"This guy and two others tried to kidnap Ethie Faute, sheriff\," Linda told him. "I'm a Pinkerton agent hired to protect her and three other ladies who are shopping in this store."

"I suppose you're responsible for killing that guy laying over there?"

"You got that right," Linda answered firmly. "Him and another two men, both armed, entered the store and tried to kidnap us. Ethie Faute took care of this scum by herself. I shot the one you're asking about. And, one man got away from us. That's his rifle over on the floor."

"Oh. I see," He responded. "You're staying with the Stanitzeks, I understand."

"Yes, we are," Linda said. "Peg Stanitzek is upstairs shopping. I was led to believe you were going to provide some kind of protection for us when we were in town."

"I would have had you let me know in advance you were going to be here," The sheriff protested. "Can't help if I don't know you're here, don't you know."

"Got us there, sheriff,"

"You seem ta be able ta take care of yourself, lady," The sheriff's deputy added.

"Speakin a' that," Ethie spoke up. "I want ta ask this guy a few questions. Any objections, sheriff?"

"I take by your tone lady that you expect to be forceful about questioning this lout. I'll just get out your way over there by the dead guy."

Ethie looked at the sheriff, 'Good idea. You best go about your business," she said. "I'll not be long with this Yankee piece a' crap."

With that, she and Linda dragged the fellow up the stairs to the second floor.

The sheriff commented to his deputy, "I learned a long time ago not to get in the way of a pissed-off Southern lady intent on her work."

Atlanta

It was late afternoon and the hot noonday sun was low in the blue sky. Mike and his men were just arriving at the Freedman's Bureau school several miles west of Atlanta. There were no students in the building at the time. The young ones had left to walk home before dark and the adult students would not arrive until after their work day was completed, usually after dark.

"Frank," he directed. "You and Stan cut those trees over the road west of the school house. Then position yourselves on that rise behind the building.

"Bob," Mike continued. "You, I and Henry will position ourselves on the hillside east of the school. After the League's troopers pass us, we will finish felling trees to block the path of their retreat.

"Remember to hold your fire till I fire a flare to illuminate the killing ground," Mike ordered. "Then you fired a flare, too."

"Do we kill them all, Mike?" Frank asked. "I thought we wanted to question some about where they're keeping Craig."

"If they all die in our crossfire, so be it, Frank," Mike decided. "But I'm sure there will be a survivor or two who we can question."

The men went to work cutting trees and preparing brush to block the road to the west. By the time they were finished preparing the road obstructions, the sun had almost disappeared over the horizon and dusk was settling over the land.

By the time it was dark, Mike and his men were in position ready to spring their trap.

They had a bit of a wait. It was nearly midnight before the lead riders appeared on the road east of the school house. The main body was one hundred yards behind.

Henry was the first to see them coming.

"Four men in the advance party and looks like twenty or so in the main body, Mike." He reported.

"They're carrying so many torches you'd think they're staging a parade, or something," Bob observed.

"That just makes it easier for us to pick 'em off, Bob."

"You got that right, Mike." He responded.

"Let them all get to the school before you push that tree over the road," Mike reminded Bob and Henry. "Then, set up behind it while I pull all that brush we cut onto the road."

The raiders gathered around the school. They had a Negro man tied to a horse which they led under a tree. When a rope had been thrown over a low hanging branch, they tied a noose around the man's neck.

"Massar," the man pleaded. "Don hang me. Let me go, massar."

"Too late fer that, boy," The leader of the raiders told him. "Gotta string you up for all to see."

Just as someone spooked the Negro's horse, a shot rang out and the man who had just spoken fell to the ground. Then, a flare burst over them. and, for a moment it seemed like daylight. Then, another flare burst above them.

That started Frank and Stan firing from the west, too. The mass of men turned and headed back the way they had come. But the felled tree and brush prevented escape that way. The high slope to the south and the deep ravine to the north kept them on a narrow road; a trap. Bob and Henry fired into the mass of men from that direction, while Mike threw sticks of dynamite into their midst. Flares continued to burst above.

Many of the riders turned back and spurred their mounts along the road to the west. There, they found another tree and more brush blocked that escape route, too. Frank and Stan Killeen were there and poured rifle fire into the group of raiders. Flares continued to burst above. Frank stopped firing his Spencer repeating rifle and threw sticks of dynamite into the midst of the riders.

Meanwhile, Mike, Bob and Henry continued to fire from the east into the confused, leaderless group of men.

Finally, many of the surviving few, spurred their horses into the darkness of the deep ravine and disappeared from sight. Mike's men stopped firing. The torches on the ground went out and the killing ground was lit by the flickering fire of the burning school house.

Mike and his men walked slowly toward the burning building. In the open area, they examined the bodies looking for men who were still alive. All but one of the fallen were Negroes.

"I got a live one here, Mike," Bob shouted. "I'll search him for weapons and tie him up."

"Another wounded man over here, Mike," Killeen said.

"Tie his hands behind him after you search him, Stan."

And, so it went for over half an hour.

"There must be fifteen or so men on the ground, Mike."

"How many alive?" he asked.

"Probably half a dozen."

"The horses aren't going anyplace with both ends of the road blocked," Mike said. "So, leave them be and let's get to talking with these wounded fellows. Take one at a time into the remains of the school house. They'll be more talkative alone, I'm thinking.

"Killeen, you n' Frank are in charge of the questioning. The rest of us will wait out here with the rest of the wounded. Got your knife, Stan?"

"Never leave home without it; good and sharp, too."

After seven men were taken into the school house and questioned, one at a time, Killeen and Frank came out.

"All of the men we questioned said the same thing," Frank reported.

"Major Murphy went off to Macon with a few men to kidnap our wives."

"And, all a' them know about Craig being kidnapped. But they don't know where he is being held captive. They all think he is alive some wears." Stan added.

"Damn it to hell," Mike spat. "The hotel people couldn't wait to tell Greenhoe our wives went to Macon. I should have known that would happen."

"Nothing we can do about it now, Mike," Bob Stephan reminded him. "What do we do with these wounded men here?"

"Tie 'em on horses," Mike ordered. "We'll take them back into town and turn 'em over to the Federal Marshal in Atlanta. We'll let him decide what to do with them. Bring the poor fella they hung, too."

"And our wives," Frank asked. "What about them?"

"We'll leave with our mounts on the first train tomorrow," Mike decided. "Tonight, we'll telegraph the sheriff in Macon when we get back to Atlanta. We'll alert him with the information we have. Hopefully, the girls are still safe."

Lowell

Eleanor and Nurse Kathy Lippincott were reviewing the patient list for Dr. Murphy.

"Seems like any time the weather changes, this time of year," Nurse Kathy recalled, "It seems like we get all kinds a' people in here with runny noses, sore throats and coughs."

"What can we do for them?" Eleanor asked.

"The traditional treatment is for them to get plenty of sleep, drink a lot of water and keep warm. Most a' the time, all the symptoms ago away in a week or so. Actually, I'm not sure we do much of anything."

Eleanor added, "Our nanny, Helen, has us sit by a steaming pot of water with a towel over our head and inhale the steam. My grandmother Hecht puts a poultice of some kind on our chest. It stinks to high heaven and is hot, too. But it seems to clear up the stuffiness and our cough."

"She's the healer you visit, isn't she?" Nurse Kathy remembered. "Do you have any of that stuff around the house?"

"I think Helen does," Eleanor thought. "Want me to bring some of it in tomorrow?"

"It sure can't hurt. I don't think we can do much good for our patience the way it is at present."

"I'll do that, then,"

"By the way," Nurse Kathy added. "Tomorrow at the Saturday clinic, a student from the University of Michigan medical school will be working with us. She is requited to spend so many hours working in a hospital or a clinic. So, she volunteered to work with us one Saturday a month.

"I'm gonna to be pretty busy getting the patients organized for the doctors. So, you'll have to show her where everything is. All right?"

"Sure," Eleanor said. "Be happy to."

*   *   *

There was quite a line-up of people on Saturday morning, waiting for the medical clinic to open.

Eleanor unlocked the door and let them into the office. Nurse Kathy took their name and gave each a number.

"Please fill out the form I've just given you," she directed. "My nurse's aides, Eleanor or Ms. Seldon, will help you. Keep the card I gave you. It has a number on it. Write that number at the top of the form I gave you. After you turn in your completed form, I will call your number when it is your turn to see the doctor. For now, please take a seat in the waiting room to your right."

"Miss Sheldon," Nurse Kathy said. "Will you join Eleanor and help the patients fill out the form I gave them. Some can't read or see very well I expect."

Miss. Seldon asked Eleanor. "Do you always have a big crowd like this on Saturday?"

"Ever since the weather became so cold, we have," Eleanor told her. "It's a shame, though. There's not much we can do for sniffles and sore throats."

"At least, I haven't come across anyone with a life-threatening problem, yet." Miss Seldon said.

"That's a blessing," Eleanor responded.

"Since we'll be working together, Eleanor," Ms. Seldon said. "Call me Mary."

"All right," Eleanor responded.

The two women worked with the patients for over an hour. The line dwindled some, but was pretty steady. Nurse Kathy kept calling numbers and sending Eleanor or Ms. Seldon to take patients into one of the small examining rooms to see one of the doctors on duty that morning.

"Nurse Kathy told me you want to become a doctor. Is that right?"

"Yes, I do."

"You might be interested, then in the new program at the University of Michigan. I'm in my second year there. If all goes well, I'll become doctor in two more years."

"My grandfather, Dr. Murphy, told me of that program," Eleanor responded. "Are you well treated there?"

"Not all of the professors like it that women are in their classes or even the school of medicine for that matter. But we all do so well in our studies, they can't ignore us. We outscore the male students by far.

"The Saturdays I'm spending here in the Grand Rapids Medical Clinic is just an example. I don't have to do these, and few of the males in my class do it. But I want to be the best, so I spend time here to better understand the routine ills every day patients complain about."

Eleanor explained, "I've been working here on Saturdays for the last month. I also work three afternoons a week in my grandfather's medical office. I certainly know that I've learned a lot."

"Nurse Kathy told me your grandmother who lives in Lowell is a healer. Is that right?"

"Yes, she is," Eleanor said. "I've spent two weekends at her home this fall. She took me on a birthing visit once. That was really exciting."

"'ll bet it was," Mary gushed. "You know, I've never assisted a birthing. I don't think any of my classmates have either. We've just read about it or heard lectures about it. I envy you having had that experience."

"There goes Nurse Kathy calling another number," Eleanor said. "I think it's my turn to take the patient back to the doctor."

And, so it went till well after the noon closing time. By the time Eleanor and her new companion, Mary cleaned up the office, it was near one in the afternoon.

Mary was housed at the Murphy home for the weekend. So, she walked there with Eleanor after closing the clinic.

"I hadn't realized just how tiring our work was this morning," Mary told Eleanor. "I'm ready for a nap."

"I am too," Eleanor said.

"So, you and your brother are staying with Dr. Murphy while your parents are away?"

"Yes," Eleanor explained. "My father is a United states Marshal. He is in Georgia somewhere helping to rescue a friend of his captured from some terror group or another. My brother Charles and I are staying with our mother's parents while our parents are away."

"Wow!" Mary exclaimed. "One grandparent a healer and another a doctor. That's quite a heritage to live up to."

"I suppose so," Eleanor agreed. "That probably has a lot to do with my determination to become a doctor myself."

At the supper table that evening the Murphy's got acquainted with their weekend guest.

"Where were yu raised Miss Seldon?" Mrs. Murphy asked.

"I was born and raised in Detroit, Mrs. Murphy."

"How large is your family there?"

"I am the youngest of four children, ma'am. And, I'm the first to attend college."

"Was there anything special that got you interested in the medical field?" Dr. Murphy asked.

"I suppose my secondary school biology teacher noticed that I had a talent for the sciences. But I think the greatest influence was my older brother's experience in the war. He was badly wounded at Gettysburg. I was so shocked by the medical treatment he received, I wanted to do something better."

"What in particular shocked you about his medical treatment?"

"For example," Mary Seldon responded. "He was refused water but was offered all the whiskey he wanted. My secondary school science teacher told his class that this practice is insane. Water is essential to contain fevers and for proper recovery of the injured."

"Would you give water to a man with a belly wound, Miss Seldon?" Dr. Murphy asked.

"No sir," she responded quickly. "That is probably the only exception to the general rule that water is good for the injured. And, another thing; many of the wounded returned home addicted to pain killers like laudanum and even heroin. This stuff was given to the wounded without regard to the potential problem of addiction. In fact, you can buy laudanum over the counter of any store selling medical supplies and treatments."

Eleanor joined this conversation at this point. "My father told me about a doctor who served the Union. He established a treatment center in New York some place for people addicted to drugs like the ones you mentioned. He told me that it was a problem many soldiers suffered from."

"I agree that doctors must be careful in the use of such pain killers," Dr. Murphy said, "But believe me, as these drugs are invaluable to a surgeon. We have to be careful to monitor their use outside of the operating rooms so that our patients do not become addicted. "

"I intend to be one of those doctors," Mary Seldon said.

"Good for you, young lady," Mrs. Murphy added.

"Miss Seldon," Dr. Murphy asked. "Would you mind talking with my granddaughter about your experiences in medical school?"

"Certainly Dr. Murphy," She responded. "I would be most willing to do so. In fact, when you have some time off from school this spring, Eleanor, possibly you could come visit me at the university. Then you could talk to some of my fellow students and even sit in on a few classes."

"Oh! that would be exciting," Eleanor exclaimed. "I'd love to."

Dr. Murphy endorsed that idea, too. "Possibly we could escort you there, Eleanor. I'd like to talk with the President of the university, too. He and I might explore the type of internship you are doing in my clinic, Miss Seldon. My colleagues and I can use the type of help you gave in our clinic today and I believe such work would be good for you, too."

"His name is James Burrell Angel, doctor," Mary Seldon informed Dr. Murphy.

She continued, "Such an opportunity would be welcomed by at least the medical students I know," But I must tell you, if you had not offered me what amounts to board and room this weekend, I could not have afforded to take advantage of the opportunity you gave me. In fact, Doctor, the rail ticket cost put a severe dent in my budget. I don't know how often I can afford to spend a weekend like this at your clinic, however helpful it is to my future career in medicine."

"That's certainly good to know, Miss Seldon," Dr. Murphy responded. "Let me talk this over with my colleagues. I am sure the board and room arrangement we have offered you could be expanded to others. And, I assure you, we will reimburse you for your travel cost."

"Thank you, Dr. Murphy," Mary Seldon said. "That is much appreciated. I assure you. My fellow students have to be just as tight with their money and I am."

*　　*　　*

Later that evening, Eleanor and Charles were talking.

"So, you are really serious about this medical school business, aren't you, Eleanor." Charles said.

"That's right, Charles," She responded. "If I can get into medical school at the University of Michigan next year, I'm going."

"Well, you can take it to the bank, that I'm not signing up for any more school after I'm done at Central Secondary School. It's time for me to stretch my legs and spread my wings."

"If that's the case," Eleanor suggested. "Why don't you write the man who is managing Grandfather Pope's land down in South Carolina. Maybe he would welcome you there."

"That's a great idea, Eleanor," Charles said. "Will you help me write it?"

"Sure," she said. "I'll get some paper. We can do it tonight."

After they had gotten all the writing materials around, they began.

"What is the man's name, Charles?"

"I don't remember." He said.

"But mother would know, for sure. but she's in Georgia," Eleanor said. "I'll bet my Uncle Joe at the Old Kent Bank would know. He handles all our mother's South Carolina business. We can go to his bank Tuesday after school. We can't go Monday, we have to work, remember?"

"Ya, I remember," Charles said. "Can't we write the letter without knowing his name."

"Sure," Eleanor assured her brother. "

"How do we start then?" Charles asked.

"Dear Mr. Something. That's how."

"What's next, though?"

"I think you should introduce yourself," Eleanor suggested. "After all, you've been gone from there for a bunch of years. He doesn't know anything about you."

"Right. How about, I am Charles Pope Drieborg. My father was Charles Pope who died during the Civil War. Then, my mother married Michael Drieborg. My grandfather was Colonel Pope. I am graduating from secondary school next spring and would like to visit you in South Carolina. I am told that you are managing the lands left me by my grandfather. Would it be possible for me to spend some time with you next summer and become better acquainted with that operation? Right now, I am working part time at my Uncle George's restaurant as a bus-boy."

"Slow down, Charles. I can't keep up," Eleanor complained. "Say that last part again."

"The part about the work I'm doing now?"

"Yes."

Charles repeated what he had said and then waited for Eleanor to catch-up.

"I think I'll ask my manager at the restaurant to write a letter for me about how I'm doing. I can send that to this fellow, too."

"Great idea, Charles," Eleanor said. "Think he'd do it?"

"Only one way to find out. I'll ask." Charles said.

"By the way, Charles," Eleanor said. "Are you planning to go to the Thanksgiving dance at school?"

"I haven't thought about it much," he responded. "Are you?"

"A bunch of us girls are going," Eleanor told him. "After, we plan to have a sleep-over at one of the houses. It should be fun."

"So, you're not going with a boy to the dance?"

"I don't think so," Eleanor told him. "No one I know really wants to be stuck with one guy all evening. We'd much prefer to dance with different guys and have our own fun as a group."

"You did that last school year for the Spring dance, too."

"Yup," Eleanor remembered too. "My group had a great time. So, we decided we'd do it again."

"Your group has all the good-lookers in it, too" Charles observed. "Not much left to pick from either."

"What about Sharon Glass," Eleanor asked. "I know she'd break a leg to go out with you."

"Yah! But she's gone out with a whole bunch of guys," Charles told his sister. "The word among the other guys is that she's easy."

"I've heard that, too," Eleanor agreed. "She's probably just looking for a husband."

"Well, believe you me," Charles was quick to point out. "I'm not looking for a wife and family. Not for a long while, anyway.

"I think I'll pass on Sharon and go to the dance with a bunch of guys. It's sure safer."

"Good idea, Charles," Eleanor concluded. "I think I'm going to bed. It's been a long day and grandmother said we're going to early church tomorrow."

"I wish just once, that grandmother would let us sleep in one day a week. We could go to a later Mass, ya know."

"Yes, I know, Charles," Eleanor said. "But she didn't."

With that, Eleanor went upstairs to her room. Charles went to his own room.

Atlanta

Mike and his team led their captives to the sheriff's office in Atlanta. He told the deputy on duty what had happened.

"They hung this dead Negro, ya' say?" a deputy sheriff asked. "An' you're a Federal Marshal ya' say?"

"That's right deputy," Mike said. "Tell your sheriff he can check us out with Mr. Kellogg who is deputy to the military governor here in Atlanta.

"These wounded men were part of the Union League force that burned a Freedman's school and hung this Negro last night. Their white leader is dead. He's lying back there by the burned-out school, along with a dozen or so of his troopers."

"Don't know what to tell you, mister," the deputy told Mike. "I gotta say, though. We don't often get something like this. Ya know. A Federal Marshal shows up with a dead Negro and six or seven wounded coloreds, too. It's pretty unusual. The sheriffs at a meeting across town this morning. An' I'm the only one on duty right now.

"Be quite honest," the deputy continued. "I don't know what to do about this situation with him gone and these fellas wounded an' all. Specially since, I got no way ta' take care a' them. So, I don't think I should take responsibility fer 'im. Ya see?"

"Tell ya what deputy," Mike said. "Why don't I go into your office and write a statement of what happened out there. While I'm doing that, you fetch a doctor to come by and look after these Negros. We can't just let them go and they need treatment. What do ya say? My men will watch the prisoners while you're getting a doctor. That sound good to you."

"I spose."

Mike's men led the wounded Union League troopers into cells at the jail to await the doctor. Then, he sat at one of the desks and wrote a statement about what happened at the Freedman's school the previous evening. By the time he had finished, the deputy had returned with a doctor.

"You sure you don't want to wait for the sheriff to return, Marshal?" the deputy asked.

"We've been up all night at the freedman's school, deputy. We are exhausted. I'll be available over at our hotel until tomorrow morning.

"Then, my men and I intend to board the train to Macon. After that, your sheriff can find me at the sheriff's office in Macon, if he needs to. As I told you, deputy, our wives are in danger down there. The men we captured last night told us our women are targets for other Union League people. We need to see to their safety as soon as possible. "

"I get ya, Marshal. An' I'll tell the sheriff when he returns." The deputy promised.

*   *   *

Mike was awakened by a pounding on his hotel room door.

"All right, all right, I'm coming," He sort a' shouted while tying his robe closed.

He opened the door to find an agitated sheriff standing there.

"I take it you're federal Marshal Drieborg?"

"Yes, I am," Mike responded. "What can I do for you?"

"You can let me in and explain this report my deputy gave me. He says you wrote it."

"Come on in then. I assume you're Sheriff Alexander." Mike said. He shut the door and turned to his visitor and held out his right hand.

"I'm Michael Drieborg a federal marshal working with the Military Governor's office. Pleased to meet you. I think that's the report I gave your deputy to give to you. What do you need to know, sheriff?"

"I can read, don't ya know," the sheriff said somewhat irritably. "So's, I don't need you to translate for me. But what in hell were you and your people doing out there last night?"

"We received word that an element of the Union League was going to burn that school and blame it on the local Klan. So, we went there to greet them. What we didn't anticipate was that they dragged along a Negro to hang, too. Before we could stop that, they hung the poor fellow.

"As you read in the report, we killed a few of the members of that bunch and dropped off a few wounded ones at your place."

"What the hell am I supposed to do with them, pray tell?"

"They committed a crime," Mike reminded the sheriff. "Arrest them."

"Says, you?"

"That's right sheriff," Mike said. "Bring them before a Judge and my men and I will testify against them. We saw them hang that Negro fellow and set fire to the school. What more do you need?"

"All right," the sheriff said calmly. "You be at the courthouse tomorrow morning at eight sharps. I'll have the District Judge there to hear your eyewitness testimony. That'll do it for those birds you dropped off at my door. Then you can run off to Macon or where ever the hell you want. Agreed?"

"Yes, sheriff, agreed," Mike hastily said. "My men and I will be there at eight sharp tomorrow morning."

As Sheriff Alexander turned and walked out the door, he muttered,

"You Yankees will be the death of me yet."

Over supper that evening, Mike told his men about Sheriff Alexander's visit. He also told them of the telegram he received from the sheriff at Macon.

"So, the ladies are safe and sound, eh?" Bob Stephan responded.

"It appears that while the ladies were shipping yesterday morning, four men attacked them," Mike told them. "Linda Gostkowski killed one and wounded another. Bose, your wife captured another and had a knife at his throat when the sheriff stopped her from cutting his jugular vein or some other part of his body.

"What a' gal." Bose exclaimed. "Tis a shame he stopped her."

"You haven't heard the best part, Bose."

"Well, hells bells man," Bost taunted Mike. "Get on with it will ya?"

"It seems that Ethie objected to the sheriff's interference. So, he allowed her a few minutes alone with this guy to have a conversation. During their time alone, she convinced the man that unless he answered her questions, he would lose his ears. She probably got that idea from you.

"Anyway," Mike continued. "Rather than lose his ears, he told her that Major Murphy had led the attack on them and was camped just south of town a mile or two. He also told her that Haynes is alive. With some more persuasion, he also told her that Murphy led the kidnapping and knew where Haynes is being held."

"Ain't that woman a' mine something?"

Frank asked. "Are all the women safe, Mike?"

"Yes, Frank, they are."

"Thank the Lord."

"The sheriff was a little miffed that the ladies didn't tell him they were coming into town. The only reason he was at the scene was because he heard the firing. That's when he and his deputies came running.

"After our court appearance tomorrow morning, we'll get take the train to Macon along with our horses and weapons, just in case.

Kellogg is going to join us for a drink after supper. We can fill him in on everything, then."

"I wish we could get to Macon sooner, Mike," Frank said. "The ladies are probably shaken by their experience today."

"Frank," Mike said. "I don't think so. After the attack, the killing and everything else they experienced, the gals continued shopping and had lunch downtown. That doesn't sound to me like they were too shaken."

The men couldn't help but laugh at that news. Even Frank had to laugh.

"I guess not, Mike." he said.

Macon

"You're sure the sheriff sent a telegram to Mike explaining what happened today?" Mary Jacqueline asked Ethie Faute.

"Yep, he did," Ethie assured her. "In fact, he said it was the longest telegram he had ever sent. I want ta tell ya, gals, it was long. I helped him write it down and was there when it was sent by the telegraph guy. It told everything that happened."

"They know we're safe?"

"They know that and everything else ta boot." Ethie assured her friends.

"Did he get an answer?"

"As a matter a' fact, he did," Ethie revealed. "The boys will be here on tomorrow's afternoon train."

"Where you gonna put us all, Peg?" Mary Alice Stephan asked.

"Not a problem sweetie," Peg responded.

"Before the war, we build this place for two boys and their two sisters. So, we have four bedrooms in the main house. In the farm manager's house, he has another three bedrooms. We have bunks in the field hand building on top a' that. So, we have no problem taking care of visitors, Mary Alice."

"Gosh," Mary Alice said. "I was just askin."

Ethie Faute entered this conversation. "I'm think we should be celebrating our victory over the rascals who attacked us this day.

"And since this is our last ladies' night without the man hoverin' about," she continued. "Do you have any alcohol around here, Peggy?"

All the ladies clapped and cheered.

"You are a devil Ethie Fault," Peggy said amid the noise. "I think I can find some around. Do ya have anything special in mind, though?"

"I'm partial to Tennessee Bourbon, but any good whisky will do in a pinch."

"I think the rest of us gals would prefer wine," Mary Jacqueline said. "What have you around in that vein?"

"It just so happens, you're both in luck," Peg answered. "I have some very tasty port and some dry white. I also have some Southern Comfort Whiskey. That should suit both tastes, don't you think.?"

And, so the evening began with a glass of wine or a slug of whiskey before supper was served.

The drinks continued during the pork roast meal. Following their very active and harrowing day, the liquor toped it off. All the ladies were ready for an early bed time that night.

*   *   *

At the breakfast table the following morning, some of the ladies appeared a bit groggy.

"Seems like my tongue has grown hair on it. Yuk!!" Ethie confessed. "I need some strong coffee this morning."

Mary Alice complained, too. "I have a headache this morning," she said. "It's sort of like someone is pounding on a drum right behind my eyes."

Peg and Mary Jacqueline however, were bright and cheerful.

"Will you two stop being so perky?" Ethie Faut ordered. "It's downright disgusting the way you two are carrying-on. A body would think you didn't drink last night at all."

"We both drank some, Ethie," Peg informed her complaining guest. "But we evidently didn't drink too much. I feel great this morning; How about you Mary Jacqueline?"

"I'm raring ta' go, Peg. Got something in mind?"

"I thought we'd take a tour of our place on horseback," she suggested. "It's a beautiful brisk day. We shouldn't let it go to waste. How about it ladies?"

"I'm going back ta bed," Ethie said.

"Me too," Mary Alice joined. In."

"How about you Linda?"

"Mike will skin me alive if I let you two go off on your own. Especially after the shoot-out we had yesterday," she told her host. "Besides, after last night, I need some fresh air to clear my head."

Peg wasn't done making fun at Ethie and Mary Alice's expense.

"Before we go, though," she said. "I need some more of these fried eggs with biscuits and sausage gravy. How about you, ladies?"

"Oh! ugg," Ethie faked a wretch. "You are truly a devil to talk right in front of me about greasy food like that, Peg, I'm suffering here an' you're making me sick to my stomach just talking about that stuff. I'm off to my room before you make me throw-up. You coming Mary Alice?"

"I'm right behind you, Ethie."

Peg and Mary Jacqueline laughed and dug into their breakfast. Linda just gulped more black coffee.

Breakfast over, the three ladies began their tour of the farm, on horseback.

"This farm is bigger than I imagined, Peg." Mary Jacqueline said.

"We started out with only one section twenty-five years ago," Peg told her companions.

"If I recall correctly, that would be 640 acres?" Linda asked.

"That's correct, Linda," Peg said. "But we've purchas4ed three more sections; two since the war. Because we have available cash, we've been able to buy land from landowners who just couldn't pay the high land taxes our Reconstruction government levied. They found themselves land poor."

"Why aren't you, land poor?" Mary Jacqueline asked.

"So, we grown all the grain we need for our herd. And we grow enough cotton and harvest enough wool from our sheep herds to provide us good cash flow as well. Remember, we have to pay those high land taxes, too."

"Sounds like you have a pretty good balance, Peg," Linda judged.

"I think we do, Linda," Peg continued. "But meat is still our best cash crop; beef, pork and lamb. People love our meats.

"Remember, ladies," Peg told them. "We have virtually no goods manufactured in the South. So, besides needing cash to pay our heavy taxes, we need cash buy manufactured goods from either Europe or the North."

*   *   *

The ladies were wiping down their horses in the barn when their husbands walked in.

Hugs were shared all around.

"It's about time you gals showed up," Frank scolded. "We've been worried about you."

"Just out for a tour of our place, dear," Peg told her husband. "You needn't worry."

"From what the sheriff told us, I guess you gals can take care of yourselves," Mike judged giving his wife another squeezed. "We worried, just the same."

"We worried about you, too." Mary Jacqueline responded.

"Let's get some coffee," Frank suggested. "We can both share our adventures."

Once everyone was inside and had their coffee, Linda told the men what happened in town during their shipping trip.

"The sheriff confirmed all of that Linda," Mike told her. "Seems that you did a good job protecting the ladies."

"Thank you," Linda said. "You can thank Ethie for getting one of the attackers to spill the beans about their plan and the location of their camp."

"I'll do just that," Mike said. "In fact, Stan and Bose are with the sheriff and his deputies rounding up Murphy and the last member of his team, right now."

Ethie and Mary Alice Stephan walked into the dining room.

"Whose making all that noise down here," Ethie complained. "A body can't even sleep around here with such a racket."

Bob hugged his wife and offered her a seat.

"Where's my ol' man, Mike?" she asked.

"He's off with the sheriff rounding up the last of your attackers," Mike told her. "He had some questioning in mind. He said something about cutting off an ear or two."

Everyone laughed at that.

"That's pretty effective in getting a body to talk, I hear." Ethie revealed.

"Seems like you Fauts have perfected that method of conversation." Frank chuckled.

"I guess we have, Frank," Ethie admitted. "When you boys figure Bose an' Stan will be getting back?"

'I have no idea," Mike told her. "Could be tomorrow by the time they get back with their prisoners to Macon. They'll be here when they get done with their work with the sheriff, I expect."

*   *   *

It was the next afternoon before the two men arrived at the Stanitzek farm.

Bose gave his wife a big hug. "How are ya' ol' girl?" He asked.

I'm fine, no thanks ta' you," she responded. "You get Murphy and his side-kick tucked away in the Macon jail?"

"Ya we did," Bose told her. "I'll tell everyone about it soon's as I get me a drink a' something stronger than the water I've been drinkin. What a' you sippin there Ethie?"

"All Peggy had on hand was this Kentucky Bourbon," she told her husband. "Not nearly as good as our moonshine. But it'll do."

"Any left for a thirsty mountain man, Peg?"

"I'll see if your wife has left any for ya,"

"When you gonna tell us what happened with the sheriff?" Bob Stephan asked.

"Don't get your drawers in a knot, Bobby," Bose snapped. "I'm not the only one who was there. Let Stan tell ya."

"What happened, Stan?" Frank asked.

"Your sheriff is sure a no-nonsense guy, Frank," Stan began. "He seems ta know right were Murphy's camp would be. An we went directly there. Took 'em by surprise, no trouble.

"Sheriff wasted no time beating on Murphy and his side-kick until they gave up the information he wanted. Rather than get hung

211

right on the spot, Murphy said that his boss, Greenhoe ordered the attack on the ladies. He also said that they had intended to kidnap a couple of the gal. But the sheriff told us Linda here foiled their plan."

"I wasn't going to let Mike blame me again for letting something bad happen," Linda said.

"Did either man say anything useful about Haynes?" Mike asked.

"Matter a' fact, Murphy's side-kick did," Bose said. "He tol' us that Haynes is alive and being kept in a barn up near Atlanta."

"Where near Atlanta?" Frank asked.

"Neither Bose nor I know what the guy was talking about," Stan said. "But the sheriff will let Mike take one a' these two there to point it out for us."

"What's he gonna' do with the other prisoner?" Gerry Gostkowski asked.

"Being a good ol 'southern boy," Bose said smiling. "I think he intends to see these northern boys sentenced to a Georgia chain-gang fer a spell."

Stan shared a thought. "I don't think the sheriff likes Murphy much, him being the head of the Union League in this area."

"I actually think he'd like to string Murphy up," Stan judged.

"Naw," Bose said. "I suspect the sheriff figures it'd be more painful fer Murphy to spend time working on a chain gang and having ta live with some Negro prisoners, too."

Bob Stephan agreed, "I think the sheriff has a fine idea."

"Such a sentence couldn't happen to a more deserving fellow," Frank said.

"Hanging's too easy for Murphy, if'n ya ask me," Ethie said.

"Remember, everyone," Mike interrupted. "We need those two guys to help us find Craig back in Atlanta and to testify against Greenhoe at his trial for kidnapping."

"I'd plumb forgotten about that scum-bag," Mary Alice Stephan said.

"The Macon sheriff intends to get the sheriff up in Atlanta to arrest Greenhoe and jail the man to await a trial down here in Macon," Stan told everyone.

"Kidnapping Haynes and ordering the kidnapping of our wives should be enough to get Greenhoe some jail time," Bob Stephan told everyone. "Even under Yankee laws."

Everyone laughed at that.

*   *   *

"Miss Peggy," a serving girl announced. "Supper is served."

Everyone got up and went into the dining room to take a seat at the long dinner table.

"Will you look at that spread," Stan said. "Meat an' potatoes. That's a meal to melt a man's heart, fer sure."

Frank added. "This is a far cry from those oysters Mike wanted us to eat back in Washington City."

"Ya got that right," Bose said."

"I remember going back to the boarding house and eating left-over stew," Stan reminded everyone. "Anything was better than those slimy oysters."

Peg told her guests, "We have meatloaf made with fresh beef and pork loin. So, suit yourselves. There's potatoes an' gravy with applesauce and of course catchup. Boiled carrots and onions are served, too. Does anyone want coffee with their meal or will water do?"

The room became quiet as the plates were passed and food eaten.

"I haven't had this kind of cooking since Ethie and I left Cade's Cove, Peggy," Bose said.

"I don't think I've ever seen such a spread, Peg; except at Christmas," Bob Stephan said.

"You best not go away from my table hungry, Robert," Peg warned him.

"Don't you worry about that," he responded. "You'll have to help me up the stairs tonight, though."

Everyone laughed at that.

"Pie, too?" Mary Jacqueline exclaimed.

"My goodness, Peg," Mary Alice added. "I don't know where I'll put it all."

"We still have some dried peaches from the spring harvest," Peg told everyone. "I thought it might be a nice change with all the apple pie being baked up North right now."

Of course, everyone felt obliged to have a piece. Coffee was served as well. Mike had a glass of chilled mile with his pie.

"Thank you for the milk, Peg," Mike said. "I don't mean to be a bother, but I can't have pie without my milk."

"That's not a problem, Michael," Peg told him. "You might notice that Frank is having milk, too."

"Oh, my stars, Peg," Mary Alice Stephan exclaimed. "I think I'm going to faint this is so good."

"Thank you, Mary Alice," Peg said. "You get many peaches up your way Linda?"

"Peaches are grown a bit north of Detroit, actually" Linda Gostkowski told her. "The season is pretty short, though. So, this desert is a real treat for us. Right, Gerry."

"Absolutely. It is." He said between bites of pie.

More coffee was poured. This time, Mike had some, too.

It wasn't long before the Stanitzek's dinner guests drifted away from the table. Ethie joined her husband on the porch to have a smoke. Others went for a stroll while one couple went right up the stairs to heir room.

Mike and Mary Jacqueline were the two who went to their room, arm in arm.

As they horridly undressed, Mike told his wife,

"A week without you has been seven days too many,"

"Just you get in this bed with me, right now." Mary Jacqueline ordered.

It was some time before they talked again.

Atlanta

Mike and his team met with Mr. Kellogg. This time, Craig Haynes was with them.

"Safe and sound, eh Craig?" asked Kellogg

"Yes sir," he responded. "But I must admit that I was sure happy to see Mike and the boys walk into that shed where I was kept."

"Not worse for wear?" he asked.

"Aside for nearly starved for food and conversation, I'm fine, sir." Craig Haynes answered.

"I have one regret, though," He added.

"What's that?" Kellogg asked.

"I wish that I had the opportunity to have a few minutes alone with Murphy,"

"We can't have everything we want in this life, ya know," Stan told him.

"At least I will be along to arrest Greenhoe later today. That's something, anyway," Craig admitted.

"Well, tell me everything that's happened since we last met, Michael," Kellogg asked. "And how are the ladies?"

"They are fine, Congressman," Mike told him. "As it turned out, they were quite up to taking care of themselves when push came to shove. Down in Macon, Linda Gostkowski stopped a kidnapping, killed one Union League attacker, captured another and ran off Murphy and a fourth fellow. She did quite a job. I'm glad we had her assigned to protect the ladies."

"But what did you and your team do after you left here ten days ago?"

"Oh, yes," Mike remembered that he had kept it from Kellogg when they last met.

So, he told Kellogg about the ambush of the Union Leaguers on the Freedman's school.

"You have been a busy bunch," He judged. "Sheriff Alexander told me of the Union Leaguers you dropped off at his prison before you went to Macon. He wasn't too prepared for them, but he was pleased to have the opportunity of tweaking Greenhoe's nose by jailing some of his raiders. Locals hate them, you know."

"Before we left for Macon, he made us testify at the trial he held here," Mike added. "The judge sent the prisoners to work on a chain gang. I'll bet that will serve as a warning to the rest of that bunch of just what is in store for them if they're caught."

Bob Stephan joined the conversation. "Did my heart good to see the judge come down hard on those birds. All the stealing of white people's property they've done, they deserve the punishment he handed out."

"Gotta admit it," Stan said. "They deserved it, seems ta me."

"What's this?" Bose said in mock surprise. "A Yank who agrees with me?"

"Fairs, fair, Bose. That judge handed out a just sentence,"

"Well, let's go see if Greenhoe will get his due," Mike said.

The men said their good-byes to Bill Kellogg and left the meeting.

*   *   *

Mike and his team walked into the Freedman's Bureau offices.

"What do you mean coming in here armed like you are?" the man at the front counter asked.

Drieborg's crew carried their Spencer rifles in plain view.

Mike waved his men to go directly into Greenhoe's office. He stopped at the front desk.

"Listen to me carefully," he demanded. "After we rescued the federal deputy to the General of the Military District from your Union League thugs, we thought it best if we protected ourselves when we came to arrest the Director of the Atlanta Freedman's Bureau. Does that explain clearly enough why we came in here armed?"

Mike looked directed into the man's eyes.

"I'm waiting for an answer from you," He demanded.

"Yes, it does," The man timidly answered.

By this time Craig Haynes came back into the room. Greenhoe was in handcuffs and being dragged along by Haynes. The other men of Drieborg's group followed.

Greenhoe shouted. "This is an outrage," As he passed the front counter, he shouted at the clerk who was standing in front of Drieborg. "Don't just stand there, go get our attorney. Tell him I'm at the sheriff's office."

Bose poked Greenhoe with his rifle. "Get along with ya. No Yankee lawyer's gonna get you outta this fix, scum-bag."

"We got ya dead ta rights this time," Bob Stephan assured him.

"It's the chain-gang for you, Greenhoe," Mike added.

"You 'all be doing some real work soon enough," Bose chuckled. "No sittin behind a desk fer you anymore."

They marched the Director of the Atlanta Freedman's Bureau through the heart of downtown Atlanta to the sheriff's jail.

The following morning, the municipal judge heard the charges.

"Are there any witnesses?" he asked.

At that point Murphy and another prisoner were brought into the court.

"Who are these two men?" the judge asked the sheriff.

"This one calls himself, Major Murphy. Says he commands the Union League in these parts."

"Is that right, Yank?"

"Yes, sir,"

"What have you got to say for yourself?"

"That man," Murphy pointed at Greenhoe, "ordered me to kidnap the Deputy to the Military Governor, a man named Haynes. So, I had my men do it. I held him prisoner at the camp where my Union League was camped."

"He's lying," Greenhoe shouted. "I never ordered him to do that."

"Quiet in my court," The judged ordered "You 'all will get your chance to talk."

The sheriff brought the other man up in front of the Judge.

"What you got to say?" The Judge asked.

"I was in the room when Greenhoe ordered my boss, Major Murphy, to kidnap that fellow, Deputy Haynes, your honor."

"He's lying, too!" Greenhow shouted.

The judge banged his gavel. "Didn't I tell you to keep quiet?"

While this was going on, Greenhoe's lawyer came into the courtroom.

The judge looked at him. "You this man's lawyer?"

"Yes, I am your honor," He said.

"You have any good reason I shouldn't pronounce a verdict and a sentence right now?"

The lawyer looked around the room at all the armed men.

"I heard the two witnesses," Your honor. "So, since I can't refute their testimony, I see no reason for you not to pronounce a verdict."

"What the hell!" Greenhoe shouted. "This is not a fair trial. I'm being railroaded. Wait till my friends in Washington hear of it. They won't allow you Southern traitors to get away with this."

William Kellogg had come into the courtroom. He asked the judge.

"Your honor. May I address the court?"

"And who are you, may I ask?"

"I am former Congressman William Kellogg and current Chief Deputy to the Governor of the Military District headquartered here in Atlanta."

"If you have something germane to this case, go ahead and say it, Deputy Kellogg."

"This man, Greenhoe has been a blight on the honor of the United States government both here in Atlanta and in the Indian Territories before that. His corrupt administrations in both these areas have been documented beyond any doubt. His direction of the Union League's rapacious actions against the citizens of this state both white and black are also well know. I hope this court finds him guilty of the charges and imposes the harshest of sentences possible.

"Thank you, your honor," Kellogg concluded.

"Thank you, Mr. Kellogg. Your comments are appreciated." The judge banged his gavel and said,

"Mr. Greenhow, this court finds you guilty of ordering the kidnapping of a federal officer," The judge announced. "And I sentence you to five years at hard labor in a state of Georgia facility.

"Sheriff, you are ordered to carry out the sentence immediately.

"As for the two witnesses, I order you sent to the sheriff of Macon for the execution of the prison sentence demanded by the municipal judge of that county for your crimes committed there. When that sentence is completed, you are to serve an additional year in prison for the crime you committed here of kidnapping the federal official.

"This court is adjourned."

As Greenhoe was escorted out of the court, he told the sheriff,

"You reb hicks won't hold me for long, As soon as my powerful friends in Washington hear of this, they'll get me free in no time."

"Gotta find ya first, don't ya know, Yank." The sheriff responded.

Stan asked Bose who had been listening to the exchange. "What do ya think the sheriff meant by that?"

"The way I hear it, this state has chain gangs operating all over the back-country. Lots a' that is just swamp land. Back in there it'd be hard to find somebody even if 'in ya know where you're going. They jus move their prisoners around, from camp to camp. Greenhow's Yankee friends ain't going ta find him unless the sheriff wants him found."

"Ain't that a shame." Stan chuckled.

Lowell

Eleanor and Charles had finished their supper and were helping to clear the table and wash the dishes.

Charles was clearing while Eleanor washed. They would both dry and put dishes and pans away.

"We received two letters today, Charles." Eleanor told him as they worked.

"Ok," Charles said. "I'd guess one was from our folks. Who the hell else would send both of us a letter?'

"You don't have to use swear words, Charles." Eleanor complained. "Can't we have a civil conversation?"

"Sorry," Charles offered. "I guess I hear that kind a' language all the time at work. It just slips out."

"I'd think that the mark of a true gentleman is to be able to gauge his audience and alter his vocabulary accordingly."

"What do ya mean by that?"

"What I mean is when you are at work, you hear and even use the rough language you used a minute ago. At home and in polite society, you don't. Simple as that."

"Oh, all right, Eleanor. I get your point.

"Now, will you tell me about the two letters?"

"You're right," she revealed. "One is from mother, to the both of us. The other is from a Mr. Mikell. Remember, he's the man our

Uncle Joe told us is managing the Pope land on Edisto Island in South Carolina for your estate."

"Wow!" Charles exclaimed. "He surely got back to me quickly. What did he have to say?"

"I didn't open your mail, Charles. "Eleanor told her brother. "I thought we'd read both of them later tonight."

"Good idea. Let's get these chores done and open those letters."

It wasn't long before they were in Charles's room.

"Let's open mother's letter first," Eleanor suggested. "Ok?"

"Sure," Charles told her.

So, Eleanor opened the letter from their mother.

November 10, 1874

Dear Children

I hope this letter finds you both in good health, doing well in school as well as on your jobs. Good news, your father and I are coming home. For all I know, this letter will not get to you before we do. I am so anxious to see you both and little Maxine, too. I can hardly wait to get back into our own house.

Be prepared to tell me everything. I'll want to know about how school is going. How is working at the restaurant and in Grandfather Murphy's office going? Have you two visited the Drieborgs and Hechts in Lowell? I hope so. They get so lonely for you. Especially you Eleanor. Of course, the Hechts have those two little girls now. But just the same they are your grandparents and they love you dearly.

I want to get this letter to the post office as soon as possible, so I will end now. Love you and miss you both terribly.

Love

Mother

"Hey," Charles said. "they're almost home?"

"I guess so. Just in time for Thanksgiving, too."

"That's great. We'll see all the cousins then. That'll be fun."

*   *   *

"Now, open the other one, Eleanor," Charles urged.

 "You want me to read it to you?'

"Sure," Charles said.

Eleanor opened that letter.

November 8, 1874

Dear Mr. Charles Pope Drieborg,

I was surprised to receive your recent letter. I must admit I had forgotten how old you must be about now. The last time I saw you was so long ago I only remember a pre-teenage boy holding his mother's hand as you two stood on our island's dock awaiting our boat to take you to Charleston and your life up North.

Life on Edisto Island has been very challenging since the end of the war. But we have all managed to survive and to some degree, prosper. Your family holdings have yielded a good annual return despite the challenges of weather and the market.

I say I was surprised to hear of your interest because I had just assumed you would pursue a professional career after a college education. But I consider working the land to be a noble profession, too. Let me be frank with you, though. Those of us who work the land work long days. We are subject to the whims of nature and the market-place. Neither can be predicted with accuracy. Both affect all classes and races of people; sometimes very negatively.

So, if you are interested in 'learning' this business, as you said in your letter, you must also experience the life. That is easier said than done. I urge you to talk this over with your parents.

You are certainly welcome to visit for a week or so. But I am not a tour guide. I am a farmer who is up at dawn to work in the fields and barns. In the evening, my lamp burns well after dark as I go over my accounts and such.

You are welcome to stay beyond a short visit, too. If you do however, you must take you place in the fields and in our barns. You will earn the title of farmer from the ground up, so to speak.

I look forward to hearing from you.

Sincerely,

Townshend Mikell

"What do you think, Charles?"

"I think he means I'm welcome but only if I'm willing to work like a field hand."

"Surely doesn't sound like you, Charles," Eleanor chuckled.

"What'd you mean?" he snapped. "I'm not afraid of work."

"Charles, be realistic," Eleanor urged. "Every time you get back from a visit to Grampa Dieborg's farm you complain about all the work he makes you do. You hate the dirt, getting up so early, milking cow, fetching wood and other farm chores. You complain about all of it.

"You think farm life will be so different on an Edisto Island farm?"

"But I'll own the place, Eleanor," Charles told her. "Uncle George doesn't seem to work all that hard at the restaurant he owns."

Eleanor wasn't going to allow her brother to get away with that argument.

"This Mr. Mikell owns his place too," his sister reminded him. "He just wrote you that he's up at dawn and works till after dark, every day. What does that tell you?"

"If he has to do it, I guess I could too," Charles said.

"When have you done anything like he does every day? You don't even pick up your dirty clothing."

"I do pretty well at the restaurant," Charles protested. "You don't hear any complaints about my work from Uncle George. Do you?"

"No, I must admit, I don't."

"And you don't hear me complaining about work, do you?"

"No, Charles, I don't," Eleanor admitted. "So, what's your point?"

"My point, miss negative opinion, is that if I could work in that smelly restaurant and put up with my ignorant fellow workers, every day, I can do whatever this Mr. Mikell demands of me, too."

"That's a good way to look at it, Charles," Eleanor said. "I was just reminding you of all the complaining you have done after visiting Grandpa Drieborg's farm.:

"Well, Eleanor," Charles decided. "Maybe I've gotten a better attitude since I went to work at Uncle George's restaurant."

"Glory be!" Eleanor exclaimed. "But I want to know one thing, Charles."

"What's that?"

"When are you going to start picking up your dirty clothing?"

Charles grabbed some dirty underwear from the pile on the floor and threw it at his sister.

"Will you ever stop being critical?" He shouted.

"Never!" she shouted as she ran out of his room.

More dirty clothing hit the door to her room as she slammed it shut.

Atlanta

Once the trial was completed, Kellogg invited Mike and his men to have supper with him at the hotel. His assistant, Craig Haynes was present as well.

After the meal, the men sat around the table and enjoyed a smoke and an after-dinner drink. Most drank brandy, but Bose, Bob and Frank sipped some southern bourbon.

"It's certainly good to have you back, Craig, safe and sound," Kellogg began. "As usual, Mike. You and your team have come through again." He raised his glass, "I salute you. Every one of you." He concluded.

"You're welcome, sir," Mike responded. "All of us served with Craig. So, we were grateful for the opportunity to rescue him."

Bob Stephan spoke up, "I was especially happy to have been a part of the successful effort to rid this area of the U.on League thugs. They have been a plague on the South."

"Hear, Hear!" Frank agreed.

Craig interrupted and said, "I can't tell you how grateful I am for your effort. If not for you I'd still be in that cage they had me in, or worse." He raised his glass. "Many thanks my friends."

"Hear, Hear!" They all chorused.

"I was a bit surprised though, that you Rebs joined in this effort. For all you knew, my captors could have been the thugs on your side, the KKK," Craig added. "So, why did you come?"

"Nothin personal, Craig," Bose responded first. "I jus couldn't pass up a trip to Atlanta, on the government's dime. Sides, Yank, all the crops were in. I had nothin better ta do."

"Actually, Craig," Frank Stanitzek added. "My wife Peg took sort of a' liking to ya when we met ya back there in Washington City. I couldn't turn her down, don't ya see."

"What about you, Bob?" Craig asked. "What crazy reason did you have for joining this motley crew?"

"My legal practice was slowing down, the holidays coming an all. And the deciding factor, my wife had never been to Atlanta or Macon."

Everyone laughed at that one.

"I knew there were good reasons you agreed to help Mike rescue me," Craig concluded.

"What are you gonna do now, Craig?" Henry asked.

"Having been beaten up physically, so I need some time to hear. But I think I need some time to recharge my mental batteries, too," Craig responded. "William has offered me my old job back, but it's too soon to return to that, I think."

"Frank and Peg have offered to put me up for a while at their place. Living and working at their place might be just the ticket for me right now. The climate down here is perfect and their hospitality will help me recover my strength."

Peg spoke up, "You're welcome to stay as long as you need to, Craig."

"See, I told ya'll, that Peg has taken a shine to Craig," Frank said. "It's been a long while since she assured that I was welcome to stay around."

"I'm a Catholic. I'm stuck with you, Frank," Peg said to the laughter of the others.

Ethie got serious, though. "If'n Peggy gets tired of ya at her table, Craig, you're welcome to stay with us up in Cade's Cove, anytime."

"Thanks, Ethie," Craig said. "But right now, despite your warm welcome, it's too cold up there. These bruised up bones a' mine need some sunshine and warmth."

Mike concluded the discussion. "I think we all understand, my friend. Just so you know, you are welcome at each of our homes. We all wish you a speedy recovery and a blessed future,"

"Hear, hear!" everyone shouted.

*   *   *

Mike and Mary Jacqueline were riding the train North. The weather was turning colder as they neared Nashville, Tennessee.

Ethie and Bose Faute had gotten off in Chattanooga for the last leg of their train trip to Gattlenburg, Tennessee. There, they would rent a buggy and driver for the few miles to their home up the nearby mountains to Cades Cove.

Back on the train heading for Nashville, Mary Jacqueline snuggled close to her husband. "It was nice to spend some time with our friends, wasn't it Michael."

"It was, dear," he responded giving her a squeeze. "Seems that each time we do, we also have a crisis of some sort."

"It would be nice if we got together to just visit."

"Right."

"Maybe we could arrange that for next year."

"We'll see,"

"Before we know it, Eleanor and Charles will be out of secondary school and Maxine will be in fourth grade at St. Andrew's. What a combination that will be."

"That combination will certainly keep us busy, I'm sure," Michael responded. "Eleanor will want to go to college. I wonder what Charles will do with himself?"

"Right now, Michael," Mary Jaqueline said. "I haven't a clue what he'll do. I know he does not like schoolwork. So, college is probably not attractive to him. It would seem strange if he just kept working at George and Susan's restaurant. So, I just hope he graduates."

Mike thought out loud, "It seems like yesterday that the two of them were working at the kitchen table on their arithmetic problems and reading to us each evening."

"And now, they are about to leave home already. Makes me feel old," Mary Jacqueline complained.

"Little Maxine will cure us of that feeling, dear. She's a fireball rearing to go all the time," Mike said. "We'll either run to keep up or be left in her dust." He chuckled.

"You got that right, Michael. I'm not sure whether to laugh or cry at the prospect of this coming year."

"We might just as well put a smile on our faces, dear. Our children will need our support as they each face the challenges of 1878."

"Just hug me, Michael," Mary Jacqueline asked. "It all makes me shiver just to think of it."

"Don't worry, sweetheart," Mike told her. "Whatever the year brings, we'll face it together."

"I know. But I still worry."

Grand Rapids

Bill Anderson was waiting at the town's train station with a carriage.

Mike was surprised. "What's this? An official welcome?"

"Someone had to pick you up," I'm the only one who wasn't too busy. Besides, I drew the short straw."

"That makes me feel real welcome," Mike said.

"And really missed," Mary Jacqueline added.

Anderson commented as he loaded their luggage on the buggy.

"You know the old saying, don't ya?"

"I can hardly wait to hear it, Bill," Mike said with a smile. "Which saying is that?"

"Out of sight, out of mind?"

"Oh! thanks," Mary Jacqueline responded. "I needed that."

"Yas can always count on me for a warm welcome, don't ya know." Bill reminded everyone.

"Welcome home to ya, by the way."

Everyone got into the buggy.

Bill directed the horse-drawn vehicle up to Division Street and then to Fulton Avenue. The horse pulled them up the steep hill to Prospect Street and then turned right to their home.

As he turned around the corner, a three-member band stood on the front steps of their house and struck up a welcoming tune. People crowded on the porch and cheered.

"Oh. My goodness!" Mary Jacqueline exclaimed, hugging her husband's arm.

Michael pointed, "Look at all the decorations, too."

Sure enough, a banner covered the front of the house over the porch, it read; **Welcome Home.**

Welcome Home

"I guess I was mistaken about that old saying of being out 'a mind," Bill Anderson said.

"Nothing unusual about that, Bill." Mike commented.

"Thanks, ta' you too."

Bill stopped the buggy in front of the house.

Their children ran down the steps to the buggy to greet their parents.

Everyone was hugging. Mary Jacqueline and Eleanor were crying.

Michael picked up Maxine., his eight-year old daughter.

"Oh, my goodness!" he exclaimed. "You've gotten so big, sweetheart." Over her shoulder, he saw his parents walking toward them.

When his mother reached them, she hugged them both. "I hope this is the last of your adventures, Michael." She said.

"I hope so, too Momma," He responded. returning her hug.

"Don't count on it, Rose," His father said smiling. "There's something about this boy of ours."

The Murphy's had gone into the house. So, had Susan and her husband George, Ann and her husband Joe, and Mike's brother Jake with his wife Judy. Helen and her husband Amos were in the house waiting, too. Even Mrs. Bacon was on hand to greet the two returning travelers.

"Tis good ta see ya home, safe an' sound, lad," Michael's deputy Pat Riley said shaking his hand and slapping him on the back.

"My gosh, everyone seems to be here," Mike said. "Who's guarding the prisoners at the jail?"

"We got it covered, lad," Riley assured him. "Don't ya worry none. Where's that rascal of an Irishman, Killeen? Ya didn't lose him down South, did ya now?"

"I couldn't shake him if I'd a tried," Mike chuckled. "I think he's outside still talking with Bill Anderson."

"I think I'll go an join 'em," Riley told Mike who was already turning to talk with someone else.

Mary Jacqueline was carrying Maxine and talking with her sisters-in-law. She finally reached her parents.

Without even a welcome home or a hug, her father said, "I hope this is the last of this rescuing nonsense you husband seems so fond of."

"Now, Miles," his wife Judy whispered a bit too loudly. "It's none of our business. Besides, people depend upon Michael. It's a good thing he can help. Welcome home, dear." The two women hugged.

"I suppose," Dr. Murphy responded reluctantly.

"Good to see you too, father," Mary Jacqueline said, softly reminding her father that he had not yet even greeted her. "it's good to be home safe and sound."

"It is, of course," he quickly agreed. "Welcome home, daughter." He gave her a hug, too.

"We so appreciate all you have done with the children, and all," Mary Jacqueline told her parents. "When things calm down some, we'll talk."

"Don't fret about it, dear," her mother assured her. "The children have been fine. They've been a joy to have in our home. Haven't they Miles."

"Yes, of course, they have," He quickly added. "A real joy."

*   *   *

Some two hours later, everyone had eaten and left. The workers from George and Susan's restaurant who delivered the food, were just cleaning up.

The Drieborgs were relaxing with their children in their living room. Mike was enjoying a pipe and Mary Jacqueline was sitting on the floor playing dolls with her five-year-old daughter, Maxine.

"Wasn't that nice of your sister and George to have provided supper for everyone."

"Sure was," Michael agreed. "With no food in the house and arriving very tired, I'd hate to think of having to provide that spread by ourselves."

"Right," Mary Jacqueline said. "And we have left-overs for tomorrow."

"Oh, ya," Mike asked. "I just remembered, I wanted to ask you something. Is Helen coming tomorrow morning?"

"She said she intended to resume her routine."

"Do you really need her?" Mike asked.

"I don't know, Michael," Mary Jacqueline responded. "I'll have to think about that."

"Seems to me she's more of a friend than an employee, anyway," Mike observed.

"That's just it, Michael It's not that she does anything I can't do, anymore. But she's been a friend to me since before Charles was born. I can't imagine beginning my day without her."

"That's a tough one, for sure," Michael told his wife. "Whatever you and Helen decide is fine with me. But I'll sure miss her grits and hot coffee in the morning. Especially with it getting so cold in Michigan."

"Me, too," Charles joined in. "I'd miss the smell of her bread baking in the morning, too."

"Who would walk Maxine to St. Andrews in the morning if Helen wasn't here," Eleanor asked.

"Well, what about me, Eleanor?" her mother reminded her.

"No offense, mother," Eleanor responded. "I was only reminding everyone that Helen has done that forever with Charles and me. Now she does it for Maxine. I think it has become sort of a tradition. I'm sure the nuns just expect to see Helen in the morning."

Her father commented. "Things change, dear. That's something that might change, too."

"Just will seem strange if she's not around every day, that's all," Charles concluded.

"When are we gonna talk about our stuff?" Eleanor asked. She had a slight edge to her voice.

"Like what, dear?" her mother inquired.

"I thought we were going to talk about what we have been doing while you were gone."

"We want to do that, for sure," Mike told his daughter. "But I think we need to catch our breath first; at least tonight"

"How about right after supper tomorrow?" Mary Jacqueline suggested. "We'll stay right at the supper table and go over everything. I'm anxious to hear everything right now. But your father's right, we are exhausted. At least I am."

"Your mother's right, Eleanor," her father said. "We've been traveling since early this morning. Right now, it will be all I can do to take our bags upstairs to our room. Charles, will you help me?" he asked standing up and walking toward the stairway closet where their luggage had been placed.

"Sure, Mike."

Mary Jacqueline took this opportunity to involve Eleanor in getting Maxine ready for bed.

"Will you help me get Maxine's bath ready?"

"Sure, Mother," She agreed. "I'll put some water on to warm while you get your cloths unpacked."

"Thank you much, dear. My bed clothing and my personal items are in the carpet-bag. I think I'll leave the unpacking of everything else for after you leave for school in the morning. I'm just too tired to tackle that tonight."

"That sounds good," Eleanor said. "You get Maxine ready and I'll bring the water upstairs when it gets warm."

"Come-on Max," her mother challenged. "I'll race you to the top of the stairs."

"I'll beat," Maxine shouted. And, off she ran ahead of her mother. She did win the race.

During the sponge bath both mother and daughter had gotten pretty wet, too.

"You little dickens," Mary Jacqueline shouted. "You splashed me."

"I didn't warn you, mother," Eleanor said. "Maxine has gotten pretty frisky since you left."

"Well, I never!" Mary Jacqueline said. Then, she wrapped her youngest with a large bath towel and began to tickled her.

"Oh, stop," Maxine shouted.

"That's what you get for splashing me," Her mother told her.

Eleanor and her mother got Maxine into her bed cloths.

"I've missed this routine," Mary Jacqueline told her daughters.

After they had tucked Maxine in, Mary Jacqueline joined Eleanor in her room.

"I see you've kept this room nice and neat," She told her daughter.

"Thank you for noticing, mother. But don't be shocked when you go into Charles's room, though. It is a mess."

"I suppose."

"How is school going?"

"Fine, mother." Eleanor said. "I expect to be tops in my class this semester."

"That's great," She told Eleanor. "How is Charles doing?"

"He gets by. You know Charles. He doesn't do any more than he absolutely has to. So, I think he'll graduate next June."

"I expect you have continued to help him with his studies. I thank you for that."

"I haven't done much of that lately," Eleanor revealed. "Since you left, he's pretty much wanted to do all the homework on his own. I think he could get better grades if he thought it was important. But he doesn't. As I said, he does enough to get by."

"And, your work?" Mary Jacqueline asked. "You enjoying that?"

"That is the high point of my day," Eleanor gushed. "I can't wait to get to grandfather Murphy's office after school. My work there is so interesting. I'm surer than ever that's what I want to do with the rest of my life."

"I'm not surprised, dear," Mary Jacqueline told her daughter. "You grandmother Hecht is quite a healer. So, I think you come by your interest in medicine naturally. Have you spent much time with the Hechts while your father and I have been away?"

"Oh, yes," Eleanor responded excitedly. "Every time I got a Saturday off from the clinic I went to their home. One time, grandma took me with her to help with a birthing. It was so exciting. Even the medical students at the university have told me they have not done that."

"Your grandmother Murphy wrote me that you were working with a University of Michigan medical student on Saturdays. How is that going?"

"It's great," Eleanor gushed. "Mary is her name. She has invited me to visit her in Ann Arbor over the Christmas vacation. You think I can do that?"

"I don't see why not, Eleanor."

"Mary is all alone. Would you mind if I invite her to spend Thanksgiving with us?"

"Certainly," Mary Jacqueline approved. "As long as she doesn't mind a house full of people. It's our turn to host thanksgiving dinner, remember."

"I'm sure Mary won't mind," Eleanor judged. You'll love her, mother."

"I'm sure I will, dear," She assured Eleanor. "Now, you must excuse me. Not only am I extremely tired, but I think I am virtually brain dead. I must get myself to bed."

"I understand, Mother," Eleanor said. The two ladies hugged and Mary Jacqueline left her daughter's room.

Back in their own room, Mike and his wife got ready for bed.

"You and Charles have a little talk, did you, Michael?"

"Yes, we did. He couldn't wait to tell me that he and the store manager fought off two thugs who attacked them on the way home one night. One was a fellow worker at George's place, who had been fired for giving Charles a difficult time."

"I never heard about any of that," Mary Jacqueline said, surprised. "Did you know?"

"Nope. Charles said your mother told him it should be kept from us."

"Why ever would she tell the children not to write us about such a thing""

"Charles said that your mother thought that we would worry unnecessarily."

"Why would she think that?"

"She told the children that being in Georgia, there wasn't much we could do. Besides, the matter was already taken care of by the local authorities and Charles was not hurt.

"I suppose she was right."

"Charles also told me that George was right on top of it with the rest of his employees. So, Charles has had no more trouble at work."

Mike continued the story. "Anyway, one of the two men involved in the attack was arrested and convicted of assault. The other fellow is still at large. But he has been identified and is being sought. I'll go over all of this with the men at the office tomorrow and let you know the details.

"You get a chance to talk with Eleanor at all?"

"Yes, I did," Mary Jacqueline reported getting into bed. "She was bursting with enthusiasm about her work in my father's office. She also has made a friend who works with her on Saturdays in the clinic. The lady is a medical student at the University of Michigan."

"You know something?" Mike asked his wife.

"What, Michael?"

"I still get excited watching you undress."

"I'm happy to hear that, dear," Mary Jacqueline responded. "As much as I love you, I am too tired right now to share more than a good night."

"Me, too."

"By the way, Michael. I told Eleanor she could have the medical student she works with stay with us over the Thanksgiving holiday. Is that all right with you?"

"Of course, it is."

"I thought you would agree."

The two got wearily into bed.

Mike leaned back, "Oh, he sighed." He relaxed for the first time that day. "This feel so good."

"Right," his wife agreed. "My own bed at last."

"Good night, sweetheart." Mike said.

She didn't answer. She was already asleep.

*   *   *

Getting up the next morning wasn't easy for the Drieborgs either.

Not long after the sun rose, Maxine was standing at the bedside.

"Get up Mother," she urged. "I have to go to school this morning."

A groggy Mary Jacqueline opened her eyes but was rather slow remembering just where she was.

Maxine was not about to let her mother fall back to sleep.

"Get up, Mother," she insisted. "I need to get dressed and eat breakfast."

This time, Mary Jacqueline gave it up, and got out of bed.

"Where did I put my bathrobe and slippers?" she wondered.

"Go to your room, Maxine," she directed. "I'll be right there."

Robe and slippers found, she headed for the bathroom for a quick morning stop.

In her daughter's room at last, she saw that Maxine had taken off her pajamas and started to dress for school all by herself.

"Why, you don't seem to need my help, dear," she encouraged. "You know just what to do."

"I think you're right, Mother," Maxine agreed. "Eleanor has been helping me, but I think I can do most of it alone now. I might need help getting on my shoes and stockings, though."

"Why don't I just wait and see?" her mother said.

"Ok."

Maxine got as far as tying her shoes.

"I keep forgetting how to do this," She confessed. "Will you help me?"

"Sure," her mother said. "Sit on your bed and I'll tie them."

"Before we go to the kitchen, mother," Maxine advised. "We should wake up Charles. Eleanor is probably downstairs already. But I'm sure Charles will still be in bed."

The two entered Charles's room. Sure enough, he was still burrowed under the covers.

"All right, lazybones," Mary Jacqueline yelled to her son. "Up and at 'em. Time for school." With that, she pulled the covers off the bed.

"Hey, what the hell!" her son shouted.

"Don't you swear around me, young man," she cautioned him. "You want me to get your father in here."

"But it's cold, mother," He complained. "Besides, I'm got plenty of time."

"Hit the deck kiddo," she demanded. "If you're not downstairs in ten minutes, I'll send your father up here."

"Oh, all right," Charles said. "I'll be right down."

"Don't forget to brush your teeth."

"Yes, mother!" he agreed.

*   *   *

Mary Jacqueline and Maxine walked into the kitchen.

"Helen," Mary Jacqueline greeted. "It's so good to see you." The two women hugged. "I'm sorry I couldn't spend more time with you yesterday. I had hoped you would come in today."

"Now jus where else would I be?" Helen scolded. "Haven't you an I ben in a kitchen somewhers every morning since a'fore Charles was born?

"Sit yourself down now an have a cup a' hot freshly made coffee. Maxine you get up in that chair an I'll get you some oatmeal an warm milk."

"I thought Eleanor was here."

"Dat girl don already eat," Helen told her. "She be off fer school some time ago cause she got some important thing ta do before class starts."

"Don't she and Charles walk to school together anymore?" Mary Jacqueline asked.

Helen shook her head. "Since Eleanor been helping Doctor Murphy with sick people, she don't wait on Master Charles no more. She tol him after you left dat he be on his own getting to school an work."

"How'd he take that, Helen?"

"Pretty good, I'd say," she answered "He be still a bear getting out a' bed. But he ben pretty good about getting ready an' out a' the house to school on time. He ben pretty good on his own, I'd say."

"Well, I'll be," Mary Jacqueline exclaimed. "That's a nice change."

"I'd say." Helen agreed.

"Are you going to walk Maxine to St. Andrews this morning?"

"Why dis morning be any different dan any other?" Helen asked. "Something happened to your memory chile, while you down in Georgia an all?"

Mary Jacqueline chuckled. "No, nothing happened to my memory, Helen. I just wondered if that was still part of the daily routine."

"Yes, ma'am," Helen confirmed. "Jus like oatmeal or grits with warm milk fer da children, grits an hot coffee fer da marshal an you. An' da bread baking in da oven."

"Everyone looks forward to your warm kitchen and your hot breakfasts, too."

"Now," Helen continued. "When I gets back from walking Maxine to school, why don't I help you unpack an hang up all your tings? Dat be a help some?"

"Oh, yes, Helen," Mary Jacqueline said. "That would be a big help. I'll be dressed by then and ready to go to work on that."

Just then, Charles walked into the kitchen.

"Can I have some grits, Helen?"

"It's in da pan on da stove. Bowls are in da cupboard. You can serve yourself. I ain't your slave no more." She told him.

"If this is what happens when a fella grows up, I think I just as soon stay a kid."

"You brush your teeth, boy?" Helen asked as he was taking a loaf of bread out of the oven.

"Yes, Helen," Charles said, "I brushed my teeth."

"That be the case, I think you should have a slice of warm bread with sugar and cinnamon sprinkled on it."

"Oh, yes, Helen," Charles sighed. "That sounds so good. Thank you."

In a few minutes he was up and out the door, the bread in one hand and his lunch pail in the other.

"See you after school, Mother," he said in parting. "Remember, I have work at the restaurant after school."

Mary Jacqueline had been silent throughout all of this.

"Helen," she began. "I didn't hear any complaints or whining from Charles since he got up this morning. He brushed his teeth, ate his breakfast and was out of the door in plenty of time, too. To top it off, he remembered that he must report for work after school."

"I noticed dat, too." Helen said.

"Are you sure this is my son, Charles? Or did you sneak another mother's son into this house?"

*   *   *

Mike arrived at the marshal's offices early. He had a lot of catching-up to do today.

Pat Riley came in early, too.

"I've made us some coffee, Mike. Want me to pour you a cup?"

"Please do," Mike requested. "I've been going over these reports. Seems all in order. Every year when it turns cold, we seem to take on more prisoners. I wonder if there's a connection?"

"Probably a nice warm cell is better than a cold park bench, don't ya know." Riley assumed.

"Did you go to Marquette when the judge held court up there last month?"

"Yes, I did," Riley told Mike. "Anderson held down the fort here. Nothing much happened here or there as it turned out. Beautiful country in the Upper Peninsula. Great country for fishing and hunting I was told. I'd like to return some time to test that out."

Mike suggested that they plan a trip up there, next fall.

"You know that Killeen spent years up there working in the forest cutting trees." Riley recalled.

"That's right," Mike said. "I remember now. He used to talk about that all the time. He had some tall tales of a lumberman called Paul Bunyan. Pretty colorful stories. Killeen might want to go with us.

"Before I forget, Pat," Mike told his deputy. "Mary Jacqueline wanted me to ask you and Colleen to join us for Thanksgiving Dinner. My brother Jake, your daughter and their kids will be there as well. Think you can make it?"

"Thank your dear wife, Mike," he answered. "I'll tell the fair Colleen. Judy and Jake will probably bunk with us over the weekend. So, the holiday dinner at your place sounds like a good plan ta me."

"Don't let me forget to invite Stand and Bill, too," Mike asked. "Seems my memory is going on me some."

"Happens when you get older." Riley told him. "You're too young to have that problem, I'm thinking."

Later that morning, Mike met with Killeen and the deputies who policed the area.

"What's the word on this at-large fellow who attacked my son?"

"We haven't heard a thing from the locals about him, Marshal," One of the men responded.

"I'm going to arrange a lunch with the Grand Rapids Chief of Police later this week. Get me the file on the incident so I can be up to-date on it beforehand."

"Will do, Marshal."

"Put out a notice of a $50 reward for information leading to the arrest and conviction of the man. And bring in the men from George's restaurant who worked with him. I want to talk to each of them separately."

"When, Marshal?"

"I'm going to see George this noon," Mike told his deputies. "I'll arrange it then. You can plan to pick them up later this afternoon. I'm guessing they work afternoons over there."

"Stan," Mike said. "You come with me to lunch today and make the arrangement with George."

"Good," Stan said. "I haven't had any of Amos's great Gumbo soup in a long time."

"Neither have I, come to think of it," Mike agreed. "Think I'll have a bowl of that, too."

Later that day, Mike was sitting with a scruffy looking fellow in one of the cells at his office.

"I don't understand why I'm here," The man complained. "I ain't done nothing."

"That's why we're here," Mike told him. "You and I are going to decide whether or not you belong in one of these cells."

"I ain't done nothing."

"You know Phil Richards?"

"Used ta work with him."

"What happened to him."

"Don't know."

"There ya go, telling me a story that's going to land you in one of these cells."

"What happened to Phil?" Mike asked again.

"I tol ya," the man insisted. "I don't know."

Mike stood up and said. "Stand up and give me your chair."

The man did as he was told. Mike took both chairs, left the cell and slammed the door shut.

"Hey!" the man shouted. "I ain't done nothing."

Mike went to another cell where another man sat in the dark waiting. He repeated the same questioning. After he slammed the door on that cell, he returned to the first one.

He opened the door. "Are you ready to tell me the truth? Or am I gonna leave you here overnight?"

"All I know about Richards is that he used ta live at a boarding house over on Bridge Street and hang out at the bar on the corner of Bridge and Water street."

"We'll check that out tonight and see." He slammed the door shut again.

Killeen knocked on the door to a rooming house on Bridge Street. With him was a deputy and a man in manacles. Another deputy was around the back guarding the back-exit stairway from the building.

"Ya?," from the landing on the second-floor shouted down the stairs. "Whose there?"

"Deputy Marshal Killeen. I need ta talk with ya Mr. Richards."

"I got nothin ta say ta ya." He shouted. Killeen heard a door slam from inside the building.

Before long, his deputy came from in back pushing a man in handcuffs in front of him.

"That Richards?" Killeen asked his prisoner.

"Ya, that's him. Now, can I go?"

"When we get back to the Marshal's office, we'll see."

"I did what ya asked."

"It would seem so," Killeen responded. "But I gotta get someone else to confirm it."

Back at the Marshal's office, the other fellow who had worked with Richards confirmed the earlier identification. So did George Neal his former employer.

"is this the guy who attacked you and Charles last month?" Stan asked the afternoon restaurant manager.

"That's the guy."

Tom Russell said. "Yup, that's him all right."

Later that day, Mike visited Richard's cell.

"What do you want?" Richards asked.

"I hear you attack young boys." He said. Mike didn't wait for an answer. He hit the man in the jaw with his fist.

Richards lay on the floor of the cell, sort a' dazed. "What ya hit me for?"

"That boy you attacked is my son; that's why." He pulled Richards to his feet and punched him again.

In his office later, Pat Riley asked. "How'd ya rough up yer knuckles, lad?"

"My right hand ran into an obstacle a couple of times."

"An, I spose that new prisoner of ours, Richards bruised his face against a wall or something?"

"Probably," Mike said. "When the paper-work on him is finished run him over to the local police office. And send a copy of the witness list and their statements to the county prosecutor, will you, Pat"

"I'll have Killeen do that a'fore closing today."

"Thanks."

*   *   *

That evening the Drieborg's were at the supper table. The children and Mary Jacqueline had cleaned their plates but Mike was still enjoying his apple pie and coffee.

Eleanor was clearly tired of waiting. "Who do you want to go first, Mother?' she asked.

"Are you ready, dear?" Mary Jacqueline asked her husband.

"Sure, He said. "My mouth may be full of your delicious desert. But my ears are open."

"God ahead, Eleanor," Her mother urged.

Eleanor told them all about her work in Dr. Murphy's office and in the clinic on Saturdays. She also told them about a school play she had been in and also reviewed her grades.

She concluded her review by telling them she wanted to contact the University of Michigan admission department about being accepted as a pre-med student.

Her father asked. "You're sure you want to be a doctor, Eleanor?"

"Yes, father." She answered immediately.

"Have you talked to grandfather Murphy about this?"

"Yes, I have mother," She answered. "He thought I had a real gentle way with sick people and a real talent with healing."

"Sounds like your grandmother Hecht," Mike offered. "Except the gentle part."

"What does that mean, father?" she asked.

"There comes a time with many patients when the healer must be firm to the point of seemingly being cruel."

"Really, father?" she said.

"Ask your grandfather Drieborg about Nurse Kathy," Mike suggested. "He virtually hated to see her visit him here when he was recovering from that burst appendix. At first, she demanded he stay in bed to allow things to heal. Then, she drove him, without pity, he thought, to get out of bed and move around.

"Ask your grandmother Hecht about my recovery at her farm in Maryland\," Mike continued. "She tore off my bandages daily and scrubbed my wound until it was raw. I hated it. But it was necessary for me to avoid further infection and heal.

"Can you be like that, if necessary?" her father asked.

"Right now," she responded honestly."Probably not. But I think I will be if I see that it is necessary for the recovery of the patient."

"Good answer, Eleanor," Mike said. "You find out from your friend Mary who to contact and we will apply as soon as possible. No sense waiting. Right?

"You agree, mother?" he asked.

"Absolutely."

"Oh, thank you!" Eleanor gushed. "I can hardly wait."

"What about you son?" his mother asked. "What have you been doing while we've been gone?"

Charles began sort of hesitantly. "Not much, Mother," He said. "You know I've been working at Uncle George's restaurant after school and on Saturdays. My boss, Mr. Russell told grandfather and grandmother Murphy that I was a good worker."

"Good to hear that, son," Mike complimented him.

Eleanor interrupted. "I told Mother last night that I wasn't helping Charles with his homework since you left. And I told her that he gets off to school on his own and doesn't whine about everything anymore."

"That true, son?" his mother asked.

"I think so," He confirmed. "Thank you, Eleanor."

Mike asked. "Will you graduate next June, son?"

"I think so, father." He said. "I won't be at the top of the class like Eleanor. But I will graduate with my class."

"Good to hear that, son." His mother said.

"Have you given any thought to what you will do after graduation?" Mike asked.

"Yes, I have," he assured his father.

"I definitely don't want to keep going to school; not any kind. I'm tired of all that book stuff." He told them firmly.

"What then?" his mother asked.

"While you were gone, I wrote Mr. Mikell in South Carolina," Charles began. "I asked him if I could visit and learn the business down there."

"Oh, my heavens," His mother gasped.

"He wrote back inviting me to visit this summer and sort of try it out."

Both parents were quiet. No one said a word for the longest time.

"Tell them what he said in his letter, Charles." Eleanor urged.

"Here, you can read it for yourselves," Charles handed Mikell's letter to his mother.

After she read it, she handed it to her husband.

Mike put the letter on the table and asked.

"Do you have any idea just what you would have to do if you accepted his offer?"

"No, I don't," Charles admitted. "But I didn't know what the restaurant job would demand of me either, father. I managed that pretty well according to Mr. Russell. Would this be so different?"

"Yes, it would," his mother said.

"How so, mother?"

"First off, you would be far away from home. Next, you would be a field hand working from early in the morning until sundown. I shudder to think of you doing that."

"Mother," he responded. "I may not be able to handle that kind of work. But I think I want to try it. I may not like living so far away from my family. I may not be able to stand the work Mr. Mikell told me about. He did it successfully. I'd like to think that I can, too.

"Anyway, I want to try."

"So," Mike said. "What do you propose to do, son?"

"I haven't thought this all out. But if I go to South Carolina after I graduate, I'll spend the summer there working for Mr. Mikell. If I do all right and if I still want to, I'll stay until the cotton and rice crops are harvested. "

"What then, Charles?" Mike pressed.

"If I still think that is the place for me, I'll stay. If not, I come back here and look for something else to try."

Everyone was quiet once again.

"My goodness," Mary Jacqueline said, tearing up. "You two aren't children any, more are you?"

She stood and went around the table to hug Eleanor and then, Charles. Mike joined them.

Still quiet in her chair, Maxine shouted. "What about me?"

Everyone laughed and moved over to hug her, too.

Thanksgiving Celebration

Somehow, everyone had a room and a bed for the weekend in town. But the Drieborg home was full of adults and children from the kitchen to the front porch. What a crowd gathered to celebrate Thanksgiving.

Joe and Ann Deeb lived in Grand Rapids, now. They brought baked salmon. Susan and George Neal also lived in town. They brought rolls and deserts from the restaurant. Amos and his wife Helen brought a pot of his famous gumbo. Jake and Judy Drieborg lived in Lowell and were staying with her parents the Riley's in Grand Rapids. They brought hard boiled eggs and raw potatoes. Grandfather and grandmother Drieborg were staying with the Murphy's. They brought fresh milk and some cheese. Pat and Colleen Riley brought pumpkin pie. Stan Killeen and Bill Anderson each brought red wine. Even Mrs. Carl Bacon was there, too. She brought a sweet potato casserole.

The host and hostess provided the turkey with homemade stuffing, gravy, fresh cranberries, freshly baked bread and a fruit salad.

It was a surprisingly mild day, so the men were on the front porch with their drinks, pipes and cigars. George Neal smoked one of those new cigarettes. Mike and Dr. Murphy had snuck in some bourbon to bolster the punch. It was good sipping stuff, too.

The women were bustling around the kitchen and the dining room, getting everything on the table. Charles and Eleanor, the eldest of the cousins by far, were trying to stay out of the way. Neither wanted the job of controlling all their out of control cousins. Charles hid in his room, Eleanor was in her father's upstairs study with her guest, Mary.

Their aunt Ann shouted up the stairs. "You two get down here and help us!"

Eleanor knocked on her brother's bedroom door.

"Our absence has been discovered, brother. They want us downstairs right now."

Charles opened the door. "Oh, geese," he said. "Do we have to, Eleanor?"

"It's once a year with our cousins, Charles," She reminded him. "It's only for a couple of hours. If I can stand it, so can you."

"I suppose."

The eight children were seated at tables set up in the living room. The moms supervised getting the various foods on their plates and filling their glasses with milk. The adults sat at the family's dining room table. With all the extensions put in, it barely seated every adult. Charles, Eleanor, her guest Mary and their cousin, Robert took their food laden plates to the kitchen table.

The hostess, Mary Jacqueline led the prayer.

Bless us oh Lord

For these thy gifts

And for what we are about to receive

From Thy bounty

From Christ out Lord, Amen.

Out in the kitchen, Eleanor said,

"What a relief, we don't have to eat or help with the children,"

"You think we can sneak out after we eat?" Charles asked his sister.

"Where do you want to go?"

"I want to meet some of the guys."

"Are you thinking about going to that that Polish bar on the West side, I've heard about?"

"I'm not sure where we're going, Eleanor. "

"And just after I told our folks how mature you were acting lately." Eleanor snapped at her brother.

"It's only a few beers, Eleanor."

"Can you have beer at home, Charles?" she asked knowing the answer.

"No."

"So, doesn't that tell you something?" Eleanor asked sarcastically.

"It's not a big deal."

"Can you imagine what would happen if you got arrested or something? Your father is the Federal Marshal here, for God's sake. Can't you see the embarrassment you would cause him?"

"You're such a worry-wart, Eleanor. Nothing bad is going to happen."

"I hope not, Charles."

Ann Arbor

Eleanor, her mother and father arrived at the boarding house on the corner of Division and Jefferson late in the afternoon.

Mary Seldon greeted them at the door.

"Welcome to my residence." she greeted.

Eleanor and her parents entered the residence.

"Thank you for inviting us," Eleanor's mother said.

"Allow me to show you to your rooms. Then we can talk in the sitting room down here." Mary told them.

In short order, the four of them met in the main sitting room.

After an exchange of pleasantries, Mary told them. "You have an appointment with the Dean of Admissions tomorrow morning at ten. He will review your application and supporting documents. I expect he will decide on your admission, on the spot."

"Oh, I hope he will admit me to the program, Mary," Eleanor said.

"I can't imagine him not doing so, Eleanor."

"Will we be able to visit the Medical School, too?" Eleanor asked.

"Yes," Mary assured her. "I've gotten permission for us to tour the facility after the noon meal tomorrow. It's called lunch around here, by the way, not dinner."

"I suppose you will discover many things here that are different here, Eleanor," Her father noted.

"I suppose." She responded.

A lady entered the room.

"Mrs. Foster," Mary said "Let me introduce you to Eleanor Drieborg and her parents. Mrs. Foster is the landlady of this rooming house."

"Good afternoon," she said extending her hand. "Welcome to my boarding house for women. She looked at Eleanor.

"So, child," she continued. "You intend to attend this university next fall, do you?"

"Yes, ma'am. I do."

"Well, Mary has shown me you letter requesting lodging here and your letters of recommendation. So, I look forward to having you here when the next term begins.

"You've seen the room you will have, Ms. Foster continued. "Let me show you and your parents the rest of the place."

After they toured the home, Mrs. Foster asked Mike to fill out some paperwork and give her a deposit for the first three months of room and board.

"Tonight's supper will be served at five," She told them. "Then, you will meet a few of the girls and sort of sample a typical evening meal here.'

"Thank you, Mrs. Foster," Mary Jacqueline told her. "We appreciate your hospitality."

"You're most welcome, Mrs. Drieborg. I look forward to having your daughter as one of my girls. Don't worry. I'll look after her, fer sure."

"Thank you," Mary Jacqueline said. "That is most comforting."

The evening meal was roast beef over biscuits. Apple pie milk or coffee was served, too.

"The meal was delicious, Mrs. Foster." Mary Jacqueline assured her.

"I've discovered that the girls are running at such a fast pace they forget to take the time to eat, Sometimes, they run out a' here with no breakfast a'tal. I can imagine they often miss lunch, too. So, I have a good solid evening meal every evening. Most of my girls do make this meal at least."

"It is good to hear that, Mrs. Foster," Mike told her.

"I have started putting up a small bag lunch for each of my girls." Mrs. Foster revealed. "Some of my girls have gotten in the habit of taking one with them in the morning. I keep telling them they need nourishment for the mind as well as the body."

"Thank you for that, Mrs. Foster," Mary Jacqueline said.

"You've got a big day tomorrow, meeting the admissions people, an all."

"Yes," Mike responded. "We do."

Mary Jacqueline added. "We're excited about it. Nervous, too."

"I wouldn't worry," Mrs. Foster assured them. "From what Mary has told me of your daughter, you have nothing to fear. She'll be admitted to the program, I'm sure."

"Thank you," Mary Jacqueline said. "I hope you're right."

$$* \qquad * \qquad *$$

At ten sharp the next morning, the Drieborgs were in the waiting room of the President of the University Dr. James Angels.

"Good morning Mr. and Mrs. Drieborg and Miss Dreiborg," he said extending his hand to Mike. "I am James Angels. You saw my title on the door to this office perhaps that I am President of the University. I am also temporally, I hope, the Dean of Admissions. Please come in my office and have a seat.

"So, this is your daughter, Eleanor is it?" Once everyone was seated, he asked.

"Please tell me, young lady. Why do you want to attend the University of Michigan?"

"Aside from the well-known fact that it is the best University in the entire mid-west, your Board of Regents began to admit women to its medical school a few years back. Few universities in the nation have had the courage and for-sight to do that."

"So, you are interested in the medical training we offer? Nursing perhaps?" the he asked.

"No, sir," Eleanor quickly told him. "I intend to become a medical doctor.

"My mother's father is Dr. Miles Murphy who has a practice in Grand Rapids, Michigan. He taught at the University of Pennsylvania Medical School for many years before coming to Michigan. I have worked in his office as a nurse's aide after school and in the Grand Rapids Medical Clinic on Saturdays in the same capacity.

"I have also gone on calls with my grandmother Hecht who is a well-known healer in the Lowell area. Recently, I assisted her in delivering a baby."

"We don't have a program to train healers, miss." President Angels informed her.

"I do intend to become a healer," Eleanor smiled. "But a healer with a license from this university as a medical doctor."

"Well said, young lady," The President assured Eleanor with a smile. "But being a woman among the men in our medical program will be a challenge. Women are in a definite minority to men in that program. I want you to know that before-hand. I also want you to know that you will not be given any allowance for your gender. On the contrary, I expect that you to be seriously challenged if you do enroll in our medical program."

Eleanor straightened her back and said with firmness.

"President Angels, I intend to become a doctor. I hope my formal training will be here at the University of Michigan. But I will become a doctor."

"Is there anything else you would like to add, Miss Drieborg?"

"No, sir," She responded. "Is there anything else you would like to ask, me?"

He smiled at her quick response and paused.

"No, miss," He responded. "I feel confident that I know enough about you to make a decision on your application.

"Very well, Miss Drieborg," he began. "I have reviewed your records and the outstanding recommendations you have received from several doctors who practice in Grand Rapids. I see no reason to doubt their opinion of you. So, allow me to inform you here and now that you have been accepted for enrollment the University of Michigan as a student in our medical program. Congratulations, young lady."

With that he stood and extended his hand to Eleanor. She took his hand in both of hers.

"You will not be disappointed in your decision, President Angels," She assured him. "I will be a credit to the University."

"I applaud your determination, Ms. Drieborg. And, I wish you every success."

Eleanor hugged her father and mother.

"Thank you, President Angels," Michael Drieborg told him. "I am sure you will not be disappointed with your decision."

"The steel I saw in your daughter's eyes, Mr. Drieborg told me that you are most probably correct. Now, if you will visit with my secretary, there are some forms to fill out before you leave."

"Of course."

For the next hour, the Drieborgs filled out form after form to formally enroll Eleanor as a student at the University of Michigan. She would report for introductory classes in the medical program the third week in June. The fall semester would begin the third week of September.

When they had finished the forms, they went to the accounting department and paid for tuition and fees for the summer and fall programs. Eleanor was also given a list of text books she was expected to have for the introductory summer courses.

"Mary has already told me I could use her books this summer until I buy my own." Eleanor told her parents.

"That's good news," Mike told his wife. "Our bank account is already straining to cover everything else."

"I wouldn't worry, Michael," Mary Jacqueline told her husband with a wry smile. "Remember, we have that account at Old Kent Bank for the children with funds from the Pope Estate."

"I had forgotten that fund," Mike admitted. "You've had income from the Pope lands deposited there for several years for them. "My brother-in -law, Joseph Deeb manages that fund for you at the bank. What a god-send that will be. Will there be enough money for all three children, do you think?"

"I believe so, especially if Charles does not choose to attend a college," Mary Jacqueline told her husband. "We will add to it each year going forward in any case. So, I am not worried about there being sufficient."

"Good to hear, dear," Michael told his wife.

After they left the administration building, they walked into the small downtown of Ann Arbor.

First, they stopped at the telegraph office and sent a message to Dr. and Mrs. Murphy. Then, they sent one to the Drieborgs in Lowell and another to the Hechts in the same town.

"Are you sure the telegrams will be delivered?" Eleanor asked.

"Sure," her father assured her. "At the Marshal's office in Grand Rapids, we are sent telegrams all the time. Messengers deliver them right to our office. The payment I made today for these three messages covers delivery, too."

271

"I didn't know that," Eleanor said.

At a small eatery, they ordered soup for lunch.

"Their soup and home-made bread were delicious, weren't they?" Mary Jacqueline said,

"Almost as good as in your kitchen, dear," Mike assured her.

Mary Jacqueline give her husband's arm a squeeze. "Thank you, dear."

They walked to the building that housed the labs and classrooms for the medical school.

Mary Seldon was waiting for them in the vestibule.

AS soon as Eleanor walked in the door, Mary asked.

"Well?"

"I'm in!" Eleanor virtually shouted.

The girls hugged and sort of danced around a bit.

"I told you, didn't I?"

"I was so nervous," Eleanor revealed. "But he seemed pleased with my responses to his questions."

"Oh, Mary," Eleanor remembered. "Don't let me forget to take the books I need for the summer program. The ones you are going to lend me."

"I've thought about that, Eleanor," Mary said. "I still use them for reference occasionally. So, I had better hold on to them. I'm sorry. I hope you don't mind."

"Not a problem," Eleanor assured her friend. "I was going to buy a set of my own anyway. Is there a store in town that sells them?"

"We'll go there after the tour."

Then, Mary led them around the building. In the amphitheater below, they watched as students cut into a woman's body.

"Oh, my," Mary Jacqueline said. "Does every student have to do that," she asked Mary."

"Yes, ma'am. We all have to."

"How excitin,," Eleanor exclaimed.

"Really?" Mary Jacqueline was astonished. "You find that exciting, Eleanor?"

'Of course, mother," Eleanor responded. "If I am to learn how to stop internal bleeding like the kind that killed my own mother, I must know all about the blood vessels, bones and muscles and how they interact. That's what is exciting."

"Eleanor is no longer a child, dear," Michael commented. "She is a woman embarking on an adventure. Get used to it, sweetheart."

"I suppose you're going to tell me to buckle up, with Charles being next out of the nest?"

"You got that right. No telling what he'll be up to after he graduates this coming June."

"I can hardly wait," Mary Jacqueline sighed.

After Eleanor carried a stack of books to her room, the Drieborgs joined Mrs. Foster and several other girls for supper.

In their room later, Mary Jacqueline told Michael. "This evening's meal was as good as last nights. Don't you think?"

"Did you or Eleanor tell Mrs. Foster that meatloaf was one of my favorites?"

"No, I didn't," Mary Jacqueline laughed.

"Gotta tell ya, then," Mike said. "Eleanor is going to put on weight here. Tonight's meal was great."

Grand Rapids

During the following week, a story about her acceptance was even printed in the Grand Rapids Eagle daily newspaper. On Saturday evening of the that same week, the entire family gathered at the Drieborg home to celebrate the occasion.

While everyone was told not to brings gifts, word got around that it would be nice to give her a gift of spending money. So, as she opened each card, there was some cash included. The group decided to tell her it was her, mad money; just in case money; or an emergency fund, of sorts.

Whatever, it was called, she gave it all to her uncle Joe Deeb for him to deposit in a personal account in her name at the Old Kent Bank. There was a branch in Ann Arbor, so she could use the newly issued checks to pay for things or just take cash out of the account directly, with no difficulty.

Anyway, the gathering was a great success except that Charles felt sort of left out.

As things quieted down, his grandfather Murphy asked him.

"What are you going to do after graduation, Charles?"

Without any hesitation, Charles answered.

"I intend to work on the Pope land in South Carolina, grandfather."

"Oh, my goodness," his grandmother Judy whispered rather loudly.

The entire group was silent for a minute. His announcement, made so quickly and firmly, had taken them by surprise.

His uncle George broke the silence, "That will be quite an adventure, Charles. I'll hate to see you go. You're a good worker. Are you sure that will be the best choice for you?"

"Thank you, Uncle George," Charles said. "I'm not sure, to be honest about it. But I've got to get on with my life too. Eleanor seems all set to become a doctor. I need to find something that suits me, also."

His grandfather Murphy added, "Well spoken, son."

His grandfather Drieborg spoke up next. "You've done very well at George and Susan's restaurant, Charles. I don't see any reason you won't do well on that land in South Carolina, too."

"Thank you, grandfather," He said.

"Hear, hear!" was heard around the table from the men. The ladies all clapped. Charles looked surprised at the approval and blushed, some.

His mother lowered her head some and brushed a tear from her cheek. She was clapping, too.

"He's no longer a child, either," She thought.

After everyone had left and the mess was cleaned up, the family was talking in their sitting-room.

Mike said to Charles. "So, you're serious about joining Mr. Mikell in South Carolina?"

"Yes, I am father," Charles confirmed. "I don't think I am well suited to attend a college. I'm afraid I'd just waste my time and your money at that. I can't continue to be a bus-boy. And, I don't want to just sleep in and hang around local bars an' such.

"Besides, I'd never know if I really am up to the challenge, I'm being offered by Mr. Mikell."

"I think you've reasoned this out very well, Charles," Mike responded. "If you still feel that way this spring and mother agrees, we'll take you down there after Eleanor gets settled in Ann Arbor next June. What do you think, dear?"

"I don't know how I feel about it, actually," she said. "We're going to lose Eleanor to college and now it's hard for me to imagine losing my son, too."

Charles asked, "Mother, do you have a different suggestion?"

"No, Charles. I don't."

"Well, then?" he asked her.

"I have to agree with your father," She admitted. "It appears that you have thought this out pretty well, son. I can't deny that. But you'll have to give me some time to adjust to not having either of you in this house. And you, Charles, so far away." Tears were running down her face by now.

"Excuse me., Mary Jacqueline rose from her chair and headed for the stairway upstairs.

"Father, you think we should go to mother?" Eleanor asked.

"No, Eleanor," he responded. "I believe she wants some time alone, right now. None of this is going to happen for a while. We'll all talk of it again. In the meantime, you have to concentrate on finishing your studies in order to graduate next June. Right?"

Both Eleanor and Charles said. "Yes, father."

"I think you should write Mr. Mikell, Charles. Thank him for his response to your letter Also, tell him that you are inclined to accept his invitation. But that you must talk to your parents about it first. Then ask him if it will be all right if you get back to him with your decision after the first of the year."

"Do you want to read the letter before I send it?"

"No, Charles," Mike told him. "But I suggest that you share it with your mother, first. She's sort 'a grieving right now, just thinking about both of you leaving. I believe it will comfort her to know that you are still discussing it with us."

"All right, father. I will share it with mother before I send it," Charles assured him.

"Hey, Maxine," Mike said to his eight-year old daughter." Do you realize that you are way past your bedtime?"

"Do I have to?" she complained.

"And, you need a bath, too," Her father continued.

"Eleanor will you heat up some water for Max's bath?"

"Just don't try to brush my hair after it's washed, father."

"Why not?"

"Because it hurts when you do it," Maxine told her father. "Let Eleanor or mother do it."

"Why does it hurt when I brush out your hair?"

"You pull on the tangles, and it hurts."

"Is that why you holler when I brush your hair after you wash it?"

"Let Eleanor do it, please!"

"Oh, all right. Have it your way, crybaby."

It wasn't long before Maxine was in her bed. Eleanor and Charles were in their rooms and their father and mother in theirs.

Still dressed, Charles knocked on Eleanor's door.

"Yes?" she asked.

"Can I come in for a minute, Eleanor?"

"Sure. I'm decent."

Once inside her room, Charles asked.

"Will you help me write my letter to Mr. Mikell?"

"Sure," Eleanor said; "You're pretty serious about this aren't you, Charles."

"Yes, I am," He responded to his sister. "I didn't realize that mother would take it so hard. But I have to do something with my life. Going back south to work with Mr. Mikell seems to make the most sense to me, right now."

"I think you're right, Charles," Eleanor told her brother. "But I'm not sure I'd have the courage to try working the fields and such in South Carolina."

Charles told Eleanor, "I'd rather do that than sit in a classroom for hours and study my head off like you're going to do."

Eleanor laughed first; then Charles.

"We each must pick our own poison, I suppose." Eleanor decided.

"Maybe tomorrow after church we can write that letter. Ok?" Charles asked.

"Sounds good, Tomorrow then."

"Goodnight Eleanor."

"Goodnight, Charles. This has been quite an evening."

"Sure has."

*   *   *

Down the hallway in the Drieborg house, Mary Jacqueline and Mike were under the covers, talking.

"Are you going to be ok?" Mike asked his wife.

"Oh, yes. I feel so foolish carrying on like I did."

"I thought your reaction was rather normal."

"But I made it sound like the children were doing something bad. When actually, they are doing what we had hoped they would do; carve a life for themselves outside of this house."

"But sweetheart," Mike hugged his wife. "They needed to know how much you love them and will miss them, too. What's so bad about that?"

"Put that way, nothing," Mary Jacqueline had an issued of her own to share.

"But I've got a bone to pick with you, buddy." She added.

"What did I do?"

"It's what you haven't done, mister big shot marshal."

"What, already?"

"You haven't shown me how much you love me, lately. We haven't made love in over a week>"

"Oh, that." Mike realized.

"Yes, that," She teased. "You've been neglecting your responsibilities." Then she ran her hand under Michael's night gown and up his leg.

"Hey, your hand is cold."

"You want me to stop?"

"Never!" Mike whispered and turned toward his wife.

That ended their conversation for the evening.

Christmas Time in Grand Rapids

The children were out of school for the Christmas holiday

 Eleanor took the opportunity to work daily at her grandfather's medical office or at the Grand Rapids Medical Clinic. Nurse Kathy and Mary her medical student friend worked with her some on the long list of terms and medical instruments she would have to know next summer.

Charles was offered the opportunity of coming into work to help serve the morning coffee hour. Everyone was surprised he made it into the restaurant by seven in the morning.

Maxine stayed at home.

Helen was still helping Mary Jacqueline during the morning. During the December vacation, she brought her two children with her to the Drieborg home. They played with Maxine. Her oldest, daughter Mary, attended S t. Andrew's elementary school with Maxine. Her youngest, son John, was too young for formal school. So, the two girls used him as their student when they played school each day.

Both girls complained to Helen that John was not cooperating. In fact, they said he was naughty and should be punished. Helen was not sympathetic.

"Don you girls ask me to do your work fer you. He don want to play school I think he be tired of always being da student, never da teacher. Leave him out of it. He'll join ya'all when he be ready, I speck."

All was not work for Charles and Eleanor, though.

Eleanor was invited to join her mother and her aunts for lunch one day at George and Susan's restaurant.

"It is so nice my aunts invited me to join them for their annual Christmas lunch next week." Eleanor told her mother.

"I think they've decided that since you're going to the University of Michigan next June, you should be part of their annual lunch."

"It's still nice of them."

"Of course, it is," Her mother agreed. "What do you intend to order?"

"I've always wanted to try some of Uncle Amos's soups," Eleanor told her mother. "Also, I've never had any of those tiny sandwiches they feature on the menu."

"They are called, finger food, Eleanor,"

"That's a cute name for them,"

She also arranged a lunch for several of her closest friends. Of course, it was held at her aunt and uncle's restaurant as well.

Not to be left out, Charles arranged an after-work meeting with several of his buddies. He was busy working through the lunch hour, so the gathering had to be after he completed his shift.

They decided to go to a place on the West side of town called, The Polish Falcons. It was a neighborhood place that served polish food and didn't mind serving beer to underaged drinkers. The city had an ordinance prohibiting the sale of alcoholic beverages to anyone under eighteen. Charles had just turned that age, but most of his friends had not. Despite the ordinance, this would not be the first time his group had gone there for a beer.

By six that evening, he and his friends had finished their meal of kielbasa sausage and red sauerkraut. But as they drank a second and a third beer, their talk and laughter became rather loud. Too loud, it seemed, for some men at a nearby table.

One of those men came over to the boy's table and suggested they tone it down. He was told to bug off mind his own business; rather rudely as only teenage boys can do.

Another man from the same table returned and without saying a word, poured a mug of beer over the head of the boy who had made the rude dismissive comment.

Charles stood up and punched the man in the jaw.

Men from several tables quickly surrounded the boys. After a brief flurry of fists, he boys were subdued. They were forced to sit on the floor and each was told to place his hands his head.

"This is our place," one of the men said. "We'll not let you trash it or disrespect us. You are no longer welcome here. In fact, if you try to come here again, we will not be as kind to you as we were just now.

"Now, pay your bill and leave before we change our minds,"

When Charles arrived home, it was a bit after seven o'clock.

His family was in the front room.

They heard the back-door slam shut.

"Is that you, Charles?" his mother called.

"Yes, mother," he called back from the kitchen. "I'm going up to bed, I don't feel too well."

"Come in here, first, Charles," His father called out.

Charles entered the hallway but stayed out of the front room.

"Is something wrong, son?" Mike said. "Come in here. Let me see you."

As soon as Charles entered the room, his mother gasped and put her hand over her mouth in surprise.

"What happened to you?" Mike asked.

"I got into a fight, that's all. I'm fine."

Mike had moved to stand in front of his son. "You stink like a brewery. Where did you get the beer?"

"One of the guys had it. I just had one swig of it,"

"Don't lie to me, Charles," Mike told him. "Where did you get the beer."

"We had supper at the Polish Falcons and some beer got splashed around."

"Is that where you got that shiner, too?"

"Yes, sir."

"They throw you and your friends out, did they?"

"Yes, sir."

"Get your coat," Mike ordered his son. "We're going for a little ride."

It wasn't long before Mike pulled his buggy up in front of the Polish Falcon bar.

"Come with me," He ordered his son.

Inside, Mike walked directly to the bar, Charles in tow.

"Are you in charge here?

"Yes, I am. I'm the manager,"

"Were you here when this boy and some others caused a commotion?"

"Yes, I was,"

"Tell me what happened, please," Mike asked.

The manager told Mike what had happened.

"So, this boy, the one standing right here started the fight?"

"Yes, he did. He threw the first punch,"

"How did this boy get his shiner?"

"Can't tell ya. He must 'a fallen or run into a door,"

"Any damage done to your place, here?"

"I don't see any. Do you?"

Mike looked around. "Can't say that I do," he agreed.

"Does my son owe you any money?"

"Nope. He and his friends paid their bill before we kicked them out,"

"Thank you for the information," Mike told the manager. He turned and told Charles,

"We're leaving,"

Mike didn't speak all the way to their house. When they arrived home, he told his son,

"Go to your room and stay there until I call you,"

After Mike told Charles's mother what had happened, she asked,

"What do you think we should do, now?"

"I think we should let him stew for a day or so before we talk with him," Mike suggested. "Let him think about what he did, how he lied to us and embarrassed us in public. Let's see if he realizes how he damaged our trust in his judgement."

"You think he'll apologize?"

"I hope so, dear," Mike said. "That would be a good start. I'd like to chalk this up to a teenager feeling his oats and who just made a poor decision; a kid who had a learning experience."

*   *   *

The next day at work, Charles ran into his boss, George Neal.

"Quite a shiner you have there, Charles," He teased. "Run into a door or a fist maybe?"

"It looks worse than it is," Charles meekly responded.

"I heard you were thrown out of the Falcons's last night after you started a brawl there,"

" I didn't start the fight, another customer did,"

"That's not the word going around town, Charles," George related. "The word is that you got drunk with some buddies, started a fight and then got thrown out of the place. What part of that story is wrong?"

"I wasn't drunk. How did you find out Uncle George? Did my father tell you?"

"Nope. Haven't seen him today. I was told about this before you even got out of bed this morning. See, I meet with my fellow restaurant owners on occasion. This morning Ron Maximowski told me of your escapade at his place last night.

"You might remember in the future, Charles, Grand Rapids is still a small town. Members of important families seldom do anything out of the ordinary that is not noticed and then spoken about."

"I'm not important, Uncle George,"

"You got that right, kid. But your father is and your mother is highly respected, too. When you screw up like you did last night, it reflects on them. Nobody gives a shit about you; for sure. But many welcome an opportunity to use what you did to trash your parents and damage their reputation and therefore their influence."

"I didn't think of that,"

"Well, then think about this tough guy. By just going to a bar and acting stupidly, you virtually made them laughing stocks in this town. And, you thereby damaged you father's ability to enforce the law.

"My father didn't do anything wrong. Neither did my mother," Charles protested. "Besides, what I did wasn't all that bad."

"Sure, it was." George insisted. "You dad's employees, regular citizens, members of the legal community, even criminals will think,

"Big shot Drieborg can't even control his own kids. He can't preach to me anymore about proper behavior, when even his kid doesn't listen to him. Why should anybody else, etc. etc."

"And, the snooty women who resent your mother for all her charm and kindness will whisper,

"What must go on in that fancy house on Prospect for her son to go out, get drunk and start a brawl?"

"But it wasn't a big deal, Uncle George."

"It obviously wasn't to you, kid," George repeated. "But as I told you, it is in this community. Think about that next time, before you act stupidly Now get back to work."

"Yes, sir."

Charles worked the rest of the day without anyone mentioning his black eye or the incident at the Polish Falcons restaurant.

*   *   *

The people around the Drieborg supper table were unusually quiet that evening.

Eleanor, who was usually the first to tease Charles about something he did, said or did not do at school, did not mention his black eye. Nor did she repeat the story going around school about the incident at the Polish Falcons.

289

Finally, Charles had had enough of the silence.

"Isn't anyone going to say anything?"

Mary Jacqueline calmly asked. "About what, dear?'

"About what happened last night."

His mother pushed on, "Please, dear," she asked. "Tell me what happened last night. Would you?"

"You don't know, mother?"

"Your mother asked you to tell her what happened last night," Mike snapped at his son. "Tell her, tough guy."

Charles colored, but answered his mother's question.

"Oh, I see now," Mary Jacqueline said. "When I was at the butcher shop today, Mrs. Wentworth asked me if you had recovered from the brawl you were in last night.

"She usually won't give me the time of day." Charles's mother continued. "So, I gather she was taking the opportunity to remind me publicly that my family is less than perfect. That's probably why she was smiling when she asked me about my son."

"When I was at the federal court-house today, Judge Yared asked me why the local police weren't called to break up the brawl you started at the Polish Falcone."

"What did you tell him, dear," His wife asked.

"I told him that the manager had taken care of it without police help."

Charles pushed back his chair and stood up to leave the room.

"Where the hell do you think you're going, tough guy?" Mike snapped.

"I don't need to hear all of this," Charles snapped back.

Mike stood, his face red with anger. "You brought this up. You wanted to know why we weren't talking to you. So, sit back down before I knock you down. You'll go when we tell you to go."

Eleanor was shocked. *"I've never heard my father swear. I've never seen him so angry about anything, either. Phew!"* She thought.

Charles sat down.

Mike sat and collected himself.

Finally, he asked.

"Did you hear about this from anyone else, mother?"

"Yes," his wife answered. "When Helen brought Maxine home from school today, she asked me how Charles was. It seems that her husband heard when he was delivering his soups around town about the big fight at the Falcons restaurant last night. She said it sounded terrible; some high school boys after too much beer, got into a fight with customers of the restaurant. Then, he told her that he heard over at George and Susan's place that Charles had started the fight"

"What did you tell her, dear?" Mike asked.

"I just told her that Charles was not injured and was at work today. She wasn't spreading rumors maliciously. She helped raise Charles from the time he was born. She was simply concerned about him."

"I'm sure that was the case." Mike agreed.

"If what that snooty Mrs. Wentworth said today is any example, I'm sure I'll hear about it in the days to come from others who resent me."

"You're not alone in that, dear. I expect to hear more subtle questions and comments, too."

"Geez!" Charles said.

"What did you say?" Mike actually shouted. Even little Maxine jumped at his outburst.

"Nothing." Charles sort of whispered.

"Nothing? I'll give you nothing, young man." Mike continued very stridently. "You will return home immediately after work each day going forward. You will not leave this house any evening for as long as your mother and I decide. There will be no Christmas parties for you, fella. When you are in this house, you will stay in your room. Am I quite clear?"

"Yes."

"Yes, what?"

"Yes, sir."

"Mother," Mike asked more calmly. "Do you have anything more?"

"One thing, dear. I don't think either of us have heard an apology from our son." she said. "And that hurts me more than a dozen snide remarks from the Mrs. Wentworths of this town."

Charles dropped his chin to his chest. "Shit. *How could I have forgotten to say I'm sorry?*" He thought.

292

"Way to go, Charles." His father chided. "Now, you can go to your room."

*   *   *

The Christmas season went as they always do, quickly. But this year, the Drieborg house celebrated rather quietly. Non-the-less, Eleanor was determined to help Charles return to the good graced of her parents.

One evening after the dinning-room episode, she joined Charles in his room. She had not yet talked with her brother about the situation since that night.

"Are you going to jump on me, too?"

"No. And I'm not even going to say that I told you not to go to that bar,"

"Thanks for that, at least."

"But I am willing to talk with you about making it up to our parents."

"What can you do?"

"You want my help or not, Charles?"

Her brother heaved a deep sigh and was silent.

"If you don't want my help, you're on your own. Well?"

"Yes, I want your help." He finally said.

He added, "At least our parents are talking to you. Even my friends at school have been avoiding me. Like the whole thing was all my fault. Geeze."

"Rumor at school has it that's their parents told their kids to avoid you. None of them want what you and their son did at the Falcons to taint their local reputations. Our father's job is a federal appointment and sort of insulated from local public opinion. But all the rest of your friends have fathers whose income is affected by what the townspeople think of them. If people don't want to do business with them, they're goose is cooked."

"Lucky me. So, I get the cool treatment."

"They figure that their financial and social survival is more important for their families than their son's friendship with you. I can understand that. Why can't you?"

"Now that you explain it, I do understand." Charles told his sister. "But do I have to like it?"

"No, you don't." Eleanor said. "But you can stop moaning and whining about it. You could get off your behind and at least make amends with our parents."

"What do you suggest miss smarty?"

"For starters, you can apologize." She responded. "After supper tonight, we clean up, then you and I join them in the sitting room. "I'll say that you have something to say to them.

"Then, you follow me into the room and say you're sorry."

"You make it sound so easy." Charles complained.

"Look," Eleanor snapped. "It's not going to get any easier if you wait. It's only going to get harder. And, in the meantime,

Christmas is no fun around here for any of us. Besides, if you don't do it, I'll stop speaking to you, and I won't write that letter to Mr. Mikell for you wither."

"All right, already." Charles held up his hand. "I'll do it. What do I say?

"When we enter the room, I will announce that you have something to say." Eleanor told him. "Then you will say,

"I'm sorry for causing you embarrassment. Then, you might add that they can be sure you'll never do such a thing again."

"That's it?"

"Yep," Eleanor assured her brother. "Remember what our speech teacher told us; the old KISS saying?"

"I forgot. What's that?"

"Keep it simple, stupid."

*   *   *

Charles gave his painful performance that same night. His mother hugged him. His father shook his hand. And things around the Drieborg house eventually returned to normal, for Christmas anyway. People at work soon tired of kidding him about being thrown out of the Falcons Bar and when his black eye faded away, it stopped reminding people of the fight he lost there, too.

But he was still grounded for the rest of that year's holiday break.

"Geeze," he grumbled. "I said I was sorry." He complained to his father. "Can't you give me a break?"

295

"I don't think so. But you're a tough guy. You can take it. Right?" Mike said, slapping him on the back a little too hard.

Preparations

Thorough out the winter and spring, both Eleanor and Charles looked forward to graduation. They also prepared for the next step in their life.

Eleanor increased preparation for summer school in Ann Arbor. At her grandfather's office, she rarely made a mistake in identifying instruments used in the medical profession. She knew all the medical terms her instructors would use as well. And, after struggling, the complexity of the human anatomy ceased to be as much of a mystery to her, either.

Charles, on the other hand had been given a serious challenge by Mr. Miklell. Responding to the young man's Christmas letter, he urged Charles to learn to fire a repeating rifle, to develop horsemanship skills and to become adept at farm animal management. All would be a challenge to the boy.

But he was willing to learn. So, Mike bought Charles a Henry repeating rifle. He and Pat Riley taught him how to fire and clean it. Stan Killeen and Bill Anderson volunteered to work with him on horsemanship.

Grandfather Jake welcomed the opportunity to teach Charles how to milk cows and goats, clean a barn properly, repair tack and chop wood. All these skills were pretty basic to a farmer, but foreign to Charles.

Of all these things, Charles disliked working around animals and the barn most. But he kept at it. His Grandfather was a good teacher.

"No, Charles," he repeated. "You're not in a hurry. Treat da animal gently. Squeeze slowly as you pull. Take your time as you milk."

By the third or fourth weekend of milking, he had earned praise from his grandfather.

"Dat's good, Charles."

Cleaning the barn was the most difficult for Charles.

"How can you stand the smell, grandfather?" he would say.

"It is something you get used to, Charles. Breathe through your mouth und the smell won't bodder you."

Firing a rifle was another matter. The kick of the weapon not only gave him a black eye, his shoulder was sore as well. It took a while for him to toughened up. Then, target practice was more fun. And, he was pretty good at it. Shooting deer and fowl was a different matter. He needed more practice at moving targets.

Stan's patience was tried as Charles attempted to saddle the riding horse. The horse would move, or step on his foot or bump Charles against the stall. It took several sessions for the boy to gain control of the situation. Riding was another challenge.

Like most city kids, Charles had no need to ride a horse. The family had a buggy pulled by a single horse trained for that purpose. So, his parents rented a horse that had been broken to accept a rider. Never-the-less, Charles had to convince the animal that he, not it, was in charge.

"Ya have ta be firm, but at the same time gentle," Bill Anderson repeatedly told him.

Not a concept easily grasped, Charles would protest. "This nag doesn't understand gentle, Uncle Bill."

It took several weeks of riding to learn. But Charles's horsemanship did improve.

Finally, Stan gave him the ultimate compliment. "I think you're getting it, Charles."

Bill Anderson added. "More importantly, I think the horse is."

With work at the restaurant, time spent at the Drieborg farm, shooting and riding, Charles had no time to complain or go out with his friends. He was either too busy or too tired.

But like his sister Eleanor, he grew in skill and in confidence.

A New Life

Graduation time came quickly, too. Eleanor was at the top of her class as expected and began preparations for college. As for Charles, everyone was happy he simply graduated. It seemed he was headed off to work in South Carolina.

As was customary, everyone in the Drieborg, Murphy, Neal and Deeb clan celebrated the event with a gathering. Helen and her family, the Riley's, Stan Killeen and Bill Anderson all joined them, too. Even the Hechts of Lowell were on hand to celebrate their granddaughter' Eleanor's graduation. This time, it was an outdoor affair in the Murphy's big front yard on Cherry Street.

The Neels had begun to cater such events earlier that year as part of their restaurant business., So, they took care of all the food and refreshments. Charles even helped them cater to other graduation parties around town that weekend. He almost missed his and Eleanor's party.

He had matured some over the winter. So, no one heard him complain about working; not once.

He handed his uncle Joe Deeb a fresh beer. "So, Charles, are you really off to work in South Carolina?" his uncle asked.

"Yes, Uncle Joe," He responded. "After we deliver Eleanor to Ann Arbor next week, my parents are going to take me South."

Stan Killeen added his opinion. "More power to ya, lad," He said. "I spent over a month there with your dad a few years back. Bugs and heat nearly did me in. I can't think of a reason to return. But that Edisto Island a' yours was a beautiful spot, I must admit.

"I remember that Townshend Mikell fella you're gonna work for, too,"

"What do you remember about him, Uncle Stan?" Charles asked.

"He was one tough fella," Stan recalled. "He was a reb cavalryman during the war. But he had my respect. He'd go to the wall with ya if he trusted ya and believed you were right. As I recall, he defended his fella' islanders white and black from the marauders, something fierce. You'll do well to follow his lead, believe me."

"Good to know. Thanks," Charles said.

Most everyone brought a present of money for the two graduates. Eleanor gave her gifts to her Uncle Joe for deposit. Charles was advised to open an account in South Carolina when he arrived. His parent's friend Robert Stephan of Charleston would help him with that.

As the afternoon sun went down, Charles helped the Neels make the rounds of the other parties they were catering and to help with the clean-up at the various sites.

Dr. Murphy asked his daughter, "I haven't seen much of Charles. Where's he been keeping himself today, dear?"

"I haven't seen much of him today either, father. He's been busy helping Susan and George manage all the parties they've catering around town. I assume he's part of the clean-up, too."

"Seems like he learned a pretty good lesson back in December from that business at the Polish Falcons bar."

"I think so, too father," Mary Jacqueline said. "Michael was pretty firm with him then. That seemed to have gotten the right response. Thank God."

"Indeed." Her father agreed.

*   *   *

By early evening everyone had left the Murphy's. Once everything was cleaned up, the Drieborg grandparents returned to Lowell. Maxine was put to sleep. But Eleanor and Charles joined classmates at one of the other graduate's home to have their own party.

"When are you leaving for Ann Arbor, Eleanor," one of her girlfriends asked.

"Classes start a week from Monday," She revealed. "So, my parents will take me to my boarding house next Saturday."

"Are you frightened,"

"Not really," Eleanor said. "I expect to be homesick some, at first. But I've been to Ann Arbor so often the past few months, it almost seems like home to me. I'll miss everyone, of course, but I think I'll be too busy for it to affect me much."

Another of her girlfriends asked.

"Is Charles really going to work in South Carolina?"

"He's planning on it," Eleanor revealed.

"Working in all that heat down there," Another girlfriend reminded everyone. "I couldn't stand it."

"I doubt if I could either," Eleanor agreed. "So, we'll see if Charles can, soon enough."

Both of the Drieborg kids arrived home later that night safe and both sober.

Ann Arbor

The train ride to Ann Arbor was uneventful.

Eleanor and Charles sat facing the opposite direction several rows away from their parents.

"Remember that time we went on the train to Washington City, Charles?" Eleanor asked.

"Man, that was years ago. We were just kids then," He recalled. "What made you think of that?"

"I just saw a barn painted red," Eleanor said. "Didn't we have a contest of about which of us could count the most barns painted red, or the most cows, or something?"

"Yah." Charles agreed. "We tried to occupy ourselves with stuff like that. All I clearly remember is that I was hungry and it was going to be a long time before mother would let us get into her picnic basket to have a sandwich."

"I warned you that morning to eat all your oatmeal and toast. But no. You said, you were too excited about the train trip to eat. I remember all your whining about it back then, too."

"I don't whine," Charles protested.

"Not now, maybe," Eleanor chuckled. "But you used to be a champion whiner."

"You sure have a selective memory, Eleanor," Charles protested.

"Maybe I do," She admitted. "But I remember the good stuff too, Charles. We have had a lot of good times, too. Don't you think?"

"Yes, we have,"

"I know I tease you about stuff," She continued. "But I will miss you terribly." She reached over and took his hand in hers.

Charles was sort of embarrassed by her move. It had an intimacy about it that surprised him. It had never happened before.

He looked at Eleanor and saw a tear running down her cheek. Then, she waited a moment before she asked.

"Promise me something, Charles?"

"What's that, Eleanor?"

"You watch yourself down there in South Carolina. You come back to me safe and sound. You hear?"

He had to turn away from her so she wouldn't see the tears welling up in his eyes. He couldn't answer her right away either.

South Carolina

A week later, Charles and his parents were headed for South Carolina. They planned to stop the first night in Pittsburg and the second in Washington City. The last time they were in that city, they stayed at Congressman Kellogg's home. This time, they were welcomed at the home of his daughter Patricia and her husband George Krupp.

After their bags were taken upstairs, they all sat in the front room, visiting.

"Patricia and I thought it would be fun to go for supper at the Oyster Bar restaurant," George suggested. "How does that sound to you?"

"Fine with me," Mike answered. "What do you think of that Mary Jacqueline?"

"I'm fine with it, too. I Haven't had oysters since you took all the ladies there years ago. Remember that, Patricia?"

"You bet, I do," She responded. "That reminds me. How is my old buddy Ethie Faute?"

"She's fine. They were with us last fall in Atlanta," Mary Jacqueline responded. "Mike and several of the old team were working with your father to rescue his deputy, Craig Haynes. By the way, I have a good story to tell you later about Ethie."

"Good. I'll look forward to hearing it. I remember Haynes," Pat said. "Wasn't he the guy who rescued me from Congressman Taft's house a million years ago?"

"The very one."

Charles asked them. "Have I ever had oysters?"

"No," his mother said. "I don't think so."

"Will I like them?"

"You had better, son," Mike told him. "They eat a lot of that kind of seafood on Edisto Island. Might just as well get used to it, now."

"I suppose," Charles said in resignation.

That evening, the two families entered Harvey's Oyster Bar. As usual, it was crowded. Many diners stood at elevated tables.

"Why are they standing up to eat?" Charles asked.

"Those tables are unique to this restaurant, Charles," George told him. "Now they also have regular tables, too. What's your preference? Stand or sit?"

"Charles has worked in his uncle's restaurant for almost a year. But he has never eaten standing up. Have you Charles." His mother told their hosts.

"Well, then," Pat said. 'By all means, let's stand up."

So, they did.

Pretty quickly, a waiter brought over some hot bread, soft butter, salt and pepper. Charles watched his parents to see what they did with these things. Before he could decide another waiter brought over a bucket full of steamed oysters and dumped them on the raised table.

Each adult picked up a shell and sucked the oyster out. Pat sprinkled on some salt first. George buttered a piece of bread and took a bite. His parents did the same. They threw the empty oyster shell on the floor.

So, he followed their lead, sucked an oyster out of its shell and swallowed.

Each of the adults took a swig of beer, too.

"Do you mind if I have a beer, mother? He asked.

"You're of age, son," She responded. "As I recall, you're familiar with beer." she teased. "Go ahead and have one."

Charles smiled. He remembered the episode at the Polish Falcon's bar in Grand Rapids last fall. He and a few of his high school friends had gotten into trouble drinking beer there one night.

Everyone was quiet. They were too busy swallowing oysters, eating bread and chugging their beer. Another bucket was delivered with more bread and butter and of course, another mug of beer.

Patricia and Mary Jacqueline stopped eating first. The three men were working on the third bucket before they were full, too.

"Well, Charles. What do you think?"

"Pretty tasty, father." He said.

"You say they eat this kind of thing on Edisto Island?"

"Yep. They probably harvest the oysters from beds right off the shore," Mike told him. "Another tasty dish I ate when we were on the island was scallops. They probably also harvest them right at the island, too. Pretty tasty stuff as I recall."

The Drieborgs were off to Charleston early the next morning.

Charleston, South Carolina

They arrived late the next evening in Charleston. Mary Jacqueline had spent the war in this city at her father-in-law, Colonel Pope's home. This was the city where Mike first met her. Michael thought of that as they entered the city by train.

"I first saw this lady dressed in black, a young boy at her side, and a Negro-servant girl were about to inter St. Mary's Catholic church for Sunday Mass. But the doorway was blocked by several colored Union soldiers. I could hear the soldiers verbally hassling them.

I was headed for the same doorway. Three of my deputies were behind me. We were all armed.

"You men have a problem with these ladies and the boy? "I asked.

"What's it to you, mister?" A Corporal in a Union uniform challenged.

"I'm Federal Marshal Drieborg," I snapped and raised the rifle I carried.

"Those armed men behind you are my deputies. Order your men to step out of the way and lay down their arms. Now!" I could hear my men chamber a round in their rifles.

I recall the soldier looked at me, confused. But after some hesitation, he did as I ordered.

I then escorted the women and the boy into church and sat in the pew behind them during the service. The servant girl sat in the balcony with the other Negroes in attendance.

After the Mass, we escorted them to their home. While she said thank you, she didn't even give me her name.

Later that day, a messenger came to our boarding house. I was invited to visit that same house by its owner, Colonel Pope. That visit resulted in an invitation to Edisto Island and a second meeting with Mary Jacqueline.

That time, I knew her name. Now, here we are again as man and wife with that same boy, all grown up, returning him to his grandfather's land."

*   *   *

Bob and Mary Alice Stephan met the Drieborg family at the train station. It had only been a few months since they were together last in Atlanta, Georgia. But Mike and Mary Jacqueline were excited to be reunited with their friends.

"So, is this is that young squirt I last saw in Philadelphia years ago?" Bob asked Charles when shaking his hand.

"I guess so, sir," Charles said. "I really don't remember."

"Welcome to my home, young fella, just the same," Bob assured. him. He slapped him on the back as he said it.

It had been a long day for them so, Mary Alice suggested they all eat supper at home that evening.

Afterward, they visited some over coffee for the ladies, brandy and cigars for the men. Charles drank a mug of hot chockalott. As the center of attention, he answered questions about what he was going to do on Edisto Island.

Bob Stephan concluded the evening with,

"Just remember, son," he assured Charles. "Should you need assistance, we are here for you."

"Thank you, sir," Charles responded. "I'll remember that. And, thank you for setting up that account at the bank for me."

Mike told everyone. "Our plan is for Charles to buy what he needs in the way of proper clothing at the island store. Mary Jacqueline will bring the remaining cash back. Bob will deposit it in the account he set up for Charles here in Charleston."

"Happy to do it."

Mary Alice asked. "Are you up early tomorrow?"

"I'm afraid so," Mary Jacqueline told her. "The boat to Edisto leaves rather early."

"If we have breakfast ready by 6:30," She asked. "Will that be early enough?"

"That would work nicely. The boat leave at eight am."

"When will you return to Charleston, Mary Jacqueline?" Bob asked.

"We probably will stay two days on the island. Counting most of one day to get there and another to return, I'd say we should be back here by the end of the week. We'll telegraph you the day before we plan to leave the island."

"That sounds good," Bob Stephan said.

"See you in the morning, everyone," Alize Mary said as the Drieborgs walked up the stairway to their rooms.

Edisto Island

The ocean was rather calm. So, the Drieborgs just lounged on the forward deck of the steamship.

"Uncle stan told me if he never traveled on the ocean again, it would be too soon," Charles said.

"Years ago, on one of our return trips to Charleston from the island, he got very sea sick," Mike remembered." Our Charleston boarding house owner, a Mrs. O'Brien, made Stan drink something to settle his stomach. He said it was awful; worse than the sea sickness. The guys gave him a lot of kidding about his tender stomach after that."

"Stan is quite a character," Mary Jacqueline said.

"You got that right, dear," Mike agreed. "But there's hardly a man I'd rather have by my side in a pinch.

"He and Bill did a nice job teaching Charles horsemanship this past spring."

"They did that, I must agree. I think they took a shine to Charles, too."

"That fondness goes back to our time on Edisto Island years ago.

"Last fall, when those two thugs attacked Charles and his manager. Stan was with us. But my word, was Bill Anderson tough on the guy they caught the night of the attack. Phew! To hear Riley tell it, that guy was lucky Bill didn't break his neck.

"After we returned from Atlanta, we picked up the second thug, Stan was with me, then. Gosh, I had to restrain him from beating the guy to death.

"Yes, dear," Mike concluded. "I think it's safe to say those two guys are fond of Charles."

"I didn't think so when they were making me saddle and ride that darn horse," Charles interrupted. "They were downright mean to me; especially Uncle Stan. I swear, he was going to beat me with the riding crop if I screwed up one more time."

"Did it work, son?" Mike asked, chuckling. "Can you ride with confidence?"

"I suppose," Charles admitted.

"Case closed."

Mary Alice had packed a picnic basket full of goodies for their sea voyage. In the afternoon sun and the gentle roll of the ship, the Drieborgs enjoyed some fried chicken, cheese, crackers and fruit as well as water for Charles and wine for Mike and Mary Jacqueline.

After eating, they all relaxed in the sway of the ship, the warm sun and the gentle breezes of the afternoon. They even slept some.

They arrived at the Edisto Island docks in the late afternoon.

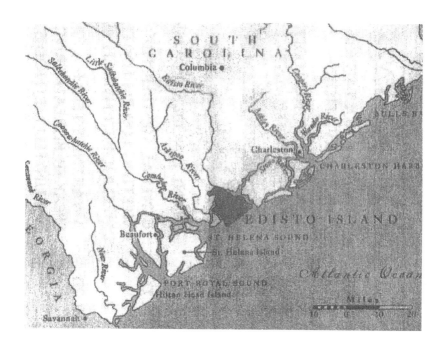

*   *   *

Townshend Mikell met that at the dock.

"Good to see you again, Mike," He said as the two men shook hands.

He turned to Mary Jacqueline, "Mrs. Drieborg," he said bowing slightly. "Welcome back to Edisto Island."

"Please call me Mary Jacqueline," She responded. "It is exciting to be back, Townshend. Can I address you that way?"

"Of course," he smiled. "And, I suppose you are Charles Pope Drieborg?"

"Yes, sir. I am," Charles confirmed shaking Mikell's offered hand.

"But you must also call me Townshend," He instructed. "Everyone on the island does. So, you must as well. All right?"

"Yes, sir. I mean, Townshend."

"Come now," He instructed. "We've a lot to do. So, let us get to the house. Charles, help me get all the bags into the wagon. Mike, you take care of your wife."

Once at the Mikell home and settled in their rooms, Townshend told Mike and Mary Jacqueline.

"We are still in our siesta time of the day. So, please rest for the next couple of hours. I'll call you for supper at five. Then we'll talk.

"Charles," he directed. "You come with me."

In their room, Mary Jacqueline said. "That was sort of abrupt of Townshend. Didn't you think, Michael?"

"What I think, dear," Mike decided. "Is that Townshend is telling Charles that he is in charge on Edisto, not us. Besides, I suspect he has some things he wants to show Charles before our son must decide to stay here or leave with us when we return to Charleston."

"I suppose," Mary Jacqueline said. She sat on their bed and unlaced her shoes. "Oh, that feels good." She lay back and dozed off.

Mike decided he wasn't tired. He quietly left the room and went outside to sit on the porch. There, he lite a pipe and just look around. Everything was quiet and no one was moving about.

"Oh, ya. Its siesta time," He remembered.

Instead of relighting his pipe, he lay his head back on the high-back cane chair and fell dozed off.

*   *   *

Before he knew it, Mike felt someone nudging him. It was Charles.

"Father," Charles said. "Townshend wants you to awaken mother and join us in the front room."

A bit embarrassed being caught catnapping by his son, he got up and went upstairs to get Mary Jacqueline.

They joined their host and Charles as requested.

"Cook will call us when our meal is ready," Townshend informed them. "So, I thought we could take this time to talk. First though, I'd like to introduce you to my wife, Charlotte.:

Introductions were made all 'round before the men went out to the front porch.
Charlotte and Mary Jacqueline went on a tour of the house.

"Just in case you're wondering, I took Charles around and introduced him to some of my people and a few of the group leaders. He had a chance to pick out a horse for his personal use. And, I wanted to give him a chance to ask whatever questions he had of me before we had this meeting.

"Did I answer all the questions you had, Charles?" he asked.

"Yes, sir, I mean Townshend. I did although I expect to have many more in the future."

"As expected," Townshend assured. him.

316

"Let me begin with you, Mike," Townshend said. "Has Charles had an opportunity to learn to fire his rifle?"

"Yes," Mike responded. "We've taken him into the woods and to a range as well. He needs more practice with moving targets, but he is fine with the basics of rifle use and care."

"Good. How about horsemanship skills?"

"Two of my deputies who were in my cavalry troop worked with him throughout the spring. They think he has learned the basics of horse care and riding pretty well. He has not had an opportunity to work with a team of riders, however."

"We'll take care of that," Townshend responded.

Mary Jacqueline walked in accompanied by a blond-haired lady, Townshend's wife.

The men stood and Townshend greeted them.

"Please join us ladies, He asked. "I see you ladies have met. Mike and Charles, this is my wife Charlotte. We were just getting started. Please have a seat."

Mary Jacqueline got into the conversation at this point. "Did I hear you say that Charles will be part of a team? What is that about?"

"Let me be clear about this, Mrs. Drieborg," Townshend revealed. "We have a colony, a community of sorts here that is very unique in South Carolina. While you can see the racial divide here, we work together irrespective of race. Our accounts are kept accurately and everyone shares in the profits, have political meetings and vote at elections for the candidates of their choice. We are all equal before the law and have a voice in the governance of our island and our economy.

"Unfortunately, our system is unique in South Carolina. Many don't want the colored's treated as equals in any way. So, we have been attacked by raiders who wish to destroy this way of life. We must, therefore patrol our boarders constantly. Everyone here can ride and shoot. Charles too, must be prepared to play a role in that defense, if necessary."

"Oh, my Lord," Charles's mother exclaimed.

"Are you talking about the Klan?" Mike asked.

"The Klan is one such group, Mike. After the feds passed a law in 1871 pretty much outlawing that terror group, they just changed the name to Red Shirts. In South Carolina, we also have other groups of armed men called Regulators or Marauders and just plain outlaws who wish to steal from us or to destroy what we have here.

"If Charles is to live here, he must embrace a role in the defense of the Edisto community or he cannot stay here. He must also be willing to work every day, shoulder to shoulder with the rest of us, whites as well as blacks, in the support of our economy.

"You see, everyone one contributes here. Just like in the slavery days when each man woman and child had daily tasks. We still do that on the island today. Tasks are assigned each person according to their age, strength, skills and gender just as they were in the pre-emancipation days.

"You, Charles have no special skills. You're not a carpenter, an artisan or a man skilled as a blacksmith, not even an agricultural worker. But if you're willing to work and learn, you have value and are welcome to this community."

"Are you willing to do that, Charles?" His father asked.

"I am willing, father," He answered. And, looking his mother in the eye he added. "Whether I am able to shoulder my share of the work, like Townshend said I must. I don't know yet."

"Is that good enough for you, Townshend?" Mike asked.

"For a start it is. More importantly, it is an honest answer. And, I accept it."

"So," Mike continued. "Let me review the plan you two propose. Charles will work with you during the next two weeks. His mother will stay with friends in Charleston until the end of that period.

"Beyond that, if he desires, and you accept his offer, he will stay and work until the fall harvest is completed as a full working member of your community here on Edisto. Then, he will return North for a Christmas break. If all remains well, he will return South for the planting season."

"I think I understand what is being suggested, Townshend? Do you, Charles?" Mike asked.

Charles said, yes.

Mike turned to his wife, "You haven't said much, dear. What do you think?"

"I'd like to talk with you alone, Michael."

*   *   *

Townshend and Charles left the room for the front porch.

"Michael," Mary Jacqueline began. "I am frightened to death for Charles." She dabbed her tears with a handkerchief.

319

"For us to get on that boat tomorrow and leave him here, is frightening for me as well." Mike responded.

"How do we handle that fear, Michael?"

"As hard as it is for us, dear," Michael. "if Charles is allowed a chance to succeed, we must allow him to fail. I can't think of a more qualified mentor than Townshend Mikell. I can't think of a person in whose hands I would feel more confident to place our son's life than Townshend Mikell."

Mary Jacqueline responded. "I know that at some point, Charles must be allowed to be free of our control. But this is so far away and so dangerous, Michael. Will I ever see him again?"

"Now you know how your parents probably felt when you married Charles Pope at your son's age. Back in 1861, with war eminent, you left home with a virtual stranger and went South to live in the very city where the war began. Don't you think they were frightened, too?"

"I hadn't thought of that."

"My parents saw me go off to war at the very age Charles is right now. How they must have dreaded that. I know my mother did. Or, how they must have worried when my seventeen-year-old brother ran away from home to join the cavalry out West in Indian country.

"We must all face this moment, sweetheart; just as our parents did."

Mike moved to her side and put his arms around her.

"I know, but it is so hard," Mary Jacqueline complained.

"That's just part of being a loving parent, dear," Mike said. "We have to let go."

"I know you're right, Michael."

And so, it was. The rest of the evening was spent touring the island. Townshend showed Charles and his parents the various work areas: the fields devoted to long stem cotton, corn, the rice paddies and the Indigo growing area; the grazing fields for their cattle and sheep; the barns with their milking cows, goats and pigs; their barnyard with chickens, and ducks.

He drove them around in a buggy and Charles rode his newly assigned horse, Rebel. After sundown, they gathered in the main house before a fire. Mary Jacqueline told Charles stories of his grandfather Pope and of the struggles on the island after the war. Townshend told him the Indian history of the island and of his early eighteenth-century ancestor settlers.

Work Begins

At five in the morning Townshend had Charles awake and at the cow barn with the milking team. Charles's parents were still asleep.

After his parents left later that morning, he sat Charles down and laid out a plan.

"During the next two weeks, you are going to work with several teams. For starters, you will continue to work with the morning milking crew. So, right after you have breakfast tomorrow, you will report for your first work assignment of the day in the cow barn, just like you did this morning. The team leader will assign you your work there.

"With the completion of your work there, you will ride over to the rice paddies. Since planting time last spring, that crop is well along in its growth pattern. We won't harvest rice till the fall. But right now, the paddies have to be drained, cultivated, weeded and then flooded again. The team leader, Mr. Curtis, will assign you your tasks for today when you report to him there.

"You and I will meet for the noon dinner and talk during our siesta time about your other work assignments. Any questions right now?"

"How will I know it's five in the morning?"

"A bell will ring. But for now, I'll wake you, just like I did this morning."

"Then, I don't have any questions that my team leaders won't answer when I report to them."

"Correct," Townshend agreed. "Right now, let's go to the General Store so you can get the proper hat, clothing and shoes. Then, I want you to go right over to the rice paddies. That's where my father had me start working when I was a teenaged boy. After your work is completed there, return here for your noon meal and siesta. Got it?"

"Yes, I got it," Charles and Townshend left the house and rode to the store.

"I don't have any money to pay for this stuff," Charles said.

"You mother already set up an account for you," Townshend told him. "You're all set for now. If your purchases exceed the money in your account, the balance will be paid from your share of income at the end of the season."

"I understand." Charles said.

*   *   *

His work in the rice paddy was rude introduction to life on Edisto Island. Charles had to stand in water up to his knees pulling weeds from between the rice shoots. Bent over in the hot sun, this work was not pleasant for anyone especially for a light skinned Caucasian boy not used to bending over.

But until the noon bell rang, Charles kept at it.

He didn't say a word about the task to Townshend when they met after dinner. But Charles was certainly ready for his siesta. Before he went to his room to rest, Townshend told him.

"This evening you and I are going to ride the road patrol until sunset. Be sure to bring your rifle with you, fully loaded. Then, when our shift is over, we'll come back here and take care of our mounts. Your work day will be over. I'll still have some book work to finish. But I suggest you get to bed. Five in the morning will come sooner than you can imagine."

That evening, Charles was shown the road defenses. The road to Edisto Island was a narrow strip of land with swamp on both sides. So, Mikell had the road blocked with a heavy gate. Downed trees and brush were placed behind the gate. Two armed men were on duty 'round the clock behind the blocked entrance.

"All of us take a two hour turn on guard duty here every week; women are included," He explained. "Tomorrow evening I'll show you our ocean side coastal defenses."

"Have you been attacked before?" Charles asked.

"Yes, we have," He was told. "Unfortunately, we were not well prepared. And, as a result, several people were killed, some of our buildings were burned and some of our stock was stolen. We are determined that will not happen again."

Townshend was right, Charles was not ready to get up when the morning bell sounded.

Charleston

Mary Jacqueline was at the Stephan home in Charleston. Michael had returned to Michigan.

"If I know the type of work done on Edisto Island, it will be a couple of weeks at least for Charles just to get used to getting up at five in the morning let alone adjusting to the back-breaking work probably required of him."

"He has never gotten out of bed that early," Mary Jacqueline told the Bob and Mary Alice Stephan. "In fact, either Eleanor or I had to pull of his covers and threaten to throw a pail of water on him just to get him up for school."

"He worked there for, what? Five days?" Mary Alice thought out loud. "I can't imagine how sore he must be with all that field work Mikell has made him do."

"It's sort of strange," Mary Jacqueline went on. I sort of want to laugh and cry at the same time. I feel for him, but I want to laugh too at the image my son picking cotton or doing most any kind of physical labor. If Charles had been raised on a farm, like Michael was, maybe. But it has been a pampered city boy."

"Until now," Bob Stephan reminded her. "I suspect he'll do just fine. Mikell is a good man. He'll look after you son. I wouldn't worry."

"Aside from all of that, I worry about the Klan or the Regulators or whatever they call themselves. Mikell told us he has his people guarding the island round the clock."

"What is that all about?"

Mary Alice said, "Unfortunately, the Klan is really big in South Carolina. So are the other armed bands of men."

"What is that all about?" Mary Jacqueline asked.

"Let me refresh our wine, and I'll explain a few things to you," Bob told her.

After he had done so, he returned to his seat and began.

"Folks up North think the war ended after General Lee surrendered what was left of his army ad Appomattox in April 1865 and General Johnston surrendered his army to Sherman in May of the same year. The war between armies in the field did end then. But the war of southern rebellion did not.

"To force the Southern states back into the union, Federal armies destroyed most of an entire generation of southern young men, our economy and our social structure."

"Don't forget, Robert," Mary Jacqueline said. "I lost my southern bred husband and brother-in-law fighting for the South. I experienced the entire war here in Charleston. And I spent most every night huddled in the cellar of Colonel Pope's house while Lincoln's people bombed the city."

"Excuse me, I didn't mean to talk down to you Mary Jacqueline," He responded. "I just wanted to begin my answer about the Klan at the beginning."

"I didn't take it that way, Robert. Pardon me for interrupting," She responded. "I guess the pain of that time is closer to the surface than I realized. Please continue."

"It must be understood that only the military battles ended in 1865. The fighting did not.

"When the Union armies and the Union government ended African slavery, they took away our labor force and turned our social structure upside-down. In so doing, they removed all the controls we had over four million ignorant largely unskilled Negroes.

"And, since the fighting stopped in 1865, the same men in Washington have passed laws to create a new social order for the South. They have failed in this effort except at the point of a bayonet.

"We in the South, have continued fighting for control, too. We call it a people's war. The Klan, the Regulators other para-military organizations represent only the visible elements of resistance. But every single white person, rich or poor resists the imposition of a Northern peace."

"Excuse me, Robert," Mary Jacqueline interrupted. "How can you oppose everyone being able to vote in elections?"

"Ideally, no one can," He responded. "Did you know that Negro men are allowed to vote in only five of the northern states?"

"I didn't know that."

"According to the Congressional Radicals, the real purpose of granting voting rights to all adult males, except American Indians, is to assure Republican control of the Federal government. You see, they expect that the newly freed Negros will vote Republican, if they vote.

"Without their vote, Southern white males will certainly be the ones who select local officials, state officials and members of Congress. That means Democrats will win those seats. Also, the 13th amendment requires that all Negro adult males be counted as a full voter for purposes of assigning congressional seats. This would give Southern states more seats in the House of

Representatives than they had before the war. Without the Negro vote, most all of those seats are expected to be filled by Democrats. Combined with members of that party from the North, the Democrats might control the House of Representatives.

"And, even worse," Robert continued, "Most of those newly elected representatives from these new Congressional districts would be filled with men who led the Confederacy in one way or another; even former military leaders."

"So, that justifies the brutal tactics of the Klan?" Mary Jacqueline asked.

"You got me there," Robert admitted. "I can't condone the terror that is going on. I'm just hoping you understand why it is happening."

Mary Alice interrupted. "Right now, Robert is representing a Negro who is trying to sue a white man for damages. "

"It's a simple matter of fairness," Robert Stephan explained. "The law should be applied fairly. The facts of the injury should determine the outcome of the court case. If the man I am representing were a white man, it would be an open and shut case based on that evidence. He would win his case and the matter would move on to decide the amount of damages that must be paid my client. But my client is a Negro. So, different rules are in play."

"Sounds unfair, to me," Mary Jacqueline said.

"Exactly my point," Robert said. "The law should be color-blind.

"Let me ask you something, Mary Jacqueline. Do you thing such an unfair situation would ever exist in a Michigan court?"

"I don't know."

"In my preparation for this case, I have reviewed a lot of decisions made in Northern states since the war ended. Most of them are as unfair to Negro complaints as in our courts in South Carolina."

"Oh, my goodness," Mary Jacqueline said.

"As for the questionable tactics of the Klan," Stephan continued. "The Union League is a para-military force that operates in the South. It applies similar terror tactics against whites in the South as the Klan applies to Negroes. In the south, the Union League is to the Republican party what the Klan is to the Democratic party."

"The leader of the League that operated in the Atlanta area tried to kidnap us in Macon, didn't he?" Mary Alice asked.

"I remember that," Mary Jacqueline said.

"On another matter," Robert Stephan went on. "What we in South Carolina call the 'Black Codes' have set up a system that is very biased against the Negro taking his place as an equal member of society."

"How so?" Mary Jacqueline asked.

"Take land ownership, for example," Stephan said. "Without the consent of a Judge, a Negro male cannot own property. A white man can, but not a Negro."

"But I thought Negro men owned land on Edisto Island," Mary Alice protested. "I think you told me they do."

"Sort of, dear," He told the two ladies.

"How can a man, sort of, own land," Mary Jacqueline asked. "I'm confused about that."

"I have worked with Townshend Mikell on this subject," Robert answered. "We have a District judge who resides on the island. He works with me so that Negro males who reside on the island can become part or full owners of land. So, some own as much as several hundred acres. Others only own their own house and the surrounding plots of land, maybe an acre or two.

Organized Opposition

"What the hell are we gonna do about Mikell's operation on Edisto Island?" Wade Hampton IV asked the chairman of the group. He was the eldest son of the new South Carolina governor, Wade Hampton III. He and his younger brother had been leaders of the Red Shirts. This was a large South Carolina rifle club. This club was instrumental in his father's election victory several months earlier.

The new governor had called this meeting. For security reasons, they were meeting at the Brick House, a well-known Charleston brothel. The owner was Grace Peixotto was an old friend of the governors. She also served what was considered the best sea-food in Charleston.

Wade Hampton was a rather short man who had led the cavalry forces of the Army of Northern Virginia late in the war. He had been one of three who reached the rank of Lieutenant General despite having no prior military experience. After Appomattox, he led the cavalry unit serving under General Joe Johnston in North Carolina. He was present at Johnston's surrender in May of 1865 of this last remaining Confederate army. Since that time, he led the resistance in South Carolina to Federal occupation and to the Reconstruction acts of the Republican Radicals in Washington City.

Before he ran for governor in 1876, he led the Democratic Party organization and their Red Shirt Rifle Clubs in South Carolina. These clubs took over the terror campaign against Republicans and freedmen in that state after the passage of the Ku Klux Act of 1872.

"The last time you raided the island, your attack failed. It was poorly organized," The governor reminded everyone. "You took

331

them by surprise but you didn't follow-up. You had them on their heels. But you let them off the hook and Mikell's people counter-attacked. They kicked your butts, in fact."

"We didn't know they had all that ordinance," One of the other men replied. "They had repeating rifles and they even had an artillery piece, for God's sake."

"What about the economic blockade?" Hampton continued. "How is that going?"

He was referring to the usual economic pressures the Red Shirts used in the Charleston area.

His second eldest son, John Preston replied. "That's been pretty effective, sir. We've put the clamps on any locals buying Edisto's agricultural goods or selling them any manufactured goods, either." He assured the group. "But that Edisto bunch is pretty self-reliant."

"So, how are they getting manufactured items?" Hampton pressed. "Surly they don't mine iron or copper ore on the island. Also, how are they selling their cotton and rice? Who's buying their products to provide the funds they use to pay their property taxes or pay for manufactured goods they do manage to get delivered to the island?"

"Ships come in at night, Governor." His son, William Preston replied. "The island has a docking facility that can accommodate most any moderate sized ocean-going ship. So, they have been able to get their products to Bermuda and thus they have access to both the Northern and European markets."

"Have you tried to blockade their docks with picket ships?"

"No."

"In the up-country, J Banks, James Avery, Dr. Braxton and Col. Pickins have completely shut down the Federal programs and enforced the Black Codes. Every businessman is one of our certificate holders and most of the blacks wear our red shirts. Edisto is the lone hold-out. This is not acceptable.

"The next time we meet, gentlemen," the governor said. "I want to hear that you've shut down those docks and with it their access to the outside world, too. Understood?"

"Yes, sir," His son, Wade said. "We understand."

"Unless there's something else that can't wait, gentlemen," The governor told everyone. "Grace has some fresh oysters for me." Besides owning the Brick House, Grace was also the madam of the ladies who entertained the gentlemen of Charleston.

"While you enjoy your meal, sir," his youngest son told the governor. "I'm going to enjoy one of those new girls Mrs. Peixotto has in from the up-country."

"Suit yourself, son."

The meeting was adjourned and the men left.

Edisto Island

Later in the week, Townshend asked Charles to join him for the evening meal.

As he entered the sitting-room, Charles was surprised to see Townshend pouring a glass of cider for a Negro man.

"Charles," Townshend greeted. "I want you to meet my other guests."

Charles walked over to the five men.

"This is Doctor Morgan," Charles. "He runs our medical clinic on the island."

"Nice to meet you, Doctor," Charles said shaking the outstretched hand of the doctor.

"This is Tom Curtis," Townshend continued. "You were going to meet him the other day. What I didn't tell you then, is that Tom has managed your family's cotton land and rice paddies for the past ten years."

Mr. Curtis shook hands with Charles. "I didn't get to meet you the other day, Charles when you reported for work at the rice paddies. My supervisor told me you're a good worker."

"Nice to meet you Mr. Curtis," Charles responded. "There doesn't seem to be an easy way to work in the rice paddies. It's darn hard."

Townshend laughed aloud. "My father started me as a boy working our rice fields. I've never forgotten standing in water up to my knees in the hot sun. You're right, Charles. It's darn tough work."

Townshend turned to the Negro man standing by his side.

"This is John Thorpe, Charles."

Thorpe extended his hand in greeting. Charles reacted by taking it in his own right hand in the typical gentlemen's greeting.

"Nice to see you again Mr. Pope, or should I say, Mr. Drieborg?" Thorpe asked.

"In South Carolina, Pope will do, sir. I'm sorry, sir," Charles said hesitantly. "I don't remember meeting you."

"I suppose not, son," Thorpe agreed. "You were only a tyke of nine or so when I last saw you on our island. Colonel Pope and your mother brought you here from his home in Charleston. That was the summer you and your mother left with Marshal Drieborg to go North."

"I don't remember much of that, sir."

"Please call me, John. After all, Townshend has asked me to teach you how to manage a General Store and run a cotton gin. So, we'll soon be working together rather closely."

"I think you have done a good job milking cows, Charles." Townshend chuckled. "I also need you to learn to do other things, and I trust John here to teach you. I just don't have the time to personally spend with you on everything."

"I understand, sir," Charles said. "Thank you, Mr. Thorpe. I mean John."

All four men chuckled at this.

"Here, Charles," Townshend offered. "Have a glass of cider. Just sip it now, it's pretty strong stuff. We don't have wine around here anymore. So, we make our own supper drink just like our forefathers did in the colonial days during the boycotts of imports from England."

"Thank you, sir," Charles said taking the goblet of citer.

Another man walked into the room.

"Here is someone else I want you to meet, Charles. This is Richard Dennett."

"A pleasure to meet you, sir," Charles said shaking Mr. Dennett's outstretched hand.

"You're Marshal Drieborg's son?" he asked Charles.

"I am his adopted son, yes sir."

"I met with him in Washington City back in 1868 to discuss his fact-finding mission into the South for the House Judiciary committee. I found him very astute."

"I'm sure he would appreciate your compliment, sir," Charles judged. "Why did he meet with you then?"

"I had just returned from the South. For two years I traveled the post-war South on a fact-finding mission for the Nation magazine. I wrote articles on attitudes prevalent among men and women, white and black, in the South. My articles were then published by my magazine in the North.

"His articles included interviews Richard conducted right here on Edisto, Charles," Townshend said.

"Yes, that's true," Dennett agreed. "It was interesting that I found quite a difference in the attitudes expressed by people here than elsewhere."

"What did you find sir?" Charles asked.

"The people on Edisto were much more positive in their outlook for the future." Dennette answered. "The trust between former slaves and the white land owners they were working for was much more positive here as well."

Charlotte Mikell appeared in the doorway,

"Gentlemen," she announced. "Supper is served."

"Thank you, dear," Townshend answered. "We best join the ladies in the dining room, gentlemen or we are in deep trouble."

A light skinned Negro lady was already standing beside the table.

"Charles," Townshend announced. "This is Mrs. Thorpe."

"Good evening, Mrs. Thorpe." Charles said bowing slightly.

"I remember you when you used to frolic on the beach with my son, Luke."

Charles remembered. "Is he still on the island, ma'am?"

John Thorpe answered. "You'll meet him tomorrow at my cotton field. In fact, he is also the one who will teach you how to run my cotton gin. Lord knows, I don't know how."

"You're being modest that's true, John," Townshend chided his friend. "Aren't you the one who built tit?"

"Well, yes," He answered. "But Luke has made so many improvements to the thing, I don't understand much about running it anymore."

Everyone laughed at that. They knew he was proud of his son's mechanical abilities.

"I've had Luke work on my cotton gin many times," Townshend said. "I swear, it wouldn't be operating if he weren't around to fix it."

Townshend stood. "Please join me in a toast everyone," he announced. "To the continued success of the Edisto community." Everyone raised their glass of cider to join him.

"Where is Susan tonight, Townshend?" Mrs. Thorpe asked.

"She should be here any moment." Charlotte Mikell told everyone. "Some last-minute thing at the store. You know all about that, Mable."

"I surly do," She answered.

"Speak of the devil, here she is now."

In walked Susan Mikell.

"Susan," her mother said. "You have not actually met our guests from the North. This is Charles Pope. Colonel Pope was his grandfather. He's working with us now. And, this is Mr. Richard Dennett a writer who is visiting from Boston."

Both men stood as Susan approached.

"Nice to meet you Susan," Charles said.

"Likewise, Miss Mikell." Dennett said.

"Wow!" Charles thought. *"She's a beauty."*

Sure enough, Susan Mikell was about five-foot five-inches tall, a brunette with bright blue eyes and a dazzling smile.

"She sure fills out that dress she's wearing."

"Nice to meet you as well, gentlemen." She responded.

And, in her characteristic direct manner, she asked, Charles. "Mr. Pope, can I call you Charly?"

"Nobody else does, but you can if I can call you Susan."

"You got a deal, Charly." She said.

During the meal Charles was rather quiet. He listened to the conversation about island life. He heard of goings on in the Negro section and the White section; how the crops were doing and expectations for the coming fall harvest.

"Tell me of life in the North, young man," Mable Thorpe asked.

"I'm not sure where to start, ma'am," He sort of stammered.

"I recall your father had a daughter your age. What of her?"

"She and I grew up together. We both graduated from Secondary School last June, too. She's at the University of Michigan studying to be a doctor."

"My goodness," Mrs. Morgan exclaimed. "I didn't know women were allowed to study for that profession."

"My sister is a determined person," Charles boasted. "The University of Michigan started admitting women to their medical school a couple of years ago. She is just taking advantage of it. Last year, she worked in my grandfather Murphy's medical office after school. She also accompanied her grandmother, who is a healer, on her calls in the farm community near us. One way or another, my sister will become a doctor, I'm sure of it."

"Were you close, Charles?"

"Yes, ma'am," Charles said. "We shared most everything; walked to school together every day and talked over most everything. I couldn't match her with the books, so she helped me a lot in that regard. In fact, Townshend, you may not know it, but she helped me write all of the letters I sent you."

"That just demonstrates how smart you are, Charles," He said laughing.

"Did you do any work up North as hard as working in a rice paddy like you did this morning?" Tom Curtis asked.

"After school I worked at my uncle George's restaurant as a busboy. I thought that was hard work until I got on this island. I never imagined how hard work could be until Townshend had me milking cows and working in a rice field."

Everyone laughed at that.

Mrs. Morgan returned the conversation to Charles's sister, Eleanor.

"Do you miss your sister?" Mrs. Morgan asked.

"If I wasn't so busy and tired most of the time, I suppose I would," Charles answered to everyone's laughter. "It will be good to see her in December."

"And, your mother? How is she?" Charlotte Mikell asked.

"She's fine, ma'am," Charles assured them. "She is pretty busy taking care of my younger sister, Maxine and worrying about me."

And, so the conversation went. Over desert of peaches and cream, Mrs. Thorpe asked about of Amos Smith.

"He's a successful businessman in Grand Rapids, ma'am," Charles told her.

"He was my son Luke's father, you know."

"No, I didn't know, ma'am," Charles admitted.

"When he accompanied Marshal Drieborg here ten years ago," she revealed. "I was already formally married to Mr. Thorpe. As a young girl, Amos and I had lived together on the Richard Pope plantation over in the back-country, years earlier. But Amos and I were never formally married. I was sold to Colonel Pope just after the war began. At the time I was pregnant. So, Luke was born after I left there.

"Amos visited here with your step-father and then left with Marshal Drieborg. I lost track of him after that."

"Yes, ma'am," Charles acknowledged. "My father sent Amos North after that. Amos settled in Grand Rapids, Michigan and worked at my Uncle George's restaurant as a cook. After the Marshal and my mother settled there, Amos met my nanny, Helen.

'They married a few years ago. I was the ring bearer and my father was Best Man. Amos and Helen bought my uncle's old bakery and house and now have a son and a daughter. He's a big success with his soups. He sells them to all the restaurants and they are a hit at most private homes, too. Aside from the cooking, I think Helen sort of runs the business, though."

"Is she a nice lady?" Mrs. Thorpe asked.

"She's a very nice person," Charles revealed. "She lived at my mother's home and cooked for my family when we first arrived in Michigan. She would get after me to get out of bed, even on the coldest winter days. And pickup my room, boy, she sure harped on that. She had a sharp tongue.

"She would remind me all the time, "I ain't your salve no more."

Everyone laughed at that.

"Mable Thorn commented, "I can identify with that comment. In fact, I can remember saying that very thing to Colonel Pope a time or two."

Charles went on, "Then, Helen would walk my sister and I to St. Andrew's primary school every morning, rain or shine. When we got there, Sister Aquinas would let her stay as a student herself. Helen learned to read, write and cast accounts right along with us. After school we three would often do homework together. She wouldn't let me get away with anything. She was worse than my mom or dad about that.

"She has a home of her own now in Grand Rapids, but still comes to our house in the morning after she walks her two kids to the same school we went to. She and my mom are very close."

"Wasn't Helen your mother's personal slave when she lived in Colonel Pope's Charleston home?" Townshend Mikell asked.

"Yes, she was," Charles answered. "I'm told Helen was in the room when I was born and was my nanny after that. So, I think she was assigned to my mom shortly after my father brought my mother to Charleston when they were first married.

"Do you mind if I ask a question, Mr. Thorpe?" Charles asked.

"Not at all, Charles. What is it?"

"Does Luke know about Amos?"

John Thorpe answered. "He knows that I'm not his real father. But he doesn't know about what happened to his biological father; mainly because we didn't know what happened to Amos."

"If he asks me about Amos," Charles asked. "Do you want me to tell him or not?"

Mrs. Thorpe answered Charles this time. "Thank you for asking, Charles. Feel free to tell him." As John told you, we haven't told him anything, because we didn't know anything. I would like him to know that his father is such a success."

"By the way, Charles," Townshend Mikell said. "While you will be working with Luke in the Thorn cotton fields, you'll also continue to work in your rice paddies.

Susan Mikell broke into the conversation. "I thought Charly was going to work with me in our store, father."

"I was just getting to that, dear." Townshend cautioned his daughter. "I also want you to work one day a week with my daughter in our store, Charles. And on Saturdays, I want you to work at my grist mill, too."

"I see."

"I want you to know all aspects of the business on Edisto. I can't think of people better to teach you than Curtis or Mable Thorne in the cotton fields or in the rice paddies and Susan at the general store and grist mill."

Townshend went on. "After Mable arrived on Edisto, she was made the Driver on Colonel Pope's cotton fields and rice paddies.

She assigned daily work tasks and looked after the welfare of the slave workers.

"When Union forces took over control here, she continued doing that. Her workers grew a lot of cotton and rice for export and kept the island's Negro population focused on working the fields and surviving on their own. She did a marvelous job in my opinion.

"After your lands here were returned to him, Colonel Pope returned to Edisto in 1866. Then, she continued to work for him as a free person. They worked together in harmony until he passed away in 1870."

"That's true, Townshend," Mrs. Thorpe responded. "The Colonel and I worked together for many years. He was a gentleman. I mourned his passing. Thank you for complimenting my work here, Townshend. You know what it takes to supervises a successful cotton and rice plantation. Your high opinion means a lot to me."

"It is well deserved, Mable. Well deserved.

"Now she runs an honest general store for all the freedmen and their families." Her husband John commented.

"John," interrupted Townshend Mikell. "Are you suggesting that I don't run an honest store?"

"Not at all, Townshend," John said with a chuckle. "Free Negros on the island trust Mable because she was and is one of them. Their experience with whites before the war is remembered as a bad time, a slavery time. But I never heard a bad work said about how you run your store, Townshend."

"Thank you, John," Mikell responded. "I hope you never do."

Charles had a question. "Mr. Dennett," he began. "What were you writing about in the South after the war?"

"Townshend," Richard Dennett began. "Is it all right that I go back a few years to answer the question?"

"Certainly, Richard."

"After I graduated from Harvard, I went to Beaufort Island and helped on the Royal Experiment that began there after the Union forces took over the island in 1862. I spent two years there as a cotton plantation superintendent. Conditions there were no so different from what was going on at Edisto Island.

"After the war, the Nation magazine sent me into the South to report on conditions there. One of my stops was here on Edisto Island. In fact, I became pretty well acquainted with both John Thorn and Townshend Mikell at that time"

Charlotte Mikell added. "Richard stayed in our home during his time here."

"That's correct, Charlotte. During my stay here, I had long talks with your grandfather Colonel Pope, Colonel Joseph Jenkins and his wife Martha as well as with former Governor William Aiken and his wife Adele. What a fascinating trio those two men were. They were Southern were patriots of the highest order.

"But they were quite different in two other respects. Your former governor Aiken, opposed secession while Colonel Jenkins was an unrepentant Confederate. Colonel Pope was a pragmatist. He and Aiken accepted the military loss and the resultant upheaval in the social order. The Colonel Jenkins recognized the military defeat but would not accept emancipation and the social upheaval. The other two men made their peace with the new order.

"In my reports to the Nation, I concluded that the views of the Colonel Jenkins pretty much reflected the attitude of most white males in the deep South.

"My editors also held the believe that the freed slave would respond with energy and enthusiasm as a free laborer. They also thought, that the indolence reported about the Negro worker was the natural result of the condition of slavery. Southern white men told me in every part of the former Confederacy that left to his own devices, the freedman would not work but was lacy and indolent.

"But ten years later, the same editors have now concluded that the Negro has not responded properly to the free market labor system but needs stern direction. So, they now believe Colonel Jenkins was right about that.""

"What of our Edisto Island community, Mr. Dennett?" Dr. Morgan asked. "Would you consider that we are the exception to the rule?"

"Yes, I do," Dennett responded. "You have something unique here; a coalition of sorts, a working relationship of the two races that has been demonstrably successful.

"Unfortunately, the white mainland community wishes it to fail." Dennett continued.

Charles asked. "Why wouldn't everyone cheer it's success?"

"Because, Charles," Dennett told him. "The success of a biracial community such as you have here is a threat to a white dominated one. That's why the South Carolina the white elite wants you to fail. That's why their Klan wants to destroy you."

The late afternoon siesta time was coming to a close and so was the evening meal at Charlotte Mikell's home.

Townshend reminded Charles, "You best get to your post, Charles. I believe you have patrol duty on the beach tonight."

346

"Yes, sir. I do, "He responded.

John Thorn remarked. "I think Luke does, too. It's about time you two got reacquainted."

"Charles?"

"Yes, sir?"

"Tomorrow you will continue to work in the cow barn. After you're finished in the morning with that assignment, report to Mrs. Thorn at her general store. She and Luke will work out a schedule for your working with them for the next few weeks."

"Yes, sir," Before he left the Mikell home, Charles said good evening to his hostess.

"Good night Mrs. Mikell," Charles said. "Thank for the super meal. Nice to have met you Mrs. Thorn, Mr. Thorn, dr. and Mrs. Morgan, Mr. Curtis."

"Good night, Charles," Charlotte Mikell said. "You are very welcome, anytime."

"Don't I get a good night, too, Charly" Susan asked coquettishly.

"Last but not least, Susan. Nice to have met you." Charles answered.

"I'll see you in the morning, young man," Mrs. Thorn said.

"Nice to have met you, son," John Thorn said.

After Charles left, John added,

"I think you've got a keeper there, Townshend."

"I think so, too." Charlette told her guests.

347

"So far, so good," Townshend said. "We'll see if he decided to stick it out."

"I'm guessing, he will," John Thorn said. "His comment about seeing his sister in December said a lot. I believe he has some steel in that backbone of his."

"We'll see, John," Townshend said. "We'll see."

"I think he's cute," Susan whispered aloud enough for everyone to hear.

"Well you little dickens!" her mother said, chuckling as she did. "I noticed that, too."

Ann Arbor, Michigan

Eleanor Drieborg was exhausted. It was nearly midnight as she got into her bed. She had been studying her anatomy text since she finished supper. A big test tomorrow in front of everyone. She was determined the professor would not stump her on any anatomy question.

As she drifted off to sleep, she thought of Charles.

"I wonder how that scamp is doing. As busy as' I've been these past few weeks, I miss him. Look after him, Lord. Please look after him down there and bring him home safely to me."

She was up early, and in the kitchen, fixing her breakfast. Even then, she had her anatomy notes on the table for last minute review as she had her coffee and toast. It would be hot in their classroom today, so she dressed with only the minimal underclothing.

She wasn't surprised that she was the first of the freshman students to be called on. This professor seemed determined to challenge the females in his class.

"Miss Drieborg?" He began. "Describe the inner ear for us this morning."

Eleanor took a deep breath and described the various bones of the inner ear without making a mistake.

"Very good," He admitted. "Now tell your fellow students, the various problems a person can have with his hearing."

"That's sort of a stupid question," She thought." *Oh, well. Here goes."*

"A person can be born without hearing. A person can plug up the ear canal with water while swimming, or ear wax and dust can build up to block hearing. There are even reports of lost hearing during the late war after shells burst near men."

"But Miss Drieborg," the professor interrupted. "I've read studies that insist such hearing loss has nothing to do with loud noises, but is the result of freight or some such thing. What would you say to that?"

'A man my father's age was in the war," She responded. "When we talk in his presence, we have to be sure to do so in front of him, if we want him to know what we say. He says he has a buzzing in his head that makes it difficult for him to hear. So, he sort of reads our lips when we speak.

"During the war, his doctors called it shell shock," She continued. "There is no obstruction in his ear canal. Nor can they account for the buzzing sound that interferes with his hearing either. It appears that the medical people just don't know what is causing his hearing problem."

"Shell shock, eh?" Eleanor's teacher commented. "Interesting. Thank you, Miss Drieborg."

Later that day, Eleanor was with her study group in the library. She had been assigned to a four-member group as had all freshman students. She was the only female in her group.

"I think Doctor Smiley has it in for me," One of the other students complained.

"Oh, come on, Bill," Another challenged. "You just flat out got the answer wrong. You were asked about the structure of the elbow. You simply didn't give the right answer."

"Smiley always seems to ask me stuff I don't know," Bill retorted.

Everyone laughed at this excuse.

"Drieborg, you always seem to get the easy questions," Bill continued.

"Oh, really, "she snapped. "All right, smart guy. You answer the question he asked me. Tell us about the structure of the inner ear."

Everyone sat waiting for Bill's answer.

Bill didn't respond.

Another member of the group asked. "How about the shoulder? Tell us about that part."

Bill didn't respond to that either.

"Seems as though you didn't study, Billy boy," Another member of the group said. "I'd guess you're spending too much of your time over at the Wolverine Bar."

"I guess that's my business and none of yours," Bill Schultz snapped.

"Then don't whine so much when we meet here. Study or just shut up."

"Maybe we should meet before the next exam to sort of quiz one another," Eleanor suggested.

"Good idea," Tom Peterson agreed. "Who's for that?"

Bill Schultz was the only one who didn't agree to meet.

"What's with you, Schultz?"

"Why? So, you guys can just show off and make fun of me?"

"Suit yourself," Peterson said. "We'll meet right here next week the afternoon before the next exam. Whoever shows up, fine. Whoever doesn't fine, too."

*   *   *

A few days later, Eleanor was hurrying home for supper. She had been in the lab working with her group on an experiment. It was almost dusk and she was pre-occupied thinking about the lab experiment. Suddenly, someone grabbed her from behind and dragged her into some bushes by the side of the path she was on.

Her arms were pinned to her sides as she was thrown to the ground. A heavy body was quickly a-top her. As her attacker tried to pull up her skirt, she got one of her arms free. She remembered that she had a pencil in her skirt pocket on that side.

"He's too heavy for me to just push him off. The pencil; get the pencil." She told herself.

She pulled it out.

"His ear; stab him in his ear with it!"

She did, and heard a shrill scream from the man a-top her. Blood dripped on to her blouse from his head.

When he released his grip on her she pushed him off and rolled away. She grabbed her books and left the man writhing on the ground. As she ran away, she recognized her attacker. It was Bill Schultz.

Later that evening, she wrote of the incident in a journal she had begun keeping when she arrived in Ann Arbor. She wasn't quite sure what she should do about the attack. Lacking a decision to report it, she did nothing. But she was more careful about being out late in the day and she carried a sharpened pencil in both of her skirt's pockets thereafter; just in case.

When she visited home, next, she shared this experience with her mother, her father was brought into the discussion. At this point, he insisted Eleanor carry a small pistol in her skirt pocket.

Eleanor agreed only after hearing that her mother's life had been saved at Fort Sumter years earlier. Then, as she was being assaulted, she shot and killed her attacker with the small pistol she carried in her skirt pocket.

"I wish I could get my hands on that bastard," Eleanor's father exclaimed to his wife. "After I finished with him, he'd never assault a woman again."

"I understand your anger, dear, But Eleanor wants to handle this herself," Mary Jacquelin reminded her husband.

"Fine, fine. I'll stay out of it; for now, anyway."

*   *   *

In the Marshal's office at the Federal Building in downtown Grand Rapids, there was another heated discussion on this same subject.

Riley said, "Seems ta me that the lass has handled this rather well by herself."

Killeen disagreed, "Eleanor and the other women in her medical class are all at risk, seems ta me. Those pampered men in that school need to be sent a message that puts the fear of God inta them."

"I agree with Stan, on this one," Bill Anderson said.

"If Mike wanted us to do anything, he'd a said so. Don't ya think?" Riley asked them.

"Eleanor asked him to stay out of it," Killeen told his colleagues. "She didn't say anything to us."

Anderson agreed. "Maybe we ought ta take a few days off and go to Ann Arbor. We could just look around and get a sense of the place; maybe even run inta this guy Schultz."

"Never know what might happen," Killeen chuckled.

Riley backed out of the deal. "You guys can take a few days off, but I don't want ta know what you have in mind ta do. Just keep it to yourselves."

"Next week, all right, Bill?" Killeen suggested.

"Sounds good to me. If we leave on Friday, we could be back by Monday or Tuesday."

"We could take care of business, there, and be back a' fore anyone misses us."

*　　　*　　　*

It was just before duck. The two men were sitting in a carriage they had rented when they arrived in Ann Arbor that afternoon. They had parked on Library Lane, just across from the University Library building. Eleanor was still inside with her study group.

"Here she comes," Bill told Stan. "The others should be close behind."

"Yup," Noticed Stan. "There's the guy with the bandage covering his right ear."

The student they were looking for walked in the opposite direction. Bill Anderson and Stan Killeen followed in their carriage. They watched as their man turned on to East Huron. He stopped in front of the Wolverine Bar & Grill and went in.

"Why don't I go in and keep an eye on this fella?"

"Suits me," Stan answered. "While you're there order me a sandwich and a bottle of Fox beer."

Bill followed the student into the bar. Once his eyes had adjusted to the dim room, he looked around and saw him sitting alone. Bill went to the bar and ordered two corn beef sandwiches and two bottles of Fox beer, to go.

It wasn't long before his order was ready. He paid and left. Eleanor's attacker was still sitting alone nursing a pitcher of beer.

"Here's your stuff, Stan," Bill announced. "I looked around inside. There is a rear exit. So, I suggest you go around back and cover that. I'll go back inside and stay as long as our friend is there."

It was dark within an hour and Schultz was still drinking beer. About seven o'clock, he paid his bill and went for the front door. Bill did the same.

Stan had parked in such a way that he could see both doors of the Wolverine Bar & Grill. So, he got his carriage horse moving. Bill jumped in just a bit down East Huron. As soon as Schultz approached a stretch with no buildings, Stan pulled over and he and Bill jumped out.

Schultz was not too steady on his feet, sort of staggering along. The stood on either side of him.

Stan grabbed him from behind and Bill put a hood over his head. With his arms bound, they dragged him to the carriage. Bill sat with the struggling man in the second seat. Stan headed the carriage out of town.

On their way into the city that day, they had located a vacant barn a half mile or so off the road. They had decided it would be ideal for their purpose. So, they headed in that direction.

Once inside the old barn, they lit a lantern. Then they took off the hood and unbound their captive.

"What the hell are you doing?" Schultz shouted.

"We are going to have a little conversation," Stan informed him.

"This is kidnapping, you know," Schultz responded. "I'll have you arrested."

"Tell ya what, sonny," Bill said.

"After we're done here, we will take you into town and turn you over to the federal Marshal ourselves."

Schultz was puzzled at this.

"Right now, though tell us how you got that injury to your ear."

"I fell,"

"We hear tell you tried to rape one of your fellow students recently and she attacked you with a pencil. That sound about right?"

"That bitch attacked me all right," Schultz responded. "But I've got something planned for that stuck-up broad, believe you me."

"We sort a' thought you might have something like that in mind."

Stan slapped Schultz across the face. Knocked him down, actually.

"What the hell!" he shouted.

"Get up and try to hit me," Stan urged.

"Fight two of ya?"

Anderson said. "I'll stay out a this entirely. It will be just you and this old man. Are you up to that?"

Schultz was a good six-foot-tall and near 200 pounds. Stan was only five-foot-five and maybe 135 pounds. Anderson was right, Stan did look old, too.

Stan slapped Schultz again, this time on his injured ear.

"Hey!" Schultz exclaimed.

This time he didn't fall, he took a swing at Stan.

Stan ducked and as Schultz was off balance Stan hit him with a fist to his nose. Then Stan skipped away from the bigger man. Schultz wasn't able to land a punch on the smaller man.

"Stand still, will ya?" He shouted.

"You tired of getting hit, sonny?" Anderson teased.

Getting out of breath, Schultz stood in the middle of the barn room with his hands on his knees.

Stan hit him again. This time, Schultz fell back on his rear end.

"Why are you doing this?" Schultz asked. "I don't even know you."

"We're friends of the young girl you tried to rape," Bill told him. "We're here to give you a sample of what will happen to you if anything happens to that girl. Anything at all mind you; she trips and falls on the sidewalk, someone you might not even know looks cross-eyed at her; anything at all. We hear about it, we're coming to get you."

Schultz just sat there looking bewildered as Anderson talked. Stan walked by the student and punched him on his injured ear again.

"Ow!" he shouted.

"Stand up, sonny," Anderson ordered.

Schultz stood holding his right hand over his ear.

Stan punched him in his flabby belly.

Schultz doubled over and threw up.

"All that beer you drank, I expect," Anderson said. "You tired yet, Stan?"

"Not so much, "Stan responded. "But what I want to know is if this dumb ass is getting our message."

 "What about it, sonny?" Anderson asked. "Are you going to be out lady friend's protector from now on, or do we need to continue this lesson?"

Stan hit Schultz on his bad ear again.

"Ow!" he shouted again. "What do you want me to say?"

"This guy is really dense. I hope I don't ever need a doctor badly enough to have him treat me."

"Sonny," Anderson repeated. "We're here talking to you because you tried to rape our friend. We are hoping that you will never do such a thing again.

"Let me simplify this for you. Will you ever do anything to harm out friend again? Just answer yes or no."

Schultz was quiet. He just stood there looking puzzled.

Stan punched him in the midsection, again.

"Didn't you hear my question?" Bill asked. "Will you swear to never do anything to harm our brined?"

"No, I won't."

Stan punched him on his ear again.

"Ow! What's that for, I said I wouldn't."

"Just making sure," Anderson explained.

"Now," Anderson continued. "Do you promise to protect our friend from anyone else harming her?"

Once again Schultz just look puzzled with the question.

Stan hit him in the midsection again.

"Stop hitting me," Schultz begged. "I'm thinking about the question."

"Answer him already," Stan shouted back. "Or, I'll hit you again."

"I'm supposed to be her protector now?" Schultz asked.

"Yes."

"Why would I do that?"

"So, we will stop hitting you. And so, that we never have to come back here to have this conversation again. That's why," Stan shouted.

"I can't swear to that."

"Why not," Then Stan hit Schultz again.

"Because I paid a couple of toughs to rough up your friend. That's why."

"Tell us about I," Anderson ordered.

"These two men are to meet me at the Wolverine Bar tomorrow night at 7 o'clock for the rest of the money I agreed to pay them."

"So, they intend to rough our friend up before then, I assume?"

"Yes, I suppose," Schultz said.

"Here's what is going to happen, sonny," Stan told him.

"We three are going to stay here overnight. My friend here and I will meet Miss Drieborg at her rooming house early in the morning and stay with her all day. If necessary, we will be with you tomorrow night at your meeting with the two men you hired. After that, we will decide what to do with you."

"Take off your boots, sonny,"

"Why?"

"Cause, I told you to," Anderson said.

They tied the barefoot Schultz to one of the barn's support poles. Then Stan and Bill got some sleep. They didn't much care if their

360

captive got any sleep. In any case, they were in town at Eleanor's boarding house shortly after sun-up.

They met her when she left the house on her way to class.

Uncle Bill, Uncle Stan," She exclaimed. "What are you two doing here?"

They explained the situation.

"Did my father ask you to come here?" she said irritably.

"No," Stan assured her.

"In fact, if he knew, we probably be suspended from our jobs," Anderson told Eleanor.

"I truly appreciate your concern," Eleanor told them. "What do you propose now that you know about Shultz hiring those men?"

"We propose to hang around today to prevent any attack. If you get through today without anything happening, we intend to meet the men Schultz hired tonight and eliminate any future threat."

"I'll tell you right now, you can't come into my classroom or the lab while I'm working."

"Don't have to, Eleanor," Bill assured her. "We'll just hang around in the hall and sort a' follow you around between classes and such."

"What's going to happen to Schultz?" Eleanor asked.

"He's gone over the line when he hired thugs to attack you. We've decided to eliminate the threat."

"You're not going to kill him I hope."

"No," Stan said. "Although we would be doing a favor for preventing him from become a doctor. He is the dumbest man I've met in a good while. How he got this far in school causes me to question what's going on in our schools today."

Eleanor said. "I think his father was in charge of the school in their rural town."

Bill laughed. "His teachers probably passed him just to get rid of the dummy."

"So, what have you planned?" Eleanor still wanted to know.

"We're not going to harm the little piss-ant. But we intend to get him out of your hair once and for all."

"How?"

"You don't need to know that, darlin'," Stan told her. "In fact, you don't want to know it either."

"I'll take your word for It, Uncle Stan."

"We have a favor to ask of you now."

"What's that?"

"You not tell your father we were here."

"All right," Eleanor promised. "It will be our secret. If he finds out, it won't be from me."

*   *   *

Later that morning, Eleanor was walking with another female student when two men approached them from behind. Eleanor whispered to her companion and then stepped back. As one of the men put his hand on her shoulder, she turned to face him.

Not expecting resistance, he was surprised when Eleanor put a pistol under his chin. She asked him,

"This is a pistol under your chin. Do you want me to blow off the top of your head?"

Equally surprised, the second man didn't know what to do. Before he could decide, two men grabbed him. Stan pulled his arms behind him, and Bill tied his hands. Then, they and made him kneel. Afterwards, they did the same with the man Eleanor was threatening with her pistol.

Stan told her. "We'll take these birds to the police station. You'll be asked to make a statement to support our arrest. So, we need you to go with us when we deliver them and Schultz to local authorities."

Stan and Bill escorted Eleanor, Schultz and the two attackers to the police station.

"This should take care of fatty Schultz," Bill said, "I don't think he'll give you any more trouble, Eleanor."

*   *   *

When they entered the police station, they introduced themselves as Deputy Marshals who were visiting Miss Drieborg, a student at the University.

The Ann Arbor deputy asked. "This man you have here, hired these two men to attack you, Miss Drieborg?"

Bill interrupted. "That's right, Deputy. My colleague and I had been told by our prisoner, Mr. Schultz, that he hired these two thugs to attack Miss Drieborg. She is with us to sign a complaint that the two attacked her earlier today."

"You witnessed this attack did you Deputy Anderson?"

"That's right, deputy," Bill attested. "The dandiest thing. She was walking with a friend down your Library Lane and these two attacked her. Stan, here, and I were following her to a restaurant for lunch. We witnessed the entire thing.

"So, we stopped the assault on her and brought the two attackers here to you. Before we got here, they told us that this Schultz fella was waiting for them at the Wolverine Bar to pay them for attacking her. So, we rounded him up and brought him along."

The deputy turned to Schultz. "This is the fellow who paid these other two?"

"He's the one, deputy," Stan attested.

"Paying those two to attack someone in my town is a serious offense young fella."

"I didn't do nothing," Schultz mumbles. "This guy beat me up." He pointed at Stan.

"Most everyone who is brought in here says he's innocent. Is that the same over your way, Deputy Anderson?"

"I run the Federal detention center in Grand Rapids," Bill said. "Every guy who is brought in is innocent."

"You'll sign a statement?"

"We'll make a statement," Bill said. "Will the statement of the two we brought in earlier be enough to charge Schultz with assault?"

"Certainly will. I'll have to have a statement from you too, Miss Drieborg," the local police officer revealed. "Please come with me. I have a desk right over here."

Eleanor accompanied him and wrote out her statement. She also signed the complaint forms.

The two thugs were placed in separate interview rooms where they wrote out their statements implicating Schultz.

Bill and Stan made statements supporting Eleanor's and signed them.

"Will that be enough for the University to expel this Schultz?" Bill asked.

"Oh, I'm sure that will do it, deputy. Assault on a fellow student? That's pretty much automatic."

"Will you charge Mr. Schultz with assault? Eleanor asked. "Will he be put in jail?"

"I can pretty much guarantee that he will do some jail time, miss," She was told. "I can't guarantee what the University will do. I can only tell you what the administration usually does.

"For now, though, if you will sign your complaint against the two thugs your friends brought in here, we'll talk care of the rest."

*   *   *

A few days later, one of the professors in the University's Medical School was taking roll for his class. Eleanor and the other freshmen students were in attendance.

"It would appear, that Mr. Schultz will no longer be with us. He has been expelled from the University. Allow me to assure you that by the end of the term, more of you will no longer be in my class, either. Happens every term."

The male students in her study group looked over at Eleanor. She showed no reaction.

*   *   *

Stan and Bill were at their desks early Wednesday morning.

Pat Riley noticed.

"You men take care of business on your vacation?"

"Yes, we did," Bill responded with a smile.

"Our friend is well?"

"She is, now," Stan added.

"You'll have to tell me about it over lunch at the Cosmopolitan this day."

"If you're buying, I'm telling," Stan said.

"Sounds like a good deal ta me," Bill added.

"You two have no shame. None a 'tall," Riley decided.

All three men laughed at their shared secret as their boss, Marshal Michael Drieborg walked into the room with a fresh cup of coffee and sat down.

"What's new?"

"Nothing Marshal. Absolutely nothing we can't handle," Bill informed him.

Edisto Island

It was Sunday. A day of rest, sort of, on the island. Charles had milked cows for two hours that morning then cleaned up for church.

When he had last been to the island as a pre-teen, his mother took him to the Sunday service at the island's Catholic church. But sometime later, when the priest died, there was no replacement. So, now you had to choose between an Episcopal or a Baptist church service. Charles chose to go with the Mikell family to the Trinity Episcopal Church.

The three Mikell's and Charles took seats in the front pew of the church. Well into the service, Charles told Susan Mikell,

"Seems to me that the Episcopal Mass is the same as the Catholic one I'm used to attending," He commented. *"Even the communion is the same."*

Mrs. Mikell told Charles, "This is our new church. Two years ago, the old one burned right to the ground."

"I don't remember the old church, Mrs. Mikell," Charles told her. "But this one is very nice."

"Thank you," She responded. "We really like it."

Afterward, he joined the Mikell's for a noon meal at their home.

"Was our Episcopal service comfortable for you, Charles," Mrs. Mikell asked.

"Yes, it was ma'am," He responded." I was surprised how similar it was to the Catholic Mass I'm used to."

"We haven't had a Catholic priest here for some time," Mrs. Mikell told him. "I doubt if we ever will."

"If that's the case, I don't think God will mind too much if I attend your church," Charles responded.

"Well, you're welcome to join us on Sunday's, Charly," Susan added.

"Thanks," he responded. "I think I'll take you up on that as long as you'll guide me through the service, Susan."

"Be happy to, Charly," She assured him. "Now, will you please pass the plate of bacon?"

"Oh, sure."

"By the way, Susie," Charles sort of taunted. "Where do you get this Charly business?"

"I don't know actually," She responded. "I guess you just seem like a Charly. Besides, Charles is so formal.

"Hey!" she added. "Didn't I ask you if you minded? As I recall, you said it was all right as long as you could call me Susan. You do remember that, don't you?"

"You got me there, Susan," He had to admit.

"So," she challenged. "Have we put this issue to rest?"

"Yes," He said. "But I have a question for you. It's about the honey you have on the table today."

"What about it?"

"For the last month, I've used a sweetener that was granular. Now, I'm offered honey. What was I using before?"

"That granular stuff you referred to, Charles is from the Stevia leaf. It grows wild on the island. We process it much like sugar cane, which we do not grow on the island. The result of the process is the stuff you've been using."

"Why the honey now?" Charles asked.

"Most of us prefer honey on our grits and in our tea or coffee. But it is not always available for us to use at our table or to sell in my store. Bees are sort of particular about when they produce raw honey. So, I can only buy it in season. So, it is a lot easier to store the Stevia grain."

"Thank you for that lesson in living close to the land. I didn't know all of that."

"You're welcome," Susan responded. "Now, if you don't mind, will you pass the bacon?"

*   *   *

Later that day, Charles was in his room sort of catching up on things. like his laundry. One of the other things he had neglected since his arrival a month ago, was writing Eleanor.

July 1879

"Dear Eleanor,

I can't believe I've been here a month already. Townshend has had me so busy it is all I can do to get up in the very early morning and fall to sleep in the evening. This is Sunday and the first day of rest

I've been given. Even this morning I was up at five to milk cows and to help make cheese and butter. Wouldn't Grandpa Jake be surprised?

That's right, I was up at five in the morning. And without anyone waking me up, too. Can you believe it? Every day since I've been here, it is up at five and drop into bed around nine, dead tired. During the week, I work in the rice paddies, the cotton fields and in the general store. On several evenings each week, I am assigned patrol duty either on the beach or at the front entrance.

In the middle of the day, we have a four-hour siesta before the evening meal and then more work in the cooler evening. It is just too darn hot in the middle of the day. Even during the afternoon break, Townshend usually has me working with him on something or other.

He is determined that I experience everything on the island. So, I am. The only bad things down here are the bugs, the heat and being away from you and the rest of the family. That, of course, is besides worrying about the Klan which is a terror group that has been trying to destroy the community on Edisto. They hate it that a successful community has been built by the white and colored folks, working together. That's what the daily patrols are about.

I plan to travel home after the fall harvest. I really look forward to that; and seeing you, of course. I hope you will be able to spend some time at home then, too. After the first of the year, I plan to return here for the winter planting and so on.

I hope you are doing well in your studies. Actually, I am sure that you are. Take care of yourself El, and God bless.

Love, Charles

*   *   *

Later that evening, Charles was riding alongside Luke along the
beach defensives. They were on the bluff that overlooked the
beach and the canal that led from the Atlantic Ocean to their
docks. The moon was high in a dark clear sky. In fact, the
reflection off the ocean made the whole area sort of, glow.

Suddenly, Luke's dogs ran down the bluff on to the ocean beach
barking furiously. Luke fired a flare into the sky to illuminate the
area.

Charles noticed something a few hundred yards out to sea.

 "That looks like a long-boat out there moving toward the canal
entrance to the Steamboat Landing docks." He told Luke.

"Looks like two boats, ta me," Luke corrected. "I think I see a
bunch of men rowing like mad in each of the boat, too. Come 'on,
we need to sound the alarm."

They reached the alarm tower rather quickly, climbed the ladder
and began ringing the large bell fixed there. Soon, other bells
echoed their alarm. People began to stream out of their lodgings
and run to their defensive stations.

Luke and Charles took positions behind a prepared trench near
the alarm tower.

"You fire on the men in the boat to the left," Luke directed. "I'll
take the boat on the right."

"Damn!" Charles thought. *"I'm supposed to kill men in that boat."*

*He hesitated while Luke began to pump shells into the chamber of
his repeating rifle and fire at the boat on the right.*

372

"Come on, Charles," Luke shouted. "Why do you think you've got that rifle? Get shooting man!"

The guys in those boats are going to kill us."

"Luke's right. These guys are not here on a friendly visit," He decided. *"Shit or get off the pot, Charles my boy. Now or never."*

Charles began to fire his rifle at the boat, too. Pull the trigger; lever a fresh round into the chamber and pull the trigger again; and again.

The boats were now only fifty or so yards from shore. Suddenly, there was an explosion between the two approaching boats. Both boats rose over the ocean and overturned. All the men in the boats were thrown into the churning sea.

"What the hell was that, Luke?" Charles asked excitedly.

"My guess is that they were towing a barrel of oil and explosives to blow up our dock. One of us must have hit it."

By this time, others joined them in the trench. They joined the firing on the two overturned boats and the men in the water. Another flair drifted over the scene and bodies could be seen in the water. Some of the attackers were just floating face down. A few others were swimming toward the shore.

Defenders were waiting on the beach to capture and question the survivors.

The defenders stopped firing.

In the sudden silence, firing could be heard from the West. Evidently, there was an attack under way on the land road, too. After a few minutes that firing stopped, too.

*   *   *

Townshend Mikell approached Charles in the trench.

"Come with us, Charles," He ordered. "We're going to question the survivors. You might as well hear what they have to say. Luke, you stay here and help secure the beach."

Behind the beach, in a grove of trees, six men were tied up and sitting on the ground under guard. There was a small barn nearby.

Inside, Mikell and one of his supervisors were in charge of the interrogation.

"Bring them in one at a time," Mikell ordered. "Observe and learn, Charles. "He directed.

The first prisoner was brought in and tied to a chair that was set against a support post.

"If you cooperate, you will not be killed," The man was told. "If you do not answer our questions, we will punish you severely."

"What is your name?

No response was given.

"Who is the leader of your group?"

No response was given.

"What was your mission?"

No response was given.

"Get the rope, Billy," Mikell ordered.

A rope was thrown over the beam above the prisoner. There was already a noose prepared on one end. This was put over the prisoner's neck and secured tightly around his neck.

"Every time you refuse to answer a question, we will pull you up by the neck and count to five or some such number. We will then lower you to the ground, let you catch your breath. Then we will start again. Each time you refuse, the count will increase. If you continue to refuse, at some point, you will die. It will be up to you.

"What is your name?" Billy asked.

The prisoner did not answer.

"Pull him off the ground, Billie," Mikell ordered.

"Charles," Mikell ordered. "Count slowly to five again, out loud, so this the man being questioned can hear the count."

"One, two, three, four, five," Charles almost shouted.

"Let him down, Billy."

After a brief interval, Mikell asked him, "What is your name?"

No answer.

"Pull him up again, Billy," Mikell ordered. "Count to seven, Charles."

After he was lowered again, and given a chance to regain his breath. He was asked his name again.

"Roscoe Johnson," He quickly answered.

"That wasn't so hard, was it, Roscoe?" Mikell told him. "I was in the Confederate cavalry during the war. How about you, infantry, cavalry or artillery?"

"Cavalry," Was the one-word answer given.

"You must 'a been in Hampton's Brigade. A tough bunch that was. Eh?"

"Ya, we were. Hampton was a good leader. We should 'a never surrendered."

"Such a decision was way above my pay grade, Roscoe." Mikell told him. "I went in a private and came out a sergeant. Never trusted them officers much. Did the Governor lead you or was it Major Wade Hampton IV?"

"We was led by Hampton IV."

"Heard a lot 'a good things about him." Mikell continued. "You still with him, aren't you?"

"Pretty much."

"Be a damn shame if we killed him in this fracas. Ya think he survived?"

"I don't know."

"We know you were towing that barrel of oil an such to blow up our dock facility." Mikell revealed to Roscoe. "I can only figure the purpose was to stop sea-going ships from docking here. You figure that too?"

"I don't know," Roscoe commented. "I just follow orders. Will you answer a question a' mine?"

"Sure, Roscoe," Mikell responded. "What do you want to know."

"You fought for the 'Cause,' like you said? Roscoe asked.

"Yes, I did," Mikell told his prisoner. "Billy here, an I fought the whole time, from the first battle under Beauregard at Manassas in '61 on to Joe Johnston's surrender in '65."

"Why did you become a nigger-lover?"

"Survival, Roscoe," Mikell told him. "When Billy and I returned home to Edisto in '65, it was plain as day that the only way we were going to survive was to work together with the coloreds here. The Yankees sure weren't going ta help us. It was going to be all up to us who lived here.

"My father and others might have gotten their land back from the Johnson administration. But they needed the coloreds to make the land productive. Landowners like Colonel Pope saw that, so did former Governor William Aiken. Even Yankee hating Colonel Jenkins agreed with that assessment.

"Roscoe," Mikell continued. "We all swallowed our pride and anger and got down to work. Anyone who stayed knew they were going to have to work together, whites and coloreds. Many decided they couldn't stomach that, and left. Even Col. Pope's one surviving son left. But those who stayed, men and women, white and colored, all have decided that it is in their best interest to work together; and thus survive."

"How do you stand to work with niggers, though?" Roscoe asked.

"Like I told you, Roscoe, survival." Mikell reminded his prisoner. "I survived the war. After our leaders surrendered to the Yankees I went home. It was then, I decided that I'd be damned if I was going to surrender my future to hate and pride. One defeat was enough for my lifetime."

"What's going to happen ta me, now?"

"We're law-abiding here on Edisto, Roscoe," Mikell assured him. "So, our Federal Marshal, who's a colored man, will put you and the others in his jailhouse. Then, our District Judge, who is a white man, will hear the complaint against you and make a decision."

"What do ya think will happen ta' us?" Roscoe asked.

"If it were left up to a jury of people who live here, I can assure you it would be a hanging for all of you. But our judge will decide. So, I'm guessing he'll set you free since you only cost us a bunch a' sleep."

Mikell had each of the prisoners brought in one at a time. The questions were the same. So was the punishment of not answering. But he didn't learn anything new.

Sure enough, the following week, the judge ordered the six men released. They were given some water and were allowed to leave the island on foot by the main road.

Mikell and the other island leaders were fully aware, now, that the Klan, the military arm of the Democratic Party, with the support of the new governor of South Carolina, Wade Hampton III, was determined to stop Edisto's trade with the outside world.

They also knew that they had to discover a way to preserve that lifeline, or they would eventually be destroyed.

General Store

Charles walked into the Mikell store after he had worked in the dairy processing building. Susan Mikell was waiting for him.

"It's about time you got here, Charly," She greeted.

"Talk to your father. He's got me working making cheese after milking cows. That process does not obey a time clock. I am able to leave when the process is finished. Not a moment sooner. So, take your complaints to the higher authority."

"Your excuse for being late is noted and understood," Susan agreed. "Now, let me show you what you're going to be doing this Saturday morning."

She led the way to a building that housed two oxen walking around and around turning some heavy stones.

"This is our grist mill. I normally only work my oxen on Saturday when we operate the grist mill to the public. But I wanted to demonstrate the entire operation before-hand for you.

"As you've discovered, we eat a lot of things made of corn. We use some wheat, too. With both, we use this grist mill to grind the crops into a form used in that food; cornbread, mush, hoe-cakes and spoonbread, tortia and pie shells and, of course grits.

"Helen used to fix us cornbread and warm mile on cold winter mornings," Charles told Susan. "I always enjoyed grits in the morning, too with melted butter and sugar on it."

"That's the staff of life on this island," Susan said. "I think I had corn in one form or another three times a day growing up. We only get bread made from wheat on special occasions.

"Those who grow corn bring their raw grain to us and we grind it for them. We keep one bushel out of four for our share. Between harvests, we barter our stored grain for the chicken, eggs and pork they raise as well as the fish they catch and the stevia they process or the honey they harvest."

"I've notices that there's not much use for money on the island."

"Right," Suisan said. "The barter system works pretty well for everybody. The cash we get for the goods we send to the various British islands and Savannah, is used to pay the land taxes the state charges each land owner."

"I know that everyone seems to have a couple of acres of land for themselves. How do they get cash to pay the tax?" Charles asked.

"Men and women hire themselves out to the large land owners for $7.00 dollars a month. The sheriff tells every land owner, large and small, what the state's land tax will be and when it is due. So, each landowner knows how much he must save and when he must pay it.

"During the year, before the harvest even begins, people put their earned wages in our island's bank. So, the money for their land tax is there when it is needed."

"In the meantime, everyone uses bartering for things they need?" Charles asked.

"Yes," Susan responded. "It all seems to work out pretty well."

"There must be a lot of trust in that system, seems ta' me."

"The alternative is chaos," Susan told him. "The people here had to come up with a workable system or leave the island."

"Simple as that?" Charles probed.

"Simple as that, Charley," Susan said. "But enough of that lesson. Earlier this week some corn was delivered for grinding. Rather than wait for Saturday when we normally grind corn. I thought we'd do it today so you could get the feel of the process. So, let's hook up the oxen and go through grist mill operation."

"Right now?"

"Right now," Susan insisted. "The first thing to keep in mind is that when these oxen are turning the stones, it is dangerous to get anywhere near the stones. When they are turning, they could take fingers just as easily as they grind the grain.

"Got it?"

"Got it," Charles repeated.

"You fill this hopper with the corn," Susan began. "Then you get the oxen to start walking. As you can see, the top stones begin to turn. The corn drops down the chute and is ground by the top stone turning on the lower stationary one. The grain is pushed out that channel into an empty box. You keep feeding corn into the hopper. When a box is near full, or you run out of corn, stop the oxen and replace the full box with an empty one. Never touch the stones as long as the oxen are hooked up.

"Got it?"

"Got it," Charles repeated.

"No shortcuts, Charly," Susan insisted. "Shortcuts will get you injured. Maimed actually.

"Got it?"

"Got it," Charly repeated.

It wasn't long before all the corn was ground. Then they sealed the cornmeal into containers to await pick-up by those who dropped off their raw corn for grinding. The store's share was stored in another sealed container.

The oxen were taken back to their stalls, groomed, watered and fed. The top stones were raised, secured and the lower stone cleaned.

Then Susan and Charles went into the general store to begin their work there.

"We might just as well jump right into taking a look at our inventory, Charly," She said.

"It's sort of boring, but the only way we can do it is to go over all the shelves and count the items we have for sale or exchange. Same for the back room.

'Take this list of goods we stock and begin. Each sheet is marked with the number of the shelf where the goods are displayed. Just write in the number of each item we still have.

"I'm going to start in the back room doing the same thing. When we're done, we'll make out a list of the items we need from the next shipment from Bermuda and Savannah. We expect ships in from those ports at the end of the month. Might as well get the order done right now."

By the noon dinner hour, they had completed both the inventory and the order forms.

"I've noticed that you have a chicken house and a pig pen alongside the store. Are those yours, too?"

"Yes, they are," Susan told Charles. "The chickens and eggs we use for out table and we give some to our house workers in payment for their services. We eat a lot of pork to go along with the beef we raise in our pastures. But the fish we trade for."

"Where does the kerosene, coal, clothing and metal tools come from?"

"Those things come from England and Europe. Traders in Bermuda or Savannah, send them over. We sell, long stem cotton, rice, cattle and some sweetener to pay for these things. Then, people on the island buy or trade for them from either my store or Mrs. Thorpe's."

"So, as long as you can trade with the outside world the island economy functions pretty well?"

"Right,"

"That's why those men were trying to destroy the docks last week; to prevent ships from docking here."

"Exactly," Susan confirmed.

Interestingly, the two young people had corn bread. jpmeu and milk for their noon meal. Then Charles asked.

"If you have some time, why don't you join me for a ride to the beach."

"That sounds good," Susan agreed. "I'll meet you at the stable after I change into riding cloths."

Soon they were riding along the beach.

"What do you do for a social life around here, Susan?" Charles asked.

"Pretty much, nothing," Susan chuckled. "We work, eat and rest. Haven't had much time for anything else. Besides, I haven't had anyone to do much socializing with, until you arrived."

"I know what you mean about being tired at the end of a day; I['m exhausted," Charles complained.

"What do you have in mind, Charly?"

"Ever gone fishing in the afternoon?" he asked.

"Usually I'm working in the store."

"Can't you take an afternoon off once and awhile, maybe during the siesta time?"

"I suppose. I's not something I would do alone.."

"Will you think about it? Luke's got a small boat we could borrow. He showed me some really good fishing spots the other day. How about tomorrow afternoon?"

"Let me think about it," Susan said.

"Promise?"

"Yes, Charly," She said. "I promise. Race you to the that big fallen tree up ahead."

Before Charles could spur his horse, Susan had spurted ahead. He caught up with her in a few minutes, but she beat him to the fallen tree with a late burst of speed.

"Oh, my God!" she shouted turning her horse away.

Charles looked at the fallen tree and saw the limp body of a man caught amongst the branches.

"Must be one of the attackers who drowned during their attack."

"When we get back, I'll tell the Sheriff. He'll take care of it," Susan promised.

"Come' on, Susan," Charles said. "Let's ride to that clump of trees. We can sit in the shade and give the horses a rest."

The two of them tied the reins to a tree and took the saddles off their mounts. For the next hour or so, they sat in the shade and talked. Their horses grazed on the short grass and flicked off the bugs with their tails.

"So, you didn't like school, I take it," Susan said.

"No, I never did. I'd rather run with my friends on the playground and after school. Baseball was a passion of mine. I play that with my friends until it got dark any time, I could get a few of the guys together."

"We get a mainland paper once and awhile, so I've read about baseball. But I don't know anything about it. What is the purpose of trying to hit a round ball with a stick?"

Charles laughed. "The purpose is to win the game, silly."

"I suppose you were good at hitting that little round ball?"

"I was so good, my father had me play with his Grand Rapids team, the Shamrocks," Charles bragged. "This team traveled all over Michigan playing other teams. It was great fun."

"All right hot-shot. Tell me about this game you were so good at."

"After the last war, most teams around the country adopted the rules that called for nine players and the same kind of field."

Charles drew a baseball diamond in the ground. Then he explained the position of each of the players as he showed Susan where they stood as each pitch was made.

"This guy is called a pitcher. He throws that little round ball toward the man on the other team who has a bat in his hands ready to try and hit that ball as it passes him." Charles places the two players in the proper position.

"So, the guy who has the little stick is supposed to hit the ball this other guy tries to throw by him?"

"Right," Charles agreed.

"If he hits the ball on the ground, one of these guys, called infielders will try to pick it up and throw it to the first baseman over here before the batter gets there. If he does, the batter is out of the game.

"What if he doesn't?" Susan asked.

"Then the batter is called 'safe' and stands on first base," Charles continued.

"He just stands there?"

"Yes,"

"This is harder to explain than I thought," Charles realized.

"He waits for the next batter to have his turn 'at bat'. If the next batter hits the ball and reaches first base before the throw gets there, the teammate who was standing at first base, runs to second base."

"So now that team has two men standing on bases?"

"Yes. One is standing on first base and one on second base,"

"Then what?"

"remember, I told you that the pitcher tries to get three batters to either strike out or have the infielders throw the ball to first base quicker than the batter can get there. If he doesn't, the other team can continue batting.

"But if there are nine players on each side and only three bases, where do the other six go?"

"If the team that had two men standing on bases has another man reach first base without being thrown out, that team will have three men standing on bases; here, here and here. See?"

Susan was ahead of Charles, "What if a fourth man bats and reaches first base without being thrown out?"

"The man over here, one third base, runs here, to the home plate. That's called scoring a run."

"Oh, I see," Susan realized, "The team that has the most runs wins. Right?"

"Right," Charles confirmed.

"What about the other team?" Susan prodded. "Don't they get a chance to hit the ball, too?"

Charles went over how one team gets the other team 'out' and gets to bat.

"So, each team bats in an inning. And there are nine of those innings before the game is over. Right?"

"Right," Charles agreed.

"And you've played this game, right?"

"Oh, ya," Charles boasted. "My friends and I played when we were in grade school and high school. I already told you I even played on my father's team in Grand Rapids, once and awhile."

"Which one of the positions did you play?" Susan asked.

"When my friends and I played, I was usually the pitcher. When I played on the Shamrocks, my father's team, I played in the outfield." Charles pointed to the spot in right field.

"We should organize a game here on the island, Charles," Susan suggested.

"Do you think there would be enough men interested in playing?"

"I don't know that. But I'm sure there would be enough men and women interested," Susan told him.

"Women don't play baseball, Susan,"

"Haven't you noticed, Charles?" she taunted. "On Edisto Island, women do most everything a man does, and more even. Remember the night we were attacked? There were as many women in the trench firing on the attackers, as men."

"Oh, ya," Charles admitted. "I remember. But what is this 'more' comment?"

"You ever had a baby?"

"Oh, that,"

"Ya, that. Smarty," She snapped. "Tell you what. You find a flat spot on the island big enough to play this game of yours and I'll recruit the people to play. You on?"

"All right," Charles responded reliantly. "I'll get Luke to help me lay out the playing field for the game. You get around twenty players. I'll see to making a couple of bats and a ball or two."

"Sounds like a plan to me," Susan concluded. "Harvest time usually begins in September. So, how about picking a date in late August. We could sort 'a treat it as an opening of the harvest season. We'll pick a Sunday afternoon for the game and follow it with an evening potluck and dance."

"Sounds like it could be a real fun time," Charles gushed.

"No more of this guff about baseball being only a man's game?" Susan asked tauntingly.

"All right," Charles agreed. "You recruit both men and women for the two teams. After you do, I'll meet with them and organize the them properly. Ok?"

"Ok, Charly," Susan said. "It's almost time for supper. We have to take care of our horses and get washed up, too. You joining us tonight?"

"Sounds good to me."

They both stood up and brushed off their riding clothing. Susan leaned over and impulsively kissed Charles. Then she turned and walked to her horse to saddle it up. Charles was surprised by her kiss. He just stood there for a moment. Then he saddled his horse, too. The two of them rode silently for a while.

Suddenly, Susan challenged him. "Race you back to the barn!"

Spurring her horse, she got the jump on Charles. He did not win that race.

*   *   *

Late that evening, Townshend and his wife Charlotte were getting ready for bed.

"What do you think of that harvest festival the two kids were talking about at supper?"

"Nice idea," Townshend replied. "We've always celebrated at the conclusion of harvesting our crops. Makes good sense to kick off the harvest with a bit of light-hearted socializing, too."

"Seems ta me that Charles is quite taken with our daughter." Charlotte said.

"Ya really think so, dear?"

"Yes," Charlotte told her husband. "Just the way he looks at her tells me that."

"I hadn't noticed," Townshend informed his wife.

"Women notice such things, dear. Would you be troubled if Susan became interested in Charles?"

"Isn't that sort a' jumping to conclusions?" Townshend said. "Lord sakes, they only went for a ride together this afternoon."

"Answer my question, dear," Charlotte challenged. "Would you mind if the two of them became more than co-workers; if they became romantically involved?"

"No, I wouldn't mind," Townshend responded quickly. "I've worried some about Susan.
She's a good worker and is serious about the store, an all. But she has had no social life. And looking around the island, there aren't any men who I'd want her to marry.

"If she and Charles become interested in one another, it would be fine with me. I think John Thorn was right when he told us he thought Charles is a keeper. What do you think, Charlotte?"

"I think I'll not worry about it." Charlotte answered. "Right now, the two of them seem to enjoy one another's company. If they develop deeper feelings for one another, fine. If they don't and sort of move on, that's fine with me, too."

"So, we'll see," Townshend concluded.

Charlotte sat beside her husband on their bed. "Susan is right about one thing, though."

"What's that,"

"Charly is cute,"

Townshend laughed and hugged his wife to his side. There was no more talk that night.

Grand Rapids

After supper Mike Drieborg was lighting up his first pipe of the evening. "You received a letter from Charles?" he asked.

"Yes, it came this afternoon."

Their daughter Maxine was excited. "Please read it Momma."

Mary Jacqueline got out the letter from her skirt pocket.

Sunday

Dear Family,

I hope everyone is well. I am fine and doing well here. I hate all the bugs and the heat, but I feel good otherwise. I think I have replaced some weight with muscle. Townshend has me up at 5 AM bilking cows and working in the dairy making cheese.

Mother, can you believe no one gets me out of bed each morning. I must do that myself. After my duties in the dairy barn, I run to my next assignment, usually the rice paddies or now the cotton fields where my old friend Luke is in charge. In both places I hoe weeds between the rows. My back was sore as heck at first. Now, I get tired because of the constant hoeing motion but the soreness has left me.

Yesterday was the first Saturday I worked grinding corn in the Mikell gristmill. Susan Mikell is in charge of that. She showed me earlier how to run the mill. She and I are organizing a harvest party for late August. I'm organizing a baseball game, Mike. She will organize the potluck and the dancing. Aside from being very pretty, she runs the Mikell store. We're going fishing next week.

Sorry I have not written before but I get so tired by the end of the day, I just fall into bed. I've discovered that 5 AM comes around pretty fast.

The Klan's Red Shirts attacked us during the week. Luke and I were on beach patrol that night. We caught them using two longboats towing some explosives to blow up our shipping docks. Luke sounded the alarm to alert everyone. Manny of the attackers were killed in the battle. I actually fired my rifle that night. In fact, I might have killed someone. I still find it hard to believe that I would do that.

You can tell Amos that Luke is his son. Luke's mother is Mable Thorne whose husband owns cotton land and rice paddies on Edisto and the general store most of the colored's use.

Give Maxine a hug for me. Tell her that I miss her a lot. How is Eleanor doing? I haven't heard from her yet, or by the way, nor have I gotten a letter from you. Come on Mother. Your turn to write.

Love you all,

Charles

Maxine said, "I'm so excited that Charles misses me. Tell me again why he went away. I forget."

Mary Jacqueline explained once again why her brother wasn't home any more.

"When is he coming home, Mother?"

"He told me he would be home for Christmas."

"That's not until next winter-time, is it, Momma." she continued.

"Yes, almost seven more months."

"That's when Santa comes. Right?"

"That's right. But it's a long time away."

"Can I write Charles a letter?" Maxine asked.

"Of course, you can, dear. Why don't we each write one tomorrow. It's Saturday, we'll have lots of time," Mary Jacqueline told her daughter. "We'll do it after breakfast. All right?"

"Do you know what time it is, young lady?" her father asked.

"But I'm not tired,"

"It's almost ten o'clock, kiddo," He reminded her, pointing to the grandfather clock standing against the wall. "It will start ringing any moment."

"But it hasn't, yet," she reminded him.

"You're right," He answered back. "But by the time you get upstairs it will. You go on to your room and I'll bring up the hot water for your bath."

"Oh, all right," She pouted. "I'll bet Eleanor and Charles didn't have to go to bed this early."

Mary Jacqueline walked with her daughter toward the stairway. "Yes, they did, dear."

"But tonight, isn't even a school night," She continued her protest. "And I'm almost nine years old."

"Which book do you want your father to read you tonight?" Her mother asked.

"I don't," she huffed. "I can read myself, you know."

"But it's you always wanted your father to read to you." Her mother reminded her.

"You asked me what story I wanted. You didn't say I couldn't read it to myself."

"No, I didn't. You're right," Mary Jacqueline admitted.

It was Maxine's turn to remind her mother. "Sometimes, I am, you know."

*   *   *

After Maxine was in bed, her parents went to their room to prepare for bed themselves.

"I'm so worried, for Charles, Michael." Mary Jacqueline revealed as she undressed.

"You're referring to the fight with the Red Shirts?"

"Yes. I am. Reading between the lines. I think Charles was very troubled about firing at them. I have a sense that he doesn't want to kill anybody."

"This first time is a shock, believe me. I went through that, so did Stan and Bill. Charles probably realized that the attackers were not there as friends. Quite the contrary, I believe he realized that he had to help defend the island from attackers or leave.

"He seems not to have liked firing on the attackers, but he did it to defend his home on Edisto Island. Most soldiers have had to come to grips with that conflict and decide. Charles decided."

"I suppose you're right," Mikes wife said pulling on her summer nightgown.

In the night heat of July, the two of them lay on top of the sheets

Mary Jacqueline was in her light cotton nightgown, Mike wore only his boxer shorts.

Mike rolled on his side toward his wife.

"I was reminded while you read the letter from Charles how quiet it has become round our house. No bickering between Charles and Eleanor, doors slamming as they came and went.

"Thank God for Maxine. I welcome even her protests about going to bed, her school stories and her constant chatter about her newest discovery in nature."

"I know exactly what you mean," Mary Jacqueline agreed. "I look forward all day to the after- school time with Maxine and the after- supper time with both of you.

"When she gets home in the afternoon, we have milk and cookie time every day. I hear all the news of school, just like I used to with Charles and Eleanor. I treasure the time she and I spend."

"I treasure the time you and I talk like this before we fall asleep," Mike told her.

"Is that all you treasure when we're in bed?" she teased, turning toward him.

Mike began running his hand up her leg under her short summer nightgown.

"It's so hot tonight," He reminded her. "Why do you even wear this?" he asked.

"Is it permissible for a proper married woman to sleep nude?'

"What an interesting idea," Mike responded. "Queen Victoria wouldn't approve I'm sure."

"Probably not," Mary Jacqueline told her husband. "But I'm the queen of this house. I decide what's decent, around here."

"You are definitely my queen, young lady," By this time, Mike had pulled the cotton nightgown over his wife's hips. His hand moved higher.

"This queen likes what you hand is doing."

"Want me to stop, your majesty?"

"Not if you want this queen to reward your efforts."

"How could she do that?"

Mary Jacqueline sat up and pulled off her summer nightgown.

Mike told her. "This subject of yours likes what he sees."

She rolled over on top of him.

"You ain't seen nothing yet, fella."

Ann Arbor

It was after ten o'clock. After supper this evening she met with her study group at the library. The all stayed until closing time. Finally, back to the boarding house, she noticed two envelopes stuck under the door to her room.

She sat on the bed to look at her mail. One letter was from her mother, the other from Charles. She opened the one from her brother, first.

"You're right, Charles," She thought with a smile. *"I can't believe you get out of bed in the morning without serious persuasion. But at five in the morning? Not in a hundred years would I have believed that."*

She re-read the part about the various jobs he was assigned.

"Isn't it ironic. Of all the jobs you could have been assigned by Mr. Mikell, milking cows is the one you whined about the most when Grandpa Jake made you help him do that very thing at his farm."

She set his letter aside and read the one from her mother.

Later, as she was falling asleep, she prayed,

"Thank you, Lord for leading my brother, Charles to a place where he seems to have found a sense of purpose for his life. Please keep him safe."

Charleston

The governor was fuming. Striding back and forth he shouted at the men who sat before him.

The commander of all of South Carolina's gun clubs, General James Conner was present.

"General Conner, you not only failed to destroy Edisto's docks but you lost eight men in the failed effort?"

"Yes, sir," Conner answered sheepishly.

"And they captured six men who they questioned?"

"Yes, sir,"

"So, we must assume Mikell knows all about the target of our attack and who was behind it."

"Yes, sir,"

"Is this the only bad news?" Governor Wade Hampton III asked, finally sitting down.

"No, sir," His General Conner answered.

"Well," he thundered, "Out with it."

"Your son, Wade Hampton IV was killed leading the attack."

"Oh, my God!" he exclaimed slumping in his chair. "This means war. I will destroy Mikell and his people."

"Yes, sir,"

"You will hang Mikell and the other leaders on Edisto, confiscate all their lands and assign all the colored's to inland plantations. The surviving whites will become pariahs in South Carolina, destitute, wandering and homeless."

"Yes, sir,"

"You will organize another attack, General." The governor decided. "Gather all the Red Shirts and have all the rifle clubs in the state send men to join you. Every one of them, hear me?"

"Yes. Sir,"

"Let me know of any clubs fail to respond as you order. They will be dealt with later."

"Yes, Sir,"

"Also, bring all the Red Shirts to a site near Edisto as soon as possible." The governor continued. "You will overwhelm Mikell and his people with sheer numbers. I don't care what casualties you might incur."

"Yes, Sir,"

"And find my son's body."

Edisto Island

Townshend was conducting a meeting with his island Council.

Every element of the island community was represented. District Judge, William Jenkins, Sheriff Richard Green, Federal Marshal Robert Stone, Postmaster Willard Smith. Doctor John Morgan, landowner John Thorpe and crop manager Tom Curtis.

"Welcome everyone. I know how busy you all are, so we should get right down to the purpose of this meeting. I have asked Charles Pope to join us because he is a major landowner on Edisto. And despite being new to our island community he should know the danger we face.

"I also see that Mrs. Thorne is in attendance. Welcome Mable."

John Thorn, her husband spoke up. "Since Mable more closely represents the colored community than anyone else here, I thought she should be in attendance."

"I agree," Mikell announced. "Any objections?"

There were none.

"The recent attack on us will probably not be the last. The white supremist who now govern South Carolina view us as a threat to their control of the state.

"It is apparent now, that the son of our new governor, Wade Hampton III participated in that recent attack. We believe he was killed when our people repulsed the attack. His body washed up on our shore a few days ago. Since, his father, Governor Hampton, was behind that attack, I am sure that he is now more determined than ever to destroy our community.

"In fact, my informants tell me he has ordered General Conner to organize a major attack on us as soon as possible. He directed the General to rally all the Red Shirts and gun club members to gather for such an attack.

"At a recent meeting in Charleston, the governor also ordered that all of us in this room today to be killed, all our people of color be dispersed and sentenced to work farms throughout the state for life and any surviving whites to be striped of property and sent homeless away from the island."

Mikell paused to let his words sink in.

"You must inform your people of this threat, and enlist their help," He continued. "Every man woman and child, has a stake in this fight. It is up to you to bring that realization home to them."

Judge Jenkins asked, "What preparations have been made, Townshend?"

"Marshal Stone can speak to that point. Marshal?"

"I have just returned from Savannah where I met with Federal officials. I informed them of the threat to our community. They are reluctant to assist us from the land side. But I think they have found a way to help us on our Atlantic boarder."

Charlotte Mikell asked. "How can they refuse to help us on our Western boarder but agree to help us on the East?"

"It is all political, Charlotte," Marshal Stone answered. "The Hayes administration traded for South Carolina's Electoral votes in 1876. They promised not to interfere with state and local policies toward us coloreds in exchange for those disputed Electoral votes.

"So, Federal officials in the South are nervous about enforcing Federal laws prohibiting violence toward freedmen. But I think a loophole has been found.

"What's that, Marshal?"

"The ocean," He responded.

"What the hell does that have to do with the law?" Judge Jenkins asked.

"No coastal state in the Union is allowed to have a naval force of its own, certainly not one in private hands."

"So?" the Judge continued.

"So, such a force is clearly illegal, in their view," The Marshal went on to explain. "An armed vessel patrolling our coast is therefore not allowed. General Sheridan has ordered ships of the US Navy to patrol our coast effective immediately. President Hayes will not oppose Sheridan's order because it has the support of Republican Radicals in both the Congress and the Senate."

"So, as long as Hayes needs the support of the Republicans in Congress, we get the protection of the US Navy?" Mable asked.

"It would seem so, Mrs. Thorne," The Marshal told everyone.

"Will that secure our Atlantic boarder?" Charlotte asked.

"It should," Townshend answered. "But we will not assume that. On the contrary, we will assign some of our forces to that area."

"What do you have in mind to protect us in the West, at the land bridge Townshend?" the Judge asked.

"Billy has been down there for the last week with a handpicked crew, Judge."

"What's he doing?" The Judge asked.

"He'll brief us on that situation later this week," Townshend promised.

Columbia, South Carolina

Governor Hampton was meeting with General Conner in the governor's private office at the state capital.

"Are you ready to carry out the attack, General?"

"Just about, Governor," He answered.

"I don't want to hear that you're almost ready. What the devil is holding the operation up, sir?"

"My attack force is a bit slow in getting organized, sir. We should be ready in another week; ten days at the most."

"You've already had two weeks. Now you're still not ready. Maybe I've chosen the wrong person to head this thing up?"

"No, you haven't, sir. The job will get done, I assure you."

"What about my son's body. Are you any closer to recovering it?"

"I sent a messenger to Edisto seeking information. The Sheriff there promised that inquiries would be made. Just today, I received word that your son's body has been identified and would be returned as soon as arrangements could be made."

"How will that be done?"

"They have refused to make the delivery by boat. They are insisting it be done overland."

"For them to deny us access to their docks is just smart. I don't understand, though, why you are having difficulty arranging delivery by way of the land bridge to the island."

"I don't want any of their people to get a sense of the attack force we are putting together west of their island. So, it has been a bit delicate."

"Hogwash!" the governor exploded. "I want my son's body back here before you attack. Is that clear, General?"

"Yes, sir. I'll make the arrangements before we attack."

Edisto Island

Townshend was talking with Marshal Robert Stone.

"How sure are you of the naval support to told us about the other day, Robert."

"General Sheridan has assured me that as long as the Republicans in Congress and the Senate support his orders, we can expect his ships to patrol our waters for the foreseeable future.

"Federal Marshals from all over the country have wired members of the Hayes administration and the Republican members of the legislative branch in support of Sheridan's order. By the way, Townshend, Charles Pope's step-father, Michael Drieborg has been very active contacting people he knows in Washington in an effort to help us. I just hope my colleagues around the country will keep the pressure on."

"I hope so, too, Robert," Townshend replied. "You know how unreliable politicians are. To win the presidency, Hayes agreed to that unholy alliance with the Democrats here in South Carolina. He got the state's electoral votes in exchange for leaving the Negro question to them.

"I'm sure Hampton will raise all hell with Hayes about Sheridan taking sides in our favor."

"Right," Stone said. "No telling what threats and offers the Hampton people will use to get him to countermand Sheridan's order.

"But as of this moment, all I can tell you is that Sheridan is using the Navy to protect our coast. What about your contacts?"

" I don't have any political contacts, Robert; not a soul. Nor do I have any leverage with any politician, North or South., in Washington or Columbia."

"What about your friend, that writer Dennett. Can't he help us?"

"He promised to write an article for the Nation magazine about our community as the shining example of bi-racial harmony and economic success. He also said he would contact Horace Greely, editor of the New York Tribune.

"Doesn't that newspaper have the largest circulation in the United States?"

"That's what Dennett told me," Townshend confirmed. "He' also going to contact papers in Washington City, Chicago and Boston. He said that articles published in the big city newspapers is frequently picked up around the country is the weeklies and the small-town daily papers."

"Well, Townshend," Robert said. I hope they get on it in time to help us down here."

"By the way," Robert. My contact in the Hampton camp told me that Hampton's people seem well informed about what goes on here and that they expect information about our defenses.

"Do you suspect anyone who was at our meeting last week is leaking information to Hampton?"

"Now that you ask, yes, I do,"

"Who do you think it is, Robert?"

"You might not like my answer, Townshend,"

"Tell me who you suspect, damnit!"

"I wouldn't trust Judge Jenkins as far as I could throw him,"

Townshend laughed. "Neither would I, Robert,"

"Tell me," The Federal Marshal asked. "Why do you feel that way?"

"Over the years, I've caught Jenkins lying to me time and again. Also, he has told me that he wants to be appointed a judge on the United States Supreme Court. But he needs the support of our state's United States Senators and Governor Hampton's influence in Washington to make that happen.

"So, do you agree with me that he might be supplying information our enemies in exchange for Hampton's support?"

Marshal Stone answered. "Makes sense to me. Remember, he has access to Hampton by way of the court personnel stationed in Columbia. Out of our group, you, he and I are the only ones with access to the outside world. "

"Ya," Townshend agreed. "Since you and I are definitely on Hampton's list to be hung, I doubt if either of us would be the leaker."

"The good Judge could meet with an accident, you know," Marshal Stone commented.

"Not yet, Robert," Townshend cautioned. "I suggest we used the Judge as a source of leaking misleading information to Hampton's people. That has the added advantage of keeping their source secretly controlled by us rather than eliminated.

"Besides, we've gotten some pretty good judgments from the Jenkins' court. If he's gone, Hayes will have to appoint a successor who might be really in Hampton's pocket.

"No, Robert," Townshend concluded. "We'll just keep an eye on the Judge and feed him some misleading information along the way."

"Whatever you say, Townshend."

"One more thing, Robert," Townshend said.

"What's that?"

"The body of Wade Hampton IV,"

"What about it?"

"Don't give it to the Governor's people until Billy says his defenses are ready."

"You think they'll hold off attacking until they get his body back?"

"Yes, I do," Townshend said. "Their recent messages to us about the Governor's son tell me they are very anxious to retrieve it as soon as possible. So, I'm sure the Governor won't take a chance on us destroying his son's body it if they attack us while we have it."

"Fine. I'll think of some excuse to delay returning it."

"And, Robert," Townshend cautioned. "Keep this conversation to yourself for now."

"Got it."

*   *   *

It was Sunday. Susan and Charles were riding along the beach. They had attended church that morning and afterward had enjoyed lunch with her parents.

Later, Charles was in his room writing a letter home. Answering a knock on the door to his room, he found Susan standing there in her riding outfit.

"There's a special tree on the island I want to how you, Charly."

"What can be so special about a tree?" he asked.

"You'll see," Susan responded.

Unable to resist her invitation, he said. "Give me a minute to change my cloths."

Then, he followed her to the stables. They saddled their horses and headed toward the beach.

"Over this way, Charly," She directed. Then, she spurred her horse into to a gallop along the shoreline.

It wasn't long before she pulled off the beach and rode on to a rise in the sand dunes. Not far from the shore line was a very tall tree with a huge trunk. It was obviously a very old tree.

Susan reigned in her house and dismounted by the tree.

"Here we are Charly," She announced.

"What's so special about this tree?" he said. "It's just a tree."

Susan ignored the disappointment in his voice.

"Not so fast, my friend," She cautioned. "This is a very special tree."

"Why?" Charles challenged. "Because it has a swing hanging from that limb."

"No smart aleck," She snapped. "It's special because my father proposed marriage to my mother at this very spot twenty or so years ago."

Charles had to admit, "That would make it special for you, I guess."

"Come on," She urged. "Help me with this blanket and picnic basket."

She and Charles spread a blanket in the shade of the tree.

Susan opened her basket and began to put its contents on the blanket.

"Is this our supper, Susan?"

"It is unless you'd rather be at my parent's table instead of here, with me."

"That's a no-brainer," He thought.

"Well Charly," Susan snapped, hands on her hips for emphasis. "What will it be? Home with my parents or here, with me."

Charles had recovered his senses sufficiently to save the situation.

"With you, of course, Susan."

"Good answer, my man. Now help me with our meal."

He did so, without comment this time.

Later, they sat with their backs against the tree.

Charles broke the silence.

"Susan," He began. "Would you mind if I asked you a serious question?"

"Is this a trick." She asked.

"No. But I am serious about getting an answer."

"All right, Charly. Ask away"

"The last time we went riding you gave me a kiss just before we returned. What was that all about?"

Susan looked at Charles with a rather puzzled expression on her face.

"My goodness, Charly," She responded "What do you think it was about?"

"Don't do that, Susan," Charles said rather hotly. "I asked you an honest question and I expect an answer, not another question. What was that kiss about?"

"I best back off my attitude and give this guy an answer. I don't want to lose him." Susan decided.

"As you probably have discovered, Charly, I have decided in my short lifetime, that a direct approach is best in most situations."

"Were you giving me a message of some sort, Susan?"

"Not of some sort, but one of a very direct sort," She answered.

"What was that?"

"What do you think, Charly?"

"There you go again, answering my question with a question. That is so aggravating, Susan."

"My message, Charly was that I like you very much.

Charles was quiet for a minute, sort of taking in what Susan had just told him.

"Is that like loving someone?"

"I'm not sure, Charly," Susan answered. "I have not felt this way about anyone else before. But I wanted you to know about my feelings for you."

"Thank you for telling me, Susan," Charles said. "I know I like you a lot, too. But I haven't gone around just kissing you. Seems to me that is a rather serious thing to do."

"Are you sorry that I kissed you, Charly?"

"No. I liked it a lot. But I didn't want to assume anything either. I can't read your mind, you know."

"Now that we've had this conversation, what do you intend to do, Charly?" Susan asked.

"Do I have to talk with your father?"

"Just because you want to kiss me, Charly?" she chuckled. "Not hardly."

"Are you making fun of me, Susan?"

"Watch out here, girl," She told herself. *"Take it easy with the sarcasm."*

"Not at all, Charly. If we were talking about getting married, yes you would talk to my father. But to sort of court one another, no."

"Does that mean I could kiss you without you getting all made at me?"

In answer, Susan leaned over and kissed Charles.

"I wouldn't get mad, Charly; not at all."

It was quite a while until they rode their horses back to the barn.

*   *   *

Charlotte Mikell heard her daughter come into the house. It was already dark outside.

"You enjoy your picnic with Charles, dear?"

"Yes, I did Mother. I think we both had a good time."

Her father asked. "Wasn't it getting chilly on the beach?"

"I didn't notice, Father," Susan responded.

"I'm not surprised," Townshend muttered.

"What did you say, dear?" his wife asked.

"I said, you and I used to enjoy an occasional picnic on the beach."

Charlotte recalled. "We would do that all the time before we married. You remember that, don't you dear?"

Townshend responded. "When Susan walked in right now, I was remembering what we did when we spent an afternoon at the beach."

"You think?" his wife asked.

"I don't know, Charlotte," Her husband admitted. "I don't know if it is the same for them."

"I wonder," Charlotte muttered. Then she went on with her knitting.

"Exactly," Townshend said.

Work in the Fields

Charles reported for work to Mr. Curtis as directed by Townshend Mikell.

"Good morning Charles," Curtis said. "Right on time, I see."

"Yes, sir," Charles responded. "Since Townshend asked me to supervise the early milking and cheese production, it's real difficult to set up a definite time for me to get down here. Today, everything went well. Tomorrow, I might be early or late. Sorry I can't be surer."

"I understand, Charles. Get here as soon as you can. By the way, call me Ed."

"Sure thing, Ed. Now what am I to do?"

"You worked in the rice paddies two weeks ago when they were flooded. Right?"

"How could I forget walking around in all that muck. It was not very pleasant work, either."

"Well, now it's time to drain the paddies."

"How is that done?"

The two men went across the paddies on raised walkways. At the far end there were wooden barricades.

"We hold the water in the paddies by means of these barricades. In the middle of them you can see a gate of sorts. We call them sluice gates. Anyway, we raise them to drain the rice paddies. After a few days, the paddies will be dry enough for us to cultivate.

"The water we drained from the rice fields, we store in those ponds below us. Raising the sluice gates there allows us to use that water for irrigating the cotton fields. In between irrigations, we hand cultivate the cotton rows. Weeds are a serious problem so, between flooding the fields, we attack the weeds."

"The last time I weeded in the rice fields, my back was sore for days after all that bending."

"Get used to it, Charles," Curtis told him. "We will be weeding the cotton fields for the rest of this week. Then, we'll open those sluice gates and irrigate our fields. We're almost at the beginning of harvesting both rice and cotton."

Sure enough, after siesta, Charles joined people of all ages in the cotton fields, hoeing.

"They even have children out here," Charles observed.

That evening, Townshend gave Charles some good news.

"After siesta tomorrow," He told Charles. "I want you to meet with me and Mr. Curtis in my office. It is time we informed you of just what happens to what is grown on your lands.

*   *   *

Townshend welcomed Bill Bishop, Tom Curtis and Charles into his office.

"Thanks for joining me here, gentlemen," He greeted. "I thought it time to introduce Charles, here to how crops are handled after the harvest; in particular those taken from his lands. He has had a

418

brief opportunity of working those fields, but he needs to become aware of the next steps in the process here on Edisto."

"Happy to help, Townshend." Curtis assured him.

"Absolutely," Bill Bishop added.

"Charles," Townshend began. "You are one of the very few large landowners on this island. There's me, Thorn, Jenkins, Aiken and you. These five landowners produce most of the cotton, corn and rice grown annually on the island. This group also raises the most livestock.

"The production of cotton, rice and corn are all below pre-1860 levels. We just don't have the workers here now, to cultivate more land. Our major crop, long stem cotton is doing very well, though. Last year we exported over 250,000 bales. This is our most important cash crop. Rice is next. We also export most of the beef cattle we raise and a good deal of our excess corn meal.

"The sale of these crops gives us the cash we need to pay our state land taxes and the money to buy all sorts of things we cannot produce ourselves. Items like, kerosene, arms, coffee, glass, paper, shoes, tobacco, oil, tea, manufactured goods, iron rods, wire, oil, wheat & dry goods are all imported. "

Mr. Curtis added, "There's a lot of activity on the island that is not associated with export, though."

"Right, Tom," Townshend agreed.

Curtis went on, "You know all about the production of dairy products, Charles."

"I should, Mr. Curtis, "He chuckled. "I'm over in the dairy barn every morning by 6 AM or so."

"Right," Townshend admitted.

"All of that stuff, milk, butter and cheese is consumed here on the island. The herds of cows and swine, too are for island use. But the beef cattle are almost all exported to Bermuda."

"I've noticed that every family has a pretty large garden on the few acres they own. They all seem to have goats, chickens & ducks running all around, too. Susan told me that they bring corn into the store for grinding, so they must grow that as well.

"Susan also told me that many of those families trade chickens, eggs and fish at the store in exchange for use of the grist mill and as payment for goods stocked on the shelves like clothing, shoes, tobacco and coffee."

"You're observant, Charles," Townshend told him. "Do you know why all those workers are in your fields weeding?"

"Because Mr. Curtis told them to, I think."

The three men laughed at that notion.

"Hardly, Charles," Tom Curtis told him. "You pay them."

"How do I do that?" Charles asked.

"From the cash you receive from the sale of your cotton and rice."

"But we haven't even harvested anything this year."

"You're right. This year's crop is not yet in, processed or shipped. But you have funds in our bank from last year's crop.

"That's where I come in, son," Mr. Bishop told Charles.

"Your workers are paid monthly from funds in your account. You accumulated those funds after last year's harvest of your cotton and rice was sold and sent to Bermuda."

"How much do I pay each worker?" Charles asked.

Tom Curtis explained, "As your representative here on Edisto Island, I negotiated contracts with residents who were willing to work in your cotton fields or in you rice paddies. Some work in both places. Years ago, the Freedman's Bureau represented the workers. That organization is no longer on the island. So, we use those old contracts as sort of a guide each time we negotiate a new contract. Our Federal Marshal sits in on any of the current negotiations. He represents the workers.

"This season we're paying a top hand in the rice fields, eight dollars a month. We pay a top hand in the cotton fields, seven dollars a month."

"But I've seen children and women working," Charles asked. "Do they each get that much?"

"No," Curtis answered. "Even young healthy females do not make the top wage. Some have gotten pretty close to being considered a top hand, though. Children would never earn the top wage. They don't often work a full day, either."

The banker, Bill Bishop reinterred the conversation at this point.

"Mr. Curtis here deposits the wages earned in a bank account for each family or individual. I set aside a certain portion for the expected land taxes for each landowner's account. The account holder gets a quarterly statement which includes a bill for goods purchased and charged at one of the two general stores.

"The coloreds seem to prefer shopping at Mrs. Thorne's store. The white people shop at Susan Mikell's store. Should a customer have a complaint about the bill, the Sheriff and I review the account with one or the other of them and the complaining customer. One of our local teachers can help them read or decipher the billing, if they need it. That usually settles things."

"I can certainly see why we pay more for work in the rice paddies than the cotton fields. Pretty grueling work in those rice fields." Charles said.

"Now you know why I asked you to work there," Townshend told him. "As the employer, you must know what it is like. My father did the same for me before the war."

"The cotton fields are no piece of cake either, Townshend." Charles added. No one disagreed with that opinion.

"If you think the work is rough now, Charles," Townshend informed him. "Wait until you're in the midst of harvesting wither of those crops."

"I can hardly wait."

Everyone laughed

"There are exceptions to the wages I mentioned," Curtis said.

"What's that?"

"Susan has hired help to clerk in her store and assist her with running the grist mill and cotton gin. The same is true with Mrs. Thorne. Some of our people work in the dairy, others in the fields and barns with animals. Loading cattle, cotton bales and barrels of rice and grain at our dock is an infrequent job. But those workers have to be paid. Sometimes, they are the same men who harvested the crop or raised the cattle being loaded." Curtis added.

"My bank helps landowners and workers arrive at equitable wages for all those tasks." Bill Bishop concluded.

"Sounds complicated," Charles told the gathered men. "Does it all work out pretty well."

"Yes, it does, Charles, "Townshend said. "Judge Jenkins is the final arbiter of complaints. But we only had one or two disputes get as far as his court all last year. "

"I think he settled both of them without difficulty," Bishop remembered.

"Right," Townshend judged. "None of us likes things to fester. That only causes distrust and anger. We want issues settled quickly.

"That's enough for tonight, gentlemen. I think we've given Charles plenty to think about."

"You mean that there's more?"

Once again, the other men laughed.

"There's a lot more, Charles. But we'll tackle those things another time. All right?" Townshend promised.

*   *

After the meeting, Charles and Susan rode to their favorite spot on the beach. They were sitting on a horse blanket and leaning against the big oak tree. Looking out to sea beneath the darkening sky, they hugged and kissed. A slight breeze had picked up.

"Charly, would you get me the blanket I tied to the back of my saddle." Susan asked. "I'm getting a bit chilly."

Charles walked over to their favorite tree where they had hobbled their horses.

"I can' imagine Susan is cold. I feel hot and I'll bet my face is flushed from all the kissing we've been doing."

He brought the blanket back and draped it over Susan's shoulders.

"Sit close to me, Charly. And tell me about your meeting tonight." She asked.

After they were settled, Charles went over all the information he had been given in his meeting with Susan's father and the others.

"I never realized how interconnected everything is on the island." He concluded.

"Surprise you, Charly?" Susan asked.

"Yes, and the complexity of it all stunned me, too.

"But the most stunning thing was when I realized that these important men were telling me how responsible I was for the livelihood of so many people. The entire system it appears depends upon the cash crops produced on the land owned by me and four others.

"Now, I realize that I have men, women and even children working for me. They earn wages that allow them to pay their land tax and buy stuff from your store or the one the Thornes' own. The workers bring stuff to barter for things you buy with the cash we earn from the export of cotton, rice and cattle. Just thinking about how it is all connected makes me feel responsible."

"Sounds like you're beginning to understand the system," Susan decided.

"The amazing thing is how it seems to work so well."

"Everyone has worked hard over the years to make it work. Our survival has depended upon it working," Susan told Charles.

"I'm beginning to see that."

"Sit closer Charly, and I'll share the blanket with you."

He nudged closer to her and Susan moved the blanket around Charles. She snuggled close. Charles lowered his head and kissed her. They didn't talk much more that evening.

*   *   *

The next day was Sunday. After services at the Trinity Episcopal Church, Charles joined the Mikell family for their noon meal.

"How about a picnic on the beach later, Charly?" Susan asked.

"Sounds great, Susan." Charles responded. "I've got a few things to do in my room right now. How about going at three o'clock?"

"That will work. I'll meet you in the barn at three, Charly."

Back in his room, Charles began his chores by gathering bedsheets and clothing that needed cleaning. Then he sat down to write a letter to his parents.

Hi Everyone,

What a week I've had. Townshend put me in charge of the dairy operation when the supervisor there came down sick. Now, I not only milk cows each morning, but I oversee the people who make butter and cheese. It is nice to know he has confidence in me. I also spent time with Mr. Curtis who has managed Grandpa Pope's lands since, forever. I worked with him draining the rice paddies and hoeing weeds in the cotton fields. Everyone works, even the boses.

Townshend had me meet with Curtis and a Mr. Bigelow, the island's banker. These three men explained what happens on grandpa's lands before, during and after harvests of our cotton and rice cash crops.

They even got into how wages are set for the workers. I knew none of this.

Susan Mikell told me all about bartering and showed me the gist mill and cotton gin operations. There is so much more to learn about agriculture, I can't begin to tell you. My head spins sometimes. I have been helping Susan some in the Mikell General Store, too. Lately, she and I have ridden our horses on the beach in the evening and sometimes we have taken a picnic lunch with us. I like her a lot.

I haven't gotten any mail from my Michigan family, though. What is going on with that? Maybe its because of being blockaded by the Red Shirts that we only get one or two mail deliveries a month, and that's from Savannah. It appears that Charleston is closed to us. All pat of the attempt by Governor Hampton to destroy the Edisto community, I'm told.

Maxine, how are you doing in school? Can you write me a letter and send me a drawing I can hang on the wall in my room? I know

426

what; send me a photograph of you and Momma. Can you do that?

There is a lot of excitement around here since Governor Hampton vowed to wipe us out. His son was killed here in the last attack of the Red Shirts, so he is determined to have revenge. Townshend and the other leaders are preparing for the attack they are sure will come soon. Pray for us, please.

Please tell Eleanor that I would like to hear from her, too. I wrote her last month. It is her turn.

I love you all and miss you, too.

Charles."

*   *   *

The late afternoon August sun seemed especially hot this Sunday and there was not much of a breeze either.

"Let's go for a swim, Charly," Susan suggested.

"I didn't bring anything to wear swimming," Charles protested.

"You're wearing underwear, aren't you?" Susan asked."

"Well, ya. But…"

"But what? Come, on. Nobody will see us."

Susan sat and took off her riding boots. Then, she stood and slipped off her riding pants and jacket."

Off she ran toward the water. "Beat you into the water, Charly," She shouted.

He was right behind and dove into a wave that was breaking on to the shallow sand of the shore. The two of them lay in the shallows.

"Isn't this heaven, Charly?"

"The water is way warmer than I thought it would be,"

"Because the water is shallow here,"

"Probably," he agreed.

"Back home, we have two small lakes nearby. On one of them called Fisk Lake. Some of the guys and I would swim out from shore to a dock right after the ice had melted. It was really cold. We did that very thing this past spring; in April, actually."

"The ocean here will get cold this fall, for sure," Susan told him. "Was the water deep under that dock?"

"Deep enough to dive off," He told her. "We would have a ball that we'd throw and try to catch as we jumped off the dock. Then, we'd lay on the dock, get dry and then jump in the water again whenever the sun got too hot.

"Seems like I did that a long time ago,"

"You miss it, Charly?"

"You asking if I miss my friends?"

"That and not having any responsibilities. You know, just a few guys having fun; no worries. Do you miss all of that?"

428

"Honestly, Susan," Charles admitted. "I've not had time to think about those guys or my life back North. I'm either working or too tired or enjoying myself with you.

"Besides, I have come to realize that here, on Edisto Island, I have a purpose in life. I had none in my life up North. So, no I don't miss it, Susan."

"And me, Charly?" Susan asked. "Am I any part of your new purpose in life?"

"Well, sure," He told her. "Where else would I get a nice picnic lunch?"

Susan splashed water in his face and shouted. "You scamp. I was being serious!"

"So was I," Charles snapped back running toward their blanket on the beach.

Sitting on the blanket in the hot sun their underwear was quickly dry. But they didn't seem in a hurry to put on their riding clothes. Instead, just as they were, they moved their blanket into the shade of the big oak tree and had their picnic lunch.

Once they finished eating and everything was put back into the basket, Susan said,

"I was serious, Charly,"

"About what?"

"Where do I fit in this new life you've discovered here on Edisto Island?"

"I best be serious now. No more smart aleck answers. This lady wants an answer, a serious one."

Charles moved closer to Susan and put his arm around her.

"No, none of that," Susan shoved his arm away. "You answer my question,"

"None of this life would mean very much to me without you," He said.

"Are you saying that you love me, Charly Pope?"

"Maybe I do, Susan," Charles said tentatively. "I don't know if what I feel for you is love. I do know that I can't be around you without wanting to hug and kiss you. Whenever I walk into your store, I have a devil of a time concentrating on the work I'm supposed to be doing. If that's love, then I guess I'm saying that I love you."

This time, Susan put her arms around Charles.

"That's exactly the way I feel about you, Charly Pope."

They lay alongside one another on the beach blanket. They kissed and touched one another until the sun went down and the sea breezes chilled the air.

Susan sat up and straightened her hair. "I need to get dressed, Charly." Susan said. "I'm getting cold."

The put on their riding cloths and prepared to return to their house.

Once back at the barn, they watered and fed their horses. While they each groomed their mounts, they talked, some.

"Remember, Susan," Charles asked her. "When I thought I needed to talk to your father because I wanted to kiss you?"

"I remember, Charly," She responded. "And I said it wasn't necessary."

"Now that we've think we love one another, is It necessary now?"

"I'd like to wait a bit, Charly," Susan said. "Let's see if what we feel lasts. If that's all right."

"I'm real new to having feeling like this for someone, Susan. It never happened to me before. You really think our feelings for one another might just go away?"

"I don't know, Charly," Susan admitted. "I'm new to this, too."

"So, you're suggesting that we wait and see before we talk with your parents?"

"I guess I am," Susan concluded.

Preparations for Battle

It was late, and Billy Kussy, Marshal Robert Stone and John Thorne were sitting in Townshend's office. Billy was born and raised on Edisto; grew up with Townshend. During the Civil War, he served in the Edisto Mounted Rifles with Townshend, too.

Of typical size for a cavalryman, Bill was five-foot six and slightly built. Since they both had returned from the war, he had been Townshend's right-hand man on the island. Now, he was in charge of planning its Western defenses.

Federal Marshal Stone

Marshal Stone was a freedman himself. He had been appointed a Federal marshal a few years earlier by the Grand administration. He and Townshend had become close. The Marshal served on the island's council and helped settle disputes within the island community.

John Thorne was one of the largest landowners on the island and a leader in the colored community.

"I want to review our preparations, gentlemen," Townshend told them. "We've stalled Hampton as long as we can on returning the body of his son. As soon as we do, I expect them to mount their attack.

"How are your preparations coming, Billy?"

"I think we're as well prepared as we can be, Townshend,"

"Does that mean you believe you can handle most any attack from the West?"

"Yes, I do," Kussy judged. "I don't believe any force can gain entry to the island from that direction. In fact, I believe any force that tries will pay a bloody price."

"Tell me about it."

"Before I get into that, let me tell you about the assumptions I've made,"

"Go ahead."

Kussy began to explain the assumptions on which he made his battle plan:

"First, the attacking force will have to use Wilcox Road. There is simply no other road available.

"Second, they will have to stay on that narrow surface because of the marshes and ditches on either side of Wilcox road.

"Third, our road blockades will force them to use the only large clearing between the mainland settlements and us on Wescott Rd. to reorganize and prepare their attack force. That dry clearing is approximately two miles from our entrance, well within range of our heavy guns.

"Fourth, the marshes on either side of the road will discourage any flanking effort by them.

"Fifth, we have sufficient ammunition to defeat the attackers.

"Sixth, we are defending our homes, they are just driven by hate.

"And, lastly our men know the swamps, the attackers do not and are afraid of what's in them."

Townshend had listened without interruption to his deputy.

"Can you think of any others?" Kussy asked.

"I have nothing to add to those assumptions, Billy. Can you show me what you've planned?"

"I'd rather not take you out there, Townshend. I think it would be just as clear to you if I showed you our battle plan, I've laid out on paper."

"Fine with me. Lay it out on the table, Billy,"

Kussy rolled out the paper and weighted it down on all four corners.

"Excuse the rough nature of this lay-out. But it's the best I could manage out in the field."

"It will do, Billy," Townshend assured him. "Tell me what I'm looking at here."

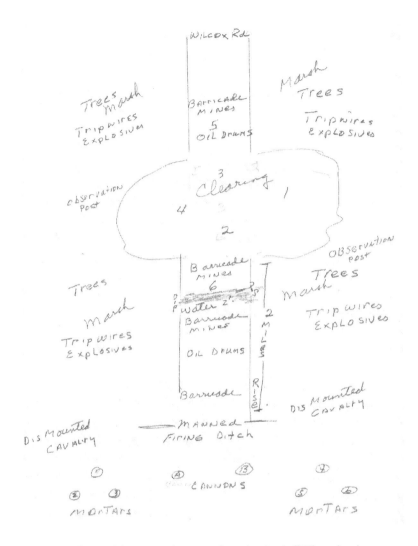

Before Billy could respond, Townshend asked. "Who else has seen this, Billy?"

"Two or three of my men. But this is the only copy of our preparations for the expected battle site,"

"Let's keep it that way. I don't want anyone else seeing this or the actual ground."

"What if the Judge or one of his people rides out to take a look?"

"Put a guard on the road in back of your entrenchments. Tell your guards not to allow anyone beyond their guard post without a pass from you or me."

"Will do,"

"What about pickets forward of this clearing?" Townshend pointed to the clearing marked on Billy's map.

"I've tied that in with our defenses in case they have artillery,"

"How so?" Townshend asked.

"Well, Townshend," Billy said. "I anticipate they'll have an artillery piece or two. After all, I assume that they have access to the state's militia stores."

"So, what do you have planned to handle that?"

"I have some men camped out near the settlement a few miles west of Wescott Rd. they will attack the horse drawn artillery with dynamite satchels and escape East on a trail we've established through the swamp."

"Sounds like a suicide mission, Billy, Townshend said. "I hope none of your men have families."

"They are volunteers and know the risks. Anyway, their escape route will not disrupt our preparations on the main road,"

"What have you placed there?"

"We've got trip wires placed along the road west of the clearing and in the swampy areas on each side of the road. They're attached to explosives."

"Too bad we can't have that road under visual observation, too," Townshend mused.

"Given the situation, I can't see how to do that. If we have mounted pickets out there, how are they going to get back to warn us? Remember, the road is mined and barricaded. And I'm counting on the swamp being impassable,"

"So, you're early warning system is the attack on the artillery and the tripping of those wires on the road attached to explosives?"

"Not exclusively, Townshend.

"I also have a few men a 'top Willtown Bluff. As soon as they spot Hampton's force, they'll fire a red flair. If they have artillery, a second flair will be fired. This time a green one."

"All right," Townshend said. "What are these numbers in the clearing?"

"Each of those numbers represents a target," Billy explained. "We've zeroed in a mortar on each number where we've placed a barrel of oil at each, too. As soon as we feel a sufficient number of the attackers have entered the clearing, we'll open fire, with each mortar having its dedicated target.

"When the mortar fire begins, we anticipate that the oil drums will explode and cover that whole area with fire, too."

"How are you going to initiate and direct that fire?"

"We have visual observation of the clearing. I have men high in trees using well camouflaged platforms on both sides of the clearing: here and here. They are connected to my command post behind the mortars by telegraph. The platforms have clear view of the clearing."

"How about the swamps?" Townshend asked. "It looks as though the attackers could use those to get access to the island."

"Trees have been felled all over the swampy areas. Generally, mucky ground under the water make it very difficult for a anyone much less a large force to use those routes. In addition, we've placed torpedoes in lower water level areas of the swamp. Those spots have been identified and are also under visual observation.

"We also have the mortars zeroed in on the barricades you see on the map. Those barriers are mined and barrels of oil have been placed there, too. So, any assault on our barricades will be met with powerful explosions.

"And finally, I have a mounted platoon of our Edisto Rifles in reserve, here and here. Should we suspect an attempt to use the swamp to flank our positions, this force will be employed."

"How will they get though the swamp?"

"We have identified a shallow path on each side of the road and cleared it for our cavalry. In addition, the men manning our mortars and six-inch cannon are prepared to shift targets and cover the swamp area being used by the attackers.

"Do you see anything else, Townshend?" Kussy asked when he had finished.

"No. And I hope neither of us have missed anything, Billy. A heavy rain would help, though."

"Right, a good thunderstorm would be great."

"But I think you've covered it," Townshend decided. "Now, it's needs to be executed."

"I think we're ready." Kussy assured Townshend. "Remember, everyone here is fighting for survival."

"You got that right."

"How about the coastal defenses?" Billy asked. "I know we expect the major attack to come on Wescott Rd. from the West. But how about the coastal area?"

"We aren't ignoring that area, Billy. Not at all," Townshend assured him.

"The Marshal and John are in charge of that part," Townshend said. "How are your preparations coming along, gentlemen?"

"We have come up with a different set of assumptions, Townshend." Marshal Stone began.

"What are they?"

"First, we have to assume that the attack could come from any one or all three sides of the island. You have the fourth side covered to the West, Billy.

"Second, the various swamps on the coastal areas are not easily penetrated and are therefore effective barriers.

"Third, our area is so vast, we have to depend upon patrols and mounted units rather than fixed positions.

"Fourth, we cannot depend upon concentrated firepower as you can on Wescott Road.

"So, how does that effect you defenses, John?"

"Let me lay out this crude map to give you an idea, Townshend," John said. He laid out the rough map on the table. "I'm afraid it's not as finely tuned as yours, Billy. But it will at least provide focus for our discussion."

Billy looked over the map of Edisto Island the Marshal had laid on the table.

"You're right about crude, Marshal," He judged. "Following this map, I might drown or at least get lost. Are you sure this is our island?" Everyone laughed at Billy's remark.

"Thanks a bunch, hot shot," The co-author of the map snapped.

"As you can see, we have water on three sides. So, we have observation towers at these three corners and patrols operating between. Each tower is supported by manned trenches, as well. In addition, we have established a cross fire between the trenches."

"What do the letters A and B represent?"

"Those are our six-inch canon. They can be moved in any direction and have a three-mile range. We have ammunition to explode above any attacking force, cannister for direct fire or penetrating projectiles. We can even direct fire your way, Billy, if you request it."

"I hope I don't need it,"

"Right."

"You have so damn much coast to cover," Townshend observed. "You think the Edisto River; the Seabrook River and the swamps are deterrent enough?" he asked.

"We're not actually sure of that, Townshend." Robert Morgan admitted.

Thorne added. "That's why we have several roving mounted patrols in those areas. And to speed up our response to any surprise attacks form those areas, we also have established telegraph communication to our central headquarters. Each patrol area has a telegraph station within a few hundred yards of their patrol area."

"Have you tested this at all?"

"Yes, we have. Our drills have demonstrated that the mounted patrols can send a rider to their telegraph station and get us messages faster than a rider could. Once received, we have directed reinforcements to the besieged area. We've done it all very quickly in our drills.

"We've also assigned women and youngsters to the trenches. They have practiced leaving their work stations or homes upon hearing the bells. They have also helped fortify the approaches to their trenches and created obstacles on the beaches."

"How have they responded participating like this?" Townshend asked.

"They've welcomed the opportunity of being asked to help in defending the island in this way."

"Where are you on your patrols?" Billy asked.

"The patrols are operating right now, around the clock," Morgan related. "Starting yesterday, we have had people in the trenches around the clock, too"

"Our kitchen people have also started bringing food to the trenches and to our central headquarters near the beach."

Ata this point, Billy asked.

"Can your kitchens bring us hot meals, too? Thus far, we've only brewed coffee and provided hardtack to our people."

"I'll check with them," Thorne promised. "Shouldn't be a problem, especially since your people are just sitting around on their asses."

"Thanks," Billy said. "I'll be grateful for the food, John. But you can shove that sarcasm where the sun don't shine."

Everyone laughed at this exchange.

Thorne asked. "Townshend, do you have any idea when the attack will come?"

"We're returning the body of Hampton's son, tomorrow," Townshend told them. "My informants tell me the Governor was waiting for that before he allowed his people to begin the attack. So, I expect them to attack any time after tomorrow morning."

Grand Rapids, Michigan

Miles and Judy Murphy were having supper at the Drieborg home on Prospect Street. Jake and Rose Drieborg were at the table too. They were in from Lowell for the weekend.

The three couples were relaxing in the living-room after the meal.

"How is my grandson doing?" Miles Murphy asked.

"It's sort of complicated, father," Mary Jacqueline told everyone.

"He seems to be well and fitting in with the island's routine well, too. Grandfather Drieborg, you will especially enjoy this. Since the second morning Charles was on the island, he has been assigned to milking cows."

"I can't believe it," Jake Drieborg responded. "Who drags him out of bed?"

"He tells us that he gets himself up," Mike answered his father. "He says bells ring all over the island at five and he just gets up, has something to eat and reports to the milking barn for his milking duty."

Mary Jacqueline added, "In his most recent letter, he told us that he has been made supervisor of the morning milking and dairy crew. It seems that they make butter and cheese there in addition to milking cows."

"Well, I'll be," Jake exclaimed. "When I put him to work in my barn, I knew he could milk a cow, if he decided to put his mind to it. But to get up that early on his own and be given the job of supervising an entire operation is really something."

"I am so proud of him," Mary Jacqueline told everyone.

"I think he has a girlfriend, too," Mike announced.

"What's that about?" Judy Murphy asked.

"He told us he has been horseback riding and going on picnics with Townshend Mikell's daughter. She runs the Mikell General Store and Charles has been assigned to spend time with her there in order to learn that phase of the business. Anyway, he says she is very pretty and he thinks she is very nice, for whatever that's worth."

"Well, I'll be," Jake said again. "The young man seems to be growing up on us."

"Tell us what his day is like down there, Mary Jacqueline," Rose Drieborg asked.

So, she and Mike told their guests the usual schedule Charles had told them about.

"This Mikell fellow seems to be in charge of things on the island, does he?" Miles asked.

"Yes, he is. He is one of the five largest landowners there. And, he has managed the Pope holdings there since Charles's grandfather died almost ten years ago. Charles wrote him about working on Edisto and learning how to manage the Pope lands there.

"You may not realize it, but Charles is one of those five large landowners I mentioned."

Jake asked. "I recall a fellow named Mikell invited Charles to come down and work on the island. Is that the same man?"

"Yes, father," Mike answered. "We met with him when we took Charles there last June. He told us then that if Charles stayed, he would be required to learn what the economy of the island is all about by working in the barns, the fields, the General Store and the cotton gin. He promised to require that Charles fully participate by working in all the activities that support the island's economy."

Miles Murphy asked. "So, what exactly is his daily schedule like?"

Mary Jacqueline described what she knew.

"Your grandson is up at five every morning, including Sundays. He must be at his first work station in a barn, milking cows by six. When he is done, he reports for work at either the rice paddies, the cotton fields, the corn fields, the cattle fields or the General Store. Then he has the noon meal. Everyone on the island then has a siesta until the supper hour around four. After that he reports to another field assignment followed by patrol duty on either the beach or the land entrance to the island. He says that he falls into bed around nine, dead tired."

"Well, I'll be," Jake Drieborg said once again. "I would never have believed it."

Rose Drieborg asked, "What is this patrol business you mentioned. That doesn't seem to have anything to do with farming."

Mike answered his mother. "You're sort of right. Mother But it does."

"How so?" Judy asked.

"Being a farmer yourself, Mother, I'm surprised you even had to ask," Mike chuckled at his mother's expense.

"Farmers are survivors," he began his explanation.

"Michael," his mother interrupted. "What has riding patrol have to do with farming?"

"They ride patrol in order to protect their community from attack by people who want to kill them."

Now everyone was talking and asking questions.

The one question that dominated the confused response to what Mike had told the grandparents was asked by Judy Murphy.

"Is my grandson in danger of being killed down there?" she didn't receive an answer.

She looked directly at her daughter, and asked again, "Is he, Mary Jacqueline?"

Her daughter put her hand over her mouth and teared-up. "Yes, Mother, he is."

"Michael," Miles Murphy asked rather loudly. "What the hell is going on down there?"

"All of you are aware of the turmoil in the South since the war ended. Right?" he began.

"Sort of," Judy responded.

"Is that why Charles was told to practice firing a rifle and learn to ride a horse before he went down there?" Miles asked.

"Yes, to your question, Miles, "Mike responded. "Everyone on Edisto is involved in protecting their community from attack. Everyone over sixteen is required to be involved, that is. They all work and they all patrol."

"Who wants to kill them?" Rose asked.

So, Mike gave them a history lesson.

"Before I begin," he said. "I must tell you that this answer will take some time to explain. Before I begin, can I get anyone more coffee or something stronger?"

"I'll have some hot water going in a minute for tea, anyone joining me?" Mary Jacqueline announced.

"If your fixing some, I will," Judy said.

"So, will I, dear," Rose said.

"What about you, two?" Mike asked his father and Miles Murphy.

"What have you got?" Miles asked.

Mike told them.

"I think I'll have some of that bourbon you brought back from your last trip South," Miles decided.

"You mean the moonshine from my friend in Tennessee?"

"Yes. That was pretty smooth stuff, as I recall," Murphy added.

"I haven't tried that, son," Jake said. "Give me a taste of that, too."

Once everyone was settled with their drink, Mike began to explain what was going on in the South generally and in South Carolina in particular.

"In May of 1865 the last Confederate military force surrendered. So, the military conflict ended. Earlier that year, the 13th Amendment to the Constitution outlawing slavery everywhere in the United States was passed. It was quickly adopted by the necessary number of states. Thus, the entire social structure of the South was altered.

"The question then became, what was to become of the almost four million former slaves living in the states of the former Confederacy? The Johnson administration felt that the state and local governments in the South should take the lead is managing the situation. President Johnson believed that since issues like voting rights, vagrancy laws, firearm ownership, and legal status had been state and local responsibility before the war, they should be the responsibility of government at those levels after the war.

"But the Republicans in Congress became concerned when they saw that the postwar Southern leaders were taking steps to control the newly freed coloreds in unacceptable ways. They were alarmed that the new rules being promulgated in the post-war Southern states were just another form of slavery. Actually, they were legal bondage

"The Republicans in Congress reacted with civil rights legislation and the 14rh and 15th Amendments to the Constitution. They suspended the existing state governments and divided the territory of the former Confederacy into several military districts presided over by a military governor. Colored adult males were given the vote. Federal soldiers were sent South to enforce federal law and see to it that adult Negro men could vote and that the rights of freedmen were protected.

"The reaction in the South was to resist. A new war began; a silent one. All over the South secret organizations like the Klu Klux Klan, Regulators, Rifle Clubs and Marauder bands attempted to subvert the Federal attempt to create a place in society for the freedmen. Where federal troops were present, the colored men voted, Republicans won elections; even coloreds often won public office.

"When I went to South Carolina for the Congressional Judiciary Committee back in 1867, we got caught in the middle of this secret war. Roving gangs terrorized freedmen. Amos, who you all know, was one of them who we rescued and sent North. I'm sure he would have eventually been lynched by the mob we encountered in Charleston.

"Any freedman who seemed to become successful was terrorized. Leaders throughout the South supported by much of society would not accept successful former slaves. Local law enforcement and the courts would not accept complaints of abuse from freedmen or court testimony from Negros. So, crimes against freedmen were not prosecuted or even punished.

"It eventually became so obviously bad for freedmen in the South that Congress passed what was called the Ku Klux Klan Act of 1871. That law made terrorism of freedmen a federal crime. It thus took enforcement of their rights out of the hands of local southern officials.

"That helped a lot. As long as federal officials had troops at their disposal in the South, freedmen had a chance for justice. But the presidential election of 1876 changed all of that. The Republican candidate, Hayes and the Democratic candidate, Tilden came down to the wire in the Electoral College voting. The Electoral votes in several Southern states were in dispute. Whichever candidate was awarded those votes would win the presidency. Behind the scenes, the Hayes people promised to end all Reconstruction efforts if Mr. Hayes was awarded the disputed votes.

"So, it happened, the congressional committee in charge of this matter awarded the disputed electoral votes to Mr. Hayes. He became President and all federal troops were withdrawn from the South. In addition, any support of federal law specifically in place to protect the rights of the freemen ceased to be enforced. The resistance movement in the South now had a free hand to manage what the press has called, the 'Negro Problem'."

"When Mary Jacqueline and I were in Georgia recently, we encountered that war up close."

Mike's wife added, "A group allied with the Freedman's Bureau called the Union League was very strong in Georgia. Led by former white Union military officers, their membership was primarily made up of former Union colored troops.

"The Atlanta based group kidnapped Congressman Kellogg's aide Craig Haynes and tried to blame it on the Klan. They also attempted to kidnap me and the wives of the other deputies in Mike's group when we were visiting in Macon."

"You never told me about that, Mary Jacqueline," Her father snapped.

"We ladies managed to protect ourselves without any help from the men, father. The problem was solved so I didn't see any sense in worrying you."

"I always knew that going on these wild adventures with your husband would put you in harms way."

Mary Jacqueline went on. "The Union League stole from whites to support their activities and they terrorized freedmen into voting Republican."

Jake Drieborg observed. "It would seem, that the coloreds were getting it from both sides in the South."

"It seemed so to us too, father," Mike agreed.

"With the election of Hayes and the demise of the Freedman's Bureau, the Union League lost its semi-official support and disappeared." Mike added.

"Getting back to South Carolina," Mike signaled. "A former Confederate general and a staunch supporter of the Klan and this secret war, Wade Hampton III was elected governor in 1878. He publicly ordered the destruction of the Edisto Island community. Last month, his people, now called the Red Shirts, instead of the Klan, attacked the island from the sea. Charles was on patrol that night and participated in repulsing the attackers."

"Was he hurt?" Ruth asked in alarm.

"No, mother. He told us that he is fine."

"Did he actually shoot his rifle at another person?" Ruth continued.

"Yes, he did."

"Well, I'll be," Jake Drieborg continued to express his astonishment.

"And, in the attack it would appear that the governor's son was killed," Mike revealed.

"So, now, Governor Hampton has vowed to do whatever is necessary to destroy the Edisto community," Mary Jacqueline added.

"Why did Hampton even care about Edisto Island? Did they pay their taxes and otherwise obey all the laws?" Miles asked Michael.

"You might remember meeting Robert Stephans, Miles," Mike said. "You met him in Philadelphia at your home when Maxine was born a few years ago. Anyway, he is a prominent resident in

Charleston and the lawyer for the Edisto community. He told me that everything is in good order, legally. He said that the islanders had paid their land taxers and obeyed all the laws of South Carolina.

"He also told me that Edisto is a multi-racial community. There, the coloreds and whites work together and govern together, successfully. That's a problem for the resist movement. Their fundamental driving force, is to destroy any semblance of racial cooperation and harmony. The new social order forbids it.

"They want any successful community like exists on Edisto, to be destroyed."

"And our grandson is in the middle of that?"

"Yes, father, he is." Mary Jacqueline said. "That's why I am so worried."

"Well, pull him out of there!" Miles told Mike.

"He won't leave, father," Mary Jacqueline said.

"I would never have guessed the boy had that much sand, that much spirit," Jake Drieborg told everyone.

"It appears that he has found a new home, father," Mike judged. "He believes that he's found a cause, something in which he can strongly believe." Mike added.

"Charles has matured in a remarkably short period of time," Jake Drieborg told everyone.

"My grandson is in danger of loosing his life defending a bunch of coloreds, and you call it maturity? By God, I find that delusional, Jacob."

Mike interrupted that exchange. "You can call it whatever you like, gentlemen, But the community is in danger. My staff and I have paid for a shipment of surplus military gear that is being shipped to the island as we speak. The stuff is pretty inexpensive. You want to contribute?"

Jake responded. "Would $100 buy very much?"

"Yes, it would, father" Mike said. "How about you, Doctor Murphy?"

"I'll match Jake's contribution. And I'll ask at the clinic about sending medical supplies. Sounds as though they'll need those, too."

"Thank you, father," Mary Jacqueline said.

"If they're blockaded by these Red Shirts, how will this stuff get through to them?" Jake asked.

"Townshend told me that they have a small ship that carries things like mail back and forth as well as some barrels of rice and some cotton bales to Savannah. The ship returns with mail and supplies like kerosene, barrels of oil and whatever else they can find room for on the ship."

At this point, Ruth Murphy suggested. "When we all go to St. Andrews church tomorrow morning, I believe we each should light a candle and pray for the people of that community."

"That's a great idea, Ruth," Rose Drieborg agreed.

"Mother," Miles Murphy said. "I'm exhausted just talking about this and worried to death for our grandson I need to go home."

"You want me to hitch up the buggy, grandmother Murphy?" Mike asked.

"I think not, Michael," She said. "Miles and I both need some fresh air and a walk. Thanks, just the same. Come Miles. Our coats are in the vestibule closet."

"See you at St. Andrews, Ruth," Rose Drieborg said. "Nine thirty good for you?"

"Sounds fine. Breakfast at our place after Mass, everyone."

Charleston

Meeting in a room at the Brick House in Charleston, Governor Hampton asked,

"Are you ready to attack?"

"I think everything is in order, Governor," General Conner told him.

"What about my son's body? The governor asked. "Has it been returned?"

"We meet with representatives of the Edisto people next Sunday afternoon," Conner answered. "They have promised to have return it then."

"So, when do you attack?"

"We plan to launch by mid-week."

"What is you attack plan?"

"We have gathered over one hundred mounted Red Shirts several miles off the island. We have another one hundred infantrymen."

"What preparations do you think they've made, General?"

"Our information has dried up in the past few weeks. You man there, Judge Jenkins has been shut out, it appears. But I would expect the usual things like road barricades and road mines covered by riflemen.

"Can you flank the defenders?" the governor asked.

"The marsh land on each side of Wescott Rd. precludes flanking action. But I have several squads of men hitting their coast in long-boats. We actually have a better chance of breaking through by way of the coast than the road to the West.

"What about those federal Coast Guard ships?" the Governor asked. "Didn't they chase off our boats earlier this month?"

"We can't control their patrol schedule," Conner answered. "But we might get lucky and have our long-boats get through their blockade. Then again, we might not. I believe It's worth a try, Governor. "

"I agree, general. Get my son's body back first. Then destroy Mikell and his race mixers."

"You can depend upon it, sir."

Edisto Island

As dusk descended over the area, the look-outs on the island had been placed on alert. Everyone expected an attack to follow the return of the body Governor Hampton's son. No-one, however, had any idea just how soon after it would come.

They did not have to wait very long. Toward midnight that Sunday, one of the look-outs on Wescott Rd. saw a white flair burst in the sky over Willtown Bluffs. The attackers had been sighted. The look-outs now waited to see whether or not the green flair would appear in the sky announcing the presence of artillery. None appeared.

"Take this message to Townshend Bobby," Billy ordered one of his men. "Make sure to tell him that no green flair was seen."

Off the rider went.

"You men keep a look-out for a green flair. It just may be that artillery is at the end of the column.

"Smart to move your force after sundown, he told his men. "Darkness would make it more difficult for our look-outs to assess the enemy's real strength. I hope that same darkness will make traveling on our narrow road through a swamp slow and difficult, too. Time would tell just who has the advantage.

It was more than an hour before the first explosion was heard and the flash seen.

"I'd guess one of their advance guards tripped a wire."

"Right. That explosion took place somewhere between Willtown Bluffs and the turn on to Wescott Road."

"That's still a few miles out from the meadow we've mined."

"In this darkness, they'll never see the other wires we've placed on the road ahead of them."

*   *   *

General Conner rode to the front of his column.

"What happened up here?" he asked. "Report."

"Our point guard tripped a wire that was attached to a bomb," he was told.

"Casualties?"

"One man killed, one wounded. Two horses lost."

"Well, get them replaced," Conner shouted. "We've got the entire column standing here. We gotta get moving."

"Yes, sir."

The new point men were much more cautious moving through the darkness. Half a mile down the road, just around a bend, another wire was tripped; another road bomb was exploded.

On Edisto Island, Billy commented, "They're a few yards from the first barricade. They won't be able to move around it."

One of his men asked. "When they begin to dismantle it, won't that trigger another bomb?"

"It should."

"Won't that ignite the oil barrels with that Greek Fire inside?"

"Yep. It should do that, too."

"Then what?"

Billy explained. "Another bunch of their men should be killed or at least severely burned.

"Look at their situation," Billy continued.

"It's so dark they can't see their outstretched hand in front of their face; at least not clearly. They've already lost three, maybe four, men. Everyone else is frightened to take a step forward in the dark. What would you do?"

"I'd probably shit my pants. For sure, I'd have second thoughts about being any part of this attack."

"Exactly," Billy told his men. "That's the whole purpose of those trip wires and bombs. Replacing men lost is not a problem for them. Doing something about their men being too frightened to move forward is."

"If I were in their shoes, I'd sure wonder what surprise waits ahead."

"Exactly."

"Now what, Billy?"

"We haven't seen that green flair. So, whoever is leading this bunch didn't figure to need artillery. Pretty confident it appears."

"Over-confident, more likely."

"It would appear so. But we'll see."

Another explosion rocked the sky.

"Your question has been answered, Billy. They're trying to dismantle the barricade."

Billy explained the dilemma the attackers faced.

"Their leader is pushing ahead. He's angry now. He chose to use darkness to approach our defenses. Now he's paying the price. His men can't see shit. So, our trip wires and roadside bombs are virtually invisible. He knows that.

"But it's too late now for him to change tactics. On that narrow road he can't turn around in the dark and go back and he can't just stay where he is. He's got to move forward.

"There are two more trip wires attached to road bombs before they get to the next barricade; and another one there. To continue moving forward, they'll have to dismantle that road block, as well. And when those men try to do that, the Greek Fire in the oil drums we placed there, will explode."

"By that time, I'd hate to be the next guy ordered to take the point." The other men in the trench had to laugh at the image of that.

Billy interrupted.

"We've only got four hours before sunrise. I want you two men to take the first watch. You others, divide the rest of the time and stand guard in one hour shifts. No sense all of you staying awake between now and dawn. Those blokes out there aren't going anywhere.

"Wake me if anything unusual occurs." With that Billy lay back in the trench, put his hat over his face and appeared to fall asleep.

461

"How can he just, do that?"

"Fall asleep, you mean?"

"Ya."

"it you rode with us during the war," the man revealed. "You'd know. We did that all the time."

*　　　*　　　*

General Conner was talking with his officers.

"I don't care what the men are saying," he vehemently told them. "It's your job to lead, damnit!

"Get some steel in your spines. Are you going to be led by your men or are you leaders of men?"

"Sir," one of his Troop commanders reminded him. "The men are really spooked. They feel trapped on this dark road with the swamps all around and the explosions. My men are volunteers, remember. The governor may be upset about his son's death, an all. But my people don't have any skin in his dispute with the folks on Edisto."

"I don't give a damn what they think about the Governor or his son," Conner insisted. "We're going to destroy the Niger lovers on this island. That's why we're here. You best make that clear in the ranks.

"Captain Smith," he ordered. "You're Troop is up. Send two men to the front of the column and take the point. Do it now Captain."

"Yes, sir."

His men grumbled, but obeyed the Captain's order, and rode to the front. That was the last time Captain Smith ever saw those two men alive. Within the hour one of them tripped another wire and exploded another road bomb.

Conner ordered the column to continue moving despite the carnage. And within the next hour, another point guard tripped a wire and another bomb exploded.

*   *   *

All was not quiet on the coast, either.

When the bombs began exploding in the West, the coastal patrols were alerted to possible assault on the beaches as well. Flairs wee fired to illuminate the coast. After several were fired, longboats were spotted coming toward the beach.

"Here they come, John," Marshal Stone told his second-in command, John Thorpe. "Order the gun crews to get the two six inchers in action."

Stone had been First Sergeant of a colored cavalry unit during the war. He was a no-nonsense bellow who commanded respect. After the war ended, he returned to his home on Edisto. In 1869, the Grant Justice Department appointed him Federal Marshal for the island community.

John Thorne was one of the largest land-owners on the island. He also owned the General Store most used by the coloreds, and a cotton gin.

He ordered their two cannons brought to bear and the boats under fire while almost a mile at sea. One boat was destroyed by a direct hit. Another boat was overturned by a near miss. Still, several others full of men were seen being rowed toward the shore.

Stone ordered a rider, "Take this message to Townshend. Make sure he knows you're from the coastal defenses."

"Yes, sir."

The longboats were still out of rifle range so the cannon continued to fire at them. The coastal bells continued to ring out their alert. It brought the old men, women and teenaged children to their assigned beach trenches. They were all armed and ready to greet the invaders.

Several longboats survived the cannon fire. When they were within fifty yards of the beach, the men women and children in the trenches were ready for them. John Thorne gave the order to fire as the boats hit the shallows.

Thorne also had one of the cannons brought to a position overlooking the beach loaded with grapeshot. When the surviving invadors were still knee deep in the surf, he opened fire. Those in the trenches were ordered to stop firing to allow cavalry to sweep on to the beach.

The few survivors were rounded up as were those still floundering the surf.

It appeared that the invasion of Edisto's coast had been defeated.

*   *   *

An hour before dawn, General Conner's force had reached the last barricade before his first objective, the clearing.

This last roadblock was especially difficult to clear because if was partially under water. Never-the-less, the General ordered it be cleared. As with the previous road obstructions, this one exploded showering the men ordered to clear it with shrapnel and hot oil.

Still, almost one hundred riders strong, the column moved on toward the clearing as the first light of dawn greeted them. This open space in the swamp was to be the jumping off point for General Connor's attack. Here, they would re-organize, receive their final orders and from here they would assault and conquer the island.

*   *   *

Meanwhile, back on the island, Billy's men were awake and ready to launch their mortar attack. From their mounted observations platforms near the clearing, the spotters had alerted Billy of the attacker's arrival.

Billy telegraphed a message to them. "Let us know when the area gets crowded."

The answer he received was, "Not long now."

*   *   *

Meanwhile, all seemed to go well for General Conner's men as they moved into the clearing. Conner's subordinates directed units to set up on various parts of the clearing. It had been a long and harrowing night. So, first thing, each rider fed, then watered and groomed his mount.

The entire area was soon crowded with horses, men and wagons full of gear and ammunition.

Conner shouted to his officers, "Get you men going. We want to hit them before the sun is up. Move it, move it! Move it, now!" His officers scattered to their areas intent on getting their units lined up for the attack.

Suddenly, there was an explosion on the far right of the clearing, then another on the left. Then shells began to land and explode all over the clearing. Barrels of Greek Fire, hidden by shrubs, began to explode throwing their fiery gell in every direction. Men and horses were sprayed with the liquid fire.

Horses that survived the initial bombardment bolted and ran about terrified. Bodies of the killed and wounded men and their mounts lay on the ground everywhere, obstructing escape. There seemed to be no end to the shelling and there was nowhere to hide.

Some men, still close to the clearing entrance, managed to make it to the road West. Others ran into the swamps to escape the deadly barrage of shells.

It wasn't long before there were few men or horses standing. Then, just as suddenly as the shelling had begun, it stopped. Cavalrymen appeared out of the swamp at the northern and southern edges of the clearing. They began to round up survivors. Those who showed signs of resistance, were shot.

The invasion had been stopped; this phase anyway.

Billy and a mounted guard came up the road from the East and entered the clearing.

Prisoners and wounded were herded into the center of the clearing. A mounted unit of defenders joined them from the West.

"You didn't tell us you had cavalry coming from the West, too, Billy."

"I wasn't about to allow riders from this bunch to escape if I could help it." he explained. "Besides, I wasn't going to let our men just stay out there waiting for artillery that wasn't going to come. "

"Now, we have to get these captives to the beach area for questioning"

"Why not just string 'em up on the nearest tree?" One of his men asked.

"Cus, we don't do things that way," Billy told him. "That's why."

"Save a lot 'a time an' trouble, Billy," Another man said. "Sides, they were going ta' hang all 'a us, weren't they?"

"Maybe so. But we'll let Marshal Stone and the Judge decide that."

"You're the boss. What da ya want us to do wit 'em now?"

"After you search each for weapons, line 'em up and march 'em to the coastal area." Billy ordered. "I think the Marshal has a holding area for 'em."

"'And the wounded?"

"Leave 'em here, under guard." Billy ordered. "Doc Morgan will be up soon. He'll take care of them."

Aftermath

Governor Hampton was meeting with several influential advisors at Charleston's Brick House. They had finished their dinner and were enjoying some cognac. The small room was filled with the smoke of their cigars.

Matthew P. Butler, the United States Senator from South Carolina asked the governor,

"Is your vendetta against Mikell and his Edisto Island community, over?"

"Not by a long shot," Hampton spat. "I just had the wrong man in charge of the attack. We'll get 'em next time."

"There's not going to be a next time, Wade," Martin W. Gary, the chairman of the state's Democratic Party organization said.

"What the hell you talking about? I decide that, not you."

"Let me explain," he went on. "John Dennett, is a writer for a Northern magazine, The Nation. He wrote a series of articles for the New York Tribune about how wonderful this Edisto Island community is and your attempts to destroy it. In case you don't know, Wade, this is the largest newspaper in the United States and it syndicates news articles all over the country.

"Anyway, this writer's stuff is all about Mikell and your attempts to crush his successful multi-racial community on Edisto Island. It has created quite a sensation throughout the North. In fact, your vendetta has made Mikell a hero: sort of a David vs Goliath story.

Hampton snapped. "So, what. That's just another northern smear against the South."

"Not this time, Wade," Butler interjected. "It appears that this firestorm has captured the attention of not only the general public in the North but folks in the border states as well."

An irritated Hampton snarled. "What in the devil has that got to do with us in South Carolina?"

"Two things, actually." Butler responded. "Just when we thought the folks in the North had given up on the Negro problem, and left it to us, you have managed to change all that.

"Your comments about confiscating the land and hanging all the whites on Edisto, and your open support of armed attacks on the people there have spawned new interest in all the old Reconstruction issues of individual rights. Thanks to you, white people, like Mikell, who fought for the 'Cause', feel threatened, too.

"That alarm has grown with such intensity that the Hayes administration has been pummeled with demands that it aggressively apply the Enforcement Act of 1871. You might remember, governor. That's the federal law that is also called the Klan Act. That law allows the Federal Justice Department to come in our state and do whatever is necessary to protect people's rights. Need I remind you, that we don't want that to happen again? "

"I resent you lecturing me, Senator."

"Someone sure has to." Another man at the table said.

The Senator continued, "Secondly, just when we were making progress getting Yankees interested in investing their money in South Carolina, we have hit a wall of reluctance. It appears, Governor, that investors are suddenly hesitant to invest in a state which has the racial turmoil you've created.

"My contacts in the Hayes administration tell me the same thing. His people are not going to use their influence to help us as long as this race turmoil continues. Get it, Wade?"

"In the Senate, I'm getting heat from my cotton state colleagues, too," Butler revealed. "They don't like all the negative publicity your actions are getting. It makes it hard for them to work with Northern senators and to interest investment in their states.

"I see Atlanta, Mobile, Nashville, Richmond, Savannah & New Orleans getting all kinds of interest and money from northern bankers and investors. How much interest are you getting in South Carolina, governor?" Butler concluded. "None, that I know about."

Another member of the group added. "It's pretty simple, Governor, you've made this Mikell fella a hero. The Northern press has painted him as the David fighting the evil Goliath.

"In short, governor," the man concluded. "You have become the evil Goliath. That makes you a liability to the future of South Carolina."

"That's a lie!" Hampton shouted. "Today, on the streets of Charleston, I could raise an army of 500 men all ready to follow me."

"That's probably true, Governor," Gary, the Democratic Party Chairman said calmly. "You are very popular with the red necks of our state. And, I expect you would get standing ovations at the Veterans of the Confederacy meetings all over the South.

"But we will not receive one Yankee dollar of investment in South Carolina as long as you continue talking about hanging white people who dare work with coloreds or as long as you pursue your vendetta against the Edisto Island community. It has got to end."

"And, another thing, Wade" Senator Butler added. "Unless you back off this thing with Mikell you will not be selected by our legislature as the next United States Senator from South Carolina."

"You-all can't be serious," Hampton responded. "All over a bunch of darkies?"

"My Lord, Wade," Senator Butler said in surprise. "What about what we've told you don't you understand?"

"Back off this business now, Governor," the Democratic Party Chairman demanded. "Or, you will not even be our candidate for governor again. We will replace you with someone who places the interests of South Carolina above his own."

"Damn!" Hampton exclaimed. "I never thought I'd hear such talk from men such as you. You value money over honor."

"Are you going to back off, or not?" Senator Butler asked.

"It would appear gentlemen," Townshend said, "that we have survived to fight again another day."

Marshal Stone said, "Hopefully, we won't have to fight again. The governor's people really took it on the chin today."

"Maybe so," Billy said. "But our governor was never known for his wisdom. We best be prepared for more of what we saw today."

"I agree with the Marshal," Judge Jenkins said. "I think the best course of action is for us to stand down and offer an olive branch."

"We're going to hope for the best, Judge. But we're going to prepare for the worst." Townshend told the group. "So, let's celebrate our victory but keep up our guard.

"Right now, we need to assess our loses and repair our defenses. Then, we can have a drink to celebrate. Get the word out to all your people. Tell them we won and thank them for a job well done. They can all return to their normal activities.

"Billy, you and the Marshal join me at the stables. I've already notified Thorne that are going to survey the area and assess our defensive situation."

"What about me," Judge Jenkins asked. "Why don't you ask me to join you?"

"Judge," Townshend reminded him. "You've got a whole lot of prisoners in the stockade to interview. Your job is to tell is what to do with them. Best get to is, sir. I want them and their wounded off our island within twenty-four hours."

"You.ve got over one hundred in that stockade and a bunch of wounded, to boot. How an I supposed to process all of them by this time tomorrow?"

Mikell was having none of the judge's resistance. "Best get at it judge. If you don't take care of it, the Marshal and I will."

*   *   *

Susan found Charly in the dairy barn. She ran up to him and gave him a warm hug.

"When I didn't see you down at the beach, I was worried that you were hurt, or something." She whispered.

Charles returned her hug as they held one another.

"Nice to know how much you cared," Charles assured her. "But I'm fine."

"Why didn't you let me know?"

"Your father sent me here as soon as the fighting ended on the beach. So, I didn't have any way to tell you."

"Why was it so important for him to send you here?"

"Because the cows were long overdue to be milked," Charles told her. "I'm told it is painful for them when milking is delayed. This morning we were several hours late. So, they must have been hurting."

The two sat and held hands.

"Charly," Susan said looking in his eyes. "I think we need to talk with my parents."

"Why now?"

"Because, when the fighting started this morning, I realized how much you mean to me."

"You think you love me?"

"I know it for sure, now."

"And that's why you think we should talk with your parents?"

"Yes."

"Are we going to tell them that we love one another."

"Yes."

"And that we think we should get married?"

"Yes."

"How about we tell them after siesta time, today."

"Yes," Susan agreed. "The best time for us to have them along is when we're having supper."

They stopped talking and kissed.

"I don't want to stop kissing you, Susan. But I have to finish up in the dairy room."

"I understand, Charly." She said giving him one last kiss, on the cheek this time.

Off she went, leaving Charles somewhat dazed.

With all the clean-up needed there wasn't much of a siesta on the island this day. Never-the-less, the Mikell family met for supper as usual, Charles was included.

As soon as they were seated, Mrs. Mikell began to pass the plates of food.

Susan immediately began the conversation.

"There is something Charly and I want to talk to you about," she said.

"And, what would that be, dear," her mother asked.

Her father set his fork down, sat back in his chair and waited.

"We love one another, mother," Susan blurted it out.

"That true, Charles?" Townshend asked.

"I believe so, sir," He responded.

"Have you ever been in love before, Charles?" he continued.

"No, sir, I haven't."

"Then, how can you tell?"

"I can't explain it, actually," Charles responded. "What I do know is that as I've gotten to know Susan, I am lonely for her when we're apart and I get this hot feeling when we're together."

"What do you intend to do about it, Charles?" Townshend asked.

"I think we should get married, sir,"

"Oh, my goodness," Mrs. Mikell exclaimed.

"I agree, father," Susan added. "I love Charly and think we should marry."

"What do you want from me and your mother, Susan?"

"We want your approval and your blessing,"

"What do you think Charlotte?" he asked his wife.

"I'm just thinking it's awfully sudden. You've only known one another for a couple of months. We don't even know if Charles intends to stay on the island. Besides you've only just turned eighteen."

"Mother," Susan challenged. "You were sixteen when you married father. Right?"

"Well yes, but there was a war on. He was going away. I might have never seen him again."

"Excuse me, Mrs. Mikell," Charles interrupted. "Aren't we in a war right now?"

Townshend Mikell was silent. But he had to smile at the comment Charles made.

"I suppose, we are," Mrs. Mikell conceded. "But it's not quite the same."

"My mother married my father when she was eighteen years old," Charles told her. "And she moved to Charleston, South Carolina at the beginning of the secession crises. At least Susan and I would be lining right here."

"There is that, I suppose." Charlotte Mikell admitted.

"Besides, mother," Susan said. "Wouldn't you rather have us living here as man and wife instead of sneaking around in the barn or at the beach?"

Townshend had to hide his smile at his daughter's frankness.

"I would hope you're not snaking around now, young lady." Her mother said.

"I'm only saying, mother."

"Susan," her father said. "I approve of your marriage to Charles."

"Thank you, father; thank you, thank you." Susan shouted. "Isn't that wonderful Charly?"

"Of course, it is," Charles responded. "But is that all you have to say, Mr. Mikell?"

"You're expecting a reservation, Charles?"

"Yes, I am,"

"I knew you would see through me, young fella." Townshend joked.

"Father," Susan exclaimed. "Don't joke about this."

"I approve of this marriage, but not until Charles returns from his trip home later this fall."

"This is my home, now, sir," Charles assured him.

"I happy to hear that, son," Mikell said. "All I am insisting on is a short engagement. I believe we should stick with the original plan of you returning to Michigan after the harvest. There, you will

477

assess your situation. If you return, and still want t marry Susan, you'll not only have my approval, but also my blessing and help. What do you think, Charlotte?"

"I agree with your proposal, dear," Mrs. Mikell said. "Let's announce the engagement at the Harvest Celebration later this month and plan on a wedding for January.

"Do you two think that is satisfactory?" she asked.

Charly spoke first. "I love your daughter, ma'am. And as much as I want to marry her now, I see the wisdom of the short engagement you want us to have. So, I agree. What about you Susan?"

"I agree, too, Charly."

With that Susan jumped up from her seat end hugged her mother, then her father. Then she turned to Charles and gave him a kiss along with a hug.

After she sat down her father said.

"I don't know about you people, but I'm hungry. Please pass the pork, Charlotte."

That sort of broke the awkward silence. Everyone filled their plates and ate.

Charles was the first to ask a question about yesterday's attack.

"I assume the men at our entrance repelled the attack there."

"Yes, they did," Townshend said. "Billy Kussy and his people absolutely destroyed the attackers. His defensive arrangements were spectacular. We've taken almost one hundred prisoners and have another twenty or so wounded in custody. I won't mention the numbers in the category of those killed while we're at the dinner table. But it was a considerable number.

"The beach attack was destroyed, too, as you know. Our cannon took out several of their boats and the rifles in the trenches took a heavy toll of the surviving invaders. The beach cavalry you were in finished the job of rounding up the rest. "

"Think they'll will try it again, father?" Susan asked

"I wouldn't, if I were them," Townshend confessed. "But our governor is a strange duck. If I were a betting man, I'd say he will try again. Hopefully, cooler heads will prevail and he will be persuaded to give it up."

"I hope that will be the case, dear," Charlotte said.

"We can't take that chance, Charlotte. So, we'll prepare our defenses as though he will attack us again."

"Which reminds, me," Charles said. "I have patrol duty tonight."

Susan was indignant. "Charly!" she exclaimed. "How could you? Tonight, is our engagement night."

"I'm sorry Susan. I didn't arrange this schedule. I knew about the patrol before tonight. I did not know that this would turn out to be the night we got engaged."

"Townshend?" Charlotte asked.

"What?"

"Do something," his wife urged. "This is their engagement night. It's important."

"Oh, all right." Townshend said. "But you two better not expect me to intervein again any time soon. Just this once. Off with ya, you two. I'll take care of your patrol duty, Charles."

*　　*　　*

Charlotte and her husband were lying in bed. The night air was hot and humid. The mosquito netting was down as they talked of their day.

"It certainly has been quite a few days." Charlotte said.

"Certainly has," Townshend said. "We survived a major attack yesterday and today we gave our permission to our only child to marry and move out."

"I'm happy for her."

"I agree, dear," Townshend said. Despite the heat, he put his arm around his wife. "Do I see tears in your eyes?"

"Yes."

"If you're so happy for Susan, why the tears?"

Because she's no longer my little girl."

"Maybe not. But I think Charles and Susan will be good for one another."

"I do think he is a fine young man." Charlotte told her husband as she turned into his embrace.

Then, Townshend kissed his wife.

480

Charlotte was still not mollified. "I'm happy for Susan. But I'm sad that I am losing her, too."

"On the positive side, dear," Townshend said. "We're gaining the son we never managed to have."

"There's that."

"And don't forget, dear," Townshend continued. "Charles is such a fine young man. We're lucky that Susan loves him."

This time, Charlotte kissed her husband.

Harvest Time on Edisto Island

The cotton fields were awash with white. The first picking of cotton was about to begin. But first there was going to be a celebration. Usually, they waited until the completion of the harvest, after the celebration of Thanksgiving and before Christmas. This year, though, Susan had convinced her father and the island's governing Board to begin that season with a celebration.

She told them that it was especially appropriate this year with the recent victory over the Governor's invasion attempt. Besides, everyone seemed ready for a break before the hard work of gathering the harvest. The Board agreed.

So, everyone brought something to an island-wide potluck. That noon meal saw a huge feast of beef, fish, scallops, clams, oysters, ham and roast chicken. Side dishes of beets, corn, sweet potatoes and apple sauce were available, too. And, instead of just laying around after the noon feast, Charles and Susan put on a baseball game.

They had recruited and trained players, laid out a baseball field and got a few balls and bats on the recent shipment of good from Savannah. The crowd was assembled for the first baseball game ever on Edisto Island.

"Boys and girls on the same team?" I never heard of such a thing." One lady lamented.

"What is baseball, anyway?" another asked.

"Beats me," a man told his wife. "But the players seem excited about throwing that little ball around."

Nine players to a team, Susan's steam took the field, first, with Luther as the pitcher. Charles's team was at bat. Charles would bat first.

The rules were simple. A pitcher threw a ball toward a batter who stood 60 feet away. The batter held a rounded stick called a bat and tried to hit the thrown ball. If the batter missed, it was called a strike. Three strikes and the batter's turn would be over. If the thrown ball was outside of a strike zone, it was called a ball. Four of those put the batter on the first of three bases.

Should the batter hit the ball the opponents in front of him tried to pick up the ball and get it to the first base before the batter got there. Should that happen the batter was out. When a team amassed three such outs, they stopped batting and traded places with the other team. When both teams had a time at bat, an inning was over. There were seven innings in a game.

During their part of the inning, should a member of a team go from first base to second, to third, and them back to what was called 'home plate', a run was scored. The team that scored the most 'runs' in seven innings, won the contest.

 Luke threw the first pitch toward Charles.

"Remember what Mike told me so often, "Be patient, wait for the ball to come to you." Wait, just wait Charly boy."

This was the first such pitch Luke had thrown in a real game. So, he was being careful to get it over the 'plate' in front of Charly, the batter. Consequently, his pitch was slow and deliberate.

The ball sort of just hung there. Charles waited, and waited. When he swung the bat, he connected and drove the ball far over the head of the defenders trying to catch it. He ran to first base, then second, then third and all the way to home plate. It was a 'home run'.

The first run was scored by the team captained by Charles. The next three batters swung and missed the balls Luke threw so many times, three outs were recorded very quickly. Now it was Luke's team members turn to try and hit the ball.

Neither side was able to score another run for the next several innings. Charles hit the ball each time he was at bat, but he didn't hit another 'home run.' So, when seven such innings were completed, Charles's team won the contest 1 run to 0.

"People up North actually pay to watch this game?" one man asked another.

"Not very exciting, is it?"

"The kids seem to enjoy it, though," another judged.

"I heard tell that some of our boys played baseball during the war."

One of the wives asked another, "You going to the Harvest Ball tonight?"

"You bet, I am," she said. "My husband hasn't danced with me since our wedding. I'm not going to let him off the hook tonight."

"I know what you mean," another said. "Besides, I want to know what big announcement Charlette Mikell has for us tonight."

"What do you think it could be?"

"I'm guessing it's about that new young man whose been staying at their house, Colonel Pope's grandson. I'm betting that the Mikell family is announcing the wedding of their daughter to him."

"Really?" was the surprised response. "How exciting. That would join the two largest land-owners into one family. I wonder if they are going to move into the old Pope plantation house?"

"I doubt it. The place needs a lot of work," was the response. "No one has lived there since the Colonel died almost ten years ago."

*   *   *

The large dairy barn had been cleaned. Banners and flags decorated the beams and walls. Tables placed against the outside displayed walls had cider and doe nuts for the guests.

A band was at the end of the barn. A couple of banjoes, a violin and a piano would supple the music for dancing. There was a caller for the square dancing, too. People began to show up shortly after supper, around 7 in the evening.

"My goodness," Charlotte whispered to Susan. "It looks as though everyone on the island is here." Well over three thousand people lived and worked on Edisto.

"I'm not surprised, mother," Susan responded. "We haven't had a dance on the island in I don't know how long.

"It might have helped when word got out about what my special announcement was." Charlotte said.

"Mother!" Susan exclaimed. "I thought you promised it would be a surprise for everyone."

"I only told a couple of my friends.," she confessed. "I never dreamed they would spread that rumor."

"You did that on purpose, mother," Susan accused. "You knew most of the women on the island felt they had to be here, just in case the rumor was true."

"I did want a crowd."

"You got it, for sure."

"I hope you're not angry with me."

"Not at all, mother," Susan assured her. "This is only going to happen once. So, enjoy it."

"Thank you dear."

It was getting dark outside and it was time for the band to take a break.

Townshend Mikell mounted the makeshift stage and called for everyone's attention.

"Ladies and gentlemen," he began. "If I could have your attention for a moment.

'I hope you are having a good time at this first of, I hope, many Edisto Island Harvest Festivals."

Everyone cheered.

"Looking over the crops this year, it appears as though we are going to enjoy a super harvest."

Everyone cheered again.

"A lot of work awaits us yet," he predicted. "But I have confidence that we are up to the task ahead."

More cheering.

"Before I welcome the band back," he continued. "My wife Charlotte has an announcement."

Charlotte replaced her husband on the stage. She waited silently as things settled down, hardly anyone spoke. It was very quiet as Charlotte stood there and waited.

"As you all know," she began. "Colonel Pope's grandson has been living and working on the island since early June. He has joined right into the work of the fields and the dairy barns since he first arrived from the North where his mother took him from our island ten years ago. He was active in defending our island from invaders recently this summer, too.

"Many of you have gotten to know him on patrol or in the barns or the fields. Townshend and I have appreciated the warm welcome you have given him. He now considers Edisto his new home."

Townshend led the clapping and the cheering.

"We have gotten to know Charles, too. And we think the world of him. So, Townshend and I have the pleasure of announcing the engagement of our daughter Susan and Charles. They will be married here this coming January."

Townshend again led the clapping and cheering.

"Because our Episcopal church is so small, we will have the wedding celebrated here in this barn."

Again, there was clapping and cheering.

"You are all invited to the wedding and the reception that will follow." Charlotte concluded.

More clapping and cheering.

Townshend then announced. "Back to the dancing!"

There was more clapping and cheering before the band began a lively tune.

One of the ladies said, "Didn't I tell you? That cute young man is going to marry into the Mikell family,"

"It certainly is unusual, having a wedding in a barn, though."

"Have you ever been in their Episcopal church?" answered another.

"No, I haven't."

"Their immediate family would have trouble fitting in that tiny church." Another speculated. "If they wanted to invite everyone, this is the only place large enough."

"I suppose."

"Come to think of it, wasn't Jesus born in a barn?"

"Oh, ya."

*   *   *

On the dance floor, Charles and Susan were dancing to a ballad.

"So, we're getting married in a barn," Charles chuckled. "I'll be."

"Too late to get out of it now, Charly," Susan decided.

"I don't have any such intention, Susan," Charly assured her. "I can hardly wait for January."

"First, you've got to survive your first harvest, my man," she challenged. "Dawn to dusk, work and more work."

"Isn't that what I've been doing ever since I got here?"

"Harvest time around here is different. Siesta time is a thing of the past, Charly," she promised. "Crops need harvesting when they ripen. Even my mother and I will be in the fields this fall. All the wives and children have their roles to play."

"Even our children, Susan?"

Susan blushed, some. "When they are old enough Charly, yes. Even our children will work."

"Tough lady!" Charles kidded her.

"It's not that," she responded. "It's a matter of survival. Everyone on the island must learn that, even our children."

Charles held Susan close.

"Thank you, Lord for bringing me here. Thank you for bringing me to Susan. Help me to always be the man You intended me to be and help me to be worthy of her love."

Once the last tune was played, everyone lent a hand in the clean-up. The ladies took the dishes in which they brought food. The men put the make-shift tables and benches away and cleared away the trash.

*   *   *

Sunday was the last day before the harvest would begin in earnest.

After church, the Mikells and Charles were easting their Sunday noon meal of eggs, ham, grits and toast.

"That was so nice last night," Susan told her parents. "Thank you for the nice announcement of our engagement."

"I don't know where I got the idea of a barn wedding," Charlotte explained. "But it is the only place big enough for either the wedding or the reception."

"I think it's a great idea, mother," Susan responded. "But if the weather is good, why don't we have it outside, maybe on the beach. Then you could give the reception in the barn."

"That might work, dear," her mother responded. "You and I have plenty of time to work out all the details. Oh, don't let me forget to get some wedding dress material from Savannah. Wherever the wedding is held, you'll need a dress specially for the wedding."

"Why don't I wear the one you were married in, mother?"

"My wedding was a hurry-up affair, dear," her mother explained. "Your father was going off for the first big battle of the war. I had no time for a special dress. As it was, we only had a two-day honeymoon."

"What did your parents do for a honeymoon, Charles?" Mrs. Mikell asked.

"I'm told they went to Bermuda," Charles answered.

"How about your mother and Marshal Drieborg? What did they do for a honeymoon?" Susan asked.

"My sister Eleanor and I were about eight years old when our parents married. We stayed in our Grandfather Murphy's house in

Philadelphia. Grandpa and Grandmother Drieborg were there, too. They traveled from Michigan to be present.

"Mike and my mother were married there. I remember, it was Thanksgiving. I think our parents were married right in the Murphy house. Then, I think they went to a downtown Philadelphia hotel for the weekend. Then, we, and the Drieborgs, traveled to Michigan."

"Where are you two planning to honeymoon?" Charlotte asked.

"Susan hasn't told me yet." Charles joked.

"Charly," Susan scolded. "That's a we decision."

Townshend laughed and said, "I see you're learning quickly, Charles."

"Father!" Susan said. "Stop it, right now."

"I'm just teasing, dear," he apologized.

"You, too, Charly," she continued. "You and I will decide where we will go and what we will do."

"Whatever you say, Susan," Charles agreed.

"Oh, you men!"

The Harvest Begins

Mr. Curtis welcome Charles to the cotton field.

"Good morning, Charles," he greeted. "Milking all done?"

"Yes, sir," he said, "All the cows are content until about four this afternoon."

"What happens then?"

"They get milked again, that's what." Charles told him.

"The first picking of cotton begins today," Curtis told Charles. "We've had pickers in the fields since six this morning. We hope to get this field picked clean today. Your other field will be tackled tomorrow. We should be done with the first picking on your fields by the end of the week."

"What do you want me to do, Mr. Curtis?"

"Grab one of those bags over there and join me."

"Put the strap over your head so the bag hangs on your right side," Curtis instructed. "Follow me down this row and watch how I pluck the white furry stuff off the cotton bush."

Charles watched as Curtis used his fingers to take cotton off the bushes to his right and then to his left. Each time he placed the cotton in the bag at his side.

"You try it now."

Charles moved alongside a bush full of white cotton. He reached out to take a cotton ball from the plant.

"Ouch!" Charles complained pulling back his right hand. "What was that?"

"The cotton boll has sharp prickles holding it in place," Curtis told him. "You'll have to develop a soft touch if you want to avoid them."

Charles reached out to pick another boll. "Damn!" he exclaimed. "That's sharp."

"I'm afraid there's no easy way to learn, Charles," Curtis told him. "I've been at this for thirty years and I still get cuts on my fingers during harvest. I'm going to leave you, now. I expect you to fill up that eight-foot long sack you're carrying before you leave the field this noon.

"I'm going to leave these two children to work with you. They'll pick the low-lying bolls. I'd watch my language around them, Charles. Parents are sensitive to profanity in front of their kids. Your Driver in this field is Stanly Blue. If you need something, call out for him. He's around here somewhere."

   The noon meal was brought out to the field. Each worker was given a plate of grits, pork ribs and cornbread. They had their choice of milk or water to wash it down. Charles chose water. He'd had his fill of fresh milk earlier in the day.

Susan joined him in the dinner line.

"How's it going, Charly?" she asked.

"No one warned me about the sharp prickles of the cotton bush. My right hand is sore as hell."

 "We all have gone through that discovery and pain, Charly," she told him.

"You, too?"

"Yup. Every person, young and old has gone through the pain of that learning process. It's no fun, I'll give you that. But there's no avoiding it either."

"Just my turn, eh?"

"Afraid so, my man," Susan told him. "Nothing I can do to help you, either. It's just something you have to learn on your own."

"What if I don't want to learn?"

Susan stopped eating and just looked at Charles.

"You mean, just leave the field?"

"Ya," he repeated. "What if I just refused to go back out there this afternoon?"

"You could do that, I suppose," Susan informed him. "But then you best not plan on a future life here on Edisto. Harvesting cotton is sort of a rite of passage for everyone. Granted, we all learned to do this as youngsters and you're learning it a bit late in life. But you have to learn if you want to take your proper place here."

"Do I have to like it?" Charles asked.

"No," Susan assured him. "But you have to do it."

"Can I whine about it?"

Susan laughed. "Sure, you can. But ya know, Charly. I never took you for a whiner. And I'm not going to marry one either." Susan stood up and prepared to leave.

"I've got to get back to my father's cotton field, I've got some picking to do, too." With that she left the makeshift lunch table and walked away.

"Damn! She sure put me in my place. Eleanor used to make fun of me when I whined. Those two women are sure not going to put up which that stuff. What a pair! No wonder I love them both."

Everyone did take a two-hour siesta that first day. But everyone except the children and old timers were expected back after supper to make up the time.

As usual, after cleaning up and catching an hour's sleep, Charles joined Susan and her parents for the evening meal.

Townshend asked. "Will you pass the chicken, Susan?"

There was mashed potatoes, gravy and cornbread, too. Of course, a bowl of grits was on the table, too.

As the plates of food were passed, Susan asked Charles.

"How'd it go this afternoon, Charly?"

"Better than the morning Susan," he informed her with a straight face. "I filled one bag by lunch and almost another before we quit for siesta. I should finish off that second one before we quit later today."

"Way to go, Charles," Townshend congratulated him. "Not bad for the first day."

"I bet you right hand is pretty sore, though," Susan said with a sly smile.

Charles put down the chicken leg he held in his right hand and flexed his fingers.

"It hurts like the devil, Susan." He confessed. "But as another worker told me, everyone has gone through it and survived. I figured, if the little kids working with me could do it without complaining, so could I."

"Good for you, Charles," Charlotte Mikell said. "I know it's not fun. But since the war an' all, we all have had to learn to do things we never expected. Picking cotton was always slave work. Now, we all have to do such things if we are to survive."

"And, next week we'll be harvesting rice," Townshend revealed. "Who among us ever thought we landowners would have to be standing side by side with our coloreds doing that?"

Susan added, "In the dried-out rice paddies, Charly," she informed him. "Instead of the fingers on your right hand being cut and stiff, your back will be sore as a boil after working a rice hook all day."

"Do you two have any good news for me?" Charles quipped to everyone's laughter.

Later, the two lovers sat on the front porch swing, relaxing before returning to the fields for more cotton picking.

Susan was holding Charles's left hand as they relaxed in the cool of the evening.

"I'm sorry about the cuts on your right hand, Charly." She assured him.

"And I'm sorry for my whining this noon, Susan," he told her. "I haven't felt sorry for myself since I got here; no matter what the challenge I faced. But I think I was just frustrated that picking cotton was so difficult. After all, even little kids were doing it without any problem."

"We've all been through it, Charly."

Charles wasn't finished. "And, thank you for talking sense to me at lunch, today. I needed that to give me a jolt, to stop feeling sorry for myself and get on with life. Thank you."

Susan pulled Charles closer and raised her lips for a soft kiss.

"Don't worry, Charly," Susan added. "the cuts on your fingers will heal before the second picking next month."

"Oh, great," Charles laughed. "I'll have to go through this all over again?"

Susan joined his laughter. "After the third picking in November, you'll have all winter to recover."

"That's sure something to look forward to," Charles commented. "Right now, though, I've a long way to go if I'm to pick 300 pounds of cotton today. I doubt if I've picked less than 150 pounds. So, I best get back to work."

"Go to it, Charly." Susan urged. She gave him a short kiss and the two of them went back to the fields.

And so it went. While the picking went on, the rice paddies were drained and allowed to dry. By the end of September, the cotton fields were picked clean and the cotton bolls ginned and packed into bales. The first shipment to Bermuda of long stem cotton was ready.

Grand Rapids

The Drieborgs were having supper. Mary Jacqueline announced.

"We have a letter from Charles."

"Oh, goody," Maxine shouted. "Can you read it to us, Mother?"

"After we finish our meal, dear," Mike told his daughter. "Finish your potato and eat another piece of meat. Then we can leave the table to read the letter."

"I've already had all the meat and potatoes I can stand," Maxine protested. "I'm stuffed."

"You know the rule," her mother reminded her. "You clean your plat of the food on it."

"But I didn't want this much."

"Maxine," her father said sternly. "You have to keep your health up. If you don't eat, you will have to go to bed and rest."

"Oh, Father," I never heard you tell Eleanor that."

"Then you weren't listening," her Mother recalled. "I can remember many times your Father reminded Eleanor and Charles of that."

"I don't intend to sit here and wait all night, young lady," her father told her. Mike took out his watch and looked at it. "I'll give you three minutes. If the plate isn't clean when that time is up, you go to bed and your mother and I go into the living room to read the letter from Charles; without you."

"Oh, Father!"

But before Mike announced that three minutes was up, Maxine had her plate clean.

`Mary Jacqueline and Mike cleared the table of left-over food and dirty plates. Mike poured himself some coffee and Mary Jacqueline made some tea.

"I thought we were going into the living room to read the letter from Charles." Maxine shouted from that room. "I'm Waiting."

"Be right there, dear." Her mother answered.

Sure enough, the door to the kitchen swung open and Maxine's parents walked through it toward the living room. Once they were settled, the letter from Charles was opened.

Hi Everyone,

Before I tell you the latest, I want ot thank Maxine for her nice letter. At lease someone in my family is writing me.

The cotton harvest is underway. Of course, I am expected to help pick cotton. It seems that no one around here can avoid that. My fingers are sore as anything. I've been picking cotton all this week. It's not easy to avoid the little prickers that hold the cotton boll in place. Even the little kids who pick the low-hanging cotton do better than me. An experienced picker can pick over 300 pounds of cotton in a day. I don't think I picked must more that 150 pounds. My total improves each day, though. Once we finish this field, we go to harvest the rice paddies.

I expect that as soon as my fingers heal, we'll be ready for thr second crop of cotton to be ready. I can hardly wait. We harvest corn and dig up sugar beets next month, too. Then, we will shear our sheep and slaughter hogs. All of these things have to be done by the end of November. I have never done any of this. But Townshend insists I be part of every step in the process, whatever the crop may be.

Even Susan knows more about this stuff than I do.

Susan and I talked to her parents about getting married. We wanted to do it now, but they insisted we wait until I return here after my Christmas trip to Michigan. We agreed to do that.

I will be leaving here by way of Savannah. Charleston still isn't safe for us. I'll write again about the definite date I'll be leaving here. It should be the first week or so of December.

I'm too tired to write any more and my fingers hurt too much. I must get some sleep. Five in the morning comes so, so quickly, I can't believe it. Remember, I'm still am in charge of the morning dairy barn.

Take care, I love you all.

Charles.

*   *   *

"Married," Mary Jacqueline exclaimed. "I wasn't ready for that."

"Don't worry right now, dear. It appears that the Susan's parents have slowed down their enthusiasm some," Mike reminded her. "We'll have a chance to talk with him when he gets home."

"I suppose," Mary Jacqueline had to agreed. "But still. Married? He's only eighteen."

"How old were you when you married Charles Pope?"

"That was different, Michael," she protested. "He was older; a doctor."

"And you were what?" Mike teased. "Seventeen or eighteen?"

"It was very different," Mary Jacqueline insisted. "There was going to be a war."

"Have you forgotten that Charles and Susan are fighting a war in South Carolina?" Mike reminded his wife. "I was only nineteen when I married Eleanor's mother. No, dear," he continued, "The only difference is that Charles is your son. We have to trust him on this."

"It doesn't sound as though we have much choice," Mary Jacqueline concluded.

"There's that, for sure," Mike commented.

Edisto Island

Charles reported to Mr. Curtis again. This time, he was at the Pope rice field. Those fields were dry now, and the plants stood high, ready for cutting.

"Just watch the experienced workers swing their sickle, Charles," he told Charles. "Notice how they are in a rhythm. No wasted motion. Just a smooth swing as they walk between the rows and cut the plants about a foot above the ground. They leave what they cut off, the sheaves, on top of the remaining part of the plant, so it can dry. Tomorrow, they'll bundle the sheaves up for transportation to the threshing house."

After watching for a while, Curtis told Charles to try his hand swinging a sickle.

"Give it a try, Charles," he directed. "Just be careful about the arch in your swing. That sickle is sharp. Watch out for the other workers."

Over the next few says, Charles got into a rhythm and even helped bundle the cut plants, the sheaves, for transport to the threshing house.

"*Susan was right again,*" He thought the next day. "Today, *my shoulders are sore as the dickens, all that swinging motion yesterday, I suppose.*"

Much of September was spent in those rice paddies and in the threshing house pounding the sheaves to release the soft rice and then putting it into to barrels for shipping.

The corn and sugar beet fields were about ready by the first week of October. So were the cotton plants ready for a second picking.

Each crop had it own particular demands; a technique different from any other fruit of the land.

Corn was picked by hand and put to dry in corn cribs to dry out for shucking. Sugar beets were dug up and transported to barns where they could be put in a presser to force their sweet juices released.

The second time around in the cotton field was little different from the first.

"Damn!" Charles thought as he recoiled from the sharp points of the cotton boll. *"You'd think I had learned to pick this blasted stuff without getting stuck."*

But he hadn't. Never-the-less, he kept at it once again and strove to pick his daily quota of cotton. He didn't do that either, but without complaining, this time, he kept at it.

"I didn't hear you whining this time about your sore fingers," Susan kidded. "You an expert picker, now?"

"No, I'm not," he admitted. "But I promised myself not to complain, this time."

"That's my Charly," Susan said, giving him a hug.

"How are your fingers, little lady?"

"Cut and sore, just like yours, smarty," She answered. "We all go through this, ya know."

"I didn't," Charles told her. "But it's good to know I'm not alone in my misery."

It was also good to know that there was only one more month of picking cotton.

"Thank God for that," He thought.

*   *   *

By the end of the November, the several thousand people who lived in the Edisto Island community cheered the end of the harvest ordeal. But it had been a successful season for all the crops. Thirty-five thousand pounds of rice, 250,000 bales of long stem cotton, 7,000,000 bushels of corn and several tons of sugar from their beets. All the cotton, most of the rice and much of the corn were prepared for export to Bermuda or Savannah. A good portion of their cattle herd would be transported to Bermuda as well.

All in all, the year had been a good one. Few were happier than Charles. He had succeeded in every task he had been given; beyond his own expectation. And, of course, he had met and won the love of Susan Mikell. Who would have thought all this was possible or even likely last June?

At the Harvest Dance, he joined everyone else in the celebration.

Susan and Charly welcomed a slow dance. They had been whirling about the barn floor to the commands of the Square Dance Caller for over an hour. So, despite the cool evening air, they were perspiring.

"Are you anxious to go North, Charly?" Susan asked.

"Not at all, Susan," he told her. "In fact, I don't want to leave your side for even a day, let alone an entire month."

"Then don't go," Susan suggested.

"I have to, Sue," he said. "I promised my mother. It will be my last trip North before I begin my new life here with you. Can you understand that?"

"Yes, Charly," she responded. "I understand it. But I don't have to like it. Do I?"

"No, you don't. I don't either. It's sort of like going back out into the cotton fields when my hand was sore and so stiff, I could hardly move my fingers. It's just something that I have to do.

"I'll be back at the beginning of January for our wedding," he promised. "Than I'll never leave your side again."

"You'd better get back here, buster," she poked him in the ribs. "Or I'll come North with a shotgun, looking for you. For sure."

The couple walked out into the evening, arm and arm. In the darkness of the night. In the shadow of the barn, they held one another and kissed until the music stopped and the kerosene lamps in the barn were extinguished.

Two days later, a ship heading for Savannah, left the Edisto docks. It was loaded with bales of long stem cotton, rice, corn grain and Charles Pope. A favorable wind and fair seas carried the ship to Savannah in two days.

Charles helped supervise the unloading of the cargo. Before he went to a hotel to await his train to Atlanta, he checked the accuracy of the goods loaded for the return trip to Edisto.

Waiting for him in the lobby of the hotel, was his father's friend, Frank Stanizek and his son.

"I expect you are Charles Pope Drieborg," Frank said, by way of introduction.

505

"Yes, sir. I am," Charles responded shaking Frank's extended hand. "I take it you are my father's friend, Mr. Stanitzek."

"Yes, I am," Frank revealed. "This is my son Fritz."

"Happy to meet you, Fritz," Charles greeted. "You two are here to escort me North?"

"That's right, son," Frank confirmed. "We're going to head to Atlanta and then to Cincinnati. Your father is going to meet us there."

"You really think I need an escort?"

"Let's go into the dining room where we can talk privately," Frank suggested. "Besides, I haven't eaten since early this morning, I'm hungry."

"Let me check my things at the desk and use a restroom," Charles suggested. "I'll be right behind you."

"Go with him, Fritz," His father told him. "By the way Charles, I don't see your revolver. Strap it on and keep it on for the remainder of this trip. No argument."

"Yes, sir."

When the three men were seated in the restaurant, Charles asked. "You were going to tell me why I need an escort for my trip North."

Frank paused, "Before I answer your question directly, let me give you some background information, Charles," he began. "You have been part of the Edisto Island community that has incurred the wrath of your Governor, Wade Hampton.

"So far, your people have successfully defended their community. And, Hampton has stopped his attacks under pressure from his political allies."

"Why has that happened?" Charles asked.

"He wants to be South Carolina's next United States Senator. But he needs the votes of the legislature to achieve that political office. The legislators want racial peace in the state in order to attract northern investments. So, to get their votes, Hampton must not pursue his vendetta against the people of Edisto Island."

"What has that to do with my trip North?"

"I'm getting to that," Frank said. "Just be patient."

"I'm sorry," Charles said. "I won't interrupt again."

"Where was I? Oh, yes. You present a very attractive target for Governor Hampton's people. By harming you they clearly punish Townshend Mikell. And to do so in Georgia or some other state, they do it without upsetting the public peace in South Carolina. Thus, Governor Hampton can pursue his vendetta against Mikell without having to take responsibility for the act and thus he can advance his political agenda, too."

"Why me?" Charles asked.

"You're Mikell's prospective son-in-law, aren't you?"

"Yes, I am."

"You're on of the four largest landowners on Edisto Island, aren't you?"

"Yes, I am."

"For the Klan of South Carolina, you represent the only successful multi-racial community in the state; maybe anywhere in the South. They hate what you for that. You are a white man and a landowner. They believe you should hate the coloreds not work side by side with them.

"If you were killed in Georgia or elsewhere on the way North, nobody could blame Hampton or his people in South Carolina."

'Oh, I see," Charles finally understood. "so, you and Fritz are going to protect me?"

"Sort of," Frank informed Charles. "I lead a Klan Den in Macon. My group is determined to maintain peace in our community. None of us are in favor of what Lincoln did, but emancipation is over, it's a fact. So, we are determined to keep a peace between the races in our area.

"But that's not true in much of Georgia. There are some pretty violent Dens operating in my state. Hampton's people have contacted one of them to kidnap you."

"So, you're going against another Klan group to protect me?"

"Yes, we are, son. That's what friends do for one another. My wife Peg and I became friends with your parents before you were born when we joined him to investigate the assassination of your Mr. Lincoln. We worked with them again last fall when they came down to Atlanta to help Congressman Kellogg.

"I heard of this plan to kidnap you and contacted your father," Frank continued. "He and I worked out a plan to get you North, safely."

"So, what is the plan, if I may ask?"

"The three of us leave on a late train tonight, for Atlanta," Frank revealed. "We'll be met there by another group of armed men for the trip to Cincinnati, Ohio. There, you father and his people will take over for the remainder of the trip to your home in Michigan."

"What about on my return trip?"

"I hadn't heard about a return trip," Frank said. "But if there is one, we will repeat the process to your ship in Savannah."

"Thank you for your help, Mr. Stanitzek."

"You're welcome, son. Now let's order, I'm hungry."

*   *

The train carrying Charles and the Stanitzeks pulled into the Atlanta station just shy of midnight.

The three man had traveled in an otherwise darkened and vacant passenger car. While the Pullman car had sleeping accommodations, none of them had slept a wink.

As he stepped off the car, Frank was met my a group of armed men.

"Any problems, Frank?" one of them asked.

"None I'm aware of, Silas," he responded. "You?"

"We've secured the area when we arrived," Silas responded. "So far, nothing seems amiss."

"Let's get to the train North," Frank suggested. "I don't want to be just standing around the station in the open."

That train left the station and headed North to Chattanooga. It would continue North to Cincinnati. A few miles outside of Atlanta, Silas entered Frank's car with a man, not a member of his group.

"What's this, Silas?"

"This bird pounded on the connecting door of the forward car," Silas told Frank. "He wants to talk with the man in charge. I searched him, Frank; he's clean."

"Pull off the hood you have over his head, and let's hear what he has to say."

"I assume you have a message?"

"Yes, I do," the man said. "The head of my Den wants you to turn over the kid to us."

"What if we don't."

"They'll be trouble before you reach Chattanooga, that's what."

"We've got a couple of hours before we arrive there. Silas, take this bird back to your car and tie him up. Put the hood back on, he's seen enough. In the meantime, I'm going to get some sleep. I suggest you do the same."

Charles witnessed the conversation and asked. "Do they want to kill me?"

"Afraid so, son," Frank told him.

"Thank you, Mr. Stanizek."

"Thank your father, son," Frank responded. "My wife and I are friends of your parents. They asked for help, they get it. They'd do the same form me and mine if I asked."

'I will thank him, for sure,"

When the train was laboring up an incline, it slowed to a stop in front of some trees laying over the tracks. Everyone in Frank's team were instantly on alert.

A hooded figure on horseback appeared at the side of the train. The man shouted.

"Stanitzek, release your passenger to me!"

Frank shouted back, "Who are you?"

"I'm the Grand Maji of the Klan den out of North Atlanta," the man on horseback responded.

"I'm the Grand Cyclops of the area south of Atlanta," Frank informed his fellow Klansman.
"Let's talk this over, privately."

"I'll meet you in the last car, alone."

"Fair enough."

Soon the two men were seated in an empty car.

"You know why we're here?"

"Yes, I do. But I'm not going to hand the boy over."

"We've been asked to help out our brothers in South Carolina, Frank. They want us to send them this kid you're protecting. What's your interest in him?"

"Do you know just who he is?"

"Not really," the man responded. "I'm just doing a favor for a brother Klansman."

"And you're willing to kill other Klansmen, Georgians, as a favor for somebody you never met?

"Let me tell you something. This young fella is the son of a doctor from Charleston who gave his life to the 'Cause' during the war. His Grandfather fought for us at Gettysburg and his uncle died from sickness as a result of being a Union prisoner at Johnson's island up in Ohio. The boy, was born in Charleston during the war and has returned to live in the home of his youth on Edisto Island. He is just going to his mother's home for a visit."

"I don't care about any of that, the Klan leader protested. "This kid probably killed other Klansmen on that island just recently."

"This boy and hundreds of others, were protecting their homes against some Red Shirts in South Carolina who were sent by Governor Hampton to get even for his son's death in a precious attack. You're helping him carry out a private vendetta. It has nothing to do with the Klan. I've checked it out. This is the governor's private war. He's recruited you because the other leaders in South Carolina have forbidden him to attack the Island again.

"He's just using you.

"The leader of the people on Edisto Island isa guy named Mikell. He fought as a cavalryman throughout the war. Went in a private and came out a sergeant.

"This boy has just finished working the harvest on Edisto. His hands are calloused from digging sugar beets, cut from pecking cotton and his upper body tanned from working the rice and corn fields.

"He's no pampered rich kid supervising others. He is the kind of young man we need here if the South is ever to prosper again. We sure as hell shouldn't be killing his sort.

"Right now, he is going North to visit his mother. He is engaged to marry a young lady on Edisto who also works with her hands every day. He wants to create a life with her and for those who are willing to work with them. Those two young people want to succeed and help others do so, as well. Can't you see, we need these kinds of young people in the South.

"You want me to kill that dream by handing him over to you, just to satisfy the anger of a grieving father, Wade Hampton?"

"So, you're not going to hand over the boy?"

"Absolutely not!" Frank told the Klansman.

"You've not enough men to stop me from taking the boy."

"Maybe not," Frank said. "but we have two members of your den prisoner already."

"You only have the messenger I sent you. Who else you got?"

"You." Frank said as he pointed a revolver at the Klansman.

"That's not fair, Frank," the man protested. "I came here to talk with you, in good faith."

"Fair? You talk to me of fair?" Frank shouted. "You tell me that you're willing to kill your fellow Georgia Klansmen as a favor for some angry Carolinian. What's fair about that?

"Fairness has mothering to do with this, my friend. I not only intend to save this boy's life, but I intend to protect the lives of my brother Klansmen, too. Hampton's anger over the killing of his son is his problem. He had better keep it in South Carolina. It's no reason for us to fight one another here in Georgia.

"I hadn't thought of it that way."

"Now, I want you to order your men to clear the tracks of all that crap you put there to stop the train. Then, a few miles up the track I'll let you and your messenger go."

Within the hour, the train was on its way once again toward Chattanooga, Tennessee.

*   *   *

The train Charles and his escort rode pulled into the railroad station in Cincinnati, Ohio the next morning. Mike and his people were waiting to board. It was chilly and a cold rain fell on the tracks. Mary Jacqueline had correctly assumed that Charles would be wearing his warm weather clothing. So, she had sent a full set more appropriate for Michigan in December with her husband for him. Mike boarded the train.

"Good to see you, Mike," Frank said offering his hand.

"I can't thank you enough, Frank," Mike told him. "You saved my son's life."

"What are friends for?" Frank assured him. "You'd do the same for me, I'm sure."

"Damn right, I would."

Then Mike noticed, Charles standing in the rail car's aisle with his rifle in hand.

"My goodness," Mike thought. *"He looks great. He looks like a man."*

Mike walked toward his son and embraced him. His eyes filled with tears of happiness. Charles dropped his bag and hugged his step-father in return.

"By God, its good to see you, son." he whispered in his son's ear.

"Thank you for sending Mr. Stanitzek," Charles said. "I'm pretty sure that he saved my life."

Mike released his son and stood back. He realized that the boy who had gone to Edisto Island several months ago, had returned a man.

"We're going to have some breakfast in the station restaurant with Frank and his team. We can talk there. First, though, your mother sent this warm clothing for you. It's darn cold outside."

"Thank goodness," Charles said. "I'm already shivering."

As soon as Charles was changed, Mike led him into the station's restaurant. Once they had ordered and were sipping hot coffee, Frank told Mike of the encounter with the Georgia Klansmen. Charles had heard this before, so he just listened and ate his breakfast while his father and Frank talked.

"Mr. Stanitzek responded to my father's request without hesitation. Mike trusted his friend with my life, without reservation. I hope I will one day have friends who are as loyal to me as these men are to one another." Charles thought.

Then, he heard Mike say,

"Remember, Frank you and Peg are welcome to visit us in Michigan. We have great summers there and Mary Jacqueline would love to have you and Peg visit."

"I'll mention it to Peg," Frank promised. "I have never been this far North before. Maybe it's time I saw those Great Lakes of yours, too. You say July is a good time to visit?"

"It is, Frank. I'll telegraph you some dates. Check your schedule and get back to me."

"I'll do that, Mike. I'll do that. Should be fun."

Frank turned to Charles.

"Young man, it has been a pleasure to talk with you during our trip North. Men like you, my sons and your bride, are the future of the South. I think the bunch of you will do your father and old codgers like me, proud."

"I'm pleased to have met you, sir," Charles said shaking Franks' hand. "Thank you again for saving my life."

"Not so fast, son," Frank warned him. "I suspect this Hampton fella will be planning something unpleasant for you if you plan to return to Edisto Island. Have your father let me know your plans and I'll meet you here for the return trip. Trust me, don't attempt it alone."

"Yes, sir, my father will contact you, for sure. "

As Frank left the table, he walked over to another.

"Good to see you, Irish," he said slapping Stan Killeen on the back. "I'd should a' known you be alongside Mike on this trip."

"Can't trust Mike to go to the outhouse alone, don't ya know. We've knowd on another since the fall of '62. I think he'd feel plumb naked without me by his side. Besides, I've grown very attached to young Charles."

Frank added. "I think you'll find your young man has grown up, Stan. In fact, I believe he's the kind of young man we need to build the new South."

"The kid comes from good stock, Frank," Stan replied. "So, I'm not surprised."

Just then Charles walked up to the two men.

"Uncle Stan," He greeted wrapping Killeen in a bear hug. "Why am I not surprised to see you here."

"That hug was pretty muscular, kid," Stan said when he had regained his breath. "Where'd you get all that strength?"

"If I am stronger than before, it's because I've been working ten hours a day, milking cows, hoeing, cutting trees and weeding the cotton and rice fields. Excuse me a minute Uncle Stan, I have to say good-by to Fritz."

Charles saw Frank's son about to leave the restaurant. He rushed over

"Fritz," he shouted. Wait up."

When he caught up, he extended his hand, "Just wanted to thank you for helping me."

"Not a problem, Charles," Fritz said. "You father and mine have been friends ever since they worked together in Washington City. When a friend of my father needs help, I'm there to give it, if needed."

"They sure are loyal to one another, aren't they," Charles told Fritz.

Fritz responded. "Yes, they are. Just remember, Charles. if you need help, I'm ready to help you, too."

Grand Rapids

It was dark when they changed trains in Detroit. They just had enough time to get something to eat at the train station. It wasn't much it being so late. Just some warmed up soup and crackers.

Stan asked Charles, "Remember years ago when we stopped in Detroit on our way to Washington City?"

"Is this the town that had the ice cream store?" Charles asked.

"Right," Stan responded. "I served with a guy in the war who invented some kind of fizzy drink. His name was Vernor, and he called his drink, Vernor's. Anyway, he turned out to be some kind of medical guy. I think he called himself a pharmacist or something. His made drugs at his store for people who were sick. and he served his drink at what he called a soda bar right in his store.

"You and your sister had some of his drink in a tall glass with a scoop of vanilla ice cream. Remember?"

'Now that you mention it, I do," Charles said. "I also remember it was really good."

"Right. I had one of those, too," Stan said. "His store is not far up from here. It's closed now, I'm sure at this hour."

"Maybe we can stop on my way back South?"

"So, you're determined to return to that island of yours?'

"Yes, I am," Charles told Stan. "It's my home now."

After they ate, they boarded the train for Lansing and Grand Rapids beyond. Everyone was still too excited to sleep. So, during that ride, Charles told Stan and his father all about his experiences on Edisto Island.

At one point, hiss father said. "Be sure to spend some quiet time with your mother, son. She needs to know how you feel about all of this. Don't wait to tell her just before you're ready to return. She'll need time to adjust to a life without you in it.

"I'm thinking, she'll not give you up easily."

"I'll do it soon after we get home, Mike."

Mike wasn't done with his advice to Charles on this matter.

"It's also important that she knows your intentions before you share it with anyone else. I'll not even tell her I know. She must believe that she is the first to know. You understand me, son?"

"Yes, Mike," he repeated.

It wasn't long before Mike returned to this subject.

"Tomorrow, your grandfather and grandmother Murphy will be at our house," Mike told Charles. "I'm warning you right now, that your grandfather will ask you what your intentions are. He has read your letters in which you mentioned marrying Susan and living on Edisto.

"I suggest you get up early tomorrow and join your mother in the kitchen. Eleanor is still in Ann Arbor, and Maxine will go off to school. I'll leave early for the office. So, you'll have your mother all to yourself for a couple of hours. "I'll even eat lunch downtown to give you more time.

"Sit her down and tell her everything," Mike urged his son. "Do not spare her your determination to return and live on Edisto Island. She must know that you are no longer just a visitor there.

Make sure she understands that you intend to marry Susan and live there, permanently.

"Stay with her as long as it takes for you to explain everything, Charles" Mike continued. "Be patient and answer all her questions honestly. It may be hard for you to do this. And it will be harder yet for your mother to hear it all. But she must hear it from you."

"Phew!" Charles exclaimed. "I hadn't thought this would be so difficult."

"You mother and I will talk about all of this privately, of course. In the end, she will accept your decision. I will assure her that we will travel South to your wedding and visit you and your future family, from time to time."

"I hadn't thought of that, Mike."

"It will be important for her to look forward to those things," Mike predicted.

"By the way Charles, you may not know it, but your grandmother Murphy traveled through Confederate lines during the war to be with your mother right after you were born."

"I never heard that," Charles said laughing. "Come to think of it, she always impressed me as determined lady."

"Evidently, she was not going to let a little thing like a war stop her from seeing her daughter or holding her new grandson; you.

"Believe me, son, your mother is no less a determined lady than your grandmother."

"I'll remember that, for sure, Mike."

"But you must impress your mother with your determination, too. If Edisto is where your future lies, tell her in no uncertain terms. Don't use words like maybe or might be. Got it, son?"

"Yes, Mike. I got it."

"When you tell your grandparents about your decision," Mike continued. "You be polite but firm. No hesitation. It is what it is, son. Tell them what you have done and what you intend to do.

"Make sure they understand that this is a visit that will end after Christmas," Mike continued. "Assure them that they will be welcome on Edisto Island, too. Got it, son?"

"Got it, Mike."

They arrived in Grand Rapids shortly after midnight. Bill Anderson was at the station with the family buggy to take them home.

"Hey, Uncle Bill," Charles greeted. The two hugged.

"Phew!" Bill said. "That's quite a hug, young fella. Where'd you get those muscles?

"Work, Uncle Bill, lots and lots of it."

They were at the Drieborg home on Prospect Street in just a few minutes. The house was full of light.

"What's going on, Mike?" Charles asked.

"Seems that everyone wants to welcome you home, son."

Sure enough, his Drieborg and Murphy grandparents along with his aunts and uncles were all there to greet him.

Of course, his mother was the first to meet him at the door with a hug and lots of tears. In her arms, he couldn't resist, he cried some too.

Bill and Stan brought his bag into the vestibule. But they didn't want anyone to see his rifle or his revolver. So, they set those inside the kitchen by the back door.

Charles made the rounds of all his relatives with hugs, kisses and a few tears, too. The dinning room table was full of finger food and punch. He had some of that between hugs. It was almost two in the morning before everyone said their good-byes and left.

Mary Jacqueline escorted her son up the stairs to his old room.

"Sleep in, son," she urged. "I'll be up to get Maxine off for school."

"You kidding, mother?" he joked. "I've been getting up at five every morning since I've been on Edisto. I doubt if my body clock will allow me to sleep in anymore. I'll join you in the kitchen firt thing in the morning. I'd like to walk my sister to school, too. Will that be all right?"

"Certainly, son," she assured him. "I may just join you on that walk. Will that be all right?" she teased.

Charles laughed, "Of course, mother," he said as he entered his old room. "See you in the morning."

"Good night, son."

Mike was already under the covers when she entered their room.

"That was quite a reception tonight, dear," he said. "Did you arrange it?"

"Not at all," she assured him as she got into her nightgown. "Everyone just kept showing up. Your parents are staying at the Murphy place. Your brother Jake and his wife are staying with Susan. Even the Riley's were here to greet Charles. I didn't dare mention his arrival time to any of his old friends."

"Good thing," Mike Chuckled. "Lord knows you would have had to rent a hall, then. Young lady, will you join me in this cold bed. I need warming up."

"So do I, Mr. Big Shot Marshal." Mary Jacqueline said as she snuggled up to her husband under the covers. "I want to hear everything about the trip but I'm too tired right now. It will have to wait until morning."

Mike pulled his wife close. The two of them were quickly asleep.

The Big Discussion

As he thought, Charles was in his mother's kitchen bright and early. She had already gotten the coffee brewing and the fresh bread baking.

"Morning, mother," Charles greeted. "You got any grits?" he asked.

"Just for you," She responded. "I made some up yesterday and left them in the ice-box. I'll warm them up in a jiffy."

"You're a coffee drinker now, I take it?"

"Coffee or tea," he informed her. "Whatever is available. It all depends upon the supply ships. But yes, I enjoy a hot cup of something in the morning before I milk my cows."

"Your grandfather Drieborg was pleasantly surprised when he found out you were doing that each morning. I think he was very proud of you."

"He has a right to be," Charles admitted. "He taught me how to do it, after all. Now I'm in charge of the entire morning dairy operation."

"I know he'll be anxious to hear all about it," his mother told him. "Be sure to ask him if you can spend some time with him at his farm. I know he'd really like that."

"I will, for sure," Charles told his mother. "I actually do have some questions for him."

"When does Maxine get up?"

"I'll tell you what," his mother said. "Why don't you go into her room and wake her up. She'd love that. She has been so waiting for you to arrive."

"When?"

"Go, now, Charles. It's time for her to get ready for school."

Charles went upstairs into his sisters darkened room.

His mother was still in the kitchen and heard her daughter's scream of surprise.

"Charles!" She heard shouted by her daughter. A few moments later the swinging door of the kitchen flew open and Charles burst in carrying his sister, still in her pajamas.

"Momma," she shouted. "It's Charles!"

"Yes, it is, dear."

"You promised to wake me up when he got here."

"It was too late for that, dear," her mother said. "You were sound asleep when he arrived."

"Are you going to be here when I come home from school, Charles?"

"Of course, I am," Charles assured her.

"Are you going to stay for Christmas?"

"Yes, I am," he promised.

"Can I stay home today, Momma?" Maxine begged. "Can I stay here with you and Charles, just today?"

"You know better than that," Mary Jacqueline told her daughter. "Sister Aquinas would be very mad if you skipped school."

"Besides, missy," Charles told her. "I will be at your school to walk you home later today. Then we can talk or anything you want to do."

"Oh, goody," Maxine said. "What are you having for breakfast, Charles?"

"Warm grits with butter and brown sugar."

"Oh, goody. Can I have some too, momma?"

"Of course," she replied. "Grits for two coming right up." .

It wasn't long before Maxine was ready for school. The three of them, mother, son and daughter bundled up and set off for St. Andrew Elementary school.

When they arrived, Maxine pulled on her brother's sleeve to go inside with her. She took him directly to the principal's office.

"I remember the last time my son was in this office. He was being punished for socking a boy on the playground. As I recall, the boy had pushed Eleanor into a snowbank or something."

"Sister," Maxine said. "This is my brother Charles. He's home for Christmas."

"I remember you Charles," Sister Aquinas said. "You're working down South somewhere aren't you?"

"Yes, I am Sister, I'm working on Edisto Island in South Carolina."

"This weather must be quite a change for you."

"It certainly is, Sister," he admitted. "I must admit, I'm freezing."

"You best get to your classroom, young lady," Sister Aquinas told Maxine.

Off she skipped. "See you later, Charles." She said.

*   *   *

Back on Prospect street, Charles and his mother were sitting in the warm kitchen. He was eating some of her freshly baked rolls and holding a hot cup of coffee.

"I had forgotten just how cold it is here in December," he said. "Just last week, Susan and I were swimming in the ocean."

"Tell me about her, Charles." Mary Jacqueline asked softly.

"She's quite a girl, mother," he began. "She runs her parent's store and their grist mill, too. She a lot like Eleanor, I think."

"How so, son?"

"To begin with, she is super determined. Just like Eleanor. When Susan takes something on it must be done just so and completely. She doesn't put up with any run-around. She's direct about everything.

"That's certainly like your sister," Mary Jacqueline admitted. "Is she kind, too?"

Charles seemed to think about that for a minute before he answered. "I think so, mother," he decided. "When we get time away from our work, she is."

"Is she pretty?"

"Oh, yes, she's pretty all right. She has brown hair not yellow like Eleanor's. And she's not as tall."

"Do you love her, Charles?"

"I believe I do, mother," Charles responded. "Neither of us knew much about that, of course. But as time went on it seemed to me that what I felt for her was love.,"

They talked more about his feelings for her.

Then Mary Jacqueline asked. "In your last letter, you said something about an engagement. What is that about?"

"When Susan and I brought marriage up to her parents, they said they would approve if we waited until I returned to Edisto this January. So, at the Harvest Festival in August, they announced that we would marry then."

There it was, Charles intended to leave Grand Rapids and returning to Edisto Island.

It appeared that his mother wasn't ready to tackle that discussion, yet.

She asked. "Tell me about the people who attack the island last summer."

So, Charles told her everything about the summer attack of Governor Hampton's people and his role in the island' defense, too.

"Sounds like a war to me," Mary Jacqueline judged.

"It sure seems like that to me, too, mother." Charles agreed.

"And you are willing to live in such a dangerous place?"

There it was. He must explain why he would choose to live on a besieged island under constant threat of extinction.

"I must admit, it is an unusual situation, mother," He admitted. "But I've become a part of a community of people who are fighting for survival, yes. But fighting for something, worthwhile, something important.

"On Edisto Island, I have found a purpose for my life," He explained. "Every day, I have important goals that I must achieve. There, I have responsibilities not only for myself, but to the community that depend upon my doing my part.

"It's is demanding, mother," He continued full of enthusiasm, "Sometimes it's dangerous, I admit. But it always has meaning. It gives me a purpose for my life that I never realized I could have. I think that's what I like about it."

Mary Jacqueline sat quietly listening to her son. Tears ran down her cheeks.

"My goodness, son," she finally managed. "I have always hoped I would see you this excited about something," Mary Jacqueline gushed.

"But this seems so dangerous and so final. I must confess, that when you walk out my door for the last time, I just know that I'll be afraid that I will have lost you forever."

Charles was silent now, too. He couldn't speak as he had tears on his cheeks now, too. He stood and went around the table to held his mother.

"You will never lose me, Momma," he muttered. "I will always be your son. But my life must have a purpose. And I've found that purpose on Edisto Island. My home will be there, but my heart will always be with you."

Mary Jacqueline stood in her son's arms and cried.

"Does your father know this?" she asked.

"Be careful here. Mike doesn't want mother to know I've told him all of this already." Charles remembered.

"He knows what I told you all in my last letter," Charles carefully said. "Can we discuss this with him tonight, maybe?"

"We are probably going to have supper with your grandparents this evening," she told her son. "I don't want your father to hear this for the first time then. So, let's take a walk downtown and have lunch with him.

"But right now, we must go over to see your grandparents. They are all at the Murphy house. I'm sure they are expecting us. Let's go over there as soon as I've cleaned up some."

"Sounds good, Momma," Charles agreed. "I'll wait for you here."

And so it went. Charles and his co-conspirator mother fielded all the questions asked by his grandparents. But at lunch, he went over everything with her for Mike as though his father was hearing this for the first time.

"Thank you, mother," he told her as they walked to the Murphy house on Cherry Street..

"For what, son?" she asked "Will I worry about you, of course I will. Am I disappointed that you will not live close by, yes, I am. At the same time, I am happy you have found purpose for your life. You have found a cause in which you can believe."

"I feared you wouldn't understand," Charles told his mother. "I feared you would try to stop me."

"That would be very selfish of me, son. Besides, how can I complain when I can clearly see you've become the kind of man, I had always hoped you would be."

"But how do I tell Maxine and Eleanor?" Charles wondered aloud.

"You leave Maxine to me," his mother told him. "But you're on your own with doctor Eleanor. She'll be the hard sell."

"That's what I'm afraid of."

*   *   *

That evening Mary Jacqueline had supper for her parents and the Drieborgs. At the first opportunity, Grandfather Murphy asked the question.

"Charles," he began. "Your mother read your last letter to us a few weeks ago. Are you going to marry that girl, Susan and live on Edisto Island?"

"Yes, grandfather, I am."

There it was, at last.

Jake Drieborg spoke first.

"Congratulations, Charles, It appears to me dat you have become a man during your stay on dat island of yours. I will miss you, but I wish you well."

"Thank you, grandfather," Charles said.

His grandmother Drieborg, added. "We will worry about you, Charles. But I will pray for your happiness and safety"

Dr. Murphy disagreed. "I think it's a damned fool decision. You've got everything a young fella could want right here. For you to go off like you intend seems reckless to me, and foolish."

At this point, Mike spoke.

"This was a difficult decision for our son," he began. "On the one hand he feared hurting his mother, and you. But on the other he knew he had found a purpose for his life on Edisto Island. And because of that, he feels he has to follow the passion he feels for that purpose.

"I for one thank God he is willing to follow that passion. I applaud him for taking the considerable risk involved. I believe his father would be proud of him. I know I am."

"Thank you, Michael." Mary Jacqueline whispered.

"I agree," Mrs. Murphy said. "You said what was in my heart."

Dr. Murphy said, "While I believe your decision to be hasty and possibly foolish, Charles, I wish you well and will certainly join your grandmother Drieborg in her prayers for your success."

"Thank you, father," Mary Jacqueline said.

In his turn, Charles spoke, too. "Thank you all," he began. "I appreciate your support. It means a great deal to me. Now, I need your prayers because I have to tell, Eleanor."

Everyone laughed.

"Lots a' luck with that, Charles," Dr. Murphy said. "She's one tough cookie."

"That's what I'm afraid of, grandfather."

Maxine had listened to all of this conversation. Finally, she asked.

"Are you going away again, Charles?"

"Yes, but not until after Christmas," he answered. "Then I have to go back to work."

Mary Jacqueline leaned over and whispered to her daughter

"I'll explain it all to you later, dear."

*   *   *

Christmas preparations were evident all over grand Rapids. Small Christmas trees were on every street corner decorated with red bows. Store windows had mannequins of reindeer and Santa's workers. The town Square held a large manger scene with life sized figures of Jesus, Mary and Joseph, the Magi and the shepherds.

On the Saturday before Christmas the town hosted a choir in the city square. Hundreds of people attend the evening concert, including the Drieborgs. And Eleanor arrived home the day before for her Christmas break.

Of course, St. Andrews Church had a manger scene on the center altar, too. Charles hadn't told anyone that he had pretty much become an Episcopalian during his stay on Edisto Island.

Early Monday morning Eleanor was In the kitchen having coffee.

When Charles walked into the warm kitchen, she said, "I can't believe you're up. I'm going to work at the Clinic this morning. But you could have slept in."

"I'm afraid that's a thing of the past, sister," Charles told her. "A lot about me is of the past."

"I did hear that you have a girlfriend now, too," Eleanor told him. "What else is new?"

"These callouses on my hands is something new." He held out his hands to her.

Eleanor examined his outstretched hands. "My lord, Charles," she exclaimed. "These are real and the cuts are recent. How'd you get these?"

"The usual way, working," he said with obvious pride. "Everyone on the island, even the children and old people, work, especially during the fall harvest. It's a matter of survival. So, I've had to pick cotton, harvest rice, dig up sugar beets, cut corn, and of course every morning at six, I milk cows and supervise the making of cheese afterward.

"That's why I pretty much have to wake up at five and that's why I have all these callouses."

"Sounds like you enjoy it."

"Not hardly," Charles admitted. "It's hard work. But it's part of the role I must play. Remember, I'm a big time land owner down there. As such, I employ hundreds of workers. So, I have to be a leader as well. That means I must work alongside the people who work for me.

"It seems sort of funny 'cause I'm usually learning more from them than they are from me."

"Hardly seems like the Charles I remember. He whined all the time when I pulled the blankets off him in the morning."

"That's all in the past, Eleanor."

"Tell me about this girlfriend of yours."

"I see you haven't changed, much though." Charles told his sister.

"What are you talking about, Charles?" Eleanor asked a little irritated.

"You always did get right to the heart of the matter."

"Oh, ya," she admitted. "I do that, don't I."

"To answer your question," Charles responded. "Susan is much like you. Maybe that's why I find her so attractive. She is all business and gets right to the point whenever she has something on her mind."

"I think I like her already," Eleanor said. "Are you in love with her?"

"Damn," Charles exclaimed. "You don't waste any time, do you?"

"I thought you just said you admired that in us girls."

"You got me there, Eleanor," Charles admitted. "Yes, I do. I've never been in love before so I'm actually not all that positive about it. But I sure get all riled up when I'm around her. When we were in a fire-fight with the Klan people from Charleston, Susan and I sure worried about one another. I suppose that tells you something."

"Tell me about all that fighting, Charles."

So, he did. He spared her some of the graphics, but he was pretty complete in his description of the attack and the fighting.

"They can just get away with trying to kill people like that."

"I'm afraid so, Eleanor," Charles informed her. "The people of the South have had a hard time accepting the freedom of millions of slaves. Negro men like Amos, for example, are not allowed to be successful, like he is here in Grand Rapids."

"Why not?"

"The way I understand it is, this. For over two hundred years in the South, the Negro had been considered a sub-human. Slavery had been considered his proper place in society. To suddenly consider him an equal is simply not acceptable. To counter his freedom under the law, many use violence to keep the Negro race in a subservient position.

"On Edisto Island, however, that's not the case. After the war, the men who owned the land on that island needed people to work their land if they were to survive. So, several of them, my grandfather Pope amongst them, decided to work with the coloreds. There was a mutual need. The coloreds needed work and the land owners like my grandfather, needed workers.

"I discovered that much of the working arrangements they fashioned years ago, are still used," Charles revealed to his sister.

"As a result, the entire community on Edisto Island functions pretty well to everyone's benefit."

"So why would anyone want to destroy that?"

"A community of whites and coloreds working successfully together is considered a threat to those who believe in the old pre-civil war days of slavery. The Klan and organizations like it want to destroy us lest others might do the same."

"Sounds like you're in the middle of a pretty nasty war, Charles," Eleanor judged. "You sure you want that?"

"I'm not happy about it, Eleanor," he admitted. "But I'm not going to turn my back on these people. They are fighting for something worthwhile. I'm just happy that they have welcomed me to work with them and to fight fight on their side."

"You've decided, then," Eleanor concluded. "that this is a cause worth risking your life for. Is that what you're telling me?"

"Exactly," Charles told his sister. "The way I figure it, Eleanor, you are becoming a doctor as your goal so that you can pursue your passion of helping people. Now, I have a determination, a passion, of working and even fighting to develop and protect an entire community of people; the one on Edisto Island."

"When did you become so smart, brother?"

"I had a pest of a sister prodding me all the time."

They both laughed at that half-truth.

"Well, brother," Eleanor said. "I don't like the danger you seem to be in down there. But I think it's great you have found purpose for your life." Eleanor embraced her brother.

"Thank you, Eleanor," Charles said. "Your understanding and support for my decision is important to me."

"Charles," Eleanor explained. "You're right. I do have a passion for medicine and a cause of being a doctor that drives me forward. So, I understand completely what you have discovered for yourself. I couldn't be happier for you." They hugged again.

Before she released her brother from her hug, she asked,

"When am I gonna meet this woman, who has stolen you heart from me?"

"Come to our wedding next month."

"I can't just leave school right at examination time." Eleanor protested.

"Let's toak about this later." She suggested.

"You have time for me later? Lunch Maybe?" Charles asked.

"If you're buying?"

Over the next few days, Charles and his sister talked over coffee and grits every morning. They had lunch with one another, too. In the evenings they both spent time with their little sister, Maxine, and talked until late with their parents after supper.

Of course, Eleanor spent time working with patients in her Grandfather Murphy's medical office, too.

Charles walked his little sister to school, talked at length with his mother and ran a few errands in town on matters that seemed important to him.

First, he talked with the executor of the Pope Estate, his uncle Joseph Deeb. Joe welcomed him into his office at the Old Kent Bank and Trust building.

"Welcome, Charles," Joe greeted. "Have a seat."

"Good morning, Uncle Joe," Charles said. "My mother told me to see you about the money you've been managing from the Pope estate on Edisto Island for the past ten years."

"Why don't I show you the account.""

"That sounds like a good place to start."

Over the next hour, Joe went over the Pope Estate account with Charles.

"My goodness, there's a lot of money in there."

"Funds have been accumulated for the past ten year, Charles. And I've just received a healthy money transfer representing the profit from this year's harvest. In my opinion, Charles, you are a wealthy man."

"I had no idea, Uncle Joe," Charles said. "Thank you for managing it so well."

"Charles, his uncle informed him. "These funds will allow you to do most anything you choose. You could buy a business here or do most anything you wish. I noticed callouses on your hand when we greeted one another. None of that effort is necessary. You cold live a very different life than the one it appears you have chosen on Edisto Island. You could live a life of leisure instead.

"Thank you, Uncle Joe," Charles answered. "Six months ago, I might have taken that advice. But the months I've spent on Edisto Island have given me a sense of purpose no money could buy. For the first time in my life I feel energized. I might change my mind later, but right now, I wouldn't exchange my life on Edisto Island for anything, despite the callouses."

"Good for you, son," Joe said to his nephew. "Good for you.

"Will there be anything else?"

"Yes, there is." Charles said. "Mike suggested that I should talk to you about a will."

"In my opinion, Charles you need a will so that if you were killed, the Probate Court would know what you wanted done with this estate.

"I can write one for you if you tell me who will inherit the funds in the estate if you suddenly died."

"For now, I think my mother and Mike should," Charles responded. "After I get married, my wife should get it. Don't you think, Uncle Joe?"

"That makes perfect sense, Charles. I will arrange for that."

"Anything else?"

"Yes," Charles said. "Can I set aside money right now for any special future purpose."

"Yes. you can."

"All right, then," he told his uncle, "I want you to pay bills I send you for the renovation of my grandfather's house on Edisto Island. I have no idea what that will cost. Can you do that?"

"Yes, I can. Anything else?"

"Yes. I want to set aside enough money to finish paying for Eleanor's education at the University of Michigan. I don't know what that amount will be, but I suppose my parents do. Also, I want you to set aside enough money for Maxine's education. I have no idea what that should be, either. I'd leave that to you and my parents."

His uncle said, "To do what you want, I will set up a separate trust for these funds and make your Mother and Mike the administrators. You'll have to authorize the transfer of the funds. But the money will become entirely separate from your estate as soon as you do sign the papers and authorize the money transfer. After that, your parents will control the fund for both of your sisters.

"Anything else?"

"Yes, I need some cash," Charles said. "How much can I have right now?"

"You can have as much as you want. You just can't exceed the amount in your account."

"Wow!" 0Charles exclaimed. "I certainly don't need that much. What do you suggest, Uncle Joe?"

"How about I give you $500 right now," his uncle suggested. "When you get ready to return South, I suggest another $50 to take with you."

'That sounds like enough. Oh, yes, there is one other thing,"

"What is it?"

"Mike told me about people taking out an insurance policy. How does that work?".

Joe explained how they worked. Charles told his uncle what his concern was.

"Because of my situation on Edisto Island, I think I should take out one of those, just to be on the safe side. What do you think?""

"I think it would be wise for you to do so, Charles."

"Fine," Charles said standing up ready to leave. "Will you arrange that as well as the will and everything? I plan to head South the first week of January.

"That would be fine, Charles. I'll have everything ready before then. If you will wait just a minute, I'll get your money for you."

After he left the bank, Charles went Christmas shopping.

His first stop was Preusser's Jewlery store on Monroe Street. It had been in Grand Rapids since 1850. Founded by William Preusser, it was the oldest such store in Michigan.

There, he bought an engagement ring for Susan. And, because the other Christmas presents Charles wanted were a bit out of the ordinary, Mr. Preusser had to order them.

"They will be here before Christmas, young man. Never fear." Mr. Preusser promised.

"Thank you, sir."

Then, he went to Grants variety store, and bought some little girl things for Maxine and a little something for all his nephews and nieces. He even bought something for Helen's children. Lastly, because none of his old clothing fit anymore, he went to Housman's clothing store. There, he bought a suite, shirt, tie and dress shoes for himself.

"This wool suite won't be worth a hoot on Edisto," he realized. *"But I don't want to look like a vagrant at Christmas time."*

Then, he went to Herpolsheimers and bought a winter coat, gloves and a knighted hat for his old nanny, Helen.

The last thing on his list was to contact Susan. So, he sent her a telegram:

"Merry Christmas, sweetheart! I will see you soon. Love, Charly."

*   *   *

It was the day before Christmas It was cold, below zero with the wind chill, and snow had been had been falling for days. Despite that, the entire family and some guests were planning to attend evening Mass at St. Andrew's Catholic church.

On Prospect Street, the Drieborg living room was resplendent with Christmas decorations. A good-sized tree was full of decorations and strung popcorn. And, as always, a manger scene was placed on the floor below its lowest branches. After church, it's candles would be lite as well.

All the church-goers planned to stop in after Christmas Eve Mass. Since they had refrained from eating before Communion, there would be sandwiches and some of Amos Smith's soup waiting along with eggnog for some, stronger drink for others.

The following day, everyone was invited to have Christmas Day dinner at the Murphy house on Cherry Street. It was their turn this year. Aside from it being Christmas and a big holiday, this celebration was a special occasion. Charles was home.

It seems that everyone they knew was either at the church or the Drieborg house, or both. All of the Drieborg clan was there, of course. The Riley family, Stan Killeen, Bill Anderson, Amos and Helen Smith and the family friend, Mrs. Bacon were there, too.

At one point, Charles stood on the upstairs landing, He looked over the crowded rooms below.

"This is wonderful. This Christmas would be complete for me if Susan and her parents were here, too. Who knows, maybe next year."

*   *   *

Once every guest had left, the Drieborgs hurried to bed. Only the perishable food was put away. Everyone was exhausted. Besides, Santa wouldn't come down the chimney unless everyone was asleep.

That didn't keep eight-year old Maxine from bursting into her parent's room, bright and early announcing,

"It's Christmas, everybody," she shouted. "Get up Santa's been here!"

Not satisfied with only waking up her parents, she went to each room, pounded on the door and shouted the same announcement.

Sure enough, there were presents under the tree and stockings hung on the mantle shock full of surprises.

Maxine sat near the tree reading the labels on each present. In the Michael Drieborg house, it was a tradition, the stockings were first, then the other stuff. Maxine got all sorts of little things, like school supplies and hard candy in her stocking. Charles found a pocket knife in his. Eleanor was surprised to find a stethoscope tucked away in her stocking.

The boxes were next. Maxine got some school clothing, but was especially thrilled to receive a doll with several outfits. Charles found a new set of work boots and Eleanor discovered a medical bag in her box.

Charles had a bag from which he took the gifts he had bought at Preusser's jewelry store. He handed one small package to each person. Each package contained a silver chain on which hung a medal of their patron saint.

Mike's was of St. George, patron saint of policemen. His mother received one of St. Monica patron saint of mothers. Maxine's medal was of St. Nicholas the patron of children. The special one was for his sister, Eleanor. It was a medal of St. Luke, the patron of doctors. He even thought to give his grandmother Drieborg a medal of St. Monica, too. For his grandfather Drieborg, he had found that the patron of farmers was St. Isadore.

"I have one of St. Isadore, too, grandfather. We're both farmers now, you know."

Grandfather Jake was so overcome, he couldn't manage say a word. He could only hug Mary Jacqueline's son, as he teared up.

Mary Jacqueline and Mike knew what Charles had arranged at the bank for his sisters. They would share news of that special gift with them, later.

 The rest of the day was full of good cheer as the assembled family and guests ate and sang until early evening. Charles gave Dr. Murphy and his grandmother Murphy their medal and chain. He also gave his uncle Jake, the Lowell Marshal, a medal of St. George, just like Mike's. His aunts and uncles enjoyed theirs, too. There was even one for his old restaurant boss, Uncle George, the patron saint of bakers, St. Phillip. And he had another special one for his lawyer uncle, Joe, of St. Thomas Moore. All in all, they all thought it was a great idea for him to leave behind with each of them, such a personal remembrance.

"I never realized how much I love these people," Charles thought. *"or how much they mean to me, or how much I will miss them. Keep them all safe Lord,"*

*   *   *

The week that followed was bitter sweet.

546

While Charles felt sad to leave his family, he looked forward with joy to seeing Susan and resuming his new life on Edisto Island.

Everyone knew Charles would be leaving early in the new year. And they were sad at that prospect. But they were excited for him too, wished him well. They also promised their prayers for hi success. He spent time with as many of his relatives as were available, especially his grandfather Jake. Facing long term separation, he and Eleanor were determined to spend as much time together as they could squeeze into the few remaining days.

Finally, New Year's Day arrived. The following day would see Eleanor returning to the university and her studies. It would also see Charles headed South and a return to his new life.

"I don't see why I can't go with you, Michael." Mary Jacqueline complained.

"You shouldn't go because it may be dangerous," Michel told his wife. "I will have enough to worry about with Charles. I don't need you to worry about, too."

"You didn't worry about that when we went on your other assignments, Washington City, Atlanta, or St. Louis."

"I must admit, you're right about that," He responded. "So, feel free to come along if you think Maxine will be all right staying here alone with everyone leaving at the same time."

Mike could see that his wife was think about this.

Finally, she said, "It would be hard for her to suddenly have all of her family leave so suddenly," Mary Jacqueline admitted. "Max would probably have trouble understanding it all.

"I want to be with my son, Michael," she insisted. "But I can see that my daughter might really suffer if I'm not there to explain what's happening. So, I had best stay here with her."

Cincinnati

As planned, Mike and his team met Frank Stantzek and his men in the Cincinnati railway station.

"No problem getting here, Mike?" Frank asked.

"Not a bit, Frank," Mike said. "Had some pretty heavy snow that slowed the train down. Cold as heck, too. But otherwise uneventful."

Frank greeted Charles, "His there, young fella. Did you have a good holiday?"

"Yes, I did, sir," Charles answered. "I hope you did, too."

"We did, thank you. Are you ready to head to some southern warmth?"

"You bet, I am. I sure missed that warm sun. Mighty cold up in Michigan. Is Fritz with you this trip?"

"He waiting for us on the train. You'll see him there." Frank informed Charles.

"We best be boarding son."

"You expect trouble, this trip Frank" Mike asked.

"No, I don't, Mike," Frank told him. "I checked around, of course and didn't hear any scuttle-but that would lead me to believe we'll encounter trouble. But you never know.

"the closer we get to Savannah, the more likely we'll encounter trouble. We'll be ready though."

"Be careful, my friend, Mike urged. "Mary Jacqueline and I should be coming your way sometime this winter for this young man's wedding. I hope to see you then."

"Married already?" Frank teased Charles. "Like your father, you don't appear to waste any time, do you?"

"I guess not," Charles said. "You think you and Jake could come for the ceremony; your wives too?"

"Don't think I've every missed a party, young fella," Frank told him. "Have to be courteous, ya know, especially when friends are doing the inviting.

"Com'on, son," frank directed. "We don['t want this train to leave without us."

Mike walked Charles to the southbound train.

"Let us know about the date of your wedding, son," He asked. "I suspect we'll be coming down for that. I doubt if your mother would miss it."

"At this point, Mike, I don't even know if I have a bride waiting for me on Edisto."

"Whatever happens, let us know."

"I will. Thank you for everything, Mike."

Mike assured him. "Anytime you want to return, you only have to let us know. You will always be welcome in our house."

"Thank you."

"Also, remember that I'm very proud of you, whatever you decide. You have behaved with honor on Edisto Island and you treated everyone with respect during the time you just spent with us in Grand Rapids. Thank you for that. We all love you and we will all pray for you.

He gave Charles a hug and said. "Take care, son, take care."

"I will. Please know, Mike, you've been a real father to me. I couldn't have asked for a better one. I believe I am what I am today because of you and mother. Thank you for all of that."

Then, Charles boarded the train. He stood for a moment on the train's platform, turned and waved to his step-father.

Mike stood on the station and watched the southbound train pull out.

"Look after him, Lord. Look after him, please." Mike prayed.

Made in the USA
Middletown, DE
14 May 2019